THE
CANDY SHOP
WAR

THE
CANDY SHOP
WAR

BRANDON MULL

SHADOW
MOUNTAIN

For Sum and Bry—the adventure we hoped to find.

© 2007 Creative Concepts LC

All rights reserved. No part of this book may be reproduced in any form or by any means without permission in writing from the publisher, Shadow Mountain®. The views expressed herein are the responsibility of the author and do not necessarily represent the position of Shadow Mountain.

All characters in this book are fictitious, and any resemblance to actual persons, living or dead, is purely coincidental.

Visit us at ShadowMountain.com

First printing in hardbound 2007.
First printing in paperbound 2010.

Library of Congress Cataloging-in-Publication Data

Mull, Brandon, 1974–
  The candy shop war / Brandon Mull.
    p. cm.
  Summary: When fifth-graders Nate, Summer, Trevor, and Pigeon meet the owner of the new candy store in town and are given a magical candy that endows them with super powers, they find that along with its benefits there are also dangerous consequences.
  ISBN 978-1-59038-783-2 (hardcover : alk. paper)
  ISBN 978-1-59038-970-6 (paperbound)
  [1. Magic—Fiction. 2. Candy—Fiction. 3. Friendship—Fiction. 4. Adventure and adventurers—Fiction.] I. Title.
PZ7.M9112Can 2007
[Fic]—dc22
                                                2007016994

Printed in the United States of America
R. R. Donnelley and Sons, Crawfordsville, IN

10 9 8 7 6 5 4 3 2 1

CONTENTS

CONTENTS

PROLOGUE

JOHN DART

The airport shuttle squeaked to a stop in the parking lot of Leslie's Diner. The generic building looked like hundreds of other cheap restaurants where you could get breakfast all day. Judging from the outdated exterior and the heavyset man in the window attacking a syrupy waffle, John Dart concluded that most items on the menu, although filling, would taste mass-produced.

The shuttle driver trotted around the front of the van and slid open the door. John stepped down. He wore a weathered overcoat and a brown fedora with a black band. John handed the driver a twenty-dollar tip.

"Thanks. No luggage, right?"

"No luggage."

Had there been bags to carry, John, tall and broad-shouldered, would have seemed a better candidate than the slight Filipino driver.

"Sure you want to be left here?" the driver asked, studying the dim parking lot.

1

John nodded.

"There's no lodging nearby."

"I like pancakes," John said.

Shrugging, the driver got back into the van and roared out of the parking lot. John had been the last passenger. The driver used his blinker when pulling onto the road, even though the world seemed deserted.

The hour was late. There were not many cars in the lot. A couple of pickups, a gray sedan, a battered minivan, an old Buick, a little hatchback, and an SUV. A man with his hands in the pockets of a faded windbreaker exited the diner and made eye contact with John. He had disheveled hair clumsily parted on one side and the beginnings of a goatee on his chin.

The man sauntered over to the old Buick, which was flecked with rust and marred by numerous nicks and scratches. John joined him, and they shook hands. The man winced slightly at John's crushing grip.

"I set up a room for you in Barcelona six years ago," the man said with a slight Spanish accent.

"I recall," John said. "How are things here?"

The man licked his lips. "A new candy shop opened in town today."

"We may have a regular convention on our hands before long," John said. "You have my supplies?"

"All the things you can't bring on a plane," the man said with a wink. He thrust a key into the trunk's lock and opened it. A dozen straitjackets of varying size were stacked inside, along with a large suitcase. The man opened the suitcase, revealing a variety of weapons: crossbows, knives, brass knuckles, truncheons, slingshots, tranquilizer guns, customized toxins, throwing stars, boomerangs, explosives, and canisters of tear gas. John picked up a heavy crossbow and examined the firing mechanism. The weapon held a pair of quarrels. He replaced the crossbow and pocketed a can of Mace.

"Looks good," John approved.

"The Council wanted me to deliver this as well," the man said, holding out a sizable seashell with vivid markings.

John accepted the shell, blew into it gently, and whispered, "John Dart, in person and in truth." When the seashell began to vibrate, he held it to his ear. At first John heard a faint whisper, like distant static. The sound progressively became more like waves heaving against a sandy shore. The deep call of a foghorn added to the sea sounds, along with the cry of gulls, and then a voice began speaking. The man who had handed John the shell strolled away to a respectful distance.

"John, we're grateful you were able to arrive so promptly," said a dignified masculine voice. John recognized it as his mentor's. "We trust that Fernando has provided you with the pertinent equipment. Samson Wells has joined the other two magicians in Colson. We now feel certain that the secret has been revealed. We must proceed under the assumption that all three are aware of what has been hidden in town, and are in pursuit of the prize. As you know, we cannot afford to allow any of our order to lay hands on it. The consequences would be catastrophic to our common interests.

"All three magicians involved have neglected warnings from the Council, so the hour for enforcing our mandate has arrived. You are hereby authorized to drive our greedy associates from the area by any necessary means."

John shuffled his feet. He was seldom authorized to confront a magician directly. Such action could provoke serious retaliation.

"Samson arrived in town only this afternoon," the voice in the shell continued. "He is spending the night at an abandoned quarry. You'll never get a better chance to catch him off guard. He may be the least experienced of the three, and strategically the least important, but apprehending him outside of a permanent lair is an advantage we cannot ignore. He will have apprentices with him. Do not underestimate his abilities. Do not enter his lair, temporary or not. Use every available precaution. Once you subdue Samson, start working on the other two.

"We cannot stress enough the crucial nature of this assignment. Success is the only option, at any cost. Work swiftly. If the secret continues to spread, nothing will stop Colson from being overrun. Mozag, signing off."

"I'd better get over my jet lag quick," John muttered. He raised the beautiful seashell high and smashed it down against the asphalt.

Fernando approached, shaking his head. "I don't envy your job." Kicking aside some shell fragments with his foot, he handed John a map. Leslie's Diner stood at the intersection of Perry Avenue and Tower Road. From that point on the map, a red marker had traced a path to a quarry not far outside of town. "Quiet place for so many weapons," Fernando sighed.

John took out a tin of Altoids and popped several into his mouth, savoring the piquant tang. "Shame," John said. "Colson isn't their kind of town. Not big enough to get lost in the crowd. Not small enough for true isolation."

"I don't need a shell to tell me something big is going on."

John gave a slight nod. "Too bad Colson wasn't built elsewhere." He offered Fernando an Altoid.

"No thanks," he said. "Unless you're hinting that I need one."

John put the tin away.

"I suppose this is where I take my leave," Fernando said, handing John the keys to the car. "I noticed that my payment is already in my account."

"You have a good reputation. Where are you off to now?"

"A job in Cordoba."

"Argentina? Good beef down there, if you know where to look."

"I usually know where to look."

"That's why you make the big bucks," John quipped.

"Something like that. Tonight's chore should go well if you approach your target discreetly. Keep to the shadows."

"I always do," John said.

Fernando paused. "I hope you never come after me," he said. "Just send me a postcard and I'll turn myself in."

"I'll keep that in mind."

"Do they ever see you coming?"

"Rarely. Colson may be different. They'll be on the lookout after tonight."

"Happy hunting," Fernando said with a two-fingered salute. "Watch your back."

"Watch yours."

Fernando climbed into the gray sedan and drove out of the parking lot. John entered the Buick, relieved as he cranked it up that the engine sounded healthier than the weathered exterior had led him to expect.

John followed the route on the map until he reached the outskirts of town, where buildings became scarce. Ridgeline Way wound around the shoulder of a hill, and his destination drew near. An abandoned quarry. Why was his work always taking him to abandoned quarries and deserted mines and seedy inner city bars? He needed a new occupation, a job that would entail extended visits to lazy tropical beaches and quaint woodland cottages.

Just over a mile from his destination, John pulled the Buick onto the shoulder of the road. If his targets were keeping a sharp lookout, they might have noticed the car heading up the road and seen the headlights go dark. Not probable, but he preferred to be ready for all contingencies.

Getting out of the car, John rummaged through the trunk, selecting gear. Handcuffs. Tear gas. A tranquilizer gun. A vial of neurotoxin. Four straitjackets. Among other things.

Taking a final peek at the map, John set off up the street. Another lonely road in the middle of the night. Not unsettling, except that it felt so familiar. Alone in the dark, he was at home.

His eyes adjusted until the moonlight seemed bright. The upkeep on the road was poor. Too many potholes. He reached an intersection where a dirt road branched out from Ridgeline. John stepped off the asphalt and paralleled the dirt road, treading silently through the brush, choosing a circuitous route in order to keep himself concealed.

After walking for several minutes, John peered into the quarry. Industry had transformed the side of the hill into a stony amphitheater. Below the chiseled cliffs sat a dilapidated school bus. John might have assumed it was derelict had he not known that Samson Wells had come to town earlier that evening. The rundown bus made for a shabby lair, but a lair nonetheless. Only a fool willingly entered the lair of a magician. But this lair was temporary—the defenses were limited. John would flush him out.

The guards posed a problem. Not unexpected, but still

troublesome. John crept along the edge of the quarry until he ascertained that two guards stood watch, one at either end of the bus.

He would have to subdue them delicately. A sloppy attack would not suffice. John could not afford to seriously harm the guards, the consequence of an unusual condition he had dealt with for decades.

Due to a powerful curse placed on him years ago, John himself suffered any direct injury he inflicted on another. If he broke someone's leg, his leg broke. If he knocked someone out, he went to sleep. If he killed a person, he would die. So finesse was always required.

One guard was tall and stocky, his face lightly pockmarked, his brown hair tied back in a ponytail. He held a wooden baseball bat. The other was a Vietnamese woman—young, short, and slim. No visible weapons. John had met Samson Wells once, and was generally familiar with his reputation, but had no idea what abilities these two apprentices might possess.

Ideally he would avoid finding out. Their positions at opposite ends of the bus kept them out of view from one another. If he disposed of one of them silently, he might overcome both without a fight.

The guy with the ponytail looked drowsy, so John opted to start with him. The school bus had come in along the dirt road and parked in a flat spot near the center of the old quarry. Boulders and rubble surrounded the bus on all sides, providing just enough cover for a stealthy approach. Staying low, moving when the man with the ponytail was looking in the wrong direction, John crept forward.

In some ways, the scarcity of decent cover was an advantage. To a less trained eye, the man with the ponytail appeared unassailable. John doubted whether his target could envision somebody successfully getting close.

John took his time, picking his moments, waiting to advance until a cloud dimmed the moonlight or the unsuspecting guard diverted his focus to pick at a hangnail. When John moved, he stayed low and silent, sometimes gliding quickly over the rocky terrain, sometimes inching forward with supreme patience. Eventually John crouched behind a meager rock pile less than fifteen feet from the man with the bat. It was the last decent piece of cover between himself and his target.

Picking up a pebble, John dropped it gently on a larger stone. The resultant sound was faint but suspicious. He heard the man approaching the rock pile, not with any urgency, just strolling over to take a closer look at what might have caused the unnatural click.

As the man came around the low rock pile to glance at the far side, John slunk in a crouch, keeping the rocks between them. Stepping quickly, John looped around and got behind the long-haired guard, who was only an inch or two shorter than John.

In one hand, John held a strip of duct tape. The adhesive side was extra sticky, and the opposite side was extra slick. From behind, John slapped the duct tape over the guard's mouth with one hand while wrenching the baseball bat from his grasp with the other.

The startled guard whirled as John set the bat down. Making a low humming sound, the guard swung a fist at John, who intercepted the punch expertly and locked the man's arm into a painful hold. Moving decisively, John grabbed the guard's other arm and handcuffed his wrists together behind his back.

A third arm grew out of the center of the guard's back and seized John by the throat. A fourth arm sprouted and tore away the remains of the guard's flimsy T-shirt, then started trying to peel away the duct tape covering his mouth. The arms that were cuffed together fell to the rocky ground and a fresh pair of arms took their place.

With a chopping motion, John broke the guard's hold on his throat and backed away. Shirtless, the guard now had six arms, two of which were clawing at the duct tape. The other four were clenched into fists.

John had not fought a Shedder in years. You didn't see many these days. They could sprout and detach limbs at will, which made them almost impossible to grapple with.

Before John could regain his composure, he heard a whooshing sound. As he turned to look in the direction of the airy noise, a sharp blow to his midsection doubled him over, and a second blow sent him reeling backwards. He only barely managed to keep his feet.

Dazed, nose bleeding, John saw the Vietnamese woman appear. She was obviously a Blur, capable of moving at tremendous speed for short periods of time, but requiring rest in between her bursts of superhuman velocity. With a Blur and a Shedder standing ready to fight, John knew that he was now in serious danger. Hand-to-hand combat was out of the question.

The Shedder lunged toward the fallen bat. John produced a crossbow from inside his overcoat. He did not mean to use it. The firing mechanism on the crossbow had a pair of safeguards, making it difficult to fire unless you knew the trick. As expected, the instant he produced the weapon, the Vietnamese woman streaked toward him and yanked it from his grasp. John lashed out with one leg along the path he expected her to take, and she collided with his shin. He spun to the ground, and she tumbled into the rock pile, dropping the crossbow.

The Shedder picked up the baseball bat while John pulled out a sleek pistol. John was frowning. He had hoped to avoid doing this the hard way. The darts in the gun were full of a sinister neurotoxin manufactured by his employer. For nearly an hour after the toxin was administered, any muscle contraction would cause a burst of excruciating pain, making movement intolerable.

As the Shedder charged with the bat raised, John tagged him in the chest with a dart. Rolling behind the rock pile as the bat swung, John put a dart into the young Vietnamese woman before she could recover. Muffled by the duct tape, the Shedder was trying to scream. John's employers knew their business. The effect of the neurotoxin was nearly instantaneous. The woman cried out as well.

"Hold still," John demanded, staying low, pain searing his jaw as he spoke. "Only movement will hurt. I want to hear you drop that bat."

Instead he heard more stifled screaming and the sound of a body slapping down against the rocks. The Shedder had tried to keep moving despite the pain, and had passed out. John had never met anyone who could endure that much pain and remain conscious. Anyone besides himself.

The toxin was one of John's most effective ways to subdue enemies. The pain kept his targets immobile or knocked them unconscious. And since the unconsciousness resulted from movements the targets chose to make, it did not affect John.

But when *he* moved, John felt pain just as sharply as they did. Muscles protesting in dizzying agony, he walked around the rock pile and retrieved the fallen bat. He had learned to cope with pain through countless injuries, most of them sustained vicariously. Over the years, he had gained the capacity to tolerate just about anything.

The Vietnamese woman glared at him, caged by the prospect of unendurable agony. Her eyes blinked, tears pooling in them.

"Even hurts to blink," John said. "Sometimes life is unfair."

John walked around the side of the school bus. All remained dark inside. Teeth grinding together against the anguish in his muscles, John hurled the wooden bat through one of the windows. "Why not come out, Samson?"

"That you, John?" a voice called from inside.

"You know it is," John said. "And you know you're cornered. A temporary lair is not going to cut it."

"Come in and get me."

John removed a canister of tear gas from his coat, opened it, and tossed it through the window. When his eyes began to sting, he knew that Samson had no emergency gas mask stashed away in there. Tears streamed down John's cheeks, and he coughed uncontrollably, the spasms triggering waves of agony throughout his body.

Samson stumbled out of the front door of the bus followed by a cloud of caustic fumes. He held a bedspread to his face, which John tore from his grasp. Samson was a thin, veiny man with his head shaved and several tattoos on his bony arms. Blinking away tears, nauseous with pain, John roughly strapped Samson into a straitjacket.

"Why are you doing this, John?" Samson gasped. "Don't you already have enough enemies?"

"You shouldn't have come here," John said. "You forced my hand. You should have known something like this would happen." John wrapped Samson in the bedspread, lashing it to him with thin, strong cords.

"I should have known some callous lackey for a despicable group of schemers would drag me from my home in the middle of the night?" Although he failed to muster much spittle, Samson spat at John. "How do you live with yourself?"

"One day at a time." John tightened the cords.

"You're not the only guy who knows I'm in town," Samson wheezed. "The other magicians have no great love for me, but they won't be pleased to learn about this."

"Maybe they'll take the hint."

Samson cackled and coughed. "They don't run, John. Me, maybe. Them? No way. You ought to be the one running." He struggled inside of the bedspread burrito.

"Thanks for the concern. Don't give me any trouble. I'm already in a lot of pain. I'd gladly suffer a bit more."

Samson grinned. He had two gold teeth. "I know the limits of what you can do to me."

"Right. Which is why I'll have a courier deliver you and your sideshow sidekicks to my employers."

Samson paled. "I'll give you ten times the money they're paying you—"

John chuckled.

"Fifty times," he pleaded.

"Friend, you made your bed, I'm just tucking you in."

CHAPTER ONE
THE BLUE FALCONS

Nate sat at the end of a sheetless mattress, bouncing a small rubber ball off the bare wall, keeping count of how many consecutive times he caught it. The ball got away from him and rolled toward the open, empty closet, coming to rest against the base of a cardboard box.

His new room was a little bigger than the old one, but felt unfamiliar and impersonal. Once the boxes were unpacked it would look a lot better.

His mom entered carrying another box with his name printed in blue marker. "You're not getting much done," she said.

"I don't know where to start," Nate replied.

"Just do this one," she said, setting the box at the foot of his bed. "After you finish you can go play outside."

"Play what? Robinson Crusoe?"

"I just saw some kids your age riding bikes."

"They're probably idiots."

"Now, don't have that attitude," she sighed. "Since when did you become shy?"

"I don't want to start all over again in a new place. I miss my old friends."

"Nate, we're here, and we're not leaving. If you make some friends in the neighborhood before school starts, you'll have a much better time."

"I'd have a better time if Tyler moved here."

His mom used a key to hack through the tape sealing the box. "That would be nice, but you'll have to settle for e-mail. Get to work." She left the room.

Still seated at the end of the mattress, Nate leaned forward and pulled back the cardboard flaps. The box contained a bunch of his old trophies cocooned in newspaper. He had a lot of trophies for a ten-year-old, having played four years of soccer and three of Little League.

He unwrapped the biggest trophy, earned last year by his first-place soccer team, the Hornets. He had been stuck at fullback all season, and had seen less action than ever. The forwards and halfbacks had generally kept the ball at the other end of the field as the team paraded unchallenged to their undefeated season. The coach, a black guy from Brazil whose son was the star forward, had spent the season yelling at Nate to stand up and stop picking grass. As if he couldn't just hop to his feet on those rare occasions when the ball visited his side of the field. Picking grass was far more entertaining than watching his teammates score goals off in the distance. They should have equipped him with binoculars instead of shin guards.

Soon the trophies were aligned on a shelf, and the newspapers were wadded on the floor. Beneath the trophies, Nate found a bunch of his books, along with a broad assortment of comics. He loaded them into the bookshelf, then heaped the wadded newspapers back inside the box.

He walked out into the hall, weaving around boxes to get to the bathroom and wash the newspaper ink off his palms. There were even boxes in the bathroom. He lived in a warehouse.

Inspiration struck while he was rinsing his hands. If they saved all the boxes, he could construct an awesome fort. He stood at the sink considering the possibilities, staring into the mirror without seeing anything. It would need a drawbridge, and secret passages, and a rope swing. How many stories tall? Where could he get barbed wire? What if the fort ended up bigger than the house, and his family chose to live there instead? He would have to weatherproof it.

"You all right, Nate?"

He turned to face his dad. "Could I have the boxes when we're done with them?"

"I'm sure we could spare a few. How come?"

"I want to build a fort."

"We'll see."

"Maybe you can glue milk cartons under it and sail to Hawaii." This comment came from his older sister, Cheryl, poking her head into the bathroom. She was referring to his failed attempt to assemble a raft out of milk cartons. He had insisted that the family store empty cartons in the garage for months after he had seen a guy on the news piloting a milk-carton barge. Eventually, overwhelmed by the logistics of joining milk cartons to form a seaworthy vessel, he had abandoned the project.

"Maybe you can go polish your braces," he retorted. "They look rusty."

His dad stuck out an arm to hold Cheryl back. "None of that," he said, suppressing a grin. "Nate, why don't you go outside for a while? I saw some kids playing out there."

"But I don't know them."

"Then go get acquainted. When I was your age, I was friends with whoever happened to be out roaming the neighborhood."

"Sounds like a good way to get stabbed by a hobo," Nate grumbled.

"You know what I mean."

"I guess. Is my bike in the garage?"

"It's buried in there somewhere. I'll dig it out for you."

* * * * *

Summer pedaled furiously up the street on her stupid pink bicycle with the white basket between the handlebars. She could hear Trevor closing in behind her. He always gained a little when they went uphill. At the top of the street, she coasted around the corner, then pumped her legs hard. She would pull farther ahead now that the road was flat, then make the lead embarrassing when they headed back down Monroe.

She rounded the last corner.

"Car!" Trevor screamed from behind her.

She hit her brakes before realizing the warning was a desperate trick. Grunting, she pedaled wildly to recover her lost momentum. Trevor almost pulled alongside her. She glimpsed his front tire out of the corner of her eye. Then it was gone, and she was stretching her lead. A kid standing on a driveway beside a bike watched her race past. The downward slope of the road was working to her advantage. Wind whistled in her ears and made her hair flutter. She passed the mailbox that served as the finish line and coasted to the bottom of the circle.

Glancing back, she saw Trevor reach the mailbox a few seconds behind her. Poor Pigeon had barely passed the kid standing in his driveway. The kid mounted his bike and followed Pigeon down the street. He looked about her age, with reddish-blond hair and a blue T-shirt. His bike looked new.

Summer stood straddling her bike. Trevor and Pigeon pulled up near her, turning to watch the new kid skid to a stop.

"What are you guys doing?" the kid asked Trevor.

"Playing water polo," Summer said.

"You're pretty funny," the kid said. "You should join the circus."

Trevor and Pigeon laughed. The kid smiled.

"Are you new here?" Trevor asked.

"My family just moved in from Southern California."

"What area?" Pigeon asked.

"Mission Viejo. Between San Diego and L.A. My name's Nate."

"I'm Trevor."

"Summer."

"Pigeon."

"Like the bird?" Nate asked.

"Yep."

"How come?"

Pigeon shrugged. "Everybody just started calling me that in second grade." He shot Trevor and Summer a meaningful glance, silently imploring them to keep the rest of the story secret.

"How long have you had that bike?" Summer asked.

"Since Christmas."

"Have you ridden it before?"

"What do you mean?"

"It looks brand-new."

"I wash it sometimes. I'll teach you how if you want."

Pigeon and Trevor chuckled. Summer glanced down at her dirty bicycle frame, groping for a comeback. She had nothing. "What grade are you in?"

"I'm going into fifth."

"So are we," Trevor said.

"What's the school again?"

"Mt. Diablo," Pigeon said. "It means Devil's Mountain."

"Sounds like a roller coaster. Have you guys always lived here?"

"I moved down here from Redding three years ago," Trevor said. "Summer and Pidge have always lived in Colson."

"Where are your houses?"

"I'm right there," Trevor said, twisting and pointing at the last house on the street. "Pigeon lives on the other side of the circle."

"And I live across the creek," Summer said.

The bottom curve of Monroe Circle had no houses. Instead there was a paved jogging path, beyond which a brushy slope descended to a creek lined with trees and shrubs. From where they were standing, Summer could see the roof of her home.

"Do you surf?" Pigeon asked.

Summer rolled her eyes. "Just because he's from Southern California doesn't make him a surfer."

"I tried it once," Nate said. "I kept wiping out. My uncle surfs a lot. What do you guys do for fun besides ride bikes?"

"We've got a club," Pigeon said.

Summer glared at him.

"What kind of club?" Nate asked.

Pigeon squinted uncertainly at Trevor. "We're still working on that," Trevor said.

"We started as a detective agency," Summer explained. "We sent out flyers, but nobody wanted to hire us, except for Pigeon's mom who sent us to buy groceries. So we became a treasure-hunting society. We didn't have much success with that either. Now we're mainly a trespassing club."

"Trespassing club?"

"We sneak into places," Summer said.

"Like where?"

"We broke into a water-processing plant," Trevor said.

"And a rich guy's barn," Pigeon added.

"Do you take stuff?" Nate asked.

"No way!" Summer said. "We don't harm anything. We just sneak in, check things out, and take off."

"And keep an eye out for treasure," Pigeon added.

"That sounds really cool," Nate said. "How do I join?"

"I don't know," Summer said. "We're pretty selective."

"Let me guess," Nate said. "Nobody has ever tried to join."

"Something like that," Summer admitted. "We need to figure out the specifics. We can't just let any random kid become a member. Why don't you go back to your house for a while and let us talk things over."

"For how long?" Nate asked.

Summer shrugged. "Come back in fifteen minutes."

"Okay."

* * * * *

"Back so soon?" his mom asked when Nate entered the kitchen from the garage. She was loading dishes from a box into the dishwasher.

"Yeah."

"Did you talk to those kids?"

"They have some club, but they're not sure if I can join."

His mom put her hands on her hips. "Do you want me to go talk with them?"

"No!" Nate exclaimed, feeling a surge of genuine alarm. Then he saw that his mom was grinning. She was teasing. "I think they're trying to make up an initiation."

"Don't eat anything unsanitary. What sort of club is it?"

"Mainly bike riding," Nate said, plopping down in a chair at the kitchen table. He pushed aside a box and began flicking a quarter to spin it, periodically checking the digital clock on the microwave.

"Are the kids nice?" his mom asked, closing the dishwasher.

"I guess. One is called Pigeon. He seems like a wuss. There's also a kid named Trevor who seems all right, and a girl named Summer who's a real comedian."

"Don't tell me she was giving you competition." His mom pressed a couple of buttons and started the dishwasher. "So why are you in here?"

"They said they need time. I'm supposed to go back after I give them a few minutes to decide what I need to do to join."

"Does the club have a name?"

"I forgot to ask."

* * * * *

After about ten minutes, Nate rode down the street to the end of the circle where the kids stood by their bikes. Summer had short brown hair and scabs on one knee. Trevor had olive skin, dark hair, and a slim build. And Pigeon was chubby with his hair buzzed short. How could such an obvious doofus be part of a club *he* was having trouble joining?

"You still want to join?" Summer asked.

"What are you guys called?"

"The Blue Falcons," Summer said.

"Come on, that sounds like a soccer team."

"You want in or not?"

"I guess."

"Follow us."

They hopped the curb and rode a short distance down the jogging path, stopping at the top of a steep slope covered in dry brush. Near the bottom of the slope, just before the ground leveled out, a ramp had been constructed. "You have to take that jump going full speed," Summer said.

"Whatever!" Nate exclaimed. "I'm not a stunt man. What are you planning to do, rob my corpse?"

"I've done it," Summer said. "We need to know you're serious about joining. If you do the jump, we'll believe you."

"You just want a free show at my expense. That has got to be the most rickety ramp I've ever seen!"

"The ramp is fine," Summer assured him. "It's wood propped up on bricks. And I jump it just for fun."

Nate rolled his eyes. "Sure you do."

"She's done it more than once," Trevor said.

"And I'm supposed to believe Pigeon jumped it?"

"He doesn't need to," Summer said. "He got in on the ground floor."

"Lucky for the ramp. Fine. You say you jump it for fun, go ahead and do it again so I can see. If you land it, I'll do it too."

They all looked at Summer. She pressed her lips together. "Okay. But if I do it and you wimp out, you're never in our club."

"Deal."

She turned her bike to face downhill. Showing no hesitation, Summer started pedaling. Nate frowned. He had dug himself into a serious hole. If he wussed out after a girl did the jump on her goofy pink bike, he would look like the biggest chicken in the world.

She gained speed, approaching the ramp in a rush as her bicycle rattled over the uneven terrain. Just before the ramp, her front wheel jagged sharply to the left, and the bike flipped over, catapulting her into an awkward flight. Summer tumbled through the brush until she came to a rest beside the splintery ramp.

Dropping their bikes, the boys dashed down the hill. Nate and Trevor reached Summer together. She stared up at them, flat on her back with her head pointed downhill. Her white shirt was torn and covered in stickers, her face was smudged with dirt, and her elbow was scraped and bleeding. But there were no tears in her brown eyes.

"You okay?" Trevor asked.

"I'm just trying to get a tan."

"That was a crazy crash!" Trevor gushed. "I wish we had a video camera. You flew like ten feet!"

She sat up, picking at some burrs in her shirt. "It knocked the wind out of me for a minute. I don't think I broke anything."

"You never break anything," Pigeon said.

She looked up at Nate. "Your turn."

"Well, you didn't actually go off the—"

Something struck Nate in the back of his head, knocking him forward in a cloud of dust. The thrown object had not come from Trevor, Pigeon, or Summer. He had been facing them with his back to the creek.

Nate heard ecstatic laughter from behind.

"Denny's in the Nest!" Trevor shouted as a second dirt clod hit the ramp, exploding in a swirl of dust.

"He's got our ammo!" Pigeon cried.

Nate whirled, swiping at the dirt in his hair and on the back of his neck. Three kids were over near the creek, half hidden by undergrowth. One had black hair and wore a faded army jacket that looked a couple of sizes too large. Another was a thickset kid with curly blond hair. The third had lots of freckles and a round, flat face.

Nate charged the strangers. It was more of an angry impulse than a rational decision. His hands were clenched into fists as he raced through the brush.

The boys looked surprised. They stooped to grab more ammunition. Flat Face chucked a dirt clod that missed to the right. Army Jacket threw one that made Nate duck.

Nate had almost reached them. Only a few bushes separated him from his targets. He planned to crash through the bushes and tackle Army Jacket, who was the tallest. He dimly hoped Trevor was following him into battle.

Suddenly something blasted Nate in the face and he crashed to the ground with dirt in his teeth. He lay there stunned, unsure whether he had temporarily lost consciousness. Surely that had been a rock. No dirt clod would hurt so much. It felt like the side of his mouth had been kicked by a horse.

"Oh, you nailed him, Denny," a voice said solemnly.

"Come on," another voice said, suppressing a laugh.

Nate heard twigs snapping as the boys ran away. Of course they were running away. They didn't want to get arrested for manslaughter.

Nate opened his eyes. Lying on his side, he touched the corner of his mouth and looked at the blood on his fingertips. He tried to spit out the gritty taste of dirt. Maybe the projectile had been a rock inside of a dirt clod.

"Are you okay?" It was Trevor, kneeling at his side.

"I'm not sure. What do I look like?"

"Your lip is bleeding and your cheek got scraped."

Nate fingered one side of his upper lip. It seemed to be swelling.

Pigeon came and squatted nearby. "You must be crazy."

"I don't let people bully me."

"Well," Summer said, her torn shirt still full of prickers, "the good news is you can skip the jump. That was way better."

"Welcome to the club," Pigeon said.

CHAPTER TWO

FIRST DAY

I t isn't too late," Nate pleaded. "Just take me back."

"You need to go," his mom replied.

"I promise I won't complain tomorrow."

"You'll feel the same way tomorrow. Except worse, because you'll be much more conspicuous."

They passed the Presidential Estates sign, leaving the neighborhood as they turned onto Greenway. Nate leaned his forehead against the window.

"With a name like Presidential Estates, shouldn't they be bigger houses?" Nate observed.

"I like our house."

"We should at least have a pool. Or some pillars. They should rename the place Typical Neighborhood Estates."

"I like our kitchen," his mom persisted.

Nate sighed. He tugged absently at the zipper on his new backpack. They hit a bump, and the window jolted against his head. He sat up. "Come on, Mom, just let me skip today."

"This is for your own good, Nate. There is no worse day to miss than the first one. Besides, your friend Summer is in your class."

"I wanted Trevor."

"You might have Pigeon."

"Great," Nate griped. "A girl and a dork. I'll be the biggest outcast ever."

They idled at an intersection. A store on the corner had a sign that read *Sweet Tooth Ice Cream and Candy Shoppe* in old-fashioned lettering.

"How about we get ice cream instead?" Nate proposed.

"Nice try. You don't hate school. What's the problem?"

"I'm too used to summer. It's hard to go back, especially starting over in a new place. I wish I could ease into it, maybe just go for an hour."

After a few cars passed, they turned onto Main. "The start of a new school year is a transition for everyone," his mom said. "You'll fit right in."

"They all know each other."

"You'd feel better if you had come to the orientation," she chided.

"An extra day at school is supposed to make me feel better?"

"Some people like to know where things are."

"Can't you home school me?" Nate pleaded.

"You would never do any work."

"Sounds perfect!"

They were driving along Main through downtown Colson. All along Main Street from Greenway to the hill topped by Mt. Diablo Elementary, the buildings looked like they were trying to belong to the Old West. Most were two stories and made of wood. Some looked like saloons, while others looked like old-fashioned houses. Plank sidewalks connected the businesses, with periodic barrels doubling as trashcans. There was a general store, a dentist's office, a town museum, a post office, a bar and grill, a craft store, an antique store, and a barbershop with a striped pole out front.

"What time does the Wild West show start?" Nate asked.

"I like this part of town."

"It looks like Frontierland."

"A little bit."

"All they need is a log ride."

"I'm glad it looks different," his mom said. "So much of America looks the same nowadays."

"Because we all live in the same time period."

"Cut it out. You like it too."

Nate shrugged.

Main curved up a slope. They turned onto Oak Grove Avenue and pulled into the Mt. Diablo Elementary parking lot. Kids poured out of cars and buses, heading into the school. Nate studied the crowd. Nobody looked too intimidating. Most of the kids were younger than him.

They reached the curb.

"All right, have a great day," his mom said. "You sure you don't want me to pick you up?"

"Trevor says they always walk home. You sure I can't just start tomorrow?"

"We wouldn't have made it this far if I wasn't."

"Mom, this school is named after the devil. That is not a good sign."

"Somehow I think you'll survive. Remember, 18-C with a blue door."

Nate opened his door. The nervous feeling in his stomach reminded him of the butterflies he had experienced before doing a lip sync in his fourth-grade talent show. Had he ever been this intimidated by a first day of school?

He stepped out of the familiar Ford Explorer onto the unfamiliar sidewalk of the unfamiliar school full of unfamiliar kids. He shut the door, waved to his mom, and joined the mass of students flowing into the school.

Covered sidewalks connected the buildings. His mom had explained that his class was in the last building on the left. He wished he had resisted begging to stay home so much. It had really gotten his hopes up for missing the day, which now made him feel even more out of place.

He heard someone crying. Glancing over his shoulder, he saw a tiny Asian kid clinging to his mother and bawling. It made Nate feel a little better. At least he wasn't that pathetic.

He moved along a crowded walkway, tapping his knuckles against a metal rail. The rail protected a grassy area between the buildings. He considered ducking the rail and cutting across the grass, but no other kids were doing it.

Up ahead, Nate identified a familiar face. The kid with black hair who had thrown dirt clods at him. He was not wearing his army jacket. It was already a hot day.

Nate touched the corner of his mouth. After five days, the bruise had faded, but he still had the remnants of a small scab. Nate adjusted how he was walking so that the kid in front of him blocked Army Jacket from view.

He had learned from Summer that the boy with the army jacket was named Kyle. The kid with the flat face was Eric. The blond with the curly hair was Denny. They were all sixth graders this year.

Although Nate had spent the last few days going to the creek and riding around the neighborhood with Trevor, Summer, and Pigeon, he had not run into the irritating trio since they had stoned him. But Trevor had warned him that those guys tried to bully them a lot, both at school and around the neighborhood. Nobody was looking forward to the bullies thinking they ruled the school as sixth graders.

Nate peeked around the kid in front of him, who looked too old to be wearing a yellow backpack with Woodstock on it. Kyle was no longer in sight.

* * * * *

Summer sat at her desk watching kids file into the room. Her backpack rested on the seat of the desk next to her. Her notebook covered the seat on her opposite side.

"Whose notebook is this?" asked a girl with long brown hair. Summer thought her name was Crystal, but had never spoken to her much.

"I'm saving that seat."

"And that other one too?"

"I have a couple of friends coming," Summer said.

As the girl claimed the desk in front of the backpack, Nate came through the door. He was in a green button-down shirt and jeans. He looked a little dazed. Then he made eye contact with Summer, and his face came to life. She waved him over. He looked a little hesitant, and then walked in her direction. She moved her backpack and he sat down.

"How are you?" he asked.

"Fine."

"Hot today."

The girl with long brown hair turned around. "Are you her boyfriend?" she asked.

Summer glanced from Crystal to Nate and back. The question made her feel a little awkward. After all, she had saved him a seat.

"No, I'm her fiancé," Nate said.

"We've been promised to each other since birth," Summer added.

"Our wedding isn't until March."

"What's your name?" Crystal asked Nate.

"Nate."

"I'm Kiersten."

That was right. Kiersten, not Crystal. Who was Crystal?

Summer glanced at the door. Her eyes widened. Pigeon had just entered wearing a black leather jacket with shiny zippers and metal studs. It was obviously brand-new.

"Nate, look at the door," Summer suggested.

"Oh, no. What is he thinking?"

Pigeon saw them and crossed the room. Summer moved her notebook and he took the desk.

"Nice jacket," she said.

He looked like he was holding back a smile. "Thanks. Remember I said I had a surprise for today?"

"Little hot for a coat, isn't it, Pidge?" Nate asked.

Summer glared at Nate. Pigeon would receive plenty of teasing today without his friends adding to it.

"This one stays pretty cool," Pigeon assured him.

"All right, class, we need to begin," said the portly woman at the front of the room. Summer checked the clock. They still had two minutes before the bell would ring. "Don't get comfortable in your seats. We will be reseating alphabetically as we take attendance. Would you all move to the back of the room?"

Summer grabbed her stuff and went to the rear of the room with everyone else. Her last name was Atler, so she was the second person seated. The bell rang as she reached her desk. Pigeon was really named Paul Bowen. He ended up two desks behind her.

"Could you just call me Pigeon?" he asked the teacher when she read his name.

"Does your mother call you Pigeon?"

"No."

"Then to me you are Paul."

Skylar Douglas sat down next to her. What was Nate's last name? She couldn't recall.

Nate was one of the last to sit.

"Nathan Sutter," the teacher read.

"Here. My mother never calls me Nathan."

"Is it Nate?"

"She calls me Honeylips."

The class exploded with laughter. Summer almost fell out of her desk. The teacher frowned. She had deep lines from her nose to the corners of her mouth from too much frowning.

"That was not a good way to start the year, Nathan," the teacher said.

"Sorry. Mom calls me Nate."

Nate ended up sitting at the second-to-last desk of the farthest row from Summer, over by the windows. After everyone was seated and accounted for, with an empty desk left for Charlotte Merrill, the teacher wrote her name in cursive on the chalkboard.

"My name is Miss Doulin," she said. She underlined the word *Miss*. "Not Mrs. Doulin. Mrs. Doulin is my mother."

Miss Doulin had to be in her late thirties. She was not a pretty woman. Her hair was shaggy, her lips were thin, and her eyes were too close together. Worse, she seemed to have a sour disposition. Summer doubted whether Miss Doulin would ever have a *Mrs.* in front of her name.

"Some of you may have heard that I don't allow a lot of horse-play," Miss Doulin continued. "This is true. You are now in the fifth grade. You are growing up. More will be required of you this year than ever before. You are preparing for junior high, and I promise you no horseplay will be tolerated there.

"This classroom is a place of learning. Without order that will never happen. If you work hard and participate in class discussions, we can have a little fun. For example, I have a trivia question. The first of you to answer correctly will have no homework tonight. But be careful. If you answer incorrectly, you will have extra work."

She gave the class a meaningful stare. Summer shook her head slightly. It was not a good sign to be talking about homework in the first five minutes of the first day of class.

"Name two men who appear on U.S. currency who were never presidents of the United States."

The class was silent.

"Currency is money," Miss Doulin clarified.

Pigeon raised his hand.

"Yes, Paul."

"Benjamin Franklin and Alexander Hamilton."

"Very good, Paul. Can you tell us where they appear?"

"On the hundred-dollar bill and the ten-dollar bill."

"Excellent. No homework for you tonight."

"Can I have a different prize?" Pigeon asked.

"Like what?"

"Could you call me Pigeon?"

She paused. "Fair enough. If you would rather have homework."

"That's fine."

* * * * *

Trevor exited the cafeteria holding a tray with a chicken sandwich, tater tots, applesauce, and a small carton of chocolate milk. The day had gotten really hot. The bright sun made Trevor squint as he scanned the rows of aluminum picnic tables for his friends.

He had watched for Nate in the lunch line. Summer and Pigeon rarely bought lunch, and he had forgotten to ask whether Nate planned to buy. Nate had never showed up.

Finally Trevor saw Summer and Nate. Who was the kid in the leather jacket? He smirked when he realized it was Pigeon. Trevor joined them at the table.

"Is that jacket keeping out the chill?"

Pigeon looked up from his bag of potato chips. "I have to keep it on. I sweated through my shirt."

"How was class, Trev?" Summer said.

"Mr. Butler seems pretty cool. Is Miss Doulin as bad as everyone says?"

"Worse," Nate said. "She already threatened me with detention."

"Nate was being a little too funny," Summer said.

Trevor ate a tater tot. "I can't believe you three ended up in the same class and I got left out."

"I wasn't sure Pigeon was in our class," Nate said. "I never knew he was named Paul, so my mom couldn't check for his name on the list."

"Pidge already got in good with Miss Doulin," Summer said.

"I didn't know he was such a brain," Nate said.

"I'm not," Pigeon said. "I just know a lot about the presidents and the Founding Fathers. I have this great book about them. I have all of the presidents memorized."

"No kidding," Nate said.

"Did you know that Thomas Jefferson and John Adams died on the same day?"

"No."

"July 4, 1826. Fifty years to the day after the Declaration of Independence was signed."

"Weird."

"They were among the last surviving signers."

A hand slapped down on Pigeon's shoulder from behind. "What's for dessert today?" It was Denny. Eric of the flat features stood at his side.

Pigeon grabbed his brown bag and folded the top down.

"For a second I thought Summer was dating the leader of a biker gang," Denny said. "Then I realized it was just a geek in disguise." Denny tried to snatch the bag from Pigeon. When Pigeon refused to let go, the bag ripped. A sandwich in a plastic bag fell out, along with a banana and two individually wrapped cupcakes.

Eric reached for the cupcakes. He got one. Nate, seated on the opposite side of the table, snagged the other.

"Two desserts?" Denny said. "Good idea! One for me, and one for . . . Eric. Maybe that jacket really has made you cooler!"

"Are you actually trying to steal his food?" Nate asked.

"That black eye healed pretty good," Denny said.

"It hit me in the mouth."

"How'd it taste?" Denny smiled. Eric chuckled.

Nate threw the cupcake at Denny as hard as he could. Denny ducked, and it flew over a couple of tables into the side of a building.

Denny was no longer smiling. "You're going to make this year interesting, Dirt Face. These guys quit fighting back at school years ago. See, Kyle's mom is the head yard duty. We never get busted."

"Maybe I'll go talk to the principal," Nate threatened.

Denny shrugged. "Try it. See what happens to you."

"Don't talk to him, Nate," Pigeon said.

"See, Nate, Pigeon knows the drill," Denny said. "Just hand over your dessert and save yourself the hassle of getting trashed."

"Should we have a talk with Dirt Face after school?" Eric asked.

Denny shook his head. "We'll let it slide today, since we already beat him up before we met him. But now that you know the rules, don't make us teach you again."

Trevor wanted to pounce across the table, grab Denny by his curly blond hair, and pound him in the nose. But Denny was a strong kid. Nate looked equally angry and hesitant.

Denny and Eric walked away.

Pigeon started peeling his banana.

"Nice try with the cupcake," Trevor said to Nate.

"Sorry to waste it," Nate said.

"Are you kidding?" Pigeon stared at Nate like he was crazy. "I wish I could lose all my desserts that way!"

"Be glad you missed him," Summer said. "Denny is a psycho. He gets worse all the time. He flunked third grade, so he's really old enough to be in junior high."

"He doesn't bug us too much at school if we do what he says," Pigeon said.

"And after school?" Nate asked.

"After school it's more like a game," Trevor said. "Like a pretend war."

"Except not always pretend," Pigeon added. "Sometimes they take things too far."

"I've noticed," Nate said, touching the scab at the corner of his mouth.

"We've tried to fight back a little," Summer said. "They don't mind so much down at the creek. But when we try to stand up to them at school, they make life miserable."

"It works out simpler to let them play their little games at school," Trevor said. "Doing anything back just encourages them."

"We'll see about that," Nate said, watching the back of that curly blond head.

"I guess I should try bringing three cupcakes," Pigeon said miserably.

CHAPTER THREE
MOON ROCKS

ate, Summer, and Pigeon met Trevor by the gate at the back of the school. From the rear of the playing field, a path zigzagged down a slope to a road that paralleled Main Street. From the gate at the top of the path, Nate could see most of Colson Valley, including his neighborhood on the side of a low hill across the basin.

"How did your day go?" Trevor asked.

"Not bad," Summer said.

"I'm soaked," Pigeon confessed. "I can't stop sweating."

"I can't believe we have nine more months of Miss Doulin," Nate groaned.

They started down the path. Dry brush and thorny weeds covered the slope behind the school, with a few oak trees adding some shade. A squirrel dashed up a trunk.

"I'm parched," Trevor said.

"Me too," Pigeon said. "Where's a drinking fountain when you need one?"

"Have you guys tried that ice cream place?" Nate asked.

"On the corner of Main and Greenway?" Summer asked.

"Yeah, I think. The one on the way home."

"It's new," Trevor said. "I'm not sure it's open yet."

"It looked open this morning," Nate said. "We should check it out."

"I'm melting," Pigeon moaned.

"You could get some ice cream," Nate suggested.

"I only have like thirty cents," Pigeon said.

"I don't have money either," Nate said. "Maybe we could get a free sample. Or at least a glass of water."

The path behind the school deposited them onto Greenway. The road was one block over from Main. The street had little traffic and was lined with small houses whose low, chain-link fences protected unkempt yards. A few other groups of kids were also walking home along Greenway. Dogs barked from behind some of the fences.

The side streets along Greenway were minor until Main curved and crossed Greenway. The intersection where Main and Greenway met marked the end of where the town continued trying to imitate the Old West. It was also the location of the Sweet Tooth Ice Cream and Candy Shoppe.

When they reached Main Street, Nate noticed that Greenway had stop signs while Main had none. An old man in an orange vest held up a stop sign and walked them across the street.

Not much farther down Greenway on the right was Nate's neighborhood. But he and the others went to the left side of the street where the ice cream shop stood on the corner. A bell jangled as they pushed through the glass doors and into the pleasantly air-conditioned store.

The floor was a white and black checkerboard. Immaculate tables and chairs with chrome legs filled much of the expansive room, leaving space to access the long, L-shaped counter that protected two shelved walls crammed with candy. Licorice, jawbreakers, caramels, gingersnaps, cookies, marshmallow treats, peppermint sticks, gumdrops, malt balls, jelly beans, lollypops, chocolate bars, and numberless other sweets burdened the shelves, some sheathed in shiny wrappers, some visible in clear jars. They had entered an extensive and sophisticated library of delicious confections.

Near the door stood a life-sized wooden Indian rendered in skillful detail, down to his pruned face and wrinkled hands. Meticulously painted, he was an ancient chief with a long feathered headdress, trinkets dangling from his neck, a buckskin shirt, moccasins, and a tomahawk in one hand. He looked weary but courageous.

The shop was empty except for an older woman behind the counter dipping an apple in molten caramel. Her hair was pinned up in a gigantic bun the color of cinnamon. She had large green eyes, and though her youth was fading, she had very pleasant features.

"Come in," she called in a sweet voice, twirling the apple to keep the caramel from dripping before crusting it in crushed nuts. "We're newly opened. Children are my favorite customers."

The children crossed the room to where the woman was placing her caramel apple on a sheet of waxed paper. "This place looks expensive," Nate ventured.

"Candy can carry a hefty price tag," she agreed. "There are brands of fine European chocolate that cost a hundred dollars for a few ounces. You see, superlative chocolate must be made with the proper care, by the correct process, and from the best cacao beans. No shortcuts. Such supreme attention to quality demands generous recompense. We carry no name brands here. Everything is handmade. But in spite of my rigid insistence on excellence, I try to stock items for every budget. I even keep a jar of penny candy near the register."

"Candy that costs a penny?" Pigeon exclaimed in hungry disbelief.

"I swap out the penny candy daily," she continued. "If you don't like what we have on sale today, you can call again tomorrow." She motioned at the large jar near the register. Already digging for change in his pocket, Pigeon hurried toward the jar.

"No name brands?" Trevor asked. "No Reese's Peanut Butter Cups? No Jolly Ranchers? No Snickers?"

"I have my own brands," the woman said. "Some from suppliers, many I concoct myself. If you like peanut butter cups, try my Peanut Butter Blast. If you like Jolly Ranchers, try my Sucker Squares. If you like Snickers, try a Riot bar. You may never go back to the brands you know."

"These are only a penny?" Pigeon asked. He was holding up a smallish pretzel smothered in white and dark chocolate.

"That's right."

Pigeon examined the change in his palm. "I'll take thirty-two, please."

The woman cocked her head sympathetically. "I neglected to mention, I sell only one penny candy per customer each day. If not, I doubt I could stay in business. But take me up on the offer every day, if you like. You'll find I never scrimp on quality, even for the least expensive treats."

"Can I get one for each of my friends?" Pigeon asked.

"Absolutely," she responded. "One per customer."

"Four, then," he said.

"How much is your ice cream?" Summer inquired. She was standing farther along the counter peering at the tubs of ice cream through the glass.

"For kids, a dollar a scoop, whether cup or cone," she said, taking a nickel from Pigeon in return for a penny and four of the chocolate-drenched pretzels. "Fixings for sundaes are extra, as are shakes and malts."

"I'm going to bring ice cream money tomorrow," Summer declared.

The others gathered as Pigeon distributed the pretzels. Nate put the whole thing in his mouth. There was so much chocolate that it overwhelmed the taste of the pretzel, which only served to add a little crunch. The chocolate was richer and creamier than any he had ever sampled. "This is awesome," he said as he finished chewing. The others agreed with wide eyes.

"How much for another one?" Trevor asked.

"You don't want to know," she said. "Tell me a little about yourselves. I have not yet met many children in town."

"I'm Summer. This is Trevor, Nate, and Pigeon."

"I'm Mrs. White," she said. "Pleased to meet you. You're on your way home from school?"

"Yes," Pigeon said.

"What grade are you in?"

"Fifth," Trevor and Summer answered together.

Mrs. White nodded thoughtfully. "Are you good students?"

"Pigeon is probably the best in the school," Summer said.

"I'm no great brain," Pigeon said, "but the three of us participate in the gifted program." He indicated Trevor and Summer.

"I did accelerated learning at my old school," Nate mentioned.

Mrs. White licked a stray drop of caramel from her knuckle. "What do you children do for fun?"

"We have a club," Pigeon said, receiving a glare from Summer.

"What sort of club?" Mrs. White asked.

Pigeon looked to Summer. "We explore stuff," Summer said.

"And ride bikes," Nate added.

"Explorers?" Mrs. White said musingly. "Do you kids like to daydream?"

"I do," Trevor said.

"Me too," Nate echoed.

"I'm always on the lookout for clever, imaginative explorers," Mrs. White said, glancing at the door of the shop. "I'm familiar with Colson, but only recently arrived in town after a long absence. It is already beginning to feel like home again."

"I'm new here too," Nate said. "My family moved here from Southern California."

"Do you have any other inexpensive candy?" Pigeon asked.

"How much money do you have?" Mrs. White inquired.

"Twenty-eight cents," he replied.

Mrs. White pressed her lips together. "Hmmm. I'm in the process of hiring help. If you kids want to assist in some chores, I could reward you with treats."

They all agreed enthusiastically.

Mrs. White walked along the counter, crouched, and arose holding spray bottles and rags. "This is for the windows," she declared, holding up one spray bottle. Nate accepted it. "This is for the tables," she said, handing the other bottle to Trevor.

"The tables look pretty clean," Pigeon observed. Summer jabbed him with her elbow.

"You can never be too tidy," Mrs. White said. "Wipe everything down and I'd be happy to share some goodies with you."

Nate and Summer attacked the windows while Trevor and Pigeon tackled the tables. The candy shop had an impressive multitude of tables, and many large windows, not to mention the glass front doors, but they worked quickly, spraying and wiping thoroughly.

Mrs. White busied herself behind the counter. Every so often Nate looked over and caught the older woman pausing in her chores, watching them.

Trevor and Pigeon finished the tables before Nate and Summer had completed the insides of the windows. Trevor and Pigeon added their rags to the window work, dragging chairs to reach the high parts, allowing Nate to concentrate on spraying. A couple of customers came and went while they wiped down the outside of the windows.

By the time they finished, the four of them were tired. They returned the rags and spray bottles to Mrs. White at the counter.

"Excellent work," Mrs. White cheered. "You four make quite a team." She placed a small glass of thick yellow fluid topped with whipped cream on the counter. Alongside it she set a tiny brownie. She cut the brownie into four bite-sized quarters and gave each of them a plastic spoon. Pigeon frowned at the miniscule portions. "Go ahead and sample my homemade eggnog and the butterscotch swirl brownie. I'll give each of you a full-sized version of whichever you like more."

The smooth, cold eggnog was thick as a milkshake, and creamy beyond description. Nate had never tasted anything like it. The chewy brownie exploded with a harmonious mix of chocolate and butterscotch.

"There's no way to decide," Pigeon moaned after sampling both.

"Maybe I should have offered some of my secret candy instead," Mrs. White sighed in a quiet tone, as if talking to herself.

"Secret candy?" Nate asked, instantly intrigued.

"My goodness," Mrs. White said. "Forget I mentioned it. I never bring up my secret candy on a first meeting. Which will it be, eggnog or brownie?"

"What kind of secret candy?" Trevor pressed.

Mrs. White stared at them. "I shouldn't allude to a secret without explaining, I suppose," she admitted reluctantly. "But I must ask for a rain check on this one. I never discuss my secret candy on a first meeting. Perhaps if you ask me some other time. Tell you what, to make up for my slip, I'll take away your choice. You may each have a brownie *and* a cup of eggnog!"

"Secret?" Pigeon said cheerily. "Any of you guys hear about a secret? I'm sure I haven't!"

"Okay," Nate consented. "But I'm asking again later."

Mrs. White began setting the treats on the counter.

* * * * *

Nate, Summer, Trevor, and Pigeon visited the candy shop every day after school. They worked hard, and Mrs. White rewarded them kindly. On Wednesday, the penny candy was cream puffs with chocolate icing, the chore was refilling the coin-operated gumball machines, and the prize was ice cream sundaes. Thursday they bought jawbreakers for a penny, then washed dishes to earn apple fritters.

It was exactly a week after their original visit to the candy shop when Nate reopened the subject of the secret candy. The four kids were seated at the counter sipping at delicious chocolate malts through sturdy straws. They had recently finished wiping down all the shelves and dusting the wooden Indian. The store was empty except for them and Mrs. White, who was polishing the counter while the kids drank their reward.

"You told us to ask about the secret candy some other time," Nate reminded Mrs. White without warning. "Has it been long enough?"

Mrs. White stopped wiping. She twisted the rag in her hands. "I was quietly hoping you had forgotten."

The kids shook their heads.

Mrs. White folded her arms and shook her head. "It is hard to put curiosity back to bed once you awaken it," she conceded. "Very well. I have a line of extra-special candy that I don't offer to the general public. The secret candy is far superior to anything on the menu, but is certainly not for everyone." She eyed each of them in turn. "That said, I pride myself on being a good judge of character, and my instincts tell me you four might appreciate it. But my secret candy must be earned by more than cleaning windows and shelves. Would you four be interested?"

"Of course," Nate said. The others nodded eagerly.

"Dear me, where do I begin?" Mrs. White asked, smoothing her hands over her frilly apron. She took a calming breath. "Some of my special candy requires extremely odd ingredients. What do you kids know about beetles?"

"There are more species of beetle than any other animal," Pigeon said.

"Very good," Mrs. White approved. "Hundreds of thousands of different species, with more being discovered all the time. There is a certain species in this area, I call them dusk bugs, whose eggs I need for a project I am working on."

Trevor spat a burst of milkshake onto the counter. "You use beetle eggs in your recipes?"

"I know it sounds peculiar," Mrs. White acknowledged. "The beetle eggs don't actually end up in any of my food; that would be distasteful. The process for producing my special candy is complicated."

"So no beetle eggs in this malt," Pigeon said, poised to take a new sip.

"There are no insect eggs in my food," Mrs. White reiterated.

"You should use that in your advertising," Nate suggested, stirring his drink with his straw.

"Where would we find these beetle eggs?" Summer asked.

"There is a trick to it," Mrs. White said. "If you follow Greenway up past the Presidential Estates, the road ends after a few blocks."

"Right," Trevor said, using a napkin from a nearby dispenser to wipe up the mess he had spewed.

"A dirt track continues where Greenway stops, running alongside a brook. One moment." Mrs. White passed through batwing doors into a back room and returned holding a can of shoe polish, a small leather drawstring pouch, and a pair of glass jars. "As the sun sets, follow the dirt road some distance along the stream until you see mushrooms growing." She uncapped the shoe polish can to reveal that it was actually full of a grainy, maroon paste. "Set this on the ground. The odor of the attractant and the time of day should summon a few dusk bugs. Open the pouch and sprinkle some of the contents on the beetles. They will soon burrow into the mushrooms. After the beetles emerge, collect the mushrooms, place them in the jars, and bring them to me tomorrow."

"You sure it will work?" Nate asked.

"I know it is a strange request," Mrs. White. "If oddness turns you off, we should forget discussing my special candy. The candy can do astounding things, but all the effects are certainly strange."

"Strange is okay," Trevor said.

"Strange is great," Nate said.

"These old bones make it harder every year for me to gather my required ingredients," Mrs. White explained. "If you will collect the eggs as I described, I will share some of my special candy with you. I am confident you will find it amazing and well worth the effort."

"With no bug eggs in it," Pigeon clarified.

"Correct," Mrs. White said.

"Can't hurt to give it a shot," Summer said. "Can you guys get away?"

"I'll just pretend it's a school assignment," Nate said.

"Good thinking," Pigeon said. "I'll have to go home, get my homework done, and eat dinner. We ought to meet up around eight. Will we be able to make it home before dark?"

"If you move swiftly, that should not be a problem," Mrs. White assured him.

* * * * *

The fat sun balanced on the horizon as Nate, Summer, Trevor, and Pigeon left Greenway and pedaled their bikes along the meandering dirt road. Brushy slopes rose on either side, and trees crowded the trickling steam. Summer occasionally stopped to check along the edge of the stream for mushrooms. On her fourth attempt, she called the others over.

The four of them huddled around a cluster of small beige mushrooms. Pigeon pointed out a second patch of mushrooms not far away. Trevor withdrew the can of shoe polish, uncapped it, and set it on the ground.

"Think any beetles will show up?" Nate asked.

"She acted like she knew what she was talking about," Summer said.

"I'm sure some crazy people are very sincere," Pigeon observed.

"This is the only way to really find out," Trevor said. "If the bugs don't show, we'll know she's a little senile. One of my great aunts was like that. Very nice, but she talked to the people on TV like they were her friends. She'd get dressed up for them to come over, introduce us to them, that sort of thing."

The last of the sun sank below the horizon, and they waited, watching the maroon paste. Insects clicked and rattled in the brush, but no beetles appeared.

"If this doesn't work," Nate said, "maybe we can still bag some mushrooms and get some special candy."

"No way!" Summer said. "I'm not taking advantage of that sweet old lady."

Pigeon chucked a pebble into the stream. "Besides, would you really want special candy from a woman with delusions about beetle eggs?"

"Good point," Trevor said. "How long do we wait?"

"Hold on," Summer said. "Look who just showed up."

A shiny black beetle crawled over the lip of the tin and began wallowing in the maroon paste.

"Get out the pouch," Pigeon said.

As Nate opened the pouch, a second beetle joined the first. By the time he sprinkled the fine gray powder on them, a third beetle had appeared. The sprinkled beetles left the paste and wandered toward the mushrooms, and several more took their place in the open shoe polish can. Nate sprinkled the new beetles. One of the beetles scaled a mushroom and began burrowing into it.

"Would you look at that?" Pigeon breathed. "To tell the truth, I didn't think there was any chance it would actually happen."

More beetles entered the shoe polish can, and more sprinkled beetles dug their way into nearby mushrooms. "How many do we need?" Nate asked, pinching powder onto the new arrivals.

"We should be fine with these," Summer said. "But keep sprinkling the newcomers just in case."

A few more beetles arrived, stragglers, and Nate powdered them. After no new beetles showed up for several minutes, Trevor picked up the can and put on the lid.

The sunset faded. Finally the first beetle emerged from a mushroom, and Summer placed the fungus in a jar. Soon, more beetles crawled out. Before long the kids had a bunch of mushrooms in each jar.

Stars were becoming visible as Summer zipped one jar into her backpack and Trevor tucked the other into his. The kids pedaled quickly down the dirt road, then onto Greenway. The four of them paused where the jogging path met Greenway, the point where Summer would split off from the rest of them.

"Mission accomplished," Summer said.

Trevor picked at a peeling sticker on the frame of his bike. "Who would have guessed it would actually work?"

"Which means Mrs. White isn't crazy," Nate said. "I wonder what her special candy is like?"

"I can't wait to find out," Pigeon exclaimed.

"See you guys tomorrow," Summer said.

They went their separate ways.

* * * * *

When Nate, Summer, Trevor, and Pigeon arrived at the candy shop the next day, Mrs. White stood at the register bagging a box of chocolates for a woman in a large red wig. The woman paid and exited the store.

"Well?" Mrs. White asked. "Was last night a success?"

In answer, Summer unzipped her backpack and held up the jar of mushrooms. Trevor did likewise.

"So many?" Mrs. White asked, sounding delighted. "Follow me into the back." She lifted a hinged segment of the counter, and the kids followed her through the batwing doors into the rear of the store. Barrels and crates dominated the gloomy room. Shelves loaded with bags and cartons and unnamed ingredients lined the walls. Various delicacies were in development on a trio of sizable worktables. Mrs. White escorted the children to a small, square table in the corner covered by a purple embroidered tablecloth. A microscope rested on the table.

Mrs. White unscrewed the lid of one of the jars and removed a mushroom. She sliced into the bulbous fungus with a scalpel, excising a flap of beige matter. Setting the sample on a slide, she peered into her microscope, adjusting the focus knob.

"Well done!" Mrs. White exclaimed, looking up at them. "You four reaped quite a harvest, better than I expected."

"I have to admit, we had our doubts about whether it would work," Pigeon said. "We were all impressed."

"Any rational person would have entertained some doubts," Mrs. White said. "What matters is that you trusted me enough to successfully carry out my instructions. I could make good use of helpers like yourselves." She rummaged beneath the table for a moment and came up with a cylindrical aluminum container.

"What's that?" Pigeon asked.

Mrs. White removed the lid of the container. "Most rock candy is nothing more than crystallized sugar," she began, removing four translucent chunks from the container. "I call these Moon Rocks. They are magical candy. I do not expect you to immediately believe this. But you will after you try them."

Nate, Summer, and Trevor shared a look expressing their mutual concern that Mrs. White might be a lunatic after all.

"Find a private place," Mrs. White suggested. "You will not want to be observed. Just suck the candy. Don't bother spitting it out to save it for later. Once you spit it out, the candy loses all potency. Biting it can be hazardous. Mark my words—if I am to share magic candy with you, for your own safety and for the well-being of others, you must learn to consume it as directed. Any questions?"

"No bug eggs?" Nate asked.

"No bug eggs," Mrs. White confirmed.

"Are you giving us drugs?" Pigeon asked warily.

Mrs. White stroked his head gently. "Why, of course not. Drugs are a terrible menace! What kind of person would I be to disguise drugs as candy and give them to children? I certainly would not be in business long! But I'm glad you're on the lookout—there are unsavory characters in the world. This is a candy shop. Some of my candy is very special. Unique in all the world, in fact, and capable of astounding things. Give the Moon Rocks a try. Like the beetles, you'll find it much easier to believe me after you put my words to the test. Find a quiet place. Suck, don't bite. Or don't try them, if you prefer. Now I must get back to minding the store and preparing goodies. Thank you for your help. If you enjoy the candy, please come visit me again."

Nate, Summer, Trevor, and Pigeon each accepted a Moon Rock and let Mrs. White usher them out of the store.

* * * * *

Near the creek below Monroe Circle was a roomy hollow canopied by five trees and sheltered by barriers of prickly undergrowth. There were only two ways in, and both were tricky to see. One required crawling. Four of the trees were quite good for climbing. The largest tree had huge, winding roots that grew out of the steep bank above the creek. The gnarled roots made for a superb emergency hiding place. This secluded hollow was the hideout of the Blue Falcons. They called it the Nest.

Summer crawled into the Nest, followed by Trevor, Pigeon, and Nate. Once inside, they stood in a circle, all still holding the sugar crystals Mrs. White had given them. "Who's going to try it first?" Nate asked.

"You're the newest member of the club," Summer replied.

"So I get to pick? Okay . . . Trevor."

"I think she meant you should try the candy first," Trevor clarified.

"What do you think it does?" Pigeon asked.

"Nothing," Summer said. "But I hope it tastes good."

"She sounded pretty convinced they were magical," Pigeon said hopefully. "And she was right about the beetles."

Trevor held up his Moon Rock, studying it. "I wonder what happens if we bite them?"

"I bet our heads will explode," said Nate. He looked around the circle; the others were all watching him with expectant looks on their faces. "Okay, I'll do it first." He popped the Moon Rock into his mouth.

"Feel any different?" Pigeon asked eagerly.

"A little," Nate said. "Sort of tingly. It tastes really good. I almost feel . . ."

He moved to take a step and floated up into the air. He rose slowly, his feet reaching the height of Trevor's eyes before he drifted downward to land gently on the ground.

" . . . lighter," Nate finished, bewildered.

They stared at each other in awed silence.

"They really are magical," Pigeon finally murmured.

Nate tried a little hop, and this time he glided over Summer's head, landing softly on the other side of her. He could almost have reached some of the overhanging branches of the trees. "It's like I'm on the moon," Nate said. "You know, the way the astronauts look on TV, bouncing around in low gravity."

"Moon Rocks," Trevor said. "I want to try." He stuck his candy into his mouth and jumped hard. He launched up into the limbs of the tree above, catching hold of one to stop his ascent. "Whoa!" he called from his lofty perch. "It felt like I was heading into orbit."

"I'm not sure *Moon Rocks* is the right name," Pigeon said, examining his piece of crystallized sugar. "The gravity on the moon is roughly one-sixth that of earth. Which means you could jump six times higher there than you could here. But that branch is more than six times higher than Trevor can jump. And he was still heading up when he caught hold."

"And you say you're not a brain?" Nate said.

"I just like books about space," Pigeon apologized.

"How do I get down?" Trevor asked. "This is freaky."

"Just drop," Pigeon said. "Since you jumped up there, it should feel no worse than falling a couple of feet."

"I don't know," Trevor fretted. "What if it stops working? I could break my legs."

Taking aim, Nate jumped toward the branch Trevor was clutching. He did not jump with everything he had, just a solid leap. He glided up through the air, feeling almost weightless. As he reached the apex of his trajectory, Nate came alongside Trevor and caught hold of the same limb.

"Watch," Nate said, letting go and floating to the ground, gradually gaining a little speed. He landed just hard enough to make his knees bend a little. Trevor let go of the branch and landed the same way.

"You guys *have* to try this," Trevor said.

"Maybe we should save ours," Summer said. "They might come in handy when we're out on adventures."

"Mrs. White acted like we could get more," Pigeon reminded her.

"For how much?" Summer replied. "A billion dollars?"

"Just try it," Nate urged. "You're not afraid, are you?"

Summer's eyes hardened and she stuck the Moon Rock into her mouth. Pigeon did likewise. They both took a few experimental leaps. Pigeon could not stop giggling. Nate and Trevor bounded around as well.

"What if the candy really is drugs?" Pigeon asked. "What if we only think we're jumping really high because our minds are warped?"

"You saw me jumping high before you tried the Moon Rock," Nate pointed out.

"Oh, yeah," Pigeon said.

"Over here," Summer called. She stood at the brink of the steep bank above the creek. The others loped over to her with long, slow-motion strides. "Who wants to jump it?"

At this point the bank of the creek was more than ten feet high. The far bank was lower, and almost thirty feet away. "Your idea," Nate said.

"I do everything first," she complained.

"I tried the candy first," Nate pointed out.

"Think I could get a running start?" she asked.

"You'd have to back up," Nate said. "You could take a few steps if you pace yourself."

"But carefully," Trevor said. "If you misjudge, you could drift right into the water."

"If you fall, be careful how you land," Pigeon warned. "It will only feel like you fell a little ways, but the creekbed is rocky."

Summer took a pair of long, low strides away from the creek and turned around. Keeping low, she started forward, pushing off tentatively with the first step, then much more forcefully with the second. Landing about four feet shy of the edge, she pushed off with all she had, soaring upward in a smooth, mild arc. She easily cleared the creekbed and had to fend off small branches before catching hold of a tree limb on the far bank. Letting go, she drifted to the ground. "Easy!" she challenged.

Duplicating the strategy Summer had used, Trevor took two

steps, but he leapt from the edge more gently and landed ten feet beyond the far bank, stumbling slightly. Nate copied Trevor and landed in almost the same spot.

"I don't know," Pigeon said, staring down at the water.

"It's no sweat, Pidge," Trevor said.

"I don't know," Pigeon repeated.

"Go for it," Nate said.

"Okay, okay." Instead of backing up for a running start, Pigeon squatted and sprang, keeping his feet together. He rose very high but had little forward momentum. After he reached the zenith of his flight, his speed lazily increased as he descended toward the center of the shallow creek.

Summer crouched and sprang, moving low and relatively swiftly on a course to intercept Pigeon. They glided past each other, just out of reach. Pigeon hit the water with a splash and ended up on his backside. Summer had not jumped very high, so she hit the side of the far bank. Pushing off from the dirt wall, she drifted back over the creek to land near Nate. Pigeon spat out his candy and waded out of the creek, his soaked jeans a much darker blue.

"That was cool of you to go after Pigeon," Nate said to Summer.

"You came close," Trevor said encouragingly. "I didn't even think to try."

"How much of your Moon Rock has dissolved?" Summer asked Nate.

"I still have a good amount," he said. "Don't worry, I'm paying attention. I don't want to run out in midflight."

Pigeon waddled over to them, pants dripping. "As soon as I spat out the Moon Rock, my weight returned to normal," Pigeon reported. "I wonder if that means you guys would seem really light to me?" He grabbed Trevor under his arms and hoisted him into the air. "Wow, it feels like you're made of Styrofoam!" He tossed Trevor, who sailed more than ten feet before landing lightly.

"That's pretty cool," Nate said. "See if you can throw me like a football."

"No!" Summer warned. "Have you ever seen Pigeon throw a ball? No offense, Pidge."

"None taken," he said. "She's right, I'm not very coordinated."

"Check it out," Trevor said. "Flying kick." He jumped into the air and glided over to a tree, lashed out with his leg, and rebounded a dozen feet after striking the trunk.

"Cool," Nate said. "We should practice jumping sideways off stuff, like Summer did with the bank. Trevor sort of did it with that kick."

"You shouldn't have spat out your Moon Rock," Trevor said to Pigeon.

"It's okay," Pigeon said. "You guys bounce around. I need to go change my pants anyhow. Seems like I'm always the one who ends up in the creek!"

CHAPTER FOUR
WHITE FUDGE

Pigeon had plans to sneak in the front door. Since his mom was a homemaker with overprotective tendencies, he didn't want to get caught in wet jeans again.

But his cousin Nile was waiting out front astride his motorcycle. Nile had picked out Pigeon's leather jacket. At seventeen, with his head shaved, he looked a lot better than Pigeon in studded black leather.

"Where were you?" Nile asked. "Taking a swim?"

"I fell in the creek."

"How'd the jacket go over?"

"I sweated like crazy," Pigeon said. "And I got teased. I decided not to wear it today."

"Those same bullies?"

"Mainly."

"You ought to let me handle them," Nile said.

"No way, that'll just make it worse."

"I'll just scare them. I'm not going to rough up sixth graders. I'll threaten to beat up their dads."

"I've got it covered," Pigeon said.

"If you say so," Nile approved. "Remember, it takes time for a new image to stick. And you can take the jacket off if it gets too hot."

"Okay."

Nile revved the engine of his bike. "Say hi to your dad." He pulled out of the driveway and noisily accelerated up the street.

Pigeon sighed. How could he be so clumsy with a cousin that cool? As Pigeon started up the steps, his mom opened the front door, a short, pudgy woman with thick black hair. She placed a hand over her mouth. "Paul, what happened to your jeans?"

"I fell in the creek," he said.

"They were brand-new!" she panicked.

"It was just water," he said.

"Filthy creek water," she lamented, rushing down the steps to fuss over him. He wished he had a Moon Rock right then so he could fly away. She always made him feel like such a baby. "It may be time to give up playing down there." He would have been worried, but she always said something like that after he drenched his shoes or got hurt.

"I'm fine. I was playing with my best friends." That was the right card to play. He had not had any friends until second grade. And it was only last year that his friendship with Summer and Trevor had become cemented. His mom had been worried about him—she was thrilled that he was finally socializing.

"Well, come inside and get cleaned up. You need to be more careful down there. How was your day?"

"Good," he said, following her inside. "I got another trivia question right. Miss Doulin seems uptight but nothing I can't handle."

"Where's your jacket? You look so sharp in it!"

"I didn't wear it today. Everybody liked it so much last week. I didn't want to look like a show-off!"

His mom beamed. Although Nile had selected the jacket, his mom had paid for it. Pigeon hurried up the stairs to his room. He ditched his wet shirt and jeans and put on tan shorts and a T-shirt. He could hear his mom scolding his sister downstairs. He had two younger sisters, ages six and three. They gave his mom people to worry about besides him, for which he was grateful.

Newly dressed, Pigeon slipped out the front door and hurried back to the creek. Upon reaching the jogging path, he noticed a single bubble the size of a baseball hovering near the Nest. It was peculiar, because instead of drifting it maintained an unwavering position about eight feet off the ground. Curious, Pigeon approached it. As he drew near, the bubble lifted higher, floating out of sight behind some trees.

In the Nest, Pigeon found Trevor, Summer, and Nate sitting on the ground. "Pigeon!" Trevor said. "Welcome back!"

"Were you guys blowing bubbles?" Pigeon asked.

"No," Summer answered. "Why?"

"I saw a bubble floating just outside the Nest. I guess you finished the candy."

"It lasted pretty long," Nate said.

"We were just talking about going back to the ice cream shop," Summer said.

"I was thinking the same thing," Pigeon said.

"I hope Mrs. White will give us more Moon Rocks now that we believe her," Trevor said.

"Who knows what other types of candy she might have," Summer said.

"I wonder why she isn't world famous," Nate mused. "If she can make magic candy, she should be a zillionaire."

"She probably wants to keep it a secret," Trevor said. "Remember how she told us to try the candy when nobody was around?"

"We've finally uncovered a true mystery," Summer said. "There's really only one way to find out more about Mrs. White."

* * * * *

The bell jingled when Nate opened the door. A tall, plain woman was paying for a caramel apple at the register. A pair of teenagers slouched at a table eating ice-cream cones. A male dwarf with spiky blond hair shaved flat on top was balanced on a stool placing candy boxes on a high shelf. Summer, Trevor, and Pigeon entered the store after Nate. Pigeon waited to hold the door as the tall woman exited.

"How can I help you?" the middle-aged dwarf asked, hopping down from the stool and mostly vanishing behind the counter.

"These are friends," Mrs. White said, raising the hinged counter-top. "Mind the shop for a moment, Arnie?"

"You got it," the dwarf said.

Nate and the others passed behind the counter and into the cluttered back room. "You hired a helper," Nate said.

"I did," Mrs. White replied. "And there will be more to come. I take it you tried the Moon Rocks."

"They were incredible," Summer raved.

"We seemed to jump a lot higher than we would on the moon," Pigeon remarked.

"Very observant," Mrs. White approved. "The Moon Rocks reduce the effect of gravity between ten and twelve times, thus imitating an environment of considerably less than lunar gravity. Did you have fun?"

"It was awesome," Nate said. "It felt amazing jumping so high. We grabbed onto tree branches, and hopped over the creek, and we practiced pushing off stuff to leap sideways."

"I'm so glad it was enjoyable," Mrs. White said, her smile creating deep dimples in her cheeks.

"I fell in the creek," Pigeon confessed.

"We were wondering if you might let us try some more," Trevor said.

"Or some other magic candy," Summer added.

"What use would a sample be if there were no more candy to be had?" Mrs. White said.

"Do you have lots of different kinds?" Pigeon asked.

"Let's not get ahead of ourselves," Mrs. White said. She lowered her voice, and her demeanor grew more serious. "I have more magic candy, but we must reach an agreement before I can share it with you. As you might imagine, magic candy is most difficult to produce, and my supplies are limited."

"I knew it," Nate huffed. "It's going to cost a fortune."

"Don't jump to conclusions," Mrs. White chided. "I know I'm dealing with children. I don't expect you to pay for the candy in cash. Its monetary value far exceeds what even your parents could afford. I am willing to give you the opportunity to earn more candy by performing small services for me. And I expect you to keep the effects of the candy secret. Should you try to tell others what my candy can do, not only will I deny your story, I will never share magic candy with any of you again." Her voice and expression softened. "I don't mean to be stern, I just want to impress upon you how earnest I am about this. Can you keep my secret?"

The kids all nodded. "What do we have to do for more candy?" Nate asked.

"Your first task is easy," Mrs. White said. "Since I'm starting up a new business, I recently whipped up a batch of one of my specialties—white fudge. I want you to distribute free samples to your family and friends. In return, I'll give you a bag of Moon Rocks."

"Can we try the fudge too?" Pigeon asked.

"There is a catch to eating the white fudge," Mrs. White cautioned. "It tastes absolutely scrumptious. Once you taste one piece, your mouth will water for more. Which is why I give them away to drum up business. But the fudge has some side effects. It dulls the effectiveness of my magic candy. It also makes it difficult for those who eat it to notice the powers my special treats grant to others. So the fudge serves a dual purpose: It will entice your friends and family into my store, so I can remain profitable, and it will help them ignore any oddities resulting from the candy I give you."

"Will it hurt anybody?" Trevor asked.

"The fudge is harmless," Mrs. White assured them. "The only reason to avoid my white fudge is if you want magic candy to work on you. After you eat the fudge, sucking on a Moon Rock won't make you a pound lighter."

"When will we get the Moon Rocks?" Nate asked.

"Take home my fudge. Share it tonight with your parents, older relatives, and any other friends, and the bag of Moon Rocks, containing at least forty pieces, will be yours tomorrow." She picked up a white rectangular box with "Sweet Tooth Ice Cream and Candy Shoppe" stamped in red and opened it. Inside were four large cubes of white fudge.

Pigeon leaned forward to sniff the contents. "Smells good."

"I'll give each of you two boxes," Mrs. White said. "Make sure you emphasize where you got the fudge, and that our shop has many other goodies. And, just in case the temptation is too great, here is some dark fudge for each of you." She handed each of them a dense square of brown fudge.

* * * * *

Sitting at his desk the next day, Nate could hardly wait for school to end. The clock seemed paralyzed. That morning, he had gotten his name written on the board for cracking jokes. A name on the board was a warning—if he got a check mark after it, he would have to stay after class, so he had forced himself to keep quiet the rest of the day.

Staying after class was not an option. He was anxious to collect his reward from Mrs. White. The previous night he had shared the white fudge with his family. His dad, mom, and sister each ate a cube. They all loved it, and wondered why he didn't eat the last piece. He explained that he had already had some. His dad ended up splitting the extra block of fudge with his mom. Everyone seemed in an unusually relaxed mood after the fudge. They all sat around watching TV together for the remainder of the evening, which was out of character for his parents.

Earlier that day at lunch, after Pigeon had lost his dessert to Denny, Eric, and Kyle, Nate learned that the others had given fudge to their families as well. Trevor had also presented a box to his neighbors. Nate still had an extra box under his bed.

Miss Doulin paced at the front of the room, droning about homework. Nate was too excited by the thought of gliding through the air again to pay attention. He doodled in his notebook, depicting a stick figure jumping from the half-court line to slam-dunk a basketball. Then he diagrammed how a stick person would leap back and forth between two skyscrapers to reach the top.

Finally, the bell rang. Pigeon went to the front of the room and presented a box of white fudge to Miss Doulin. She smiled and they chatted for a moment. Pigeon had offered a bunch of correct answers in class again today. The guy might not have much athletic ability, but he was certainly a world-class kiss up!

"I saw you giving sweets to your new girlfriend," Nate teased as he and Pigeon walked out of the room.

"She's not my girlfriend," Pigeon said.

"Not yet," Nate said. "But she's not married, she calls you by your nickname, and you're giving her chocolates. Give it time."

"Lay off," Summer said, coming up from behind. "Can't hurt for one of us to get on Miss Doulin's good side."

"It isn't just getting on her good side," Nate said. "I bet she writes about Pigeon in her diary."

"You're the one who keeps talking about it, Nate," Summer pointed out. "Maybe you're the one with the secret crush."

Nate found himself without a comeback. Fortunately, he saw Trevor walking toward them and jogged over to greet him. "Ready to go for a moonwalk?" Nate asked.

Trevor gave him a high-five. "For sure. Let's get over to Sweet Tooth."

The four friends were hurrying toward the ramp at the rear of the school when something stung the back of Nate's ear. Nate looked over his shoulder and found Denny leering at him. As usual, Eric and Kyle were following right behind. "What's your problem?" Nate said, turning away from the older boy, trying to ignore him.

Denny flicked his ear again. Nate whirled, angry. He wanted to tear out a handful of that curly blond hair. "Come on," Denny invited. "Start it."

Despite Nate's outrage, a look at Denny's stocky frame warned him that although this kid was only a year ahead of him in school, he was two or three years ahead of him in growth. If Nate tried to fight him, he would be playing right into his hands. For a moment, Nate considered swinging his backpack like a club. Instead, he just said, "Go find a better hobby."

"Actually," Denny said innocently, "I came over because I need a favor. See, I'm supposed to do an oral report about retarded kids, so I was wondering if I could follow you guys around for a few hours. Do a little firsthand research."

Eric and Kyle burst out laughing.

"Maybe you should interview your mom," Nate said. "None of us ever flunked a grade."

The laughing stopped. Nate relished the hurt expression that flashed across Denny's features. For a moment, Denny seemed to be groping for something to say, then he shoved Nate hard, sending him sprawling onto the grass. Nate looked up at him, still feeling victorious.

Denny picked up Nate's backpack and chucked it over the fence at the back of the school. The bag tumbled down the weedy hill.

"Don't cry, Dirt Face." Denny pouted theatrically, strutting away with Eric and Kyle.

"You really are insane," Summer said as Nate got to his feet.

"You burned him good, though," Trevor said.

"I'm not going to let him push me around," Nate said.

"Looks like he just did," Summer said. "I'm telling you, don't egg him on—it only makes it worse."

As they descended the ramp at the back of the school, Trevor ran off the path and grabbed Nate's bag, rejoining the others at the bottom of the slope, where they set off along Greenway. An old woman with a curly gray hairdo and checkered pants roamed her yard watering weed-choked flowers with a hose. She smiled and waved as they walked by, a beauty-queen wave, hand near her cheek.

They were nearing the intersection of Greenway and Main when a bleary-eyed man in a stained corduroy jacket came running toward them down one of the side streets. "Summer, Trevor, Pidge, Nate! Hold up! You have to listen to me."

The kids turned to face the oncoming stranger. He had lean features, a stubbly beard, and wild hair. "You guys know him?" Nate asked.

"Not by name," Summer said.

"I've noticed him roaming around town lately," Trevor said. "I think he's homeless."

"Stay away from Sweet Tooth," the stranger warned, stumbling slightly. "You can't trust Mrs. White. She's dangerous. You can't trust anyone!" He was still rushing toward them.

"That's close enough," Nate commanded.

The man stopped short. "You have to let me explain. Nate, it's me. I'm you! I'm from the future!"

"Right," Nate said. "You don't look anything like me. How do you know my name?"

"I have no time," the stranger said. He plunged his fingers into his hair. "What was I thinking? I forgot that you weren't going to believe me. I guess you guys don't want to come with me so I can fill you in on some things?"

"Sorry, we're not going anywhere with you," Summer said.

"This guy harassing you?" the crossing guard called, approaching from down the street.

"I think he's drunk," Pigeon said.

The stranger threw up his hands like he was under arrest. "No problem here, sorry to bother you kids. Keep in mind, robbing graves isn't right. I have things to do."

The man sprinted away from them down Greenway, swerving unsteadily. "What a nutcase," Trevor muttered.

"Out of his mind," Nate agreed.

"What do you think he has against Mrs. White?" Summer wondered.

"He probably can't afford her ice cream or something," Trevor said.

The man turned down a side street and vanished from view. "What if she did something to him?" Pigeon asked. "What if she made him crazy?"

"No way," Nate said. "She's too nice."

"She does make magic candy," Pigeon reminded them. "She might not be safe."

"We'll be careful," Summer said.

"Weird that he knew our names," Trevor observed.

"And that he was in such a hurry," Pigeon added. "Don't homeless drunks usually loaf around?"

"He was probably on drugs," Summer said. "Some drugs make you hyper."

They reached the crosswalk. "You kids all right?" the balding crossing guard asked. "What did that fellow want?"

"We're fine," Summer said. "He was just nuts."

"If he keeps troubling you, let me know, we'll get the police involved."

"Thanks," Pigeon said.

The guard held up his sign and helped them across Main. When they reached the door to the Sweet Tooth Ice Cream and Candy Shoppe, they found it locked. A sign in the window proclaimed that the store was closed. As they were turning away, Mrs. White hurried to the door, unlocked it, and pulled it open. "Come in, quickly!"

The kids filed in. "You're not closed?" Pigeon asked as he crossed the threshold.

"I temporarily closed the shop so we could chat uninterrupted," Mrs. White explained. She led them to the back of the store. "I know Pigeon and Trevor delivered their fudge because their mothers came into the shop this morning. And Nate's dad came by on his lunch break. I trust you delivered your fudge as well, Summer?"

"Yep. My parents are divorced. I live with my dad, and he has a pretty long commute. But he really liked the fudge. I'm sure he'll be in."

"Good enough for me," Mrs. White said, producing a large bag of Moon Rocks. "These are yours. Along with a new assignment, if you're interested."

"Jackpot," Trevor said, accepting the bag and hefting it.

Mrs. White led them into the back of the store.

"What assignment?" Nate inquired.

"You told me that you're explorers," Mrs. White said, leaning against a worktable. "I have a need specific to your talents. If you accept the mission, I will provide you with a variety of new candy to get the job done, with more as a reward upon completion."

"What kind of candy?" Summer asked.

"First, I need to know whether you accept the mission," Mrs. White countered. "Let me share some background. An ancestor of mine named Hanaver Mills used to live in Colson, back in the old days. He witnessed the Gold Rush. A rare hardbound copy of his memoirs is on display in the town museum alongside an old pocket watch he made. As a direct descendent, I have asked the museum to return my great-grandfather's memoirs and pocket watch to me, but they deny my claim to them. So I want you kids to acquire them on my behalf."

"You mean steal them?" Nate asked incredulously.

"You can't steal something that rightfully belongs to you," Mrs. White corrected. "Even so, I only intend to borrow the memorabilia. I want to read the original printing of Hanaver's memoirs, and I want to have a replica made of his timepiece. Then I will return them to the museum."

"Our club sometimes trespasses for fun, but we never take anything," Summer said.

"Or harm anything," Pigeon added.

"You needn't accept my offer," Mrs. White said. "I understand that the request may seem morally complex to you. If you are unwilling, I'm sure I can find another way to reclaim these lost heirlooms. It just isn't right. Hanaver Mills means a lot to me. It was chiefly in his memory that I chose to set up my candy shop here in Colson."

"What sort of candy will you give us to help us succeed?" Nate asked.

"Well, if you must know, the Moon Rocks will help," Mrs. White said. "The museum has a security system on the ground floor, covering all the doors and windows on that level. Nothing sophisticated—the sort of system you could find in a middle-class home. But none of the second-story windows are wired. I'll also give you some Melting Pot Mixers, to conceal your identities. Little balls of chocolate that temporarily alter your race. They're fun, you never know what you're going to end up looking like. You'll also get some Shock Bits, in case of an emergency. They generate an electrical charge inside you that infuses your touch with a burst of energy capable of stunning an attacker."

"Sweet!" Trevor exclaimed.

"And one or two other mission-specific treats," Mrs. White concluded. "What do you say?"

"Can we have some time to think it over?" Summer asked.

"Sadly, no," Mrs. White said. "I closed the shop so we could discuss this in peace. It's now or never. For the record, if you ever decline an assignment, our arrangement for sharing magic candy permanently ends at that moment. I require helpers I can count on."

"When do you want this to happen?" Nate asked.

"Late Friday night," Mrs. White responded. "Technically, early Saturday morning. Should you elect to help me out, I have a few more details for you. I've already conducted all the appropriate research. The task should be almost effortless if you follow my instructions."

"I'm not sure this is right," Pigeon said skeptically. "Remember what the guy we saw said?"

"What guy did you see?" Mrs. White asked.

"Some drunk," Trevor said. "He seemed to have something against you."

"He told us to stay away from you," Summer said. "He said you were dangerous."

"What did this man look like?" Mrs. White asked.

"Skinny and dirty," Trevor said. "I think he's homeless. I've noticed him roaming around town the past few weeks."

"He was a crackpot," Nate said. "I'll help you, Mrs. White."

"Excellent, Nate," she said, beaming at him. "This means so much to me. You other three, if any of you feel too uncomfortable, this is not an all-or-nothing proposal. Two of you can do it, or three of you. But any who refrain get no more magic candy. I'm sorry, but that is how I do business."

"I'll do it," Summer said.

"Me too," Trevor agreed.

All eyes turned to Pigeon. He looked unsure. "What if my mom finds out?" he asked.

"The white fudge will help with that," Mrs. White promised. "You'll sneak out after midnight. Since you'll be using magic candy, she won't check on you. You'll be back a couple of hours later, and she will be none the wiser."

Pigeon shuffled his feet. "Can the Shock Bits kill somebody?"

"In the quantity I recommend, a small mouthful, they will give just enough of a jolt to keep others from apprehending you. Nothing lethal, or even truly harmful. Furthermore, I doubt you'll even need to use them."

Pigeon looked at Summer, Nate, and Trevor. "I'm in," he said at last.

"Fabulous," Mrs. White said. "I would hate to break up the club. One moment." She retrieved a long cardboard cylinder from one of the worktables, uncapped it, and removed a rolled-up sheet of paper. Flattening the paper on a table, she revealed the blueprints to the William P. Colson Museum.

"You really are prepared," Summer said, glancing at her friends in surprise.

"Here are the upper-story windows," Mrs. White said, indicating marks on the plans. "I recommend using one of these two front windows. As you can see, there is plenty of roof in front of them. Reaching the other windows will be more precarious."

"How do we get through the window?" Trevor asked.

Mrs. White held up a small plastic bottle with clear fluid inside. "Squirt this solution on the glass. For a few hours, the glass will become intangible, effectively vanishing, only to reappear when the effect wears off. That way you'll do no lasting damage to the facility. I detest vandalism. I got the formula from a magician who wanted to protected her prized collection of dishware when her grandchildren visited."

Trevor accepted the container. "Does it work on people?"

Mrs. White shook her head. "Just glass and ceramics."

"Too bad," Nate lamented. "There's a certain teacher who I wouldn't mind vanishing for a few hours now and then."

"Once inside," Mrs. White continued, "you'll be in one of two rooms, depending which window you enter. Both rooms lead to the same hall." She indicated the areas she was discussing on the blueprints. "Sadly, three of the doors on the top floor are connected to the alarm system: the door that grants access from downstairs, and both doors to the room you need to enter."

"Then how do we get in?" Nate asked.

"This big room is where you'll find the memoirs and the watch," Mrs. White said, pressing a finger against the center of the largest room on the blueprint. "Over one doorway is a narrow window, about a foot high, the same width as the door. Here's where another of my prized candies comes in." She held up a thin paper tube the size of a soda straw. "This is Proxy Dust."

"Looks like a Pixie Stick," Trevor said.

"You tear open one end and sprinkle a little of the powder onto your specially prepared Proxy Doll," Mrs. White said, indicating a plastic doll seated on a nearby workbench. The doll was a ten-inch male surgeon dressed in scrubs, his nose and mouth hidden behind a pale green mask. "Then you swallow the rest. And presto! Suddenly, you're seeing through the eyes of the doll, as if your mind were inside the doll's head."

"Like remote control," Nate said.

"Exactly," Mrs. White said. "You'll want somebody with you, because while you're inhabiting the doll, you won't be aware of anything going on around you."

"Weird," Trevor said.

"To get into the room, you'll vanish the window above the door and toss the doll through the opening. Controlling the doll, make your way to the cabinet in the far corner of the room." She tapped a finger on the blueprint to clarify which corner she meant. "Do what you must to get inside the cabinet and retrieve both the pocket watch and the book. Feed some string through the broken window to recover the doll and the desired items. Break the connection with the doll by opening the eyelid of the person controlling it and blowing on the eyeball. Then bring me the memoir and the timepiece the next day, wrapped in a towel inside one of your backpacks."

"Should we walk through the museum today?" Nate asked. "To get our bearings?"

"Studying the blueprint will suffice," Mrs. White said. "I would rather you not be associated with the museum anytime this week. They do not get many visitors, and I would prefer there be no way to implicate any of you."

"Should we wear gloves?" Summer asked.

"I've tested, and the Melting Pot Mixers will alter your fingerprints," Mrs. White said. "I suggest you visit the museum around one in the morning. Wear dark clothes. Stay out of sight. Any questions?"

"You said we get reward candy?" Nate asked.

"Always," Mrs. White said. "Do you kids have any enemies?"

"There's some sixth graders who love to pick on us," Pigeon said. "They threw Nate's backpack down the hill today."

Mrs. White grinned. "I have some trick candy you might enjoy."

Nate, Trevor, and Summer shared excited looks. Pigeon giggled and clapped his hands.

* * * * *

When Nate got home, a police car was parked in front of his house. He quickened his pace, worst-case scenarios playing in his mind, and hurried through the front door. His mom was in the entry hall talking to a black female police officer.

"Is everything okay?" Nate asked.

They both turned to face him. "Our Explorer was stolen," his mom said.

"When?" Nate asked.

"Just over an hour ago, right out of the garage."

"No way!" Nate said.

"You haven't seen anyone suspicious hanging around your house?" the tall police officer inquired.

Nate thought about it. "Nobody in particular."

"I think I have the info I need," the officer said. She handed his mom a card. "You can call me if you think of anything else."

"Okay, thanks for coming so quickly."

Mom let the officer out through the front door.

"How did it happen?" Nate asked as his mom shut the door.

She tossed up her hands. "I was in the kitchen and heard the garage door open. I thought maybe your dad had come home early. I went to greet him and saw the Explorer driving away, with the garage door closing. I ran out through the front door just as the Explorer vanished around the corner—I couldn't see the driver. I called Cheryl, but she was at a friend's house, and your dad was still at the office. Want to hear the scariest part? The keys weren't on the peg by the door. Whoever it was came into the house, took the keys, opened the garage door, and drove away."

"That's freaky!" Nate said. "Sounds like it could have been somebody we know!"

"That's what the police officer said. But who do we know? We just moved in, we have no relatives in the area. Most likely, some thief cased our house, waltzed right in under my nose, and drove away in our car. Doesn't make you feel very secure, does it?"

Nate could see that the experience had left his mom feeling frazzled. He gave her a hug. "At least nobody got hurt," he said.

"Not this time," she said, biting back a sob.

"It was just some idiot who liked our car," Nate said. "It creeps me out too, but the last thing he'll do is come back here." Nate gave her a hug. "We should do something to take your mind off it. How about a treat?"

His mom held him away from her, looking at him with teary, grateful eyes. "I did pick up some more of that white fudge."

"Yeah, some fudge." Nate felt a little guilty with her gazing at him like her knight in shining armor. After all, the fudge was mostly meant to distract her so he would be free to use magic candy. But he was hoping maybe that very quality of the fudge really would calm her down about having their SUV stolen.

His mom took a deep, cleansing breath. "You want some too?"

"I'm more thirsty," Nate said. "I'm going to have some chocolate milk."

CHAPTER FIVE

THE MUSEUM

Nate sat at the family computer playing a video game called *Grim Reign,* waiting to be told to go to bed. In the game, he was a paladin exploring a desecrated temple full of fearsome creatures. Currently he was locked in combat with a pair of mummies. It was a role-playing game, so the fighting was handled automatically—he simply selected from a menu of spells and attack options.

He kept an eye on the time in the corner of the screen. By 11:15, he began to wonder what had happened to everyone. His mom never allowed him to play on the computer for this long, plus it was more than an hour past his Friday bedtime.

Pausing the game, Nate roamed the house. The lights in the other rooms were off. Cracking his parents' door, he saw the lumps of their covered bodies in bed. His sister was in her bedroom as well, door locked, no light showing underneath.

Since when did his parents go to sleep without checking on him? For that matter, since when did they go to sleep before him at all?

Friday was their date night—on the rare occasions when they stayed home, they were usually up late watching a rented movie. Tonight they had retired early without a word.

Nate returned to the computer, finished off the mummies, and found some treasure behind a sarcophagus. Feeling tired, he retreated to the nearest chamber where he could save the game, defeating a giant spider en route, and shut down the computer. After visiting the kitchen for a glass of ice water, he switched off the remaining lights and went to his room.

At his bookshelf, Nate selected a comic he had not read in a while and plopped onto his bed. As his eyes moved from panel to panel, taking in the narration and the dialogue, he began to find it difficult to focus. Having read the comic several times, he found everything too familiar. He skimmed instead of read, and could not retain the meaning of the words. He experimented with laying his head down on the bedspread for just a moment . . .

. . . and awoke with something tapping at his window. He looked around the room, disoriented, eyes settling on his clock radio. It was 12:54 A.M. He was way late.

Nate rolled off his bed and crossed to the window, where he found Trevor crouching on the roof, wearing a dark blue hooded sweatshirt. Nate unlocked the window and pushed it up. "Sorry, I dozed off," he whispered through the screen.

"No big deal," Trevor said. "So did Pigeon. I was already on his roof. Does this screen come off?"

"I'll just meet you downstairs," Nate said.

Trevor nodded. He jumped gently, gliding beyond the roof and dropping slowly out of sight. Nate quickly pulled on a black sweatshirt. Deciding that the jeans he was wearing were dark enough, he hustled down the stairs and out the front door, leaving it unlocked.

Summer and Pigeon waited on the driveway. Trevor stood in the street. Summer wore a dark jacket and black pants, and carried a backpack. Pigeon wore his studded leather jacket. Nate had not seen him in the jacket since the first day of school.

"Should I spit out this Moon Rock?" Trevor asked. "I don't want to float around while we're walking to the museum, but I have a decent amount left, and I'd rather not waste it."

"Don't spit it out," Nate said. He tapped Summer on the arm with the back of his hand. "Bring the backpack." She followed Nate across his lawn to where a whitish rock shaped roughly like a football sat between two low bushes. Grunting, Nate picked up the rock. Summer unzipped the backpack, removed the plastic surgeon doll, and held the backpack open on the grass. Waddling over, Nate dumped the rock into it.

Trevor soared over from the street, landing near them. "Is it going to be too heavy?" he asked.

"It's not that bad," Nate said. "Mainly awkward to hold. It should be fine in the backpack."

Trevor scrunched his eyebrows. "But I'm so much lighter, what if I'm not strong enough?"

"Just because gravity is pulling on you less doesn't make you weaker," Pigeon noted. "If you were weaker, you wouldn't be able to jump so high. I think Nate is right—the rock won't be too heavy to carry, but should keep you weighed down."

Nate picked up the backpack and helped Trevor slip his arms through the straps. "You're right," Trevor said. "This isn't too bad." He jumped, and although he didn't go very high, the weight of the rock twisted him around in midair and whipped him roughly to the ground. He ended up flat on his back. "On second thought, maybe I'll just lose the candy," Trevor said, spitting out the remains of the Moon Rock.

"I didn't think about how top-heavy it would make you," Nate apologized.

"Neither did I," Trevor said.

They dumped the rock back between the bushes and set off down Monroe Circle toward the creek. When they reached the jogging path that paralleled the creek, they halted. "Do we eat the Melting Pot Mixers now?" Trevor asked, fishing the chocolate balls out of his pocket.

"Okay," Summer said.

"Mrs. White said they last only about an hour, so we need to be quick," Pigeon reminded them.

Trevor handed each of them a little ball of chocolate. They peeled off the wrappers. Nate sniffed his. It smelled like regular chocolate with a trace of mint. "All together?" Summer asked.

The four kids popped the chocolate into their mouths in unison. "Pretty good," Pigeon said. They stared at each other, waiting, the expectant moment stretching longer than they had anticipated.

"Here it comes," Trevor finally said.

Tingles raced through Nate's cheeks and sparked through his hands. His muscles began to twitch involuntarily, gently at first, then with greater intensity, until the tissue between his skin and his bones seemed to liquefy and start boiling. Despite the bizarre sensation, Nate managed to stay on his feet. Of the four, only Pigeon collapsed to the jogging path.

As the sensation subsided, Nate marveled at the new appearance of his friends. Their heights and builds remained the same, but their new features made them almost unrecognizable. Summer was now Asian, with sliver eyes and black hair. Trevor had fiery red hair, pale skin, and a swarm of freckles. Pigeon, getting to his feet, was now black. Looking at his own hands, Nate saw that he was a dark brown. "Am I Mexican?" he asked.

"You look like you're from India," Trevor said. Pulling back his sleeve, he held up a pallid arm. "I'm all freckly."

"You're a redhead," Summer said, feeling her features. "Am I Chinese?"

"Something like that," Nate said.

"Cool," Pigeon said, examining himself. "I was kind of hoping for black."

"We better get moving," Nate said. "We've got only an hour in our disguises." They followed the jogging path to Greenway, then took Greenway to Main, where the Sweet Tooth Ice Cream and Candy Shoppe stood, the darkness inside making the windows opaque. With Nate in the lead, they ran across Greenway and hurried along Main. The museum was on the same side of Main as the candy shop, a couple of blocks down.

The stores and offices along Main were all dark, except for a bar on the far side of the street with neon signs glowing in the window. Antique streetlights shed a peach fluorescent luminance at regular intervals. A single car zoomed along the street, going well over the speed limit. The wooden sidewalks, carved hitching posts, and barrel garbage cans contrasted with the electric guitars in the window of the music shop Nate was passing.

With no other pedestrians on the street, Nate felt conspicuous. He noticed the silhouette of a man in an overcoat standing in front of the bar, apparently staring at them. The man had every reason to be watching them—they were a group of fifth graders walking along an empty street at one in the morning! Nate stole covert glances at the man until he turned and wandered into the bar.

Soon they arrived at the William P. Colson Museum. A hundred years ago, the two-story building might have housed the richest people in town. The sizable structure had a single turret and a covered porch. On the far side of the museum ran a side street. The neighbor on the near side was a small, old-fashioned post office. A narrow, shadowy alley ran between the post office and the museum.

Nate, Trevor, Summer, and Pigeon slipped into the alley. A cardboard box jiggled as a scrawny brown cat darted away from them. "I don't feel good about this," Pigeon whispered.

"It'll be fine," Nate said, although he had similar misgivings. Why did witnessing the fear of others tend to boost his courage? "We need to do what we planned. In and out. Pidge, you and Summer wait in the alley. You have the whistle?"

Summer unzipped a side pocket of her backpack and removed a plastic whistle, looping the string around her neck. "I'll give it one long blow if you need to abort," she said.

"Look," Pigeon said, pointing at a high corner of the alley. "The bubble."

The kids all looked up and saw a bubble the size of a baseball hovering near the roof of the post office. The bubble wobbled, drifted a bit higher, and floated out of the alley and out of sight.

"It looked the same as the bubble I saw outside the Nest," Pigeon reported.

"Weird," Nate said.

"What do you think it means?" Trevor asked.

Nobody had an answer. "I don't like it," Summer said.

"Me neither," Nate agreed. "But we can't do much about it now. We have to keep on task."

Trevor and Summer started portioning out candy. Everybody got three Moon Rocks and a small handful of Shock Bits. Nate accepted the slender tube of Proxy Dust and the surgeon doll. "Remember to spit out your Moon Rock before using the Shock Bits," Pigeon cautioned. "Mrs. White said the Mixers can be used with other candy, but that most of her sweets don't combine well." The others nodded.

"I want to come inside with you guys," Summer complained.

"It only takes two," Nate said quietly. "Keeping watch is just as important."

"And way more boring," Summer said. "Next time I'm doing the fun job."

"I'll keep watch again next time," Pigeon volunteered.

Nate and Trevor crept to the front of the alley. Trevor held a short, rusty rod they had found at the creek. The street was quiet. Stepping into the street in front of the museum's covered porch, Nate and Trevor each put a Moon Rock in their mouths. Nate recognized the familiar lightening sensation.

Trevor took a small hop and drifted mildly up toward the roof. Nate jumped as well, quickly passing Trevor and rising much higher than necessary. Nate was level with the second-story roof before he started descending. He landed lightly on the porch roof a little ways ahead of Trevor.

Two second-story windows opened onto the porch roof, just as the blueprints had indicated. Trevor glided to the window on the left, and Nate followed him, stepping carefully so he would move low and slow over the wooden shingles. At the window, Trevor spat out his

Moon Rock, as did Nate, shingles creaking underfoot as they became heavier. Nate crouched low, eyes scanning the street, wishing they had more cover. At least the street looked empty.

Trevor removed a plastic bottle from his pocket and squirted a pane of glass with the clear solution Mrs. White had given him. The pane almost immediately disappeared. He reached his hand through the vacant square, unlocked the window, and opened it. He and Nate entered, shutting the window behind them.

The room was dark, illuminated only by light filtering in from the streetlamps outside, and it contained a female mannequin positioned as if she were weaving wool yarn into cloth on a large loom. A spinning wheel stood in the corner. A velvet rope spanned the doorway opposite the window.

Trevor and Nate walked across the room and ducked under the velvet rope into a dark hall. Trevor produced a small flashlight, and it took only a moment to find the door with the narrow window above it. "Boost me," Trevor said.

Nate laced his fingers, and Trevor stepped into the impromptu stirrup. Nate held him as high as he could. Reaching up, Trevor squirted the window with the fluid and it vanished. Trevor jumped down.

"You're up," Trevor said, taking a spool of kite string from his back pocket.

Setting the surgeon doll on the floor, Nate tore off the end of the Proxy Dust tube and slipped the tiny scrap of paper into his pocket. He sprinkled a little dust onto the doll. Upending the tube, he dumped the rest into his mouth. The dust tasted like slightly sour tangerines.

Nate instantly felt lightheaded, and reached out to support

himself against the wall. The room seemed to teeter. He sat down on the floor, which swayed so steeply that he tipped onto his back, all sense of equilibrium lost.

When the room stabilized, Nate sat up, staring down at his plastic hands. He flexed his fingers, then rubbed his palms together, but felt nothing. He had no nerves. "No way," he said, his mouth soundlessly forming the shape of the words.

He glanced up at Trevor towering over him, then over at the Indian version of himself, slumped unconscious against the wall. Trevor stooped, grabbed him around the waist, and lifted him up. Nate could not feel Trevor's hand, and he experienced no sensation as Trevor raised him. If not for his sight, he would not have known that he was moving. "That you?" Trevor asked.

"Yes," Nate mouthed, making no sound. He waved an arm instead.

"I guess you can't talk," Trevor said.

Nate made an okay sign with his fingers. Trevor tied the kite string around his waist. They had decided to always keep the doll fastened to the string, in case they had to extract it hurriedly. Trevor tossed Nate through the window and lowered him to the floor.

"Nate," Trevor said, "since you can't talk, give the string three hard tugs when you want to come back. Until then, I'll feed you slack and shine the light through the window."

Although he could feel nothing, Nate found he could move pretty much like normal, right down to blinking. He ran across the room toward the corner Mrs. White had identified in the plans. The room was full of tables and displays, so he had to zigzag to reach the distant cabinet. Trevor was not tall enough to angle the flashlight beam down into the room, but enough light reflected off the roof for Nate to see fairly well.

When he arrived at the display cabinet, Nate found it was tall, with glass doors. From his ten-inch height, the cabinet looked the size of an office building. The only way in without causing damage would be to squirt the glass, but he had neglected to bring the solution.

Nate raced back the way he had come and tugged on the string. Trevor pulled him up, looking befuddled when he saw that Nate was empty-handed. Nate pointed at the window and pantomimed like he was spraying it.

"Gotcha," Trevor said, handing Nate the plastic bottle and lowering him back into the room.

Nate raced to the cabinet. Holding the bottle under his arm like bagpipes, he squirted the window with the clear solution. The glass dissipated into nothingness.

The lowest shelf held black-and-white pictures of coal miners, a pair of work gloves, and a large chunk of some green mineral. He would have to jump to reach the next shelf. There appeared to be just enough room between the cabinet door and the shelf for Nate to squeeze up to the next level. Leaving the plastic bottle behind, Nate jumped. Dangling from the lip of the higher shelf, he hoisted himself up with no strain. As a doll he was small but surprisingly strong.

The next shelf had more pictures, a pair of old glasses, a cracked glass mug shaped like a stout man in a tricornered hat, a cigarette case, and a deck of cards. Nate leaped and caught hold of the next shelf. Kicking out a leg, he boosted himself up. Here were more pictures, a leather-bound book, and a silver pocket watch with the numbers written in Roman numerals. Excited, Nate approached the book. Despite the dimness, he could read the title embossed in gold leaf: *The Collected Reflections of Hanaver Mills.*

Relative to his stature as a doll, the pocket watch was about the size of a manhole cover. Nate lifted it up, surprised that he felt no strain and bore the weight easily. Setting the timepiece down, he approached the book. It was fairly thick. He picked up one end of it. The weight was not a problem, but the shape made it unwieldy at his current size.

After trying a few methods of carrying the memoir, Nate decided he would probably have more luck sliding it, and then tying the string around it to get it up and through the window to Trevor.

The first dilemma was how to get the items down from the third shelf to the floor. His thinking was suddenly interrupted by the shrill sound of a whistle blowing. "Time to go," Trevor called in an urgent whisper. The flashlight beam wobbled as Trevor began taking in the slack of the string. Nate froze, looking from the timepiece to the book.

* * * * *

Summer peered out of the alley, waiting impatiently. How long did it take to grab two objects from a cabinet? It seemed like Nate and Trevor had been inside the museum forever. There had been a moment of tension when they first leapt up to the roof, but the action had not attracted any attention. Since then, she had seen a couple of cars go by on Main, but otherwise the uneventful waiting was mind-numbing.

"Do you think they're all right?" Pigeon asked, breaking the silence.

"Of course," Summer said. "Better off than we are, sitting in some stupid alley." Looking at Pigeon, with his dark brown skin and leather jacket, it was like she was talking to a stranger. He crept forward, scanning the street. "I wish I had a mirror," she said. "I'd love to see the Chinese rendition of myself."

"Police car," Pigeon warned, withdrawing deeper into the alley and crouching down. Summer shrank into the shadows as well, flattening herself against the wall. From farther back in the alley, she could see only a narrow slice of Main Street. The police car flashed by. Summer edged forward in time to see the taillights disappearing around the curve toward Greenway.

"Now, why are you kids hiding from the cops?" said a deep, no-nonsense voice behind her. Summer and Pigeon both whirled. Pigeon squealed. A few steps away, deeper in the alley, loomed a big man in an overcoat and a brown fedora. "What are you doing here?"

"Uh, nothing," Summer said, conscious of the Moon Rock in one hand, the Shock Bits in the other, and the whistle around her neck.

"Awful late to be hanging around a dark alley doing nothing," the man observed. He had his hands in his coat pockets.

"We could say the same to you," Summer said.

"I'm not doing nothing," the man said. "I noticed you two hiding here looking guilty and it made me curious. Where are your friends?"

"Who?" Summer asked innocently.

"The other two boys you were with. The Indian kid and the red-head."

Pigeon turned and tried to run, but the man sprang forward adroitly and seized him by the collar of his jacket. He had a big hand with thick fingers and hairy knuckles. Summer saw Pigeon stuffing the Shock Bits into his mouth, so she ran from the alley and blew hard on the whistle twice.

The man released Pigeon and chased her down the wooden sidewalk, catching up in a few long strides. He grabbed her elbow harshly in one hand and pulled the whistle off over her head with the other. Crushing the plastic whistle between his thumb and forefinger, the man hauled Summer back toward the alley. By the light of the nearest streetlamp, she could see his face better. Square jaw with a firm chin. Heavy eyebrows. Hard eyes. He was gripping her by the same arm that held the Shock Bits. She had a Moon Rock in her free hand, but didn't see how it would help her as long as he was clutching her.

Pigeon emerged from the alley just before they reached it, fingers sparking in the darkness. The man stopped just out of reach. "Shock me, shock her," the man said.

Pigeon furrowed his brow. The man changed his grip and swung Summer around, holding her out in front of him like a shield. "Shock me, shock him," Summer said.

Pigeon hesitated. "Come on," Summer insisted. He reached out a hand toward her, and the man tossed her aside and backed away. Pigeon charged him, arms outstretched, and Summer slapped her own handful of Shock Bits into her mouth. The bits of candy buzzed on her tongue and made her teeth tingle. The man twisted away from Pigeon and pulled a miniature crossbow out of his coat pocket, leveling it at him.

"That's close enough," the man ordered. Pigeon froze. After having dodged Pigeon, the man was facing mostly away from Summer.

"A crossbow?" Pigeon asked.

"I left my battle-ax in my other jeans," the man said.

Summer dove. The man must have caught the motion out of the

edge of his vision, because he swiveled toward her, but her hand grazed his shoe before he could do anything. A dazzling flash accompanied the sound of a gigantic bug zapper claiming a victim, and the man was hurled several yards down the sidewalk. His crossbow clattered into the street. Tendrils of smoke curled from Summer's mouth. The Shock Bits had entirely dissolved, leaving behind a charred, metallic aftertaste.

Pigeon rushed the sprawling man. As the man sat up, Pigeon swatted him on the side of the head. A brilliant flash accompanied by an electric crackle sent the stunned man tumbling into the street.

"Come on," Summer urged. She and Pigeon ran off down Main, turning down the side street beyond the museum. Looking back before rounding the corner, Summer no longer saw the stranger in the overcoat lying in the street.

* * * * *

Timepiece or book? Although Nate guessed that the book was more important, he knew the pocket watch would be much easier to carry, and resolved it would be better to get one item than neither. Picking up the watch, he ran to the edge of the shelf.

The slack on his string was almost gone as Trevor reeled it in, and there was no way to tell him to pause, so Nate held the pocket watch over his head and dropped down through the gap between the shelf and the cabinet door, bypassing the second shelf and landing on the first. Not only was the impact painless—he felt nothing. Despite his best efforts to hold the timepiece high, Nate heard a bad sound when he landed, and saw that the glass covering the face of the watch had cracked.

Holding the timepiece under one arm and the plastic bottle under the other, Nate flung himself through the empty space where the glass had been, hugging his possessions tightly as the string pulled him swiftly back along the route he had taken. His path had wound around several tables and displays, so the ride was not smooth. Since he felt no pain, Nate's only concern was protecting the pocket watch from further damage as he bumped around corners.

As the string dragged him, Nate managed to contort himself as needed to avoid getting hung up on anything. He promptly reached the base of the door and began to rise. He clung to the watch and the bottle as he reached the window above the door and Trevor tugged him through. Trevor kept his hands high, so instead of crashing to the floor, Nate swung wildly. A moment later Trevor set him down carefully.

From the floor, still clasping the timepiece in his unfeeling plastic arms, Nate watched as Trevor crouched down over his actual body and used his fingertips to push apart the eyelids of one eye. When Trevor blew sharply, Nate felt the wind on his eyeball. The sensation made him blink several times. When his eyelids stopped fluttering, Nate found that he was back in his own body.

"What's going on out there?" Nate whispered, patting his face experimentally, grateful to have nerves again.

"I haven't looked," Trevor said. "Can't be good."

Nate picked up the pocket watch, the plastic bottle, and the doll. The timepiece seemed so small relative to having carried it as a diminutive plastic surgeon. He shoved the doll into a pocket. Trevor took the watch and the bottle. "Mrs. White said none of the second-story windows had alarms on them, right?" Nate asked.

"Right," Trevor confirmed. "You thinking we might not want to go out the front?"

Nate pointed to a window at the end of the hall. "That should let us out over the alley," he said.

They dashed down the hall. Trevor unlocked and opened the window. There was no roof outside—just a straight drop to the alley and a view of the post office roof across the way. The window had a screen. Trevor shoved it, and the screen tumbled to the alley below.

Nate and Trevor each put a Moon Rock in their mouths. The alley remained quiet. They waited for a moment to see if the rattle of the screen would summon anyone. Nobody approached. "Think there's anybody out there?" Nate asked.

"They might be chasing the others," Trevor said.

"I guess we jump over to the post office roof," Nate said, although no sane person would have tried it without a Moon Rock.

Nodding, Trevor climbed out the window and pushed off, floating lazily over to the post office roof. Nate followed him, moving in a trajectory that lifted him comfortably over the clogged gutters and onto the relatively flat roof. Staying low and stepping gingerly, they crossed to the far side of the roof. They found a parking area on the far side of the post office that continued around to the back. The next building over was two stories high. Even with the Moon Rocks, it did not look like they could make the jump to that roof.

Trevor pointed to the back of the post office. They drifted over and looked down into a parking lot with several post office trucks. Nodding at each other, Nate and Trevor stepped off the roof, landing in an empty parking space with the force of a small hop.

"One left," Trevor said, holding up his final Moon Rock. "Summer has the rest. Do we spit and run?"

"Leave it in," Nate said. Behind the post office parking lot ran a chain-link fence that served as the rear boundary for several houses on a residential street. Nate motioned toward the fence. "Let's bounce into that neighborhood."

They sprang toward the fence, gliding high. Two more bounds and they would be over it and into the backyard. A bright beam from behind suddenly spotlighted them. "Now, there's something you don't see every day," said a gruff voice.

Nate and Trevor touched down, leaping again. Nate glanced over his shoulder. A man in an overcoat was holding a long black flashlight with a blinding beam. Tall and bulky, he could certainly be the same man who had watched them from the front of the bar. The flashlight beam wobbled and Nate heard footfalls as the man sprinted after them.

"You go left, I'll go right," Nate said as they neared the pavement only a few yards shy of the fence. When they touched down, Trevor took off diagonally to the left. Nate veered right. Both of them easily cleared the fence. The flashlight stayed on Nate.

"You can go high but you're not very fast," the man threatened. Nate heard the fence rattle as the man reached it, heard the man crunch onto the wood chips on the far side.

The backyard was fairly large, with a swimming pool shaped like a peanut. Nate was about to land on the lawn. He could hear the man in the overcoat gaining, heavy footfalls on the grass. The house was too far away for Nate to vault onto the roof in a single leap. But there was a shed on the far side of the pool that might be reachable, and the water would serve as an obstacle for his pursuer.

When Nate landed, he turned and sprang toward the shed. As he soared over the pool, a light on the back of the house switched on, flooding the yard with white radiance. Nate realized he did not have quite enough distance to reach the shed—instead he was going to land on the patio between the shed and the pool. At least he would comfortably clear the water.

The man was sprinting around the pool, but Nate could tell he would land on the patio with enough time to jump again. Nate thought he could make it up to the roof of the house with his next leap.

The man slowed as he stooped to grab something. Nate hit the patio and bounded toward the house with everything he had. At the crest of his jump, Nate judged that he was going to barely clear the gutter. His next leap would be a light skip to the top of the roof.

Nate could hear the man running directly beneath him. As he was about to land a few feet beyond the edge of the roof, something whacked into his side and thrust him brusquely down to the lawn. It took Nate a moment to realize that the man had swatted him out of the air using a long pool skimmer.

The man in the overcoat seized Nate by the front of his shirt before he could try to escape, and effortlessly lifted him into the air. "You don't weigh any more than a piñata," the man said.

"Let me go," Nate said.

"Not until you answer some questions," the man said. "What are you sucking on?"

"The people who live here are already calling the cops," Nate said, nodding toward the house.

"That was a motion-activated light," the man assured him. "The people living here are sound asleep."

"I'll scream," Nate warned.

The man instantly clapped a hard hand over his mouth and nose.

The large palm smelled faintly of cologne. "I wouldn't, if I were you. Let's try to keep this friendly."

Nate gave a curt nod. The man removed his hand. "Tell me how you and your pal manage to defy gravity," the man demanded.

The man was holding Nate high, so he had a good view of Trevor dashing toward them across the lawn. His friend obviously no longer had a Moon Rock in his mouth. "Well, if you really want to know," Nate said, talking loudly to cover the sound of Trevor's approach, "I'm one of the Lost Boys, and Peter Pan wanted us to get in some practice—"

At the last instant, the man sensed Trevor approaching and turned, but he was too late. Trevor extended a hand and touched the man on the chest, and with a burst of light the man was flung across the lawn.

Nate suffered the electric jolt as well, muscles clenching involuntarily, but while the man went cartwheeling across the lawn, Nate took off like a rocket. Recovering from the painful shock, Nate watched in horror as he rose higher and higher, body lazily rotating, first facing the ground, then the stars, then the ground, then the stars. Swinging his arms and twisting, Nate managed to minimize the rotation. Looking down on the post office, then on Main Street, he felt like a slow-motion version of a football during a kickoff. As he curved back toward the earth, Nate realized he was going to land on the roof of a building across the street from the post office. Even though the flight was much slower than it would normally have been, by the time the roof drew near, he had picked up alarming speed.

Limbs flailing, Nate failed to adjust his position for the impending impact, and he flopped jarringly against the shingles, bouncing high and twirling wildly. He caromed against the roof a second time and, after a disorienting spin through space, finally crashed down into the bushes behind the building.

Spitting out the Moon Rock, Nate sat up, dizzy and relieved to be alive. Although jostled and sore, he felt no sharp pain—no bones seemed to be broken. He considered going back to make sure Trevor was all right, but discarded the idea. Trevor had shocked the man and then surely had gotten away. If Nate went back, he would just be giving the tenacious stranger in the overcoat another opportunity to catch him.

Nate got unsteadily to his feet. Keeping his Shock Bits handy, he hurried out the back of the parking lot, avoiding Main Street, and started making his way home.

CHAPTER SIX
TRICK CANDY

O nly a tiny chip of his last Moon Rock was left, and Trevor flicked it around his mouth with his tongue. The candy was now so fragile that biting it was very tempting.

Trevor crouched atop the Sweet Tooth Ice Cream and Candy Shoppe. After shocking the man in the overcoat and sending poor Nate rocketing off into the sky, Trevor had waited to use his final Moon Rock. He had hopped the fence to the front of the house and turned down a couple of streets, winding deeper into the quiet neighborhood and farther from Main. Finding a bushy hedge with a hollow underneath, Trevor got down on his belly, wormed into the darkness, and waited.

It had not been long before the man in the overcoat came running by. He jogged halfway down the street and then doubled back, scanning the surrounding yards and rooftops, occasionally turning on his powerful flashlight to brighten a dim recess. The man had not looked closely at the hedge.

To force himself to wait, Trevor had counted slowly to three hundred after the man moved out of sight. He had not wanted to leave his hiding place prematurely and get apprehended.

When he finally did emerge from the hedge, he had become nervous walking along the sidewalks, knowing that at any moment he might happen into the man in the overcoat. So he had used his final Moon Rock and made his way home leaping through yards, over fences, and across rooftops. Aside from a few dogs barking at him, the trip from the neighborhood to the candy shop roof had been uneventful.

Confident that he had truly ditched the man in the overcoat, and with the candy in his mouth dwindling, Trevor sprang from the roof of the candy shop, glided over Greenway, and landed on the opposite sidewalk.

After taking an accidental fifteen-foot hop upon landing, Trevor spat out the thin remnant of the Moon Rock. The waning sliver of candy was now so delicate that the urge to finish it off with a bite was almost irresistible. Perhaps biting the candy when it had almost dissolved would be no big deal—Mrs. White had never spelled out the specific consequences of chewing a Moon Rock. But Trevor certainly did not want to find out the hard way.

He trotted along the path to the Nest, hoping the others would think to reunite there. His body began to tingle, his flesh began to ripple, and, an instant later, the freckles were gone and his olive complexion had returned.

Down under the trees near the creek, it became hard to see, so Trevor switched on the little flashlight that he was still carrying. Winding through the undergrowth into the Nest, the flashlight beam soon revealed Pigeon, Nate, and Summer all waiting for him. Like

Trevor, their appearances were no longer under the influence of the Melting Pot Mixers.

"Glad you made it," Nate said, sounding relieved and giving Trevor a high-five. "We were just talking about going back for you."

"I'm fine," Trevor said. "The shock to the dude chasing us gave me a good head start. That guy had me pinned down for a while, though. I wound around a lot on my way back to make sure he wasn't tailing me."

"You still have the pocket watch?" Nate asked.

Actually, Trevor had forgotten that he was carrying it. He pulled it out of a pocket and shone the flashlight at it. A crack ran across the glass shielding the face. "Did you guys break it?" Summer asked.

"My bad," Nate admitted. "When I was the doll, and you sounded the alarm, I had to rush. I jumped down from the third shelf of the cabinet."

Pigeon picked up the watch and held it to his ear. Then he wound the tiny knobs and held it to his ear again. "Sounds like it still works," he said. "Just needed to be wound."

"But on top of breaking the watch, we didn't even get the book," Summer reminded them. "I knew I should have gone inside."

"I wish you had," Nate huffed. "Then we probably wouldn't have either the pocket watch or the book, and I could be the one complaining."

"Nate did a good job," Trevor said. "We didn't have much time. Who was that guy, anyway?"

"Whoever he was, he had a crossbow," Pigeon said. "He was going to shoot me."

"Only after you approached him with lightning crackling from your fingertips," Summer said.

"He didn't seem very intimidated that we could jump so high with the Moon Rocks," Nate said. He turned to Trevor. "I already told Summer and Pidge how he chased us and how you shocked him."

"Sorry about that," Trevor said.

"About launching me to the moon?" Nate said. "Better than letting that guy have me. I ended up landing all right. You shot me all the way over Main Street, though."

"I was afraid you were going to die," Trevor said. "You really took off."

"It was scary," Nate said.

"Summer saved me when the guy had me pinned," Pigeon interjected. "She shocked him down the walkway. Then I shocked him too. We ran off, but I don't think he chased us."

"Because he ended up chasing *us*," Nate said. "You guys didn't take his weapon?"

"No," Pigeon said.

Nate folded his arms. "Then he probably had it when he was hounding me and Trevor. But he never pulled it on us. We almost got away from him—if he was really ruthless he could have shot us."

"Of course, we could've yelled and brought the whole neighborhood running," Trevor observed. "Whatever that guy is up to, he's bad news. We definitely need to tell Mrs. White about him."

"For sure," Summer said. "So what now?"

Nate shrugged. "We go home, and hope our folks don't bust us."

"Do you think they might have noticed we were gone?" Pigeon asked, sounding more terrified than he had all night.

"I doubt it," Nate said. "That fudge seems to work. My parents were really weird tonight. They went to bed early and didn't even check on me."

"Mine have been out of it too," Trevor said.

Summer pinched her lower lip thoughtfully. "Yeah, my dad usually takes a bigger interest in my day, asks lots of questions. But not lately."

"Well I just hope my mom is still asleep, or this may be the last you ever see of me," Pigeon said.

"Do we meet up again tomorrow?" Nate asked.

"My family is going to my grandma's in Walnut Creek until Sunday night," Trevor said.

"I'm not allowed to play on Sundays," Pigeon said sulkily.

"Let's just meet up at school on Monday," Summer said. "Trevor, you hang on to the watch until then. We'll bring it to Mrs. White on the way home."

"Okay," Nate said. "You want us to walk you home, Summer? You live the opposite way from the rest of us."

"I'm not worried," she said. "It isn't far, and I'm not Chinese anymore."

"Still, be careful," Nate said.

"I'm more worried about after I get home," Pigeon grumbled.

* * * * *

Pigeon lived on the other side of Monroe Circle from Nate and Trevor. He had not been understating his concerns about his fate should his mother discover he had snuck out in the middle of the night. His mom was hesitant to let him walk home from school. It had taken hours of begging for her to allow him to take the training wheels off his bicycle—and the first time he had fallen, she had insisted that his father screw them back on. What would she do if she learned he had crept out of the house well after midnight? He knew exactly what. His friends would officially go into the "bad influences" category, and he would be grounded until he left for college.

Nearing his house, Pigeon stopped walking, a cold feeling forming in the pit of his stomach. A few more steps forward confirmed what he had glimpsed. There was no doubt about it. Several downstairs lights were on. His doom was sealed.

Maybe he could run away, live in the tunnel slide at the park. Maybe he could pretend he had been sleepwalking. Maybe he could give himself black eyes, bind his wrists with duct tape, throw himself in a ditch, and wait for a police officer to discover him. His mom couldn't blame him for getting kidnapped!

Even as those ideas shuffled through his mind, Pigeon discarded them. There was no getting around this. He had to face his fate. There was no using a Moon Rock to jump up to his window and sneak inside. If the lights were on, his mom had already checked his bed and was sitting downstairs, staring at the front door, waiting for him. She had probably already called the police. And the F.B.I.

With a hopeless sigh, Pigeon trudged up the porch steps and tried the door. He was relieved to find it unlocked, as he had left it. His mom was not in the living room or the entry hall. He heard something rustle in the kitchen. She was playing it cool, pretending not to be worried. Maybe he should just sneak up to bed. No, she would only be angrier if she knew he was trying to deceive her.

Mouth dry, head hung low, Pigeon entered the kitchen, a convicted criminal reluctantly awaiting his sentence. His mom sat at the kitchen table with a tall glass of milk and a platter half covered with white fudge, reading the newspaper. She twisted when he entered, dropping the piece of fudge in her hand. "What are you doing up?" she asked, sounding unmistakably guilty.

Pigeon blinked. "I heard some noise so I came downstairs," he tried. Had she not noticed he was gone? Did she not notice he was in his street clothes?

His mom laid down the newspaper so it covered the platter of fudge. "Mommy just needed a glass of milk," she said. "She was having a tough time sleeping. You march back up to bed."

His mom was sneaking fudge! Earlier that evening, hadn't she told his dad they were all out? Whatever was going on, he had no desire to press his luck. "Okay, I'll just go back up to bed."

Her expression softened. "That's a good boy."

Pigeon left the room. Walking up the stairs, he shook his head. It was as if the laws of nature had been turned inside out. He had just escaped an inevitable punishment for no good reason. Whatever was in that fudge had saved his life!

* * * * *

"Is it just me, or has Miss Doulin mellowed out?" Nate asked as he, Summer, Trevor, and Pigeon walked along Greenway after school on Monday.

"You're right," Summer said. "She's a lot more relaxed."

"I was sort of testing the waters today," Nate said. "Getting my name on the board is a freebie, and I was in the mood to see how far I could push. No matter how many jokes I cracked, or how little attention I paid, or how much I talked to Scott Simons, I didn't even get a warning. The class has never been louder than today, and not a single name ended up on the board. And we have no homework."

"It's the fudge," Pigeon said.

"That's right!" Nate said.

"The fudge?" Trevor asked.

"I gave Miss Doulin fudge," Pigeon said, "and it took all the fight out of her. Same with my mom. This morning, as an experiment, I took my cereal into the living room and ate it over the carpet. Mom didn't say a thing. So I used a pair of scissors to pick at my teeth while I had a conversation with her. She acted like she didn't even notice. Normally she would have screamed. It's like she's been lobotomized."

"My dad forgot to drive me to school today," Summer said. "He drops me off every morning. Today, he ate breakfast with me, went out to his car, and drove away. I chased him down the block. I ended up walking to school."

"*That's* why you showed up late," Nate said. "And of course Miss Doulin didn't even seem to mind."

"I couldn't believe it," Summer said. "Dad bought a huge box of white fudge on Saturday, and has been eating lots of it."

"My mom bought a ton too," Nate said.

"My folks brought a bunch to my grandma's yesterday," Trevor said. "Grandma kept trying to get me to have one. I didn't, of course."

They reached the crosswalk. The crossing guard held up his sign and they scurried across the street and went to the front door of the Sweet Tooth Ice Cream and Candy Shoppe.

The shop was open and busy. Some kids from their school crowded the counter. Several women and a few men waited in line or sat at tables eating sundry treats. The blond dwarf bustled about filling orders, along with a young man with shaggy brown hair and a blotchy red birthmark coloring half his face and neck. A very fit woman wearing workout clothes walked away from the counter holding a large box of white fudge.

Mrs. White emerged from the back and raised the folding segment of the counter. Trevor led the others into the back of the store. Pushing through the batwing doors, he discovered a translucent plastic tarp blocking the doorway. He grabbed a corner of the tarp and lifted it, allowing the others to duck past him before entering himself.

The back of the store was frosty. Their breath plumed out in front of them with each exhalation. Icicles hung from the worktables and some of the shelves, and ice glazed many surfaces. Several large coolers were stacked around the room. One was open, filled three-quarters of the way with medallions of ice and containing a few bricks of some substance snugly wrapped in white paper. Slick patches made the floor treacherous. In a cage on one of the worktables was a pair of odd birds. Black and white, they stood about two feet tall, with heavy, colorful bills. They looked like mutant penguins.

"What planet are those birds from?" asked Nate.

"Ours," answered Pigeon. "They're puffins. They live in the Arctic."

"Very astute, Pigeon," said Mrs. White.

"The genius strikes again," Nate grumbled.

"I just like books about wildlife," Pigeon apologized.

Summer was starting to shiver. Nate and Trevor had goose bumps on their arms. Mrs. White took four heavy woolen ponchos off pegs on the wall and distributed them to the kids, then slipped another over her own head, careful not to disturb her tidy bun.

"And how are the four of you today?" Mrs. White asked.

"Better, now that I'm not freezing," Summer said. "Why is it so cold?"

"I'm creating treats called Frost Bites," Mrs. White said. "The process both requires and causes a low temperature. I'm still finishing up the last two batches."

"What do Frost Bites do?" Nate asked.

"I expect you'll find out soon enough." They gathered around the square table with the purple tablecloth. Mrs. White indicated a quartet of folding chairs, and the kids took the seats. "Business has been picking up lately," Mrs. White announced happily. "I've continued hiring extra help to man the shop. White fudge samples always do the trick. How did your Saturday morning exploits go?"

"We got this," Trevor said, pulling out the pocket watch.

Mrs. White looked delighted. "Clever children! And the book?"

"I had to leave the book," Nate said. "Some guy showed up and tried to grab us."

Mrs. White sat up a little straighter. Her smile faltered. "What guy?"

"Big guy, dark hair," Summer said. "He wore a trench coat and an old-fashioned hat."

"He had a crossbow," Pigeon said. "He tried to apprehend me and Summer, but we used the Shock Bits and got away."

"Summer blew a whistle to warn us," Trevor said. "Nate snagged the watch, and we ran off. The guy chased us. He was fast and tough-looking. He almost caught Nate, but I shocked him."

"You were using the Melting Pot Mixers?" Mrs. White asked.

"Yeah," Summer said. "He didn't see what any of us really look like."

Mrs. White was inspecting the timepiece. She fingered the glass covering the face. "Was this cracked when you found it?"

"My fault," Nate said, unable to make eye contact with Mrs.

White. "I had to jump from the cabinet after Summer sounded the alarm. I sort of panicked."

"I see," Mrs. White said, frowning. She peered at the watch from several angles and held it to her ear before setting it down on the table. "Under the circumstances, you children surpassed expectations. I did not anticipate any opposition, or you would have been better equipped. I considered this a trial run—a severe miscalculation. Shock Bits and Moon Rocks are insufficient protections from a determined foe."

"The weird thing about that guy," Nate said, "was that he didn't seem very surprised about our powers. He just came out of nowhere and chased us down."

"Do you have enemies?" Pigeon asked. "Do you know who he is?"

"I suspect who he represents," Mrs. White said, looking at each of them in turn.

"What's really going on?" Nate asked.

Mrs. White folded her hands in her lap. "I suppose you children deserve to know more about what is really transpiring. You see, I have come to town in pursuit of a hidden treasure. As you must have guessed, I am something of a magician. The treasure I am chasing is most valuable, but of particular worth to me, because it could help broaden the range of magical treats I produce. Others would like to lay hands on the treasure simply for the monetary value it represents. If you four help me find the hidden cache, you'll get your fair share. There will be plenty to go around."

"You lucked out," Summer said. "We used to be a treasure-hunting society."

"Only we couldn't find any treasures to hunt," Trevor mumbled.

"That guy who chased us is after the same treasure?" Nate asked.

"Apparently word is out that the treasure is in this vicinity," Mrs. White said. "The treasure is ancient, dating back to the mighty civilizations who inhabited the American continents before European colonization. The treasure has been relocated numerous times, and sought by many adventurers, but some recent discoveries have given those who take an interest in such matters good reason to believe its final resting place is in or near this town. My ancestor, Hanaver Mills, was in possession of clues regarding the location of the treasure. He passed out of this life without realizing his dream of uncovering it. I intend to pick up where he left off."

"That's why you wanted the book," Nate said. "To look for clues."

"Precisely," Mrs. White affirmed. "Hard to say where the clues I am seeking will be found—the book and the pocket watch are possible starting points. Hanaver was an eccentric man. It is tough to anticipate where his secrets might be hidden. You four did nice work this weekend, and should feel entitled to a reward."

Mrs. White reached under the table and lifted a metal box that had a keyhole in the front. Turning a key in the hole, she raised the top of the box and removed six pieces of candy. There appeared to be three different kinds—two of each. "Trick candy," she announced, "to baffle and dismay your enemies."

"Cool," Trevor said, stretching out the word so it lasted a few seconds.

"Like the majority of my candy, it will have little effect on individuals who have already consumed white fudge. And it is more potent on youngsters than adults."

"What does it do?" Pigeon asked.

She picked up a yellow, crystalline treat. "I call these Sun Stones. They function like the opposite of a Moon Rock, increasing the pull of gravity. The candy reinforces the anatomy of the recipient to prevent the crushing force from inflicting lasting damage." She indicated a second candy that looked like a miniature brownie. "That is a Whisker Cake. Makes hair grow at an unusual rate." She tapped the last kind of candy, which looked like a solid sphere of root beer. "And one of my trick candy masterpieces—the Dizzy Fizzer. I'll let you see for yourselves what it does. What are the names of your bullies?"

"Denny Clegg, Eric Andrews, and Kyle Knowles," Summer said.

"Any of those treats should give them a memorable payback for whatever wrongs they've inflicted," Mrs. White said.

"Do we get any candy we can use for ourselves?" asked Nate.

"You get to keep the leftover candy from the museum mission, which should include several mouthfuls of Shock Bits along with your stash of Moon Rocks. And I'll be coming up with another task for you soon, which no doubt will involve a bunch of new candy. Check back with me tomorrow." Mrs. White stood up in a way that suggested the conversation was over.

"I have a question," Pigeon said. "The white fudge seems stronger than you described. It's like my mom hardly notices me anymore."

"She notices you," Mrs. White said. "She just doesn't pay enough attention to get you in trouble. The effect will go away when I stop making white fudge. For now, be glad you have the diversion you need to go adventuring in the night."

"My dad forgot to take me to school today," Summer said.

"You may have to help your parents remember to include you in their plans from time to time," Mrs. White said. "A necessary side effect."

"Our teacher, Miss Doulin, ate the fudge and is acting strange too," Nate said. "Not just to us, to all the kids."

"I'm guessing your teacher has a fairly extreme personality," Mrs. White said.

"She's pretty strict," Nate said. "Or was."

Mrs. White nodded as if this were to be expected. "The white fudge tends to normalize extreme personalities. Again, the effect is temporary, lasting only as long as the subject continues to consume the fudge. I won't keep selling it forever. When I am done here, I'll move on, and all will return to normal." She ushered the kids toward the door.

"Are they becoming addicted to the fudge?" Trevor asked. "My parents keep buying tons."

"No more addicted than some people are to a favorite breakfast cereal," Mrs. White said. "The fudge is just really yummy."

The kids returned to the front of the store. It was even more packed with customers than before. A middle-aged man with a mustache was walking away from the counter holding a tower of stacked white fudge boxes.

"Really, really, really yummy," Nate muttered to Trevor.

* * * * *

Nate folded the lined paper and creased it, smoothing his hands over it carefully. Miss Doulin had given them thirty minutes before lunch to study. She had not specified what they should study, nor did she seem to care, as she sat at her desk, sneaking pieces of white fudge from her drawers. Nate had elected to study the science of folding and throwing paper airplanes.

He put the finishing touches on the plane and sent it sailing to the front of the room. It veered left, sliding onto the floor beside Miss Doulin's desk. She sat hunched over a stack of papers, green marker in hand, chewing with her eyes closed. She did not notice the paper airplane, just as she had not noticed the four others, including the one that had bounced off her shoulder.

The lunch bell rang, interrupting the steady murmur of talking in the room. There had not been much teaching since the first bell rang, and even less discipline. It was as if Miss Doulin were a day away from retirement and just didn't care anymore.

Miss Doulin looked up. "Have a good lunch," she said. "Get ready to hit the books when you get back."

Yesterday when class had ended, she had pledged that the next day would be very busy. Which meant today should have gone a lot differently. Somewhere in the fudge-addled haze of her mind, Miss Doulin seemed to feel guilty enough about how she was slacking to at least pretend she had plans to improve. But Nate suspected that the class would keep getting less orderly.

"You ready?" Pigeon asked.

"Of course," Nate said.

They strolled out of the room with Summer and met Trevor among the tables in the lunch area. Most of the lunch tables were either indoors or on a central concrete patio surrounded by buildings on three sides. But there were a few isolated lunch tables around the corner from the main area. They were rarely used, but Trevor, Summer, Nate, and Pigeon hurried to the exiled tables to claim their spot. They did not want the supernatural spectacle to play out in front of the whole school.

"What if they don't find us over here?" Pigeon asked.

"They'll find us," Summer assured him. "They'll think we're trying to hide because we're not in our regular spot. They'll wonder what special dessert Pigeon has today."

"Do I look like I'm eating casually?" Pigeon asked, taking a bite from his sandwich.

"Lean back a little more," Nate instructed. "And kind of dip your shoulder."

"Your right eye is open too wide," Trevor said. "Close it halfway."

"Tilt your head," Nate suggested.

Pigeon looked increasingly silly as he followed their directions.

"Knock it off, you guys," Summer said. "Pigeon, don't try to *act* casual, just *be* casual. Or be nervous. Just don't be fake."

"Hey!" called a voice coming around the corner of the building. Denny walked toward them, followed by Eric and Kyle. "What's with the new table? You guys too cool to eat with everybody else?"

"More like they're hiding," Eric said.

"Where's the jacket, Pigeon?" Kyle teased. "I'm starting to miss it!"

"At least you still have your army jacket to keep you company," Nate said. Kyle was wearing the same jacket he had worn at the creek. He wore it most days. "Does it remind you of your days serving our country?"

"Man, Dirt Face," Denny said in disbelief, "you do not know when to shut up. That mouth is going to get you in trouble one of these days. Hey, Pigeon, what's for dessert today?"

Pigeon clutched his lunch bag close to his chest. "Nothing you'd want."

"We're not picky," Eric said, reaching for the bag.

Pigeon let him have it. Eric handed it to Denny.

"See, Dirt Face, Pigeon knows how to keep things simple," Denny said, rummaging through the sack. He pulled out a sandwich bag with three unusual pieces of candy inside. "What have we here? A special treat? What are these, Pigeon?"

"Candy," he said.

"Not a lot, though," Denny said. "Only one for each of us." He sniffed the yellow crystalline candy, kept that, and handed the sandwich bag to Eric. Flat-faced Eric chose the one that looked like the little brownie, and Kyle received the root beer sphere.

"I've never seen candy like this," Kyle said, eying the brown ball. "Where'd you get it?"

"My mom picked it up somewhere," Pigeon said.

Eric started chewing his candy. Denny and Kyle popped theirs into their mouths. "Not bad," Denny said. "Like lemon meringue pie. Sort of sticks to my mouth, though." Denny swayed, a worried look crossing his face, and began to stoop. Straining, he managed to wrench himself upright. His features drooped, and his arms hung trembling at his sides. Suddenly, as if his legs were loaded with mousetrap springs, his body whipped down to the concrete patio with a mighty slap.

"What did you give us?" Eric asked, his hair already down to his shoulders, his eyebrows getting bushier, wispy whiskers emerging on his chin.

Kyle staggered and clutched the end of a lunch table to steady himself. "Oh, no," he moaned, eyes wide, one hand on his stomach.

Denny did not move. He groaned, but his entire body appeared to be glued to the patio. Eric crouched beside Denny, hair growing so swiftly that his head looked like a fountain, but he could not even budge one of Denny's arms. Kyle dropped to his knees, still gripping the end of the table.

"This is impossible!" Eric stammered, rising to his feet. The hair on his scalp already reached the ground. The long hairs of his sparse beard reached beyond his waist. Tufts of fur protruded from his ears and nostrils. "You okay, Kyle?"

Kyle opened his mouth to respond and amber foam frothed from his lips. He covered his mouth, but despite his efforts to contain it, a bubbly stream of foam gushed out, much of it splashing onto Denny's immobilized legs. Eric ran away, his hair trailing behind him on the ground like a long bridal train, his beard dangling between his legs. Froth continued to faucet from Kyle's nose and mouth, as well as to foam up from the waistband of his pants and spew out the bottoms of his pant legs.

Panicking, Kyle stumbled to his feet and tried to run, but he leaned heavily to one side and flopped to the ground after only a few paces, foam geysering from every available opening.

Summer watched the display in amazement. Nate, Trevor, and Pigeon laughed uncontrollably. Pigeon had tears streaming down his cheeks.

As the foam erupting from Kyle began to subside, leaving his clothes completely drenched, Nate tapped Summer. "We better beat it," he said.

Summer nodded.

Denny had not moved an inch. He continued to groan. While the others hurried away, Pigeon squatted beside him and said, "You better learn to watch what you eat."

CHAPTER SEVEN
A GRAVE ASSIGNMENT

Summer leaned against the flagpole at the front of Mt. Diablo Elementary, waiting for the other Blue Falcons. The parking lot was jammed with the cars of parents picking up their kids. Several buses idled at the curb, one of them near enough for the exhaust fumes to bother her.

When class had let out, Nate had accompanied Pigeon to the rest room. Ever since admonishing Denny to watch what he ate, Pigeon had grown progressively more paranoid. He was certain that vicious retaliation was inevitable, and had even discussed submitting a written apology. Summer and Nate had warned that if he showed any weakness, he would be doomed. Their best hope was to act confident and pray that Denny, Eric, and Kyle would be too intimidated by the effects of the magic candy to strike back.

As extra precautions, Nate had chaperoned Pigeon to the rest room, and they were all meeting in front of the school in order to take a different route home. If Denny opted to seek revenge, he would probably ambush them at the ramp that descended to Greenway.

Summer had mixed feelings about what they had done. Denny, Eric, and Kyle deserved to be humbled—they had ruthlessly bullied others for years. But even though the candy was designed to inflict no lasting damage, feeding it to them seemed almost too harsh, like issuing the death penalty for shoplifting. Denny had never actually beaten up any of them. He was just a pushy jerk who liked to steal lunch desserts and start dirt clod fights down at the creek. It was almost a game. Terrifying Denny and his friends with supernatural punishments might scare them into leaving the Blue Falcons alone. Or it could escalate the animosity into something much more real and dangerous.

Summer tried to picture how she would react if somebody gave her candy that made her vomit foam until she was soaked. Wouldn't she be furious? She would certainly want retribution. She might even involve the police.

Somebody tapped her on the shoulder. She looked, but nobody was there. Turning the other way, she saw Trevor. "Gotcha," he said. "Where's Nate and Pidge?"

"Pigeon had to make a pit stop," Summer said.

"I've had the best feeling all day," Trevor said. "There should be Munchkins coming out of hiding and dancing in the streets."

"Except I'm not sure the witch is dead," Summer said. "Dorothy and her friends might get assaulted on the way home."

"No way," Trevor said. "Those guys are going to stay a million miles away from us. They probably think we have super powers or know voodoo. Would you mess with somebody who could turn gravity against you?"

"No, but who knows if they'll be able to make sense of what happened? They might decide we drugged the candy and they dreamed the weird results. I mean, what happened seems impossible."

"If all else fails, we break out the Shock Bits," Trevor said, as if that idea ended the discussion.

"Don't you think that's a little extreme?"

"Depends on what they're trying to do."

"What if it stops their hearts?" she asked. "When I shocked that guy, he flew a long ways. A lot farther than any stun gun would throw him. And stun guns can give people heart attacks."

"We'll do what we have to," Trevor said. "Now that we started fighting back, we can't let up, or they'll make us pay for years."

"That's exactly right," Nate said, approaching with Pigeon. "They asked for it. Once they stop asking for it, we'll stop giving it to them. But not before. Besides, after today we should add some new weapons to our arsenal."

"I hope you guys are right," Summer said.

"You're as bad as Pigeon," Nate accused. "There is nothing wrong with giving a stupid, mean bully a taste of his own medicine."

"Except Denny isn't stupid," Summer said. "Mean, yes. Stupid, no. And unlike some bullies, he's not a coward. Last year he thrashed a sixth grader who was bigger than him."

"Tom Turrel?" Trevor said. "He was big, but it was all fat."

"Would you have fought him?" Summer asked.

"No way—what if he sat on me!"

"Sounds like Summer might have a thing for Denny," Nate said.

Summer clenched her teeth. She wanted to slap Nate for saying something so stupid and embarrassing, but managed to restrain the impulse. "I'm just saying we should be ready for Denny to come looking for revenge, no matter how scared he should be."

"We're with you there!" Trevor said. "Why do you think we're sneaking home a different way?"

"We want to be careful," Nate said diplomatically. "We're also having fun enjoying the victory."

Summer resisted a smile. "It was pretty funny," she admitted. "They were freaked out."

"It was the most hilarious thing that has ever happened," Pigeon agreed. "I'm just worried it might cost me my life. And that my mom won't be able to stop eating fudge long enough to hold a funeral. They'll probably just dump me in a hole in the backyard."

The four of them walked west along Oak Grove Avenue, the street that granted access to the school parking lot. Going home this way would make the walk nearly twice as long, since they all lived south of the school, and the first few southbound cross streets west of Mt. Diablo Elementary ended in cul-de-sacs. The slope at the rear of the school continued west for some distance before the incline diminished, allowing a road to connect the top of the ridge to the bottom.

A block down from the school on Oak Grove waited a boxy old ice cream truck. The shabby vehicle was painted a faded blue. Music chimed from hidden speakers. The words *Candy Wagon* were emblazoned on the side in black cursive. A semicircle of kids huddled around the opening in the side of the truck.

"Is that Mr. Stott?" Pigeon asked hopefully.

"Looks like it," Trevor said, hurrying forward with Pigeon at his heels.

"Who's Mr. Stott?" Nate inquired, continuing alongside Summer.

"He's the best ice cream man," she said, "but he hasn't come around for over a year."

Summer and Nate caught up to Trevor and Pigeon, who were waiting behind other kids. Mr. Stott was handing a red-white-and-blue Popsicle to a young black girl. He looked to be in his late sixties or seventies. His silver beard hung halfway down his chest and had a pair of dark streaks that ran from his chin almost to the end of his whiskers. His bushy eyebrows dipped and bobbed expressively, and he wore his silver hair smoothed back close to his scalp. Notwithstanding his age, Mr. Stott was robust, with a gruff, grandfatherly voice.

"Any of you guys have money?" Trevor begged. "I'll pay you back."

"My mom gave me a ten this morning," Pigeon said reluctantly. "I'm supposed to buy white fudge on the way home."

"Spot me?" Trevor persisted. "What I want is only fifty cents."

Pigeon had reached the front of the line. Only the four of them remained beside the truck.

"Here are some familiar faces," Mr. Stott chuckled. "Trevor, Pigeon, Summer . . . and I'm not sure I've met you."

"Nate," Summer said.

"Hi," Nate said with a little wave.

"Good to meet you," Mr. Stott boomed. "Sebastian Stott, at your service."

"Where have you been, Mr. Stott?" Trevor asked.

"Here and there," Mr. Stott said. "At my age, an extended

vacation now and again helps keep the motor running. Why, were you looking for me down at the cemetery?"

"No," Trevor and Pigeon said together.

"I hope not. I anticipate several more encores before the curtain falls. What can I get you?"

"Whatever Trevor wants and a frozen banana," Pigeon said.

"You're putting up the cash today, huh?" Mr. Stott said, pulling a chocolate-dipped banana out of the freezer. "Hope that means he'll be paying tomorrow."

"I'll pay him back," Trevor promised. "I'll have a Lightning Rod."

"Good choices," Mr. Stott said, taking a striped frozen fruit bar from the freezer. "I dip the bananas and make the Lightning Rods myself, you know."

"They're the best," Pigeon said.

"I was correct to assume you're still going by 'Pigeon'?" Mr. Stott asked.

"Yep," Pigeon said, unwrapping his treat.

"You might outgrow that moniker soon. You're going to have to upgrade to a bigger bird. Let's see . . . how about Condor?"

"Maybe," Pigeon said noncommittally. He looked over his shoulder. "You guys want anything?"

"What about your mom?" Summer said.

"Honestly, as long as I come home with fudge, I don't think she'll be counting the change," Pigeon said.

"You wouldn't be referring to fudge from that new Sweet Tooth place?" Mr. Stott interjected. "That shop is going to run me out of business."

"No way," Trevor said. "She doesn't drive around."

Mr. Stott scrunched his eyebrows. "I don't know . . . have you kids tried that white fudge of hers?"

They all shook their heads.

Mr. Stott scratched his beard just below the corner of his mouth. "Might be safer to keep it that way. I don't know what she puts in that stuff, but after the first bite, it is hard to resist. I'm not sure she needs to drive through neighborhoods in order to ruin me."

"I'll have a Tooty Fruity," Summer said.

"Sure you have enough to cover all this?" Mr. Stott asked Pigeon in a confidential tone.

Pigeon proudly flashed the ten-dollar bill.

"And Mrs. Bowen won't mind?" Mr. Stott pursued.

"I'm feeling good about my chances," Pigeon said.

"One Tooty Fruity coming up," Mr. Stott announced in a more boisterous voice. "How about you, Nate?"

"You have candy too?" Nate asked.

"It's the Candy Wagon," Mr. Stott said, slapping the poster beneath the window that listed a broad array of treats and snacks. He handed Summer her Tooty Fruity.

"I'll just have a piece of red licorice," Nate said.

"*Just* a piece of licorice? Licorice is part of a proud candy tradition. I'll even spice it up for you, if you want, make it a Powder Keg."

"A Powder Keg?" Nate repeated.

"Easiest thing in the world," Mr. Stott said. "An old favorite with some extra kick." His hands began doing the work he was describing. "Tear off the end of a piece of red licorice. Dump in the contents of a Pixie Stick. And voila! Instant Powder Keg!"

"Thanks," Nate said, accepting the candy.

Mr. Stott winked. "You stay in this business as long as I have, you learn a trick or two. That will be a dollar seventy."

"Your prices are so low," Nate remarked.

"Easier to say when you're not paying, right, Pigeon?" Mr. Stott took the ten and handed Pigeon his change. "But yes, I take pride in the fact that I have not raised my prices for almost twenty years."

"If Mrs. White is putting on the pressure with her candy shop," Trevor said, "we'd be glad to pay a little more."

"Very kind," Mr. Stott said, "but somehow I think I'll survive. You can't take those long vacations unless you've put aside a healthy nest egg." He winked. "You youngsters keep out of trouble."

"You bet," Pigeon said, trying to pocket his change with one hand while holding the frozen banana in the other. He was having trouble stuffing in the cash because his jeans fit too tight.

They turned down a road called Winding Way and descended into the little valley that housed much of Colson. Many shade trees grew along Winding Way, and the modest houses along it had tidy yards.

Summer noticed Nate eyeing her Tooty Fruity. "Want the last of it?" she offered.

"I'm okay," Nate said. "That Powder Keg was pretty good."

"I'm not sick or anything," Summer said. "Tastes like peaches and cream, with a hint of strawberry."

"Okay, you sold me," Nate said, accepting the Tooty Fruity and finishing it off.

"What do you think Mrs. White will want us to do this time?" Pigeon asked. "Rob a bank?"

"If she does," Nate said, "I think Condor is the man for the job."

Summer and Trevor giggled.

"We should make you a feathery costume," Nate said.

Pigeon rolled his eyes, trying to keep a smile from creeping onto his face. "I'm going to stick with Pigeon."

"We could still make a costume," Nate said. "You still haven't told me how you got the name. Have I been in the club long enough?"

Pigeon glanced at Trevor and Summer. "Should I tell him?"

"Up to you," Summer said.

"Tell him, it's funny," Trevor prodded.

"You tell it," Pigeon said.

"Okay," Trevor began, excited to have permission, "so, almost three years ago, during second grade, Pigeon used to sit alone at lunch. My family had moved here that year, and I hadn't really met Summer or Pigeon yet. Anyhow, you've probably noticed our school has a lot of seagulls hanging around at lunchtime. Don't ask me why, we're what, fifty miles from the ocean? Anyhow, the point is, we get lots of seagulls, but you never see any pigeons."

"Right," Nate said.

"Well, one day this pigeon shows up, and Pigeon, he was Paul back then, starts feeding it. They became friends. That same pigeon would show up at lunch and sit with Paul without fail, eating little crumbs of his sandwich or whatever."

"Then one day," Pigeon jumped in, "I put a breadcrumb on my arm. And the pigeon hops up onto my sleeve and eats it. So I put a piece of bread on my shoulder. And the pigeon perched up there and ate it."

"Everybody starts noticing this pigeon on Paul," Summer said, holding back laughter. "And everybody starts gathering around him, checking it out."

"Then the pigeon hops on top of his head," Trevor said. "It stands there for a minute, just staring at everybody."

"And then it made a mess on me," Pigeon said. Nate cracked up, and the others laughed hard as well. "I had all this gooey white gunk in my hair."

"Everybody saw it," Summer gasped through her laughter.

"And he's been Pigeon ever since," Trevor finished.

"Did you ever see the pigeon again?" Nate asked once the laughter died down.

"No, never," Pigeon said. "I've never seen another pigeon at our school, before or since. It was like he deliberately showed up long enough to humiliate me, then took off forever."

"That is hysterical," Nate said. "I guess you should be glad you aren't called Condor."

They all cackled again.

* * * * *

The line at the Sweet Tooth Ice Cream and Candy Shoppe spilled out the front door and along the walkway. Old and young, male and female, dozens of people waited anxiously for their sugar fix.

The crowd made Nate recall what Mr. Stott had said about being run out of business. Maybe he was right. To have a line like that at 3:00 P.M. on a Tuesday meant Sweet Tooth was becoming a major fad.

Nate led Summer, Trevor, and Pigeon through the front doors, shouldering past the people in line. The dwarf and the guy with the lurid birthmark looked frazzled as they hustled to fill orders. Mrs. White was handing two boxes of white fudge to a young man with stubbly facial hair and an earring. Nate noticed envious looks from many of the waiting customers as Mrs. White greeted the four of them enthusiastically, raised the counter, and escorted them into the back.

There was no indication that the back of the store had ever been as frigid as a meat locker. Dozens of trays of white fudge rested on the worktables and filled tall racks.

"Welcome, welcome," Mrs. White said, "we're in the midst of our busiest day yet. You wouldn't believe the orders we've been getting. I'll be up all night replenishing our supply of white fudge! Maybe I should spoil a batch or two, slow things down a bit. I need to do more hiring! How are you doing? Did you repay your bullies?"

"Repaid them and then some," Nate said.

"How wonderful, I'm glad the trick candy went to good use," Mrs. White said. "I'm a little overwhelmed today, so we'll have to be quick, but I do have a new assignment for you. Turns out it was fortunate you opted for the pocket watch over the book, Nate. I dismantled the watch and discovered a message on the back of the face. The letters were so miniscule, they could have been written with an eyelash. The note indicated that Hanaver Mills was buried with an important item hidden in an ivory box. By implication, the message granted permission to exhume him."

"What?" Trevor asked.

"To unbury him," Pigeon interpreted.

"Of course, we would suffer an endless runaround if we tried to obtain permission through formal channels. I would prefer you four visit the Colson Valley Cemetery tomorrow night and see what you can dig up."

"You want us to rob a grave?" Nate asked.

"Goodness, no," Mrs. White said. "I want you to seek out the item referenced in the pocket watch message. Take the item in the box, an item meant to be claimed, and rebury the rest."

"What if we get caught?" Trevor asked.

"You'll be much better equipped than last time," Mrs. White promised. "Let's see, for Summer I have a package of Flame Outs. I would prefer if she were the only person to use them. It might be gender bias, but I believe that she has the coolest head of all of you. Summer, when you put one of these in your mouth, it will emerge as a searing ball of fire. Use a Flame Out only under dire circumstances, for the effect can be lethal. Never chew it or use more than one at a time. Never use one indoors, or you may very well incinerate yourself along with your target."

"I don't want candy that could kill someone," Summer said.

Mrs. White sighed, glancing at her wristwatch. "Lots of things have the potential to kill someone, my dear. A baseball bat. A ladder. A bicycle. It all depends on how you use them. I don't give you these Flame Outs to cremate people. Maybe you'll need a distraction. Maybe you'll need to disable an unoccupied car. Who knows?" She passed the candy to Summer. "Might come in handy to have some extra fire power."

Mrs. White turned to Nate. "You did a fine job operating the Proxy Doll last time, so I am giving you more Proxy Dust, along with a new subject to control. I call him the Forty-niner." She pointed to a squat caricature of an old miner carved out of wood standing beside one of the worktables. The figure had crazed eyes, a shapeless hat, and a white beard, and stood about three feet tall. He clutched a pickax in one hand and a shovel in the other. The pickax and shovel were made of metal.

"The Forty-niner is designed for tunneling," Mrs. White went on. "Like the surgeon doll, he is stronger than he looks. Using him, you should have no trouble burrowing down to the burial vault and accessing the casket. You know what I mean by a burial vault?"

"Pigeon?" Nate asked.

"The container that encloses the coffin?" he ventured.

"In this instance made of stone," Mrs. White approved.

"Let me guess," Nate said. "You read a lot of books about undertaking."

"I actually figured that one out through context," Pigeon responded.

"You'll have to pry up the sealed lid of the burial vault," Mrs. White said. "The Forty-niner should be able to handle it." She handed Nate a dose of Proxy Dust, then gave Trevor a clear plastic container holding several white candies. "These are Frost Bites. They'll make your body radiate intense cold while you suck on them. Water will freeze in your presence, and you'll be immune to the effects of heat and fire. Using two at a time will heighten the results, but I do not suggest trying more than that."

"I'm not sure this is right, exhuming bodies," Pigeon protested.

"One body," Mrs. White corrected. "Don't fret, Pigeon, I didn't forget about you. I thought you should carry some of my Sweet Teeth." She held up a baggie with six candy corns in it. "The Sweet Tooth is a specialty of mine, so much so that it shares its name with my store. You'll feel tempted to chew them—don't. Just let them dissolve, and use only one at a time. While a Sweet Tooth is in your mouth, others will find it difficult to disobey or disbelieve your suggestions. There is an art to it. You don't want to push people too hard or contradict reality too blatantly, or the spell will collapse. You'll find that a little subtlety goes a long way. Different people will exhibit different levels of resistance. The Sweet Tooth does not work as well on those who are aware it exists—for example, you would find it tricky to influence Nate or Summer or Trevor, now that they know what the candy can do."

"How do we know you haven't used a Sweet Tooth on us?" Pigeon asked.

Mrs. White smiled. "I suppose you don't, although most of my candy works only when used by children, so I probably couldn't use a Sweet Tooth even if I so desired. In addition, I assure you that I would not share magic candy with youngsters whom I had to coerce into accepting it. There are plenty who would help me voluntarily. Can I entrust these to you?"

"Sure, but—" Pigeon began.

"I realize some of you may be uncomfortable with this new task," Mrs. White interrupted, handing Pigeon the bag of candy corns. "Keep in mind, you are a treasure-hunting club, and treasure hunters often have to raid burial grounds in search of clues and artifacts, from the pyramids, to sunken ships entombing drowned sailors, to various necropolises around the globe. In this instance, we have permission from the deceased, who is a relative of mine, so you need not fret about ethics.

"If any of you wish to back out, please take this opportunity to surrender your candy to those willing to undertake the adventure, keeping in mind that your refusal to cooperate will mark the end of our secret relationship. If none of you are willing to claim the next clue, please return all the candy and I'll find others to assist me. Naturally, whatever our relationship, I'll expect you to keep the secrets I have shared with you, not that many would give such preposterous notions much credence."

"Will all your tasks involve stealing from museums or graveyards?" Nate asked.

"Not all of them," Mrs. White assured him. "Although when it becomes necessary, you will find I am willing to bend the rules to accomplish my aims. Others are actively competing for the prize we are chasing. If you go by the museum, you will find that the memoirs of Hanaver Mills are now missing, along with his pocket watch."

"Do you know who grabbed the book?" Trevor asked.

"No idea," Mrs. White said. "Perhaps the same man who chased you the other night. At any rate, can I rely on your continued assistance? I have to get back."

"I'll do it," Nate said.

"Me too," Trevor said.

Summer and Pigeon nodded, but Pigeon looked reluctant.

"One more wrinkle that I wanted to withhold until you accepted the mission," Mrs. White said. "Hanaver Mills is not buried under the headstone with his name on it. To throw off unworthy trespassers, he was interred under a tombstone inscribed 'Margaret Spencer 1834–1893.' You'll find the monument not far from his own."

"All this was in the note," Pigeon said.

"Written by his own hand," Mrs. White said. "Here is another Melting Pot Mixer for each of you. Be careful. Do your best to disguise the fact that you have disturbed the gravesite. Here are some extra Shock Bits as well for you to share. Sadly, I really am in a rush. Good luck Wednesday night. Please bring what you find to the shop on Thursday. I'll be waiting with another reward."

CHAPTER EIGHT

UNEARTHING SECRETS

A fternoon sunlight filtered through the overlapping branches above the Nest as Summer, Nate, Trevor, and Pigeon sat on the ground facing each other. Between them, on a weathered remnant of cardboard, sat all the magic candy they had collected to date: the Moon Rocks, the Shock Bits, and three leftover pieces of trick candy, along with the new candy they had just received from Mrs. White.

Nearby stood the Forty-niner. After exiting the candy shop, the four friends had looped around back where Mrs. White had met them at an unmarked door. She had then entrusted them with the Forty-niner, bundled in a green bedsheet. The wooden figure was so heavy that Trevor and Nate had to share the load. The two of them had lugged the wooden miner directly to their hideout by the creek.

Beside the Forty-niner sat two boxes of white fudge Pigeon had purchased for his mother.

"Hear ye, hear ye," Pigeon announced, "the governing council for the Blue Falcon Treasure-Hunting Society is now in session. Our president, Summer Atler, presiding."

"I feel like such a nerd," Nate muttered.

"I appreciate all of you gathering on such short notice for this important discussion," Summer said, ignoring Nate's grumbles. "Pigeon requested we convene immediately, and, given the importance of the topic at hand, I seconded the motion. Pigeon?"

"Thank you," Pigeon said. "Guys, I'm worried that we've gotten in way over our heads. Candy that makes you float around is one thing. Candy that lets you create infernos and control people's minds is another. Whoever Mrs. White is, she is very powerful, and I'm starting to really worry she might not be one of the good guys."

"Is it because of that drunk dude?" Nate said.

"He's part of the reason," Pigeon said. "Remember how he warned us about robbing graves? What if he really did come from the future? We've seen magic candy that can produce equally impossible results."

"The psycho said he was me," Nate said. "He didn't look anything like me. There is no chance I'm going to look like that when I grow up."

"And maybe it was nothing," Summer said. "But keep it in mind, especially since he somehow knew we would be robbing graves."

"Maybe he's from Mrs. White's competition," Trevor said. "You know, trying to make us distrust her in order to slow her down."

"Another possibility," Pigeon conceded. "Don't get me wrong. I'm in no hurry to jump to hasty conclusions. I just want to make sure we've considered all the different possibilities before we keep helping her."

"But we have to do this mission," Nate said. "We already took the candy."

"We could return it," Summer said.

"Tell me this," Pigeon said. "If Mrs. White is so powerful that she can make magic candy, why is she relying on fifth graders to run all her errands?"

"She said the candy only works well on kids," Nate reminded them.

"Shouldn't there be some other way?" Pigeon persisted. "It seems irresponsible to send kids around trespassing and stealing stuff." Nate folded his arms. Trevor shifted his feet. "It seems to me like Mrs. White doesn't want to take any risks herself, and she thinks kids are easy to manipulate."

"Part of it might just be that she likes to see kids using her candy," Trevor suggested.

"She acted like that at first," Pigeon said. "Have you noticed how she has gotten more and more demanding? How she now spends more time threatening to take the candy away than offering to share it with us?"

"Just because she wants to find this treasure doesn't make her wicked," Nate argued. "Sure, I think she really wants to find it, and yeah, she wants helpers who will do their part. But that doesn't make the candy less fun, or the adventure less cool. And it doesn't make her a villain."

"I agree," Trevor said.

"We're not saying she's evil," Summer said.

"Just that she might be," Pigeon clarified. "How do we know what the message in the pocket watch really said? How do we know that she is truly related to Hanaver Mills? How do we know if there is actually a treasure? Or that she would share it with us if she finds it?"

"Here's the other question," Nate said. "Is the candy so awesome that you would do all this just to be able to use it? The answer for me is yes. I've hoped all my life that something this cool would happen to me. I used to salvage broken appliances and collect little scraps of wire and metal in hopes that someday I would assemble it all into a robot. Guess what? I never got close. I used to mix magical potions out of ingredients from the pantry. They didn't work, but my grandma was nice enough to buy them for a quarter and pretend to drink them. And I've had a million other daydreams that never happened either. But this is real. Magic candy that actually works. If I get treasure on top of it, that's just a bonus."

"But what if Mrs. White really is dangerous?" Summer asked. "We're not just concerned that she might not share the treasure. What if the white fudge is harming our families in ways she hasn't told us? What if we end up helping her carry out some terrible scheme that hurts people?"

"Don't you think that sounds a little paranoid?" Trevor asked. "I mean, the lady makes magic candy. If she wants to cause harm, she'll cause harm, whether we help or not. What reason would she have to lie to us? Why involve us at all?"

Summer and Pigeon were silent. "I don't know," Pigeon finally said. "I just want to be careful. I mean, are we really going to go dig somebody up at the cemetery tomorrow night?"

"I'll be doing the digging," Nate said. "The rest of you just have to keep watch and help collect whatever is hidden in the coffin."

"I'm not sure I totally trust Mrs. White," Trevor confessed. "I have my doubts about her. But I definitely want to see what is in that grave. And think about this: If she *is* evil, wouldn't it be best if we were in a position to keep an eye on her? Who else is going to stop her? The police? She has magic—she'll just give them white fudge and send them away."

"Or hypnotize them with a Sweet Tooth," Nate said. "I'm with Trevor—we need to watch her closely."

"I guess that makes sense," Summer said slowly. "In that case, I think we should examine whatever we find in the grave ourselves before we hand it over to her. I would have liked to have seen that note on the watch."

"For all we know, we may really be digging up Margaret Spencer," Pigeon said. "This could have nothing to do with Hanaver Mills."

"You know," Nate said, "Mrs. White could fake a note as easily as she could fake a story."

"Not if we had examined the watch ourselves when we first got it," Summer said. "That's all I'm saying."

"I'm fine with checking out what we find before turning it over to her," Nate said.

"Meet here tomorrow at midnight?" Trevor proposed.

The others agreed.

"Bring your bikes," Summer suggested. "And don't fall asleep this time."

* * * * *

Located on Main Street, the Colson General Store lacked gas pumps on the outside, and fell short of offering a broad enough selection for serious grocery shopping on the inside. It was an ideal place for snacks like doughnuts or chips or candy or jerky or soda or hot dogs or nachos, and certain essentials like milk, eggs, bread, pasta, and cereal. You could also find some auto supplies, a fair amount of hardware, and a decent assortment of over-the-counter medication. Liquor, cigarettes, magazines, paperback novels, greeting cards, helium balloons, piñatas, DVD rentals—the store boasted those as well.

On Wednesday afternoon, shopping in the Colson General Store with his mother, Trevor found himself striving to avoid the attention of the man seated on the bench beside the newspaper stand. The man had a toothpick in his mouth, and was taking his time leafing through the *Contra Costa Times*. He wore an overcoat and a brown fedora with a black band. He was definitely the same man who had chased Trevor through the neighborhood behind the William P. Colson Museum.

Trevor knew the man had only glimpsed him as a freckly redhead in the dark. There was no chance of his being recognized—Trevor was even wearing different shoes than he had worn that night. He knew that only by acting suspicious could he possibly earn any serious attention from the man.

And yet Trevor could not resist spying.

He dawdled at a rack of packaged fruit pies, brand name and generic, pretending to be torn on which to choose, handling a blackberry pie, then a vanilla pudding pie, then apple, then blackberry again. He stole glances through the rack at the profile of the man reading the newspaper on the bench.

The man was indeed reading the paper—in fact, he would occasionally take out a pen to circle or underline an item of interest. But he was also spending a lot of time studying the passersby.

From his position near the entrance the man could watch people as they came and went, as they waited in line with their purchases, and as they roamed the store. The man hardly moved his head, but his eyes were in constant motion, never lingering on anything: the page he was reading, the woman in the red coat, the young man stocking the sunflower seeds, the page he was reading, the little boy whining about wanting a doughnut, the page he was reading, the old guy in the outdated jogging suit, the young couple near the register, the page he was reading, and so on.

The man was looking for something.

Trevor felt an unsettling certainty that the man was looking for him.

He realized how lucky he was that, so far, the man had not appeared to notice him peeking through the packaged fruit pie rack. Had they made eye contact, Trevor was certain the man would have become suspicious.

Trevor chose the blackberry fruit pie and rejoined his mother. He managed to avoid looking in the direction of the man the rest of the time his mother shopped. He did not look at the man while he waited beside his mom in line, or while she paid for the groceries and his fruit pie.

But, unable to resist, on his way out the door, Trevor glanced over at the man on the bench and found the man staring at him. The man's eyes narrowed almost imperceptibly. And then Trevor was out the door, helping his mom load bags from the undersized cart into the trunk of their car.

He did not look back at the store.

Deep down, he knew the man was still watching.

* * * * *

Pigeon went through the sliding glass door into his backyard. His dog, Diego, a black Labrador, padded over to him. Pigeon crouched and petted the dog's sleek coat for a moment before jogging around to the side of the house and wheeling his bike through the gate into the front yard. He normally stored his bike in the garage, but had figured that exiting through the side gate would be quieter.

Not that subtlety mattered. His mom was a different person. She no longer asked how his day went. She no longer double-checked the clothes he selected in the morning. She paid no attention to what he ate, when he did his homework, or whether he brushed his teeth before bed. And she had not asked for the change from the white fudge, so he had kept the extra seventy-nine cents.

His dad had always been low-key, letting Mom fuss over the details. If anything, he was mellower now. Pigeon probably could have driven away in the family minivan and nobody would have noticed or cared.

Pigeon pedaled down Monroe Circle to the creek and found the others waiting on the jogging path astride their bikes. "Everybody made it," Trevor said. "Good job."

"You all have your candy?" Nate asked.

The others nodded.

Summer adjusted her backpack. "Did you get the Forty-niner to the graveyard?"

"Yeah," Nate said. "I stuck the Forty-niner in the trunk of our rental car, then told my mom I was supposed to find the grave of Hanaver Mills as part of a homework assignment."

"Rental car?" Trevor said. "That's right. They never found your Explorer, did they?"

"Nope. At least it was insured. Anyhow, my mom bought the story and drove me to the cemetery this afternoon. A lady on duty knew right where the grave was, not far from one of the little roads that wind around in there. Hanaver has a big gravestone."

"What did you do with the miner?" Pigeon asked.

"I popped the trunk, unwrapped the Forty-niner, and set him behind Hanaver's gravestone. I did it right in front of my mom and she didn't even pay attention, no questions, nothing. That guy is heavy to carry by yourself—I couldn't have gone far. It didn't look too odd sitting there; I mean, people sometimes leave weird things at graves, not just flowers. It's a safe bet that nobody will have messed with it by tonight."

"I hope you're right," Summer said.

"You know we aren't actually going to Hanaver's grave," Trevor said.

"Right, but Mrs. White said Margaret Spencer was buried near Hanaver Mills."

"Let's get going," Summer said, starting down the jogging path, heading the opposite direction from Greenway. Pigeon enjoyed the wind in his face, riding through the darkness. Not many houses had lights on at this hour. The night was warm, the stars were bright, and the horizon was beginning to glow with the approach of moonrise.

The path dumped them off at a road called Mayflower Drive before continuing on the other side of the street. They abandoned the path and followed Mayflower for quite a distance. Pigeon's legs began to burn with exertion, but the others seemed fine, so he kept his mouth shut.

Summer led them onto a road called Skyline Avenue that soon became steep. Pigeon was relieved when Trevor dismounted and started walking his bike up the slope. After taking his time up the hill, by the time they had crested the rise, Pigeon felt ready to ride again.

They turned down another street, Saddle Road, and the cemetery came into view. Pigeon had never visited the Colson Valley Cemetery. A chest-high wall made of stacked, interlocking stones surrounded the graveyard. The graves looked old. He could see a few large tombs, several tall obelisks, a couple of statues, lots of upright headstones, and many flat grave markers lying on the grass. The effect at night was intimidating. It was easy to imagine the place teeming with witches and ghosts.

Summer rode over to the wall and stopped. "The front gates will be closed, so we might as well hop the wall here. Help me with my bike." Nate and Summer lifted her bike over the top of the wall. Trevor hopped the wall and lowered the bike to the grass on the far side. They passed all the bikes over the wall that way, and then Nate and Summer boosted themselves up and over.

Pigeon placed his palms on the top of the wall like the others had, but could not boost himself high enough to get the upper half of his body draped over the top. He couldn't kick a leg high enough to hook his foot up there, either. He just kept hopping and panting and scratching up his forearms.

He felt embarrassed when Trevor climbed back over and helped him get on top of the relatively low barrier. Pigeon dropped to the grass on the far side, and Trevor landed beside him a moment later.

"This place is scary at night," Nate said, running his hand along the top of a worn old headstone. In the buttery glow from the rising moon, the fading inscription was legible. "This guy died in 1906. Just about everybody alive now hadn't even been born yet."

"There's lots of old graves," Trevor said.

"Especially on this side of the graveyard," Nate said. "They still have empty land way over that way." He waved a hand in the direction he meant. "The gravestones are more recent over there."

"Where's Hanaver?" Summer asked.

Nate looked around. "Mom and I came in through the front, so I'm a little turned around. Follow me." He started weaving among the shadowy tombstones until he reached a narrow paved road. They continued along the road to an intersection. Nate paused, looking around.

"I know where we are now," Nate said confidently. "I remember that tomb with the angels." He took the road that curved up a gentle slope. As they rounded the bend, Nate started trotting. "There it is," he said, pointing.

The tombstone for Hanaver Mills was as tall as Pigeon, and wider than it was tall. It looked old, but his name remained deeply inscribed in commanding letters. Beneath his name were the years 1821–1893, along with the words "Father—Inventor—Philanthropist."

"What's a philanthropist?" Trevor asked.

"It means he donated money to charities," Pigeon said.

Around the back of the tombstone stood the Forty-niner, looking creepier in the darkness than he had under the sun. "Did you find Margaret Spencer?" Summer asked.

"I looked around a bit, but didn't see her," Nate said. "I figured eight eyes would be better than two. I didn't want to ask anybody from the cemetery, since we were going to be digging up her grave."

They fanned out. A few minutes later, Summer called out, down the slope and farther from the road. The others hurried over. Margaret Spencer had a more modest, traditional tombstone—about waist-high, narrow with a rounded top. The inscription had almost weathered away, and a few thin cracks zigzagged across the surface. Her name and the years she lived were barely legible.

"Good eyes," Nate said. "Let's go get the Forty-niner."

Nate and Trevor returned to Hanaver's headstone and lugged the wooden miner down to the other gravesite. "Should we take the Melting Pot Mixers now?" Pigeon asked.

"Maybe we should wait until we get more of a hole dug," Summer said. "It might take a while, and the mixers only last an hour."

"She should have given us more than one each," Trevor complained.

"We definitely want them on the way home," Nate said. "I think we should wait. If somebody comes, we can always take them quickly."

"Except you," Trevor said. "You'll be unconscious."

"Good point," Nate said. "I better take mine now, just in case."

Summer unzipped a pocket of her jacket and gave Nate the little ball of chocolate. She passed Melting Pot Mixers to Trevor and Pigeon as well, so they would have one when they needed it. Nate ate his, and after a moment started convulsing. He doubled over. When he stood upright, he looked like a full-blooded Native American. His face was darker, and though some similarities persisted, the transformation had structurally altered his features.

"You guys be lookouts," Nate said. "I'll want Trevor to stay by me while I dig. Stay low. With that moon, people could see us from the road."

"I want to do the cool part this time," Summer said. "Not keep watch again."

"Mrs. White said I'm supposed to work the miner," Nate reminded her.

"Not digging, that's no fun either. I want to get the box out of the coffin."

"Be my guest," Nate said. "We'll call you when we get there. Summer, you watch the little road, and Pigeon, you watch the main one. If you see trouble, hoot like an owl."

"I'm not sure that would fool anybody," Summer said.

"Just make that the signal if you need one," Nate replied. "We don't need something as piercing as the whistle."

Nate and Trevor huddled into the shadow of the largest tombstone close to the Margaret Spencer gravestone. Summer moved in the direction of the little cemetery road and squatted behind an eight-foot obelisk. Pigeon snuck down the slope toward Saddle Road, taking up position behind a wooden supply shed.

Before long, Pigeon heard the sounds of a shovel penetrating and flinging earth, along with the occasional scrape of metal against stone. The sounds were so quick, they could have come from multiple shovels, but he never actually heard two at once, and Pigeon knew the only digging tools they had were the little shovel and pickax of the Forty-niner.

Pigeon watched the field of tombstones before him, the wall, and the dark road beyond. The rhythmic sounds of digging became hypnotic, but the tension of possible discovery and the eeriness of the setting helped keep him alert. As time passed, he recited the U.S. presidents to himself, first in the order in which they had held office, then alphabetically. Pigeon was starting on vice presidents when he saw a car cruising slowly along Saddle Road, the headlights messing up his night vision. Crawling so that the shed was between him and the road, Pigeon hooted. The sounds of shoveling had already ceased.

Pigeon leaned out, peeking around the side of the shed with half his face. The car had stopped. He was almost certain that it was a police car. Suddenly a bright light glared in his eyes. Pigeon hid his head behind the shed. A bright beam of light began sweeping the area.

"You behind the shed," crackled an electronically magnified voice. "Come out with your hands in the air."

The beam of light returned to the shed. Pigeon popped the ball of chocolate into his mouth, and a moment later his flesh began to ripple. "I saw you, come out from behind the shed. Don't make me come in after you."

"Go," Pigeon heard a low voice urge from up the slope.

The rippling had subsided, leaving Pigeon looking Latino. He stuck a Sweet Tooth in his mouth and stepped out from behind the shed, hands held high. "I'm just a kid," Pigeon yelled.

"Keep your hands where I can see them and walk slowly to me," the police officer instructed. Pigeon complied. It was a long walk. The spotlight stayed in his eyes the entire time.

When Pigeon reached the wall, he could see the police officer, a muscular man with short hair and chiseled cheekbones. The officer turned off the spotlight and approached Pigeon holding a bright flashlight, one hand near the gun at his waist. "You aren't allowed to be in the cemetery after hours," the police officer told him.

"I have special permission," Pigeon said, the Sweet Tooth nestled under his tongue.

"Special permission?" the police officer repeated in a tone that implied it was unlikely.

The only lie Pigeon could think of sounded pretty lame, but he had to say something. "I'm doing a service project for Cub Scouts. Weeding graves."

"Little late for weeding, isn't it?" the policeman said.

"I have school, and my dad works odd hours," Pigeon said. "This was the best time. The cemetery people know about it. I have to do this to get my Arrow of Light."

The police officer stared at him. "You know, as a kid, I always wanted to be a Cub Scout," the man said. "Never really knew how to join."

"Please don't report this or tell anybody," Pigeon said. "If they hear from the police, the cemetery people might back out of sponsoring my project."

The police officer winked. "I think we can keep this one off the record. Keep up the good work. Don't stay out too late."

"Thanks for being so understanding," Pigeon said. "Might not be worth remembering this ever happened."

"Might not." The police officer turned, got in his car, and drove off down the road.

Feeling traumatized but relieved, Pigeon retreated to the shed. The noise of digging had already resumed. A Hawaiian girl wearing Summer's clothes met him at the shed. "What did you tell him?" asked the Hawaiian girl in Summer's voice.

"I said I was doing a Cub Scout project," Pigeon said.

"He bought that?" she exclaimed.

"Pretty easily," Pigeon said. "I was worried at first, but then he just accepted it. Now might be a good time for a victory hula."

"Am I Hawaiian?" Summer said.

Pigeon nodded. "You should do the hula right now," he urged.

Summer started waving her arms and shaking her hips. A

moment later she quit the dance and swatted him on the arm. "I knew what you were doing and it still sort of caught me off guard," she said. "Spit that thing out."

"I don't want to waste it," he said. "I should probably keep it in."

"You're right," Summer said.

"You ought to hurry back to your post," Pigeon suggested.

"Okay," Summer said. "Good job." Crouching, she dashed up the slope.

Pigeon grinned.

* * * * *

The last time Nate had tried to dig a hole had been very frustrating. The previous year, he had decided to dig a swimming pool in his grandma's backyard. He had grabbed both of his grandpa's shovels—the one with the square head and the one with the head more shaped for scooping—and gone to a patch of ground beyond the lawn where dry weeds were withering. It had been frustrating to discover how much force was required just to jab the head of either shovel even a little ways into the unyielding ground. He ended up driving the head of the shovel just a couple of inches into the dry earth with each thrust and scraping up only a little dirt. There were roots and rocks to slow him down, and a hot sun blazing overhead. He had given up before the pathetic hole was knee-deep.

Inhabiting the Forty-niner made digging a much more satisfying experience. With every thrust, the little shovel sank deep into the earth and came up with an impressive pile of soil. Nate soon found that since he did not feel the exertion of shoveling and never grew tired, he was free to dig as fast as he wanted.

He felt satisfaction watching the hole rapidly deepen and widen, the soil soft as pudding, light as popcorn. Whenever he struck a rock, he levered the blade of the shovel beneath it and flung it out of the way without difficulty. Trevor made suggestions on where to widen the hole and where to throw the dirt, which became increasingly useful as the hole deepened. In the three-foot-tall Forty-niner's form, it did not take long before Nate could not see out of the hole.

When Trevor saw the police car, he jumped into the hole with the Forty-niner and whispered a breathless warning. After Pigeon sweet-talked the officer, Trevor climbed out, and Nate resumed the excavation.

The hole was about six feet deep when Nate struck something solid. Pitching dirt high over his shoulder, he uncovered the surface of the burial vault. He created some space on one side of the stone vault, then pantomimed for Trevor to toss in the pickax.

Nate found the line dividing the lid of the vault from the rest of the stone box, and began prying. Bits of stone chipped off under the pressure he exerted. Although he could not feel the strain, several times he wedged the pick into position but failed to raise the lid.

Nate dug more, working his way around the entire vault, creating space for him to chip away at the sealed lid. Finally, after relentlessly attacking the vault from all sides, Nate forced the lid up, got a wooden hand under it, and heaved it aside.

"Good job, Nate," Trevor applauded.

Inside the stone vault lay a long box of rotten wood. Trevor shone a flashlight at it from above. Nate bashed open the wood with the pickax, tearing away splintery chunks and casting them aside. He glimpsed the remains of a decayed skeleton inside and observed a pale box beside the collapsed skull. Nate waved up at Trevor, who called to Summer in a loud whisper.

A few moments later, Nate saw a Polynesian version of Summer appear, grimacing down into the hole. "Okay, I changed my mind, you get it." She moved out of view.

Nate retrieved the ivory box from the coffin and scrambled over to the edge of the hole. Trevor climbed partway down the least sheer side of the hole and accepted both the shovel and the rectangular box. Nate slammed the lid back onto the vault, adjusted it as snugly as he could, then used the pickax as a climbing tool to emerge from the hole. Having not exited the hole since commencing the project, he was impressed by the quantity of earth mounded around the gravesite.

"Fill it in and let's get out of here," Summer said. "It's almost two-thirty."

Nate started with the shovel, but soon he was racing around the perimeter of the hole, hurling in armfuls of soil. He would get low to the ground, spread his arms, churn his legs, and bulldoze sizable piles into the void all at once. Then he would turn around, bend over, and scoop dirt backwards between his legs, arms pawing tirelessly.

Trevor helped with the shovel, and Summer kicked at the dirt as well, but it was Nate using the Forty-niner to wrestle earth into the hole that got the job done. In the end, the grave looked recessed and grassless. Too much of the dirt had dispersed too widely as Nate had chucked it skyward during his digging. Staring at the grave, they could see how obvious it would be that somebody had dug it up.

Trevor walked over to Summer. "What do we do?" he asked.

She surveyed the area. "Nothing. Had we been thinking, we would have cut out squares of grass at the start, set them aside, and laid them back down now. At least we got the box and pretty much filled in the hole. We better get out of here."

"Should I wake you up, Nate?" Trevor asked.

The Forty-niner bobbed his head.

Nate felt the rush of wind against his eyeball and was once again back in his own body. He was already back to his original race. Summer remained Polynesian. Trevor had not ingested a Melting Pot Mixer.

Trevor and Nate hauled the Forty-niner back up to Hanaver's tombstone; then they went and found a Latino Pigeon sleeping beside the supply shed. They woke him up, retrieved their bikes, and rode home.

CHAPTER NINE
CLEAN SLATE

Nate stood at the front of Mt. Diablo Elementary, watching from beneath an overhang as rain streaked down, wondering why white sidewalks turned brown when they became wet. A nearby gutter funneled a steady flow of water from the roof. Great pools had formed in the overcrowded parking lot, where kids were trying to leap into cars without dousing their shoes.

The rain had caught him unprepared. There had been a few clouds in the sky when his mom drove him to school. The day had grown overcast by first recess, then the rain began around lunchtime, accompanied by prolonged growls of thunder. Although the thunder had passed, a ceiling of murky clouds stretched to all horizons.

Trevor exited the main office and trotted over to Nate. "My mom is coming," he said. "She'll take all of us."

"At least somebody still has parents," Nate said. He and Pigeon had both already tried to phone home and reached only voice mail.

"I'm surprised none of our families knew the rain was coming," Pigeon said. "Plenty of kids brought raincoats and umbrellas."

"Mrs. White should start printing the forecast on her fudge boxes," Summer proposed.

Trevor shifted his backpack on his shoulders. "What should we do about the thingy we found?"

The previous night, after returning from the cemetery, they had unfastened the clasp on the ivory box and opened it. Inside, bundled in silky fabric, they found what looked like a little golden spyglass. When they had looked through the spyglass, whatever image they focused on was fractured into fragments, as if someone had inserted kaleidoscope mirrors into a telescope. Upon further examination, they had discovered no other clues in the box, among the silken wrappings, or on the view-warping spyglass.

"We go home, get dressed for the weather, and meet on the path by the Nest," Nate said.

"I still say we take the telescope apart," Summer insisted.

"And I still say it isn't made to dismantle easily," Nate said. "It seems too fancy, with mirrors or whatever inside—we'll mess it up."

Summer crossed her arms. "I don't want to rely on Mrs. White. I want to see the clues myself."

"If we could see screws or something we'd give it a try," Trevor said. "I agree with Nate."

"Me too," Pigeon said quietly.

"Okay, have it your way," Summer relented. "But if Mrs. White claims she found a clue inside the telescope telling us to rob a church, I'm turning in my candy."

Nate shrugged. He gave Pigeon a playful shove. "I saw you dozing in class," he said. "Not that Miss Doulin noticed."

"I couldn't keep my eyes open for a while there," Pigeon confessed. "I hope next time Mrs. White gives us an assignment we can do during the day."

"Have you guys seen Denny or Kyle or Eric?" Summer asked.

"I saw Kyle on my way into school," Trevor said. "He noticed me and avoided me. I think we're in the clear with them. Oh, speaking of that, did I tell you guys I saw the dude with the overcoat?"

"No, where?" Summer asked.

"I was at the Colson General Store yesterday with my mom. He was sitting by the entrance reading a paper and keeping an eye on everyone. Mrs. White was right that he's definitely up to something. I forgot to tell you guys last night."

"Did you play it cool?" Nate asked.

"I think so," Trevor said. "But he gave me a look that made me nervous. Hopefully it was just in my head."

They stood listening to the patter of the rain, watching the cars in the parking lot dwindle. Miss Doulin scurried over to her little hatchback without a coat, holding a leather satchel over her head, and entered through the passenger door to avoid the puddle on the other side.

"You guys stranded?" a mellow voice asked from behind them.

They turned. It was Gary Haag, the custodian. Nate had seen him around a few times. He was a thin guy in his early thirties with a wispy mustache and a light brown mullet that dangled to the base of his neck in straggly curls. He wore a denim jacket decorated with images doodled in black ink: a Viking ship, a frowning snowman, a dollar sign made out of cobras, Homer Simpson's head, a snowflake, a scuba diver, a pair of dice, a curved sword, a biplane, an algebra equation, a hamburger. A ring with at least twenty keys dangled from his belt. The odor of cigarettes lingered about him.

"My mom's coming," Trevor said.

"Oh, right on, I was feeling bad for you guys," Gary said, brushing hair out of his eyes. "I was going to find you a ride or something." He looked up at the gray clouds. "You're not dressed to walk home, and that rain ain't letting up anytime soon."

"That's nice of you," Summer said. "We'll be all right."

"How you been doing, Pigeon?" Gary asked.

"Good," Pigeon said.

"Right on." Gary stood with his hands on his waist, examining the sky. "You ever wonder if the clouds are really just hiding alien spaceships, like in that movie? I mean, this could be a full-on invasion."

Nate could think of a few movies Gary might be referencing. "It's a big storm," he said to fill the silence.

Gary nodded. "Don't you wish rain would fall from normal-sized clouds? You know, here and there, a little at a time. You might even be able to get out of the way if you stayed on your toes. But nope, all we get is some megacloud that blankets the whole state. I bet you couldn't even get out of the way in a Ferrari."

Nate glanced sideways at Trevor, who raised his eyebrows. Pigeon scratched his scalp. Summer stared at her feet.

Gary let out a prolonged sigh. "Well, I have a bunch of stuff to do." He jangled his keys. "Going to be a soggy ride home. Hope your mom stashed a life raft in the trunk. Keep it real." He sauntered away down a covered walkway.

"Is that guy sane?" Nate asked in a low voice.

"Gary's nice," Trevor said. "He can be kind of odd. There's Mom!"

Trevor's mom was driving along Oak Grove Avenue in a dark blue sedan. She turned into the parking lot and pulled up alongside the curb. Trevor climbed into the front seat, while the others piled in the back. His mom had curly dark hair and a darker complexion than her son. "It's really coming down," she said.

"Thanks for picking us up," Summer said.

"My pleasure," Trevor's mom said, pulling out of the parking lot. "Nate, you're on Monroe?"

"Right," Nate said.

She wove around a slow-moving pickup. "We all live so close we should carpool in the mornings!"

The wipers were on high mode, pushing away each new bombardment of raindrops an instant after they splattered against the glass. Nate found himself entranced by the motion, and wondered how Trevor's mom kept her concentration on the road. The sedan splashed through the edge of a huge puddle, sending up an impressive fan of water.

"Awesome," Trevor said.

They went to Summer's house first, pulling into an empty driveway. She waved and used a key to let herself in. They returned to Main, hung a right on Greenway, and turned into the Presidential Estates, the rain still pouring. After dropping off Pigeon, they swung around to the other side of the circle and let Nate out.

Simply running from the car to his porch, Nate got surprisingly damp. He did not carry a key, but knew where the hidden spare was tucked away. He tried the knob and found the door unlocked. Nate swiveled and waved, but Trevor's car was just pulling out of sight.

"Mom?" he called.

"In here," she answered from the family room.

Nate found her on the couch in front of the television. "Where were you?" he asked. "I tried to call, the rain had us trapped at school."

"I'm sorry, honey," she said. "I wasn't thinking. Looks like you found a ride."

"Trevor's mom."

"I was looking into joining a health club. Did you know I've put on six pounds since I started eating your fudge?"

"Maybe you should stop eating it," Nate said.

"I can't," she said, making wide, guilty eyes. "Neither can your dad. Cheryl eats her fair share as well. It's like we're stuck in a fanatical fudge phase."

"Did you join the club?" Nate asked.

"No, they kept pressuring me. They wanted me to sign a two-year contract. So I went and got a few exercise DVDs instead. I got back not five minutes ago."

"Okay. I'm going to go change. I'm supposed to meet Pigeon."

"Doing homework?"

"We have an assignment to finish." Nate rushed upstairs.

* * * * *

As rain pattered against the yellow hood of her raincoat, Summer brooded about the injustice that she had the longest walk to the Nest. Unless the creek was really low, she had to go all the way over to Greenway, up to the jogging path, and back to the bottom of Monroe

Circle just to reach their hideout. It was even less fair on a rainy day like today.

Fishing a sealed sandwich bag of Moon Rocks out of her pocket, she decided to take a shortcut. She turned down a side street that granted access to the strip of wilderness along the creek, and squelched through the weeds to where the water was rushing at a much higher level than normal. It would be a long jump, even with a Moon Rock, and if she messed up, she could get swept away. She hesitated, reconsidering the longer route, then decided she was being a sissy and popped a piece of candy into her mouth. Her body swiftly felt lighter.

She had picked a spot where the far bank was only a little higher than the near bank. Crouching, she sprang forward. For a moment, instead of merely jumping, it seemed like she was soaring up into the rainstorm, rising like a superhero, the rain noisy against her coat, but soon she reached the apex of her leap and began curving down toward the far bank. Her galoshes plopped down in the oozy mud.

"Now, that was an incredible jump," said a familiar voice.

Summer whirled. Denny came out of some bushes wearing a hooded camouflage slicker. He appeared to be alone. "Jump?" Summer said, playing dumb.

"Yeah," Denny said. "I wanted to see how high the rain had made the creek. Imagine my surprise when I see you walk up to the edge of the water, eat something, and jump across. I mean, a huge jump, like you were flying."

"You must be seeing things," Summer said.

"Kind of like how we were seeing things when Eric got all hairy and Kyle was puking root beer? Kind of like how I imagined that I was pinned to the ground by a massive force? What's going on, Summer?"

Summer pretended to sneeze and spat her Moon Rock into the weeds. Her body grew heavier. "I don't have time to stand around talking," she said. "Let's just say, if I were you, I wouldn't mess around with us anymore." She turned and walked away hurriedly.

"Love the threat," Denny laughed. "Fine, go fly away to play with the magical geek squad. You don't scare me. I have my eye on you guys."

Summer did not look back. She kept her pace quick and found the others waiting on the path above the Nest. Trevor and Nate wore hooded ponchos. Pigeon had on a thick winter coat and carried a black umbrella.

Summer bit her lip. Part of her wanted to report what Denny had seen, but she felt too embarrassed that she had been so careless. They already knew Denny was suspicious of them because of the trick candy. She decided there was no need to humiliate herself by sharing what else he had witnessed. "Do you have the telescope?" Summer asked.

"Of course," Trevor said.

They started down the path together. Summer checked periodically over her shoulder to make sure Denny wasn't tailing them. It would be easy enough for him to deduce that their candy was coming from Mrs. White without their actually showing him. By the time they reached Greenway, she felt confident that Denny was not on their trail.

The Sweet Tooth Ice Cream and Candy Shoppe was not as busy as it had been during their previous visit. But considering the rainstorm, there was still a respectable crowd. The guy with the wine-colored birthmark was helping customers, but the dwarf was not behind the counter today. Instead there was a big, round guy. He had thick, shiny lips, and his cheeks and jowls were bloated with fat. His black eyebrows almost met above his knoblike nose. Pockets of blubber bulged from the backs of his huge hands.

The guy with the birthmark ducked through the batwing doors into the back of the store and returned with Mrs. White, who waved the kids over. She raised the countertop and led them into the back.

Today the rear of the store was immaculate. Everything looked freshly scrubbed, the shelves appeared orderly, and no ingredients cluttered the worktables. "I'm very excited to see what you discovered," Mrs. White said, taking a seat at the table with the purple covering.

Trevor opened his backpack and placed the ivory box on the table. Mrs. White undid the latch. They had rewrapped the spyglass in the silky material, trying to make it look exactly as they had found it. Mrs. White unfolded the fabric and held up the spyglass, peering into it. "Excellent," she said, twisting the end of the spyglass. "Well done."

"What is it?" Nate inquired.

Mrs. White lowered the spyglass. "This is a teleidoscope, undoubtedly fashioned by Hanaver Mills. I expect it will prove useful locating the treasure."

"Teleidoscope?" Pigeon asked.

"You mean you don't know?" Nate asked, enjoying the moment.

Pigeon rolled his eyes.

"A teleidoscope is a hybrid between a telescope and a kaleidoscope," Mrs. White elaborated. "A normal kaleidoscope uses optical trickery to create patterns out of bits of material built into the device.

A teleidoscope uses similar optics to reconfigure whatever you point it at. Teleidoscopes work best when aimed at vivid backgrounds—for example, a bright floral arrangement."

"Is it a clue?" Trevor asked.

"I suspect it is a tool for unlocking a clue," Mrs. White said, setting the teleidoscope aside.

"Do we get some reward candy?" Nate asked.

"You get a new magical edible to use in completing a new assignment. While I strive to unravel the secret of the teleidoscope, I have a new mission of some urgency for the four of you."

"Do we have to do it at night?" Pigeon sighed.

"Nighttime would probably be best, but you can wait until the weekend." Mrs. White held up a grainy gray cube. "As you know, most of my confections work best on children. But a few function equally well on adults, like the white fudge. Interestingly, adults tend to remain most susceptible to magic that dulls their senses and reduces their vision. This masterful creation exploits that weakness, wiping out the memory of anyone who ingests it."

"Like amnesia?" Nate asked.

"Total amnesia," Mrs. White said. "Those who consume it retain their language abilities, but lose all the specifics of their identity. They start again with a clean slate, which is where the substance derives its name. Since the effects are permanent, and each Clean Slate is indescribably difficult to produce, I do not administer it lightly."

"You want us to erase somebody's memory?" Summer verified.

"A villainous man," Mrs. White affirmed. "An enemy to me and to all humanity. Letting him start again with a clean slate will be a service to him and to the world."

"What makes him evil?" Summer asked. "Is he after your treasure?"

"He is after the treasure, and would do terrible things with the power it would grant," Mrs. White said. "Whether or not I succeed in finding the treasure, he must be stopped. We need to get him to voluntarily consume the Clean Slate. If we try to force it upon him, the magic will fail. The Clean Slate dissolves almost instantly into any liquid, so I will need you to sneak into his house and taint a drink in his refrigerator."

"That sounds really dangerous," Summer said. "Who is he?"

"I'll tell you once you agree to the assignment," Mrs. White said.

"Can you prove that he's evil?" Summer challenged.

Mrs. White pressed her lips together for a moment before regaining a look of calm. "This relationship requires trust," Mrs. White said. "I trust you with candy so powerful that most grown, responsible adults would misuse it. You trust me that the assignments I select are in our best interest. Otherwise we should end the relationship."

"You can't just expect us to blindly do whatever you say," Summer said. "You have to earn trust. How do we know you won't misuse the treasure as much as this other guy? We earn your trust by fulfilling the tasks you give us. Can't you give us some proof to earn ours?"

All eyes were on Mrs. White. "If I had evidence, I would share it. All I have is knowledge and experience. I could tell you stories about this man, but I have no tangible proof to show you."

"Can we see the note on the back of the watch face?" Summer asked.

"Now you doubt that?" Mrs. White asked. "You found the teleidoscope right where the note described!"

"Can we see the note?" Summer repeated.

"If there is no trust in this relationship, perhaps you should turn in your candy," Mrs. White said.

"My dad says people who insist that you trust them usually don't deserve it," Summer said. "You don't need to give me more candy, but I earned the candy that I have. Everything you've had us do so far has seemed shady, and this new assignment is the shadiest yet. I just don't trust you." Summer looked at her three friends. "Any of you guys coming with me?"

"I am," Pigeon said. "You probably have good intentions, Mrs. White, and your candy is amazing and fun, but I'm not cut out for this sort of stuff. I don't have all my candy with me, but I can bring it back if you want."

"Summer has a point, you earned the candy that you have," Mrs. White conceded. "You can keep your share, as long as you use it in secret, and stay out of the treasure hunt. How about you, Nate? Trevor?"

Nate cleared his throat. "I'll keep working for you," he said.

"Me too," Trevor agreed. "Sorry, Summer."

"It's okay, you guys can do whatever you want." She felt tears welling up in her eyes. "I better go. Come on, Pidge." They started walking away.

"Are you certain?" Mrs. White asked. Summer and Pigeon paused, listening. "There is no coming back if you walk away now. You'll miss many of my most amazing candies. You haven't even seen Creature Crackers!"

"We're sure," Pigeon said. He and Summer passed through the batwing doors to the front of the store. She continued holding back the tears.

"You were really brave in there," Pigeon said, putting a hand on her shoulder.

"Was I?" she said, her voice catching. "Or was I a chicken?"

They stepped out into the rain.

"It's hard to stand up to somebody like Mrs. White," Pigeon said. "I wanted to before the graveyard mission, but I didn't have the guts. I wanted to again this time, but who knows if I would have without you."

"Well, the adventure is over for us," she said. "No more treasure hunt, no more candy."

"I think I've had enough treasure hunting," Pigeon said. "We can still have some fun with the candy we have left."

They hurried across the rain-glossed asphalt of Greenway.

"I hope Nate and Trevor know what they're doing," Summer said.

"I sort of doubt it," Pigeon sighed.

* * * * *

Nate felt bad as he watched Summer go. She had looked truly hurt when he and Trevor chose not to side with her. He wished he could explain. What Summer had asked of Mrs. White had sounded really reasonable to him. Mrs. White's evasive responses had made him even more suspicious of her. Which meant it was even more important to keep working for her until he figured out what she was really doing.

"Shame they didn't want to trust us," Mrs. White said, shaking her head. "You boys sure you don't want to follow them out?"

"I'm sure," Nate said.

Trevor nodded.

Mrs. White narrowed her eyes. "I could tell you two were made of tougher stuff than those others. As we close in on our goal, things will be heating up. I need to know I can rely on you boys to the bitter end."

"You can," Trevor promised.

"Very well," Mrs. White said. "The man whose mind we must erase is a magician like me, but has lived here in town a bit longer. His name is Sebastian Stott."

"Mr. Stott, the ice cream man?" Trevor blurted.

"The very same," Mrs. White said. "You may have noticed him out on his route again. He would do anything to lay his hands on the treasure we are seeking."

"But he's so nice!" Trevor exclaimed.

Mrs. White shook her head knowingly. "Believe me, he'll be a lot nicer if we let him start over with a new memory."

Trevor looked to Nate. Using the table to shield the action, Nate nudged Trevor with his foot. Whatever they ended up actually doing, they had to play along for now.

"Will the Clean Slate work on a magician?" Nate asked.

"It will work on anyone unless forced upon them," Mrs. White said.

"So, what's the plan?" Nate asked.

"Sneaking into his home will require some ingenuity," Mrs. White said. "We magicians lay down protective spells to guard our abodes. But I know a way to bypass his defenses, an arcane technique that he would never expect. Mirror walking."

"What's that?" Trevor asked.

"Most of those who still know of this secret believe it has been lost over the passage of time." Mrs. White held up a tiny blue mint.

"Put this in your mouth, bite down hard, and for a moment you will be able to step through a looking glass into the space inhabited by reflections."

"Like *Alice in Wonderland?*" Nate asked.

"Not like Alice," Mrs. White said. "You will become a living reflection capable of dwelling in the darkness that unites all reflected space. No walls exist in the void between mirrors, no substance except floors. The feat of magic that either discovered or created this space is nothing I can take credit for. But I do know how to access it. You can pass through the blackness from one mirror to another, and gain entry to forbidden places."

"Weird," Trevor said. "That's how you want us to get into Mr. Stott's house?"

"I have done some investigating, and I know he has a mirror large enough. None suspect that this secret art endures. You'll need only take a mirror near his house, climb inside, pass through his walls in the darkness, enter his bathroom through the mirror, deposit the Clean Slate in his milk or his juice, and then exit through the mirror."

"Once we're in, can't we just go out the door?" Nate asked.

"Open no window or door," Mrs. White warned. "Do not explore his home. Go from the bathroom to the kitchen and back."

"What if he finds us?" Trevor asked.

"Don't let him find you," Mrs. White said. "If he does, run away. If you're caught, play dumb. But be careful and you won't get caught. Strike late Friday or Saturday. Be sure the house is dark. Or I suppose you could sneak in during the day if you're sure he's off driving his route. I'll leave the timing up to you. Each Mirror Mint gets one person through one mirror. You'll pass through a mirror to get into the darkness of the reflected world, and through another to get out. Should you get stuck in the reflected world without a mint, you could become trapped for all eternity."

"Eventually we'd die," Nate said.

Mrs. White shook her head. "Not true. You would stop aging, no longer require food or air, and persist as a living reflection until the last mirror in the universe was destroyed."

"So be careful with the mints," Trevor said.

"Most careful," Mrs. White agreed, handing each of them four. "Two for each of you to get into his house, and two to get out. I imagine you'll want to stay together, although it might be wiser to enter solo, leaving the other guarding the mirror outside."

"Together is better," Trevor said. "It would be too freaky alone. We'll hide the outside mirror."

"Who wants to take charge of the Clean Slate?" she asked, holding up the gray cube.

Nate accepted it. "How do we find our way if the mirror world is dark?" he asked.

"The mirrors are all you can see in the blackness," Mrs. White said. "You can peer out of them like windows. But no light shines in through them. It can be disorienting—with no walls, you can see mirrors a long ways off." From under the table Mrs. White lifted a large oval mirror in a frame. "This should be large enough for you to fit through. The closer you place it to Mr. Stott's house, the closer you will be to his bathroom mirror. I suggest you set up really close to minimize the distance you'll have to traverse in the dark."

"Can we get in through a window?" Nate asked. "Windows sometimes have reflections."

"Most reflections in windows or water are too faint to connect to the mirror realm," Mrs. White explained.

"Should we use Melting Pot Mixers?" Trevor asked.

"The Mixers will do you no good if Mr. Stott catches you," Mrs. White said. "Your only option on this mission is to avoid getting apprehended."

"Where does Mr. Stott live?" Trevor asked.

"1512 Limerick Court," she said. "Just off Greenway, between here and your school."

"Do you have blueprints of his house?" Nate asked.

"No need," Mrs. White said. "Go through the big mirror in his guest bathroom. Don't confuse it with the small mirror in the bathroom adjoining his bedroom. The guest bathroom opens onto a hall. Walking away from the bedroom doors, pass through the living room and into the kitchen. I'll wrap up this mirror so you can take it now. Any other questions?"

Nate and Trevor looked at each other. Nate shrugged.

"I think we've got it," Trevor said.

"One more thing," Mrs. White said. "Until our treasure hunt concludes, I would prefer that you limit your exposure to Summer and Pigeon. Put those friendships on hold for a week or two. All right?"

Nate and Trevor nodded.

"Good boys."

CHAPTER TEN

ICE CREAM MAN

Heather Poulson passed a folded note to Nate, not even bothering to be sneaky about it. Miss Doulin stood at the front of the room reading aloud from a textbook, having obviously not prepared an actual lesson. Seeing his name printed in blue ink, Nate unfolded the torn slip of lined paper and read the single question it posed:

You don't actually trust her, do you?

Nate looked at Summer in her desk near the front on the far side of the room. She did not look back at him. They had not talked all morning. He had caught her once giving him a sad, pensive stare.

Tearing part of a page from his notebook and uncapping his black pen, Nate wrote:

I'm not an idiot. Trust me. (Even though I have no proof ha-ha)

He folded the paper, wrote "Summer" on it, and handed it to Heather. The note traveled to the corner of the room where Summer sat. She scanned the message, shook her head, tore a fresh piece of paper, and began writing. Her reply was passed to Nate and he opened it.

I do trust you, you're my friend, no joke. I'm worried about you. The candy is fun, but that lady is hiding something. I think she's dangerous. Don't you?

This note was on a larger piece of paper, leaving space for him to reply. When he started writing, he noticed that his script appeared small and cramped compared to her loopier style.

Of course she's dangerous! I only stayed so I could keep an eye on her a little longer. She doesn't want us hanging out with you and Pigeon anymore. We'll have to meet in secret. I don't even think we should eat lunch together—she seems to have some way of knowing things. Trevor and I have some surprising info. I don't want to write it down.

He crossed out his name as the addressee, wrote hers, and sent the folded paper back to Summer. After she read his words, she gave him a look to ask, "Then what do we do?"

Nate leaned over to Heather. "Hey, Heather, trade seats with Summer."

"I'll get busted," she whispered.

"I don't think Miss Doulin will care," Nate said.

"She might."

"Never mind," Nate said. He got up and walked across the back of the classroom, then up the row to Summer's desk. Miss Doulin continued to read aloud. He squatted beside Summer. "She wants us to erase Mr. Stott's memory," he whispered.

"The ice cream man?" Summer sounded shocked.

"She says he's a magician like her."

"What are you going to do?"

"We're not going to do it," Nate said. "We've agreed on that much already. We're still trying to decide our next move."

"Go talk to Mr. Stott," Summer said. "Spill your guts and see what he has to say. Maybe he can help."

"Or maybe he really is worse than she is," Nate said.

"Even if he is a bad guy, he'll be glad you brought the info to him," Summer said. "He can at least help you figure out what the heck is really going on. If you're not going to use the Clean Slate on him, you can't keep working for Mrs. White. And she may not take it well if you quit now. You'll probably need help dealing with her."

"I guess talking to Stott is the only real option," Nate admitted. "We can't just do nothing."

"You might be able to try quitting like me and Pigeon," Summer considered. "Just return all the candy and walk away. But with what she told you about Mr. Stott, you may know too much."

"Plus if we quit and try to pretend like none of this happened, we won't be able to learn any more info," he said. "I have to find out what is going on. Mr. Stott lives at 1512 Limerick Court, just off Greenway on the way home. If you want to come, meet us there tonight at eleven."

"I'll be there. Mr. Stott has been driving that truck around since I can remember. He's always acted genuinely nice. I bet he's one of the good guys."

"I hope so," Nate said, glancing at Miss Doulin, who continued reading from the textbook. "One more strange thing. Yesterday evening, after Trevor and I left Sweet Tooth, I had my mom drive me to the cemetery. I told her it was a follow-up visit for my project, but really I wanted to pick up the Forty-niner."

"Was he there?"

"Yeah, that wasn't the strange part. While we were nearby, I took a look at Margaret Spencer's grave. It looked untouched, with grass over it and everything."

"No," Summer said.

"I'm serious. And I don't mean maybe all the rain somehow made it look a little better. The grave looked untouched. Somebody covered our tracks for us, maybe with magic, maybe with gardening, I don't know. My guess is Mrs. White did it. But weird, huh?"

"Very weird."

"See you tonight."

Nate headed back to his seat, winking at Pigeon.

"Nate?" Miss Doulin asked. "What are you doing?"

He looked over at her, a little surprised that the teacher had glanced up from her reading and noticed him crossing the room. "Can I use the rest room?" Nate asked.

"Um, sure, go ahead." Miss Doulin returned her gaze to the textbook. "Where were we? Ah, yes." She started reading aloud again.

* * * * *

The house at 1512 Limerick Court was a boxy, one-story home made of wood and white brick. A small detached garage stood at the end of the short driveway. Quirky items cluttered the yard: a sculpture made of bicycle wheels, an inflatable Elvis, an aluminum totem pole, a miniature windmill with rotating sails, a giant ceramic boot with flowers sprouting out the top, along with other more conventional eccentricities like wind chimes, bird feeders, lawn gnomes, and pink flamingos. A low chain-link fence enclosed the front yard, with a gate providing access to the brick walkway that led to the porch.

As Nate and Trevor straddled their bikes in front of the gate, only one of the house's large, rectangular windows was illuminated— a window at the right end of the squat structure, with the blinds closed. The asphalt under their tires was almost dry. The rain had tapered off during the day. Patches of stars peeked through the clouds overhead.

"Think Summer and Pigeon will show?" Trevor asked.

"Summer at least," Nate said.

"I don't like standing here on the street," Trevor said. "Somebody might see us."

Nate inclined his head toward the door. "Should we go knock?"

"We don't need to all enter together," Trevor said, reaching to open the gate.

"You have those Frost Bites ready just in case?" Nate asked.

Trevor nodded. "You have the Shock Bits?"

"Yep," Nate said. "Think he might have a dog?"

Trevor rattled the gate gently and whistled. No animal responded. "All clear," Trevor said, opening the gate and wheeling his bike through. They left their bikes propped against the inside of the low fence and walked to the front door. Artificial turf blanketed the porch. A terra-cotta Buddha sat near the door, along with a painted statue of a cheetah. Nate pulled open the screen door and knocked. When the house remained quiet, Trevor pressed the lighted doorbell. They heard it chime a few notes from "Raindrops Keep Falling on My Head."

Illumination brightened a new window, and a moment later they heard locks being unfastened. The door opened halfway. Mr. Stott was wearing flannel pajamas with fat maroon and cream stripes. He squinted at them. "Tracked me down at home, did you?" he said. "Little late for a fruit bar."

"We aren't here to buy treats," Nate promised.

"I remember Trevor, and you're Nate, correct?" Mr. Stott said.

"Right," Nate said. "We're here about Mrs. White. She has plans to harm you."

Mr. Stott's demeanor transformed instantly. His cranky half-smile drooped into a somber frown. His eyes flicked back and forth between them. "You mean by driving me out of business?"

"We mean by using magic against you," Trevor clarified.

Mr. Stott nodded, stroking his beard. "Then you had better come inside," he invited, stepping out of the way and pulling the door open wider.

"Trevor, Nate," came an urgent whisper from behind them.

Nate turned and saw Pigeon and Summer pulling up at the gate on their bikes. "They're with us," Trevor explained as he stepped across the threshold.

Pigeon and Summer parked their bikes and hurried through the doorway. Mr. Stott closed the door.

Nate and Trevor went into the living room and plopped down on a black leather sofa. A fanned-out assortment of peacock feathers decorated one wall. A print showing Easter Island statues hung on another, stone heads staring mysteriously. Several issues of *Log Home Living* magazine rested on a glass and chrome coffee table. A tall, unlit lava lamp occupied one corner. A few pedestals stood around the room, each topped by one or two little telescopes locked into position by some kind of holder.

Summer and Pigeon sat on an elaborately carved loveseat. Mr.

Stott claimed a large armchair upholstered in cowhide, adding to the ridiculousness of his striped pajamas. He leaned forward intently. "You say you are aware of a plot by Belinda White?"

"Is that her name?" Summer asked. "Belinda?"

"The name she is using here in Colson," Mr. Stott said.

"She wanted Trevor and me to use something she called a Clean Slate to erase your memory," Nate said. "She told us that you were an evil man."

Mr. Stott nodded, pinching the whiskers immediately below his lips. "I've heard rumors that she could concoct a powerful amnesiac. How did she expect to administer it?"

"She wanted Nate and me to come into your house using mirrors and mix the Clean Slate into a drink in your fridge," Trevor said.

"Using mirrors?" Mr. Stott asked dubiously.

"She said we would turn into reflections and be able to travel through walls," Nate said.

"I had no idea that technique had survived," Mr. Stott marveled. "How sloppy of me! Tell me, why are you sharing this information?"

"We didn't want to do it," Trevor said.

"We got involved with Mrs. White because she was giving us magic candy," Nate explained. "She would have us do little tasks, and then reward us with more candy. We could jump around like we were in low gravity, we could shock people, we could control dolls with our minds—"

"But the stuff she was asking us to do seemed fishy," Summer interjected. "We gave fudge to our parents that made them distracted and forgetful. We stole from the town museum. We dug up a grave."

"We wanted to figure out what she was up to," Nate said. "But we drew the line at erasing your memory."

"For which I'm most grateful," Mr. Stott said. "With that mirror technique you might have succeeded. What have you learned about her master plan?"

"We know she is here looking for a treasure," Pigeon said. "We know she wants it because it will increase her powers. She says you are looking for it as well. She somehow knows a lot about what is going on in town. We're not sure why she involves kids in her work, or whether she really is as dangerous as we worry she might be."

Mr. Stott folded his hands. "I appreciate you laying your cards on the table," he said. "I will try to be equally forthright. Mrs. White is more treacherous than you can guess. We are both magicians, but she has one of the most notorious and bloody histories of any member of our order. She craves power, and has never hesitated to lie, cheat, steal, or kill to get it."

"Are you dangerous too?" Pigeon asked.

Mr. Stott shifted in his chair. "I can be, I suppose. No magician is really safe, to himself or to others. Many of us are hermits, who mostly want to be left alone as we pursue our studies. Some have altruistic intentions; others are entirely selfish. We all generally try to maintain a low profile. A few of us take on the responsibility of policing those who attempt to blatantly use magic for sinister ends, or who operate too openly and risk revealing the long-guarded secret of our existence."

"Are you one of the policemen?" Nate asked.

"In a limited capacity, yes," Mr. Stott said. "However, I am not one of those who dedicate all their time to such matters. Belinda concerns me. I am aware of the treasure she is seeking—it is part of the reason I took up residence in this town years ago."

"What is the treasure?" Summer asked.

Mr. Stott stroked the furry length of his beard. "None know for certain. We have only rumors. Supposedly it is a talisman of significant magical power, worthy of remaining concealed these long centuries. I came here as a guardian rather than a treasure seeker. I did not want Belinda or others of her mind-set to lay hands on an item of such terrible power. But now I fear the only way to stop her and those like her may be to locate the treasure myself."

"And what would stop you from using it for bad purposes?" Summer asked. "Mrs. White makes the same claims about you as you make about her."

"No magician would trust another with a talisman such as this," Mr. Stott acknowledged. "Least of all Belinda White. But I have lived quietly for hundreds of years. In bygone days, I have inhabited seats of power and prestige, and such honor long ago lost its savor. I have lived in Colson for years, not searching for the treasure, but delivering ice cream to schoolchildren in a rundown truck. I would gladly leave the treasure hidden away if Belinda were not hot on the trail. If I gained the treasure, I would store it and protect it from others who might abuse it."

"I don't get why Mrs. White involved us," Pigeon said.

"That has as much to do with the nature of the magic we practice as it does with her greed," Mr. Stott said. "You see, magic functions much more potently on the young. Part of the paradox of becoming a magician is that by the time you know enough to manipulate magic, you are too old to use it to your full advantage. Mrs. White can engineer sweets that grant great power to the young, but those same miraculous confections would have little effect were she to use them herself."

"Why not use magic to make yourselves younger?" Pigeon asked.

Mr. Stott spread his hands. "We do what we can. Taking away years from a person is nearly impossible. Adding them is much easier. As magicians, about the best we can do is try to maintain our current age. We can't quite stop the aging process, but we can slow it considerably. That is how magicians like Belinda and myself survive for so many years."

"So Mrs. White just wanted us for our youth, because her candy would work well on us?" Nate restated.

"Basically, yes," Mr. Stott said. "Undoubtedly she believed that you four were especially bright and capable. She must have been monitoring your achievements—she would not have entrusted you with an assignment like erasing my memory unless she truly believed in your abilities. But make no mistake about it, you were being used."

"What should we do now?" Trevor asked.

Mr. Stott rose and began pacing. "That is the question of the hour. By coming to me and disclosing your assignment, you have placed yourselves in extreme jeopardy. If Belinda learns you have betrayed her, your very lives could be in peril. As I see it, you have three options. You could pretend that your attempt to erase my memory failed and continue working for her. You could resign from her service immediately, never speak of any of this to anyone, and hope for the best. Or you could try to beat her at her own game and get to the treasure ahead of her. Any of those choices is risky."

"Pigeon and I resigned yesterday when she started explaining this assignment," Summer said.

"We're mainly here for moral support," Pigeon added.

"Trevor and I were only staying with her in order to figure out what she was up to," Nate said. "We don't want to keep helping her."

"I want to beat her to the treasure," Trevor said.

"Is that realistic?" Summer asked.

"Depends," Mr. Stott said, pacing with his hands behind his back. "How much do you know?"

"We helped her steal a pocket watch that belonged to her ancestor Hanaver Mills," Nate said.

One side of Mr. Stott's mouth curved up into half a smile. "She said Hanaver Mills was her ancestor? Belinda White was making magical candy when Hanaver Mills was in diapers."

"Supposedly the watch contained a clue revealing that an important object was buried with Hanaver Mills," Pigeon said. "The clue indicated that Hanaver Mills was actually buried under a grave marker for Margaret Spencer, who died the same year. We dug up the grave and found a teleidoscope."

Mr. Stott stopped pacing and faced Pigeon. "A teleidoscope? Where is it now?"

"She has it," Summer said.

Mr. Stott shook his head slowly, wearing his lopsided grin again. He fingered the telescope on top of one of the pedestals. "Do you know what this is?" he asked.

"A teleidoscope?" Nate ventured.

"I collect them," Mr. Stott said. "Artisans create high-end teleidoscopes that sell for thousands of dollars. Those in this room function almost like kaleidoscopes, in that the teleidoscope is locked into a fixed position aimed at a certain target. This teleidoscope points at a stone ball with water trickling over it. The ball slowly turns, and the flowing water ensures that the pattern the teleidoscope observes is never quite the same twice. Feel free to look."

As the kids took turns gazing into the eyepiece and turning the wheel to rearrange the pattern, Mr. Stott crossed to a different teleidoscope, switching on a light behind it. "For this teleidoscope, you dip this hoop into this soapy solution." He pulled a lever that immersed a circle of wire into a shallow reservoir. When he raised it, the hoop had a glossy film stretched across it, as if for blowing a huge bubble. "Take a look," he offered.

Nate peered into the teleidoscope and beheld a brightly animated pattern. Twisting the end of the teleidoscope, he made the pattern dance. "It looks like a cartoon," he said.

"Just the soapy film with the light behind it," Mr. Stott affirmed.

Nate stole one more peek before allowing the others a turn. They had to dip the wire hoop again each time the film broke.

"Come with me," Mr. Stott said. He led them down a hall to a bedroom dominated by a big four-poster, complete with canopy and curtains. On a nightstand sat a small platform fashioned out of pink granite, with a single vacant mounting for a teleidoscope. Trevor, Summer, Pigeon, and Nate gathered around it.

"This base was designed and built by Hanaver Mills," Mr. Stott said. "He left it to me in his will. He was not a relative, but we were friends. A teleidoscope is meant to point at this surface." He indicated a smooth surface speckled with variegated flecks opposite the empty mounting. "Hanaver told me that the right teleidoscope would reveal a message hidden in the stone."

"You think we found the teleidoscope?" Pigeon said.

"It was this base that instigated my teleidoscope collection," Mr. Stott said. "After inheriting the platform, I tracked down several teleidoscopes attributed to Hanaver Mills. None revealed a message. I also experimented with teleidoscopes made by a variety of random craftsmen, hoping to get lucky. Again, success eluded me. I suspect Mrs. White now possesses the teleidoscope I have been seeking all these years, a vital clue to locating the treasure. I have kept this base a closely guarded secret, but perhaps she somehow learned of it. That might explain why she would want my mind erased."

"She didn't mention anything about the base to us," Nate said. "But that doesn't mean you're wrong."

"How does she know so much?" Trevor asked. "Does she sneak around at night?"

"I see that Belinda has not explained much about herself," Mr. Stott chuckled. "A magician cannot leave his or her lair. The lair is empowered with magical defenses and spells that keep them safe and postpone their aging. If Belinda abandoned her lair to snoop around, she would become a pile of bones in no time."

"But what about your ice cream truck?" Pigeon asked.

"Part of my lair," Mr. Stott said. "Although making a vehicle part of my lair creates certain vulnerabilities, to me the added mobility justifies the risk. Magicians can journey from lair to lair, setting up new abodes as needed, traveling in temporary lairs, but a price of the lives we lead is that we surrender the ability to move about freely."

"You're saying Mrs. White lives at Sweet Tooth?" Pigeon asked.

"Most assuredly," Mr. Stott said.

"Then how does she know so much?" Trevor asked again.

"Belinda has always employed henchmen," Mr. Stott said. "Most of us also have a trick or two that allows us to personally spy on the outside world. Which is why I worry about you kids. There is no way to be sure where Belinda is looking, or when. You must be most cautious."

"What are the chances of us stealing the teleidoscope from Mrs. White?" Nate asked.

Mr. Stott frowned. "It would be very difficult. Her lair will be well-guarded by spells."

"What if we use her Mirror Mints against her?" Nate suggested.

Mr. Stott's eyebrows knitted together. "I'm sure she keeps no mirrors in her lair large enough for anyone to gain access that way, since she is aware that the secret of mirror travel endures."

"What if we planted a mirror inside the candy shop?" Nate proposed.

Mr. Stott scratched his hairy cheek. "Possible," he said, eyes lost in thought. "If I could get my hands on that teleidoscope, we just might beat her to the treasure. Once we acquire the treasure, she'll start preparing to leave town the next day. She'll have no more interest in Colson, California. And if she tried anything foolish out of spite, I would have the means to protect you."

"Maybe we should go for it," Trevor said.

"Yeah," Nate said. "I'd rather take action than wait around for her to punish us."

"I can't advise you to try this," Mr. Stott said. "It is too bold. But . . . if you insisted on taking the risk, your advantage would come from the fact that Belinda probably thinks her candy shop is invulnerable. Our lairs are designed to keep intruders out. If you can discover a way in, you may not find many obstacles between you and your goal."

"She probably just keeps it stashed under that table in her workshop," Trevor said.

"On the outside chance you were daring enough to attempt such an inadvisable mission, you would probably need to do it before you were supposed to wipe my memory," Mr. Stott said. "When you fail to complete that assignment, her guard will be up."

"Good point," Nate said.

Mr. Stott put his hands behind his back and stood up straight. "Of course, this could all be an elaborate ruse by Belinda to ferret out what I know. If it is, well done, you utterly fooled me. I have laid my cards on the table. Please keep this information private. There are many others besides Belinda White who would try to destroy me simply to lay their hands on this teleidoscope base." He rubbed the pink marble platform.

"We won't blab," Summer said.

"Having heard your news, I should eliminate all mirrors from my home," Mr. Stott said. "Whether she has been peeking through windows, or having spies use mirror travel, Belinda will probably notice if I do that, so I will wait for a few days while you figure things out. Would you like my telephone number?"

"Yes," Nate said.

Mr. Stott opened a drawer and withdrew four business cards, handing one to each of the kids. His address and telephone number were on one side. On the other, they read:

SEBASTIAN STOTT
THE CANDY WAGON
Homemade and Brand Name
Ice Cream · Frozen Treats · Candy

Nate pocketed his card as Mr. Stott led them toward the front door. "Feel free to contact me if you need anything," he said. He opened the door.

"Thanks, Mr. Stott," Pigeon said.

"Thank you again for the warning," Mr. Stott said. "I'm quite fond of my identity."

They filed out the door. Nate exited last. "You'll hear from us again," Nate promised.

Mr. Stott winked. "I hope so."

CHAPTER ELEVEN
MIRROR MINTS

Summer and Pigeon crouched beside a white cake box on the jogging path about twenty paces from Greenway Avenue. Summer had purchased a mint-chocolate-chip ice cream cake from the Sweet Tooth Ice Cream and Candy Shoppe earlier that afternoon using money from the little yellow safe on her bedroom shelf. The cake now resided in her freezer, bundled in plastic wrap. The point had not been to get a cake. The point had been to acquire the box.

A round mirror rested on the bottom of the box, the reflective side facing down. The diameter of the mirror was almost too great to fit, even though the box had held quite a large cake.

Pigeon had furnished the mirror. In the bathroom that he shared with his younger sisters, a round medicine cabinet hung on the wall. Up until that afternoon, the mirror had served as the front of the cabinet. Now the cabinet had no front, exposing narrow shelves stocked with bandages, bottles, and dissolving tablets. Pigeon had no idea how

long it would be before his parents noticed, but he was much less worried about it than he would have been a week ago.

Summer and Pigeon each uncapped a tube of super glue purchased at the Colson General Store. They squeezed the colorless,
gelatinous glue all over the back of the mirror, closed the lid of the
box, picked it up, and hastened down the path to Greenway.

It was Friday evening, and the line of customers at the Sweet
Tooth Ice Cream and Candy Shoppe wrapped halfway around the
outside of the building. Cars jammed the parking lot and lined the
curbs of Greenway and Main.

Summer and Pigeon skipped the line and pushed their way
through the front door with the cake box. All of the tables inside were
occupied, with many patrons standing around nibbling at various
sweets, but an older couple was just standing up from a square table
not far from the door. Summer and Pigeon rushed over and claimed
the table before the couple had cleared their napkins.

Summer positioned herself to at least partially impede a view of
Pigeon from the counter. Setting the cake box on his lap, Pigeon
opened the top, removed the mirror, and pressed it up against the
underside of the table. He held the mirror firmly in place, fingers
splayed against the glass, and slowly counted to thirty. The glue was
supposed to work instantly, but he wanted to be safe. He kept an eye
on the customers standing or sitting near him, but none seemed to be
paying any attention to his actions. Carefully he reduced the pressure
of his hands against the glass until he was no longer supporting the
mirror.

Pigeon gave Summer a curt nod. He glanced beyond her at the
counter, manned by the big round man, the guy with the birthmark,
and the dwarf. They looked harried as they took requests, filled

orders, and made change, and gave no sign of having noticed him or Summer. Toting the cake box, Pigeon and Summer dodged around the line at the doors and fled the store.

* * * * *

The clock radio came to life playing one of the five or six songs that seemed to be incessantly on the air lately, and Trevor pawed at it, slapping the snooze button. His mattress felt deep and soft and his pillow was bunched just right. How long did the snooze button last? Seven minutes? Nine?

He pushed himself away from the mattress. That was the danger of keeping the alarm clock within arm's reach of the bed—the snooze button was too tempting. But he had wanted the alarm nearby so he could shut it off quickly. White fudge or no white fudge, he didn't want to press his luck by awakening his parents. The green digital numbers read 2:16 A.M.

Trevor put on his shoes and a lightweight jacket. All his clothes were dark. Grabbing his private stash of Moon Rocks, Shock Bits, Frost Bites, and Mirror Mints, he went downstairs. He sucked a few sips of water from the faucet in the kitchen, then exited through the front door, leaving it unlocked.

He reached the jogging path first and sat down to wait. Hopefully Nate would be sufficiently excited to get himself out of bed. Pigeon had called to report that the mirror was in place.

Trevor saw Nate walking down the street and waved. Nate waved back. He was carrying the mirror that Mrs. White had given them. Trevor got up. "You ready?" Nate asked as he approached.

"I'm freaked out," Trevor said.

"In and out," Nate said. "Hopefully it will only take a minute."

"You have your candy?" Trevor asked.

"I'm all set," Nate said.

They started down the path. "She's going to flip out when she finds the teleidoscope missing," Trevor said.

"We'll have to watch our backs."

"If we pull this off smooth enough, Mrs. White may not even know we did it. I mean, if the teleidoscope just seems to have vanished, with all the different people who are hunting for the treasure, who knows who she might suspect?"

"Good point," Nate said. "We'll have to try to play it cool."

"I left several lights on in my house, in case we need to retreat to our homes inside the mirror realm," Trevor said. "I never realized how many mirrors we had."

"I left my bathroom light on for the same reason," Nate said. "Most houses will be dark, so I hoped I would be able to find the bright mirror."

Trevor tapped the mirror that Nate was holding. "Dressed in black in the middle of the night, we look like we stole that mirror."

"Nobody will see us," Nate said. "We walk along the path, we cross Greenway, and we're there."

The night was dark and silent as they reached Greenway. No cars on the street, no cars in the candy shop parking lot, no people. Trevor and Nate trotted across the street and knelt behind a low hedge that bordered the parking lot.

"Let's lean the mirror here," Nate said, propping it against the hedge so that it faced a narrow alley between the candy shop parking lot and another building.

"I guess this is as good a place as any," Trevor said. "You have four mints?"

Nate counted them out. "One to get into the mirror, one to get out, another to get in, another to get out. Should we do it?"

"Sure."

"Who goes first?"

"I have the flashlight," Trevor said. He stuffed all his candy in his pockets and placed a Mirror Mint on his tongue. He tapped his knuckles against the surface of the mirror and it rippled, making his reflection undulate. When he pressed his palm against the glass, it flexed inward, wavering less as he stretched it. He bit down on the mint, and his hand passed through the surface of the mirror as if it were the surface of a pond. He wiggled his fingers. The space beyond the mirror felt much colder than the night air.

Switching on the flashlight, Trevor crawled through the mirror into the darkness. Although the dark space beyond the mirror was bitterly cold, he did not shiver or get goose bumps. Before him, at different heights and in all directions, a multitude of rectangles and ovals interrupted the darkness, the vast majority small and far away. Most were so dim that they were visible only because everything else was perfectly black.

Turning back to face the mirror he had just crawled through, Trevor found himself staring out at Nate, illuminated by the pinkish glow of streetlights. Although he could see Nate fine, none of the light spilled through to brighten the darkness. Trevor waved, and Nate waved back. Nate put a mint in his mouth and entered, the glass rippling as he passed through. As soon as he moved beyond the mirror, his body lost all color and was visible only as a silhouette against the dim background of the alley.

"Welcome to Wonderland," Trevor said.

"Is your flashlight on?" Nate asked.

"Yep," Trevor said. "I don't think light shines here."

"We can see the mirrors," Nate said. "Light has to be reaching our eyes."

"Sure, but it doesn't brighten anything—not us, not the ground, not even the emptiness."

"Maybe there's nothing to shine on," Nate said. "We're reflections now, which sort of means we're nothing."

"You saw me wave, right?" Trevor said.

"Sure. But look, I put my arm right next to the mirror, and absolutely no light hits it. I bet reflections are only visible from outside a mirror."

Trevor reached out and touched Nate's arm. "At least I can feel you. And I can see your outline when you're in front of the mirror."

"Touch the ground," Nate suggested.

Trevor crouched and ran his hand over the hard, smooth surface. "It's like glass."

"It certainly isn't dirt or asphalt," Nate said. "Nothing is quite real here, not the ground, not even the cold."

"Isn't the cold weird?" Trevor agreed. "You feel it, but it doesn't really get to you, it doesn't penetrate."

"That's what I mean," Nate said. "Nothing here is real. We better get going. I can see how people could get lost in here."

"If we walk directly away from this mirror, we should be inside the candy shop in about twenty steps," Trevor said. He placed his hand against the mirror, which from his current perspective looked like a window. "Let me test something." He gradually pushed harder and harder. "The mirror won't budge."

"I'm telling you, I think we're close to being nothing in here," Nate said. "We may be just about the only things in here that can think or move or talk or make a silhouette. It creeps me out."

They started taking hesitant steps away from the mirror. "If it's dark inside the candy shop, we may have a hard time spotting the way in."

"We'll find the mirror," Nate assured him. "It has to be brighter than total blackness!"

"I keep thinking I'm going to run into something," Trevor said.

"There's nothing to run into! No walls, no objects, just ground."

"What if I run into the back side of a mirror?" Trevor wondered.

"I guess that's possible," Nate said.

They continued forward. Trevor could not shake the worry that he might whack his face against something in the darkness, but it kept not happening. He paused and looked back at the mirror through which they had entered. "I think we're inside the candy shop by now," he said.

Nate gave no answer. "Nate?" Trevor asked. "Nate?" he repeated more urgently.

Nate exhaled loudly. "Sorry," he said. "Try holding your breath. You never run out of air. It seems like you will, but the point where you actually need to take another breath never comes."

Trevor held his breath. Nate was right, it felt normal at first, like his oxygen was running out and soon he would need to exhale and gulp down fresh air. But the moment of true desperation never came. "It's like if we didn't have the habit, we wouldn't need to breathe at all."

"Find your pulse," Nate said.

Trevor felt his wrist, sliding his fingers around, searching for that spot a bit off-center where the pulse was strong. He could not find it. He tried his neck instead, where it was usually easier to find his heart-beat, again to no avail. Finally he pressed his hand against his chest. Nothing. "No pulse?"

"No pulse," Nate confirmed. "Our hearts don't need to beat, we breathe only out of habit . . . no wonder Mrs. White said we could get trapped in here forever."

"This is definitely not the place I want to spend forever," Trevor said.

"Window shopping until the end of time," Nate said. "Roaming from mirror to mirror like a ghost."

They were talking fairly quietly, but Trevor lowered his voice even more. "You don't think our voices are carrying through the mirrors, do you?"

"I doubt it," Nate whispered. "But we should probably be care-ful, just in case."

Trevor spotted a less black circle floating in the darkness at about the height of his waist. "Do you see that?" Trevor asked.

"What?"

"Over here. Follow my voice."

"Oh, genius, good eyes, that has to be it."

Leaning over the circle, about the size of a medium pizza, Trevor could faintly discern the white and black checkered pattern of the candy shop floor. He could also make out some chrome table legs and chair legs. Trevor placed a hand on the circle. "Feels solid. How should we go through?"

"Stand on it," Nate recommended. "Then you'll land on your feet instead of on your head."

"Think it will hold me?"

"I think we're nothing right now. It will hold nothing."

"Come help me balance," Trevor said. Laying a hand on Nate's shoulder, he got one knee up onto the circle, then lifted his opposite foot, and in a moment he was standing on the dim disk. "Should I go for it?"

"You didn't see any sign of anybody?"

"Just our moms trying to break in and steal fudge," Trevor said.

Nate chuckled.

"It looked quiet and dark," Trevor continued. "I think the only light was trickling in through the windows from the street."

"Then go for it," Nate said.

Trevor pulled a mint from his pocket and put it in his mouth. The circle became elastic, like he was on a trampoline. Biting down, he instantly dropped through the circle to the tile floor. Raising his arms over his head, Trevor ducked down, worming the rest of himself through the round opening. There was not much room to spare, but he fit. He scooted out of the way so Nate could drop through.

Trevor had almost forgotten that he was holding his flashlight, until he saw it actually penetrating the darkness of the candy shop. The beam landed on a withered old man wearing a long feathered headdress, making Trevor feel a brief surge of panic before he recognized the figure as the wooden Indian. He switched the light off.

Sneakers slapped down against the tile floor as Nate dropped through the mirror. To Trevor it looked like a moment from a magic show—a pair of legs wearing jeans sticking out from the bottom of the table with nothing visible above it. It would make a pretty good stage trick.

Nate shimmied the rest of the way through the mirror, then

crab-walked out from under the table. "I can hardly see," Nate whispered so quietly that Trevor could barely hear him.

"Should I turn on the flashlight?" Trevor whispered back.

"Better than stumbling and making a ton of noise," Nate said.

Trevor clicked on the light. After how busy the candy shop had been lately, it was peculiar to see it empty. Nobody behind the counter, no patrons. Everything still and silent, with candy everywhere for the taking. "Where should we look first?" Trevor asked.

"In the back," Nate said. "Let's try that table where Mrs. White always sits."

After ducking under the hinged segment of the counter, they went through the batwing doors into the rear of the store. The worktables were messy, covered with various candy projects in different stages of development. On one table an oily black snake lay coiled in a cage, on another rested a fancy jade urn, on a third slouched a sack spilling burgundy powder.

Trevor shone the flashlight beam onto the table with the purple tablecloth. Nate hurried over, knelt, and lifted the tablecloth to look underneath. "Nothing," Nate growled.

"Not so loud," Trevor reminded him.

The two of them meticulously navigated the room, the flashlight beam slowly sweeping the shelves and worktables. They checked inside crates, boxes, barrels, and jars. They looked inside a spacious closet, a cramped rest room, and behind a door marked Private that led to a long staircase. They even investigated the cage with the snake.

"What now?" Nate asked in frustration, after the final cupboard yielded no teleidoscope.

"What's up the stairs?" Trevor asked.

"It's probably where Mrs. White lives," Nate said.

"Do we dare?" Trevor asked.

"If the teleidoscope isn't down here, it's probably up there," Nate said.

Trevor sighed. "After we leave, we'll have no more Mirror Mints. This is our only shot at this. Keep those Shock Bits handy."

Nate followed Trevor over to the door with the black and gold Private sign. They opened it, and Trevor shone his flashlight up the long staircase. Treading lightly, they took the stairs one at a time, tense, ready to retreat if necessary. A couple of times a step creaked, and they paused, waiting, listening, trying not to breathe.

At last they reached the top of the stairway and found a plain brown door with a peephole. Trevor placed a hand on the doorknob and slowly turned it. "It's open," he mouthed to Nate with wide eyes.

Nate motioned for him to open it further.

Switching the flashlight off, Trevor eased the door open. The room beyond was dark. Stepping through the doorway, Trevor felt thick carpeting beneath his shoes. Nate slipped in behind him. They left the door ajar.

Trevor held up a hand for Nate to wait. He could hear the sound of something large breathing. He moved his mouth near Nate's ear and whispered, "You hear that?"

"Yes," Nate whispered back.

Trevor cupped a hand over the end of the flashlight and turned it on. His fingers glowed red, and just enough light escaped to reveal the big, round man lying sideways on the couch, mouth gaping, heavy chest rising and falling rhythmically, huge head cushioned on one fleshy arm. He wore a white undershirt, and a blue knit blanket covered him.

The room was large, with two couches, two armchairs, an

entertainment unit, and several bookcases crowded with old books and glass figurines. The entrance to a hallway yawned at one end of the room. Trevor crept away from the hallway, passing the couch, moving into the adjoining dining room and kitchen. He scanned the china cabinet and the tidy counters.

A pocket door in the dining room was shut. Trevor pushed the door sideways and it slid into the wall, revealing a roomy study designed around an impressive wooden desk. Trevor uncovered the end of the flashlight, allowing the beam to shine brightly. Nate pointed at the desk. Trevor saw the pocket watch resting alongside a leather-bound copy of *The Collected Reflections of Hanaver Mills*.

"She took the book," Nate whispered.

"Still no teleidoscope," Trevor replied.

Nate tiptoed into the room and tried the desk drawers, sliding them open and closed with extraordinary care. When he opened the third one, he froze, then pulled out the teleidoscope, pumping his fist in silent triumph. Trevor motioned for them to go, once again dimming the flashlight with his hand. Nate picked up the book as well, following Trevor back into the dining room.

The instant Nate passed through the doorway, a blast of sound like a hundred trumpets blared for a solid three seconds. The unexpected clamor startled Trevor so much that he dropped his flashlight. Crouching to retrieve it, he saw that Nate had dropped the book, which Trevor grabbed as well.

Their ears ringing from the explosion of sound, Trevor and Nate hurried toward the front room, but stopped short when they found the big, round man on his feet, facing them, his hair matted and disheveled. He had just turned on a lamp. In his undershirt and athletic shorts, his tremendous girth was on display. From his rotund torso to his elephantine limbs, blubber deformed his body. He was tall, a few inches beyond six feet, and nearly as wide, an obese hill of a man with a grouchy head on top.

"This isn't what it looks like," Nate said.

The big man opened his mouth, those thick, shiny lips spreading wide, as if to take a bite from a towering sandwich. His chest convulsed, and out shot an orange glob of jelly nearly the size of a grapefruit. The glistening projectile splattered against Trevor's shoulder, about half of it continuing past him to slap the wall. The orange ooze on his shoulder writhed, shapelessly climbing toward his neck, moving like an amoeba. Shouting, Trevor wiped at the nightmare spitball, orange jelly squishing between his fingers.

The man fired another orange glob of similar size at Nate, who avoided it by diving behind the dining-room table. Having wiped away most of the ooze, Trevor joined Nate behind the table, fumbling in his pocket for the Frost Bites. Nate was also digging in his pocket.

Mouth still gaping, the big man walked toward them. Instead of expelling another glob of ooze, he sent a vast quantity of orange jelly gushing from his mouth like water from a fire hose. The stream of jelly collected on the table in a vivid, translucent mound, enough orange ooze to overflow a bathtub. The gooey pile quivered, stretched taller, and then surged off the tabletop, enveloping Nate.

Trevor scrambled away from the table back into the study, tearing open the baggie with his Frost Bites inside. Nate looked like he was drowning in orange gelatin. Only his head and one arm remained outside the rippling ooze. The big man was approaching the table, looking considerably thinner, loose skin sagging, orange jelly no longer pouring from his lips.

Trevor popped two Frost Bites into his mouth. It was his first time sampling the candy. They tasted like vanilla yogurt. For a moment he felt an intense chill sweep over him, and then his body went numb.

The translucent gelatin now totally surrounded Nate. Trevor saw his encased friend move one hand to his mouth, followed instantly by a bright flash. The electrical burst liquefied the jelly, which slopped all around him to form a dull orange pool.

Placing his palm to his mouth again, Nate arose, sparks crackling between his fingers. The pool of liquefied jelly began to flow toward the big man, who stayed on the far side of the table from Nate.

"Run to the kitchen!" Trevor called, charging the big man. Nate retreated to the kitchen, dodging around the counter. The big man backpedaled into the front room. As Trevor neared the liquefied pool, it froze solid, taking on a frosted sheen.

The big man opened his mouth and coughed a jellyball at Trevor. The sphere struck him in the chest and sent him spinning to the ground. His numbness prevented him from feeling the pain, but he heard ribs snap. It took Trevor a moment to realize that the coldness had frozen the jellyball, causing it to bash him instead of splatter.

As the big man inhaled to launch another jellyball, Trevor spat out his Frost Bites. Instantly the numbness vanished and a sharp pain blossomed in the left side of his chest. The next jellyball splashed against his forehead, soaking his hair. "Nate!" Trevor called, crawling away as the big man advanced, another jellyball slapping wetly against his back, the gelatin on his head squirming against his scalp.

Nate raced out of the kitchen, arms raised threateningly, electricity sparking from his fingertips. The big man faced Nate and spat out a glob of jelly the size of a golf ball. There was a flash as the glob struck Nate, and the tiny ball turned to liquid.

"He's shorting out my charge," Nate yelled, slapping more Shock Bits into his mouth just in time for another undersized jellyball to waste his electricity. "I don't have many Shock Bits left!"

Trevor was now crawling on slick, frozen ooze. It vibrated beneath his hands and knees. Having spat out the Frost Bites, he could feel that the temperature in the apartment had lowered significantly. His breath visibly condensed in front of his face. What were his weapons? He had Moon Rocks, a couple of Mirror Mints, some Shock Bits, and his Frost Bites. "I can't do Frost Bites!" Trevor warned, reaching for his Shock Bits. "Those balls of goo turn hard as a rock!"

"I dropped the scope," Nate said. "Snag it."

Glancing under the table, Trevor could see the teleidoscope lying on the far side, where the jelly had enveloped Nate. Trevor lunged under the table, sprawling on frozen ooze, ribs aching, and grabbed it.

"Surrender now and we may show you leniency," the big man said, cheeks drooping, baggy skin sagging from his bare arms and legs. He was considerably less rotund.

Nate stood with a handful of Shock Bits ready. "I'll eat these the second before I touch him," Nate said. "Follow me."

Trevor was back on his feet, teleidoscope in hand. Nate rushed the big guy, who ran right at him vomiting a blinding stream of orange jelly. Before Nate could get the Shock Bits into his mouth, the big guy caught hold of his wrists, continuing to expel ooze from his mouth. Pulsating gelatin cocooned Nate for the second time.

Trevor ran at them, teleidoscope in one hand, Shock Bits in the other. The instant before he reached them, Trevor slapped the Shock Bits into his mouth and sprang. His outstretched hand touched the gelatin, and with a flash like lightning, the ooze liquefied, the big man went tumbling, and Nate was hurled into the wall.

Ribs smarting, Trevor got another dose of Shock Bits ready and approached the big man, who was shakily rising, his body grotesquely deflated, a skeleton wearing skin ten sizes too big. Orange liquid ran toward the freakish man across the floor, as if the apartment were tilting in his direction. Just before reaching him, Trevor ate more Shock Bits, a larger dose than he had ever tried, and swatted the man on the shoulder. A blazing flash and a crack like a gunshot sent the man soaring into the entertainment unit, scattering DVDs and overturning the television.

Nate was on his feet and running for the front door. Trevor followed him, his last dose of Shock Bits ready in his palm. "Hold it!" ordered a voice that sounded like it had inhaled helium.

Trevor turned and saw the blond dwarf with the flat top crouched in the middle of the hall that led away from the front room, hands balled into fists. He wore a dark blue tank top and gray sweatpants. A white glimmer flickered about him, gradually intensifying. He had a look on his face like he was trying to lay an egg. Since the dwarf was not moving, and Trevor was almost to the door, he refrained from eating his final dose of Shock Bits.

The dwarf sprang, streaking toward Trevor as if he had been shot from a cannon, slamming into him with stunning force. Searing pain erupted in Trevor's ribs. The teleidoscope flew out of Trevor's hand, as did the Shock Bits, and he crashed to the ground with the dwarf's strong arms wrapped around his torso.

The teleidoscope rolled forward across the carpeting. Standing in the doorway, Nate picked it up. "Run!" Trevor gasped.

Nate shoved a handful of Shock Bits into his mouth, and a glob of orange jelly splashed into him, accompanied by a flash. "That's all I have!" Nate cried.

"Run!" Trevor repeated, clinging to the dwarf, trying to give Nate a chance.

Nate disappeared from the doorway. Trevor heard his feet thumping down the stairs. The feisty dwarf wrenched himself free and chased after him. The big man shambled over and collapsed onto Trevor, blanketing him with mushy loose skin. The man seized Trevor's wrists, pinning them to the ground at either side of his head.

"Your luck just ran out," the big man said. His breath reminded Trevor of a rotten jack-o-lantern his family had once kept on the porch too long.

Trevor bucked and struggled but, even deflated, the big man was too strong. Orange liquid began to slither over Trevor, warm and syrupy. The liquid streamed up the big man's arms and flowed into his gaping mouth. Trevor closed his eyes.

"Trevor, Trevor, Trevor," said a familiar, grandmotherly voice tinged with regret. "I could not be more disappointed." Trevor opened his eyes. Mrs. White stood above him wearing a lavender robe with lace embellishing the neck. She shook her head sadly. "I had so hoped to spare you from the horrors of my dark side."

CHAPTER TWELVE
COSTLY CLUES

Nate knew that without any more Shock Bits, he would get caught along with Trevor. Which would mean the teleidoscope would remain in the hands of Mrs. White and her sideshow henchmen. But if he managed to get away with the teleidoscope, he might be able to enlist help from Mr. Stott in defeating Mrs. White. Maybe they could even use the teleidoscope as leverage to bargain for Trevor's release.

Mind racing, Nate dashed down the stairs. In his peripheral vision, he had seen the blond dwarf streak across the room. Like the big man full of jelly, the little man had some sort of magical power. Nate debated whether he should try to get out through the mirror, through a door, or through a window. He could recall no windows in the workroom, just as he had seen no windows in the apartment. Wasn't there a back door someplace?

In answer to his question, he saw the back door at the bottom of the staircase, opposite the door to the workroom. Skipping the last five steps, Nate landed heavily, grabbed the knob, and found it locked. The door had a deadbolt that he could release, but the knob had a keyhole. He rammed the door with his shoulder but it felt sturdy, and he heard footfalls at the top of the stairs, so Nate switched tactics and charged through the door into the dark workroom. Running blindly with his free hand extended, he glanced off tables and stumbled over stools.

In the midst of his panic, he tried to strategize. Mr. Stott had warned them to exit through the mirror. The old magician had expressed concern about the spells that guarded the lair. But wasn't that just if they were trying to be stealthy? Would those spells actually harm him on his way out, or simply raise an alarm? His understanding was that the spells were in place mainly to prevent people from entering.

Could the dwarf use Mirror Mints? What about the big guy? Where was the dude with the huge birthmark? Was he a roommate as well? Nate realized that if he could just get through the mirror, even if somebody chased him, he could run as far as he wanted and get lost in the darkness. Then he could eventually exit through some random mirror anywhere in town. If he escaped the store through a window or a door, he might get zapped by some spell, and the dwarf might follow him out onto the street. He had seen the dwarf fly at Trevor only out of the corner of his eye, but had glimpsed enough to know that the little guy had some sort of ability to attack at great speed.

The flood of thoughts and questions was interrupted when Nate heard the door open behind him. Fluorescent lights flickered on overhead. Focused on reaching the mirror, Nate burst through the batwing doors and vaulted the counter, holding the teleidoscope high as he tumbled to the floor on the far side.

Regaining his feet, Nate raced toward his destination. He fumbled in his pocket to find a Mirror Mint. Sliding to his knees at the table with the mirror underneath, Nate finally glanced back. He saw the dwarf perched atop the counter, holding a chair that he must have brought from the back room, his body crouched and contorted. Shimmering light gathered around him.

Worried that the dwarf was about to take flight, Nate fell flat. A fraction of a second later, the dwarf uncoiled in a ferocious motion, hurling the chair with superhuman force. The chair flew too quickly to be anything but a blur, but Nate felt it whoosh past above him, and heard it collide violently with the table. The table flipped end over end, and the chair sailed though one of the plate-glass windows facing Main Street. As the window disintegrated, there came a tremendous blast of sound, like the horn of an ocean liner, accompanied by a fiery surge of light and heat.

The way the table had landed, Nate could see that the mirror on the underside had shattered. The gaping window through which the chair had passed was his next best option. Nate sprinted in a crouch, trading the Mirror Mint in his hand for a Moon Rock. He leaped through the huge square hole where the window had been, broken glass clinking and crunching underfoot.

Slipping the Moon Rock into his mouth, gripping the teleidoscope tightly, Nate jumped away from the candy shop with all of his might. His feet had hardly left the sidewalk when a powerful force slammed into him from behind, carrying him across the street low and fast, two bodies spiraling through the air until the dwarf hit the ground first and they rolled to a stop on the narrow front lawn of an antique store.

Thrashing to escape the dwarf's tenacious embrace, Nate heard a car screech to a halt nearby, and headlights suddenly glared at him. He heard a car door slam, and the dwarf released him. Having somehow maintained the teleidoscope in his grasp, Nate jumped, gliding considerably higher than the eaves of the antique store roof before curving back down to land on the shingles. Just before he landed, he heard a gunshot.

Head down, Nate took a low hop to the far side of the roof. Adding to the momentum of the gentle hop, he leaped hard, ascending over the small parking lot behind the antique store and rustling through leaves and twigs before grasping a half-glimpsed limb. Pulling on the limb and letting go, he drifted to a higher branch. Pushing off, he turned and wrapped his arms around the trunk of the tall tree. Not wanting to gain more altitude, Nate kicked off the trunk, floating sideways through a gap in the branches, arcing down and alighting on the weedy back lawn of a one-story home. His next jump put him on the roof of the house, and the next deposited him on the sidewalk out front.

He was now on Greenway, not far from the street where Mr. Stott lived. After the disaster at the candy shop, he wanted to deliver the teleidoscope immediately to the old magician. Nate cleared the street with a single spring, then glided up to a roof. Most of the houses in this neighborhood were one-story, and the yards were narrow, so Nate was able to jump from rooftop to rooftop most of the way to 1512 Limerick Court.

From the roof of a home neighboring Mr. Stott's, Nate leapt to the roof of the free-standing garage, then into the front yard, landing beside a turtle fashioned out of wire. All of the windows were dark. Nate spat out the Moon Rock and rushed over to the window that had been lit the first time they had visited Mr. Stott. He beat on the glass. A moment later a light came on and the blinds parted, revealing a pair of eyes. Nate held up the teleidoscope.

The blinds snapped back together, and Nate met Mr. Stott at the front door. Today his pajamas were plaid with a matching nightcap. "You got it?" he asked in wonder, stepping aside to let Nate enter.

"She caught Trevor," Nate said, coming inside.

"Oh, no," Mr. Stott said.

"I barely escaped," Nate said, his voice catching. "I was out of Shock Bits. I had to either run or get caught too." Tears stung his eyes. He clenched his jaw.

"You did the right thing," Mr. Stott said.

"Will he . . . be okay?" Nate asked.

"He was no longer fighting?"

"No, he was done."

Mr. Stott nodded. "Anything can happen during a fight, but if Belinda subdued him, she won't kill him. Losing the teleidoscope is a major blow; she'll want to use Trevor as a bargaining chip."

"Can we trade the teleidoscope for Trevor?"

Mr. Stott cocked his head slightly. "Without the base, it would do her little good. If she suspects I have the base, she may want more than the teleidoscope. But first things first. Shall we see if it actually reveals a clue?"

Nate gave a nod.

Mr. Stott led the way to his bedroom, crossed to the little marble platform beside his bed, and placed the teleidoscope in the mounting. It fit perfectly. He bent over and began turning a wheel on the teleidoscope. Nate waited, hoping the sacrifice had not been wasted.

"Mrs. White also had a book written by Hanaver Mills that she got from the museum," Nate said. "We had it, but we lost it in the fight."

"You brought the most important item," Mr. Stott said.

Mr. Stott quit peering through the teleidoscope for a moment and turned on the rest of the lights in the room, then returned to his task, slowly fingering the wheel, one eye closed. Nate folded his arms. He paced. He thought about Trevor, wondering whether Mrs. White was hurting him.

Mr. Stott backed away from the teleidoscope. "Without touching a thing, tell me if you see words."

Nate crouched and gazed into the eyepiece. The message was faint, written in sparse gold flecks mingling with the other colors, the letters warped but unmistakable:

HOLDS

THE

KEY

"Holds the key?" Nate said. "What is that supposed to mean?"

"I assume there's more," Mr. Stott said. Nate moved out of the way, and Mr. Stott resumed his position. He began turning the wheel backwards in such small increments that the motion reminded Nate of the minute hand on a clock. Patiently Mr. Stott nudged the wheel, studied the image for several seconds, and then nudged the wheel again.

"Aha!" he finally exclaimed, stepping aside. "What do you see now?"

It took Nate a moment to recognize the words, faintly inscribed in blue specks against a brilliant background of tie-dyed sunbursts, the letters highly stylized:

HOUSE
OF
HAAG

"House of Haag?" Nate said.

"Tougher to spot that one," Mr. Stott chuckled. "Not an endeavor for the color-blind. House of Haag holds the key."

"What does that mean?"

"It means I need to research the Haag family," Mr. Stott said. "I know there are numerous Haags here in town. The family has been well-represented in Colson for many years, no doubt dating back to the days of Hanaver Mills. This is a major breakthrough. The key to accessing the treasure must be a Haag family heirloom. They probably don't even know what it does." Mr. Stott hunched over the teleidoscope and began to delicately turn the wheel again.

"You think there's more?" Nate asked.

"If there are two messages, there may be ten," Mr. Stott said. "We must be thorough."

Nate sat on the edge of Mr. Stott's mattress, not really expecting Mr. Stott to find anything else. "Mrs. White has a dwarf who can jump super far and throw things really hard," he said. "He tackled me out in front of the candy shop and practically broke my back. We landed on the other side of the street. Then somebody showed up in a car, and the dwarf let me go. I heard a gunshot."

"Did you see who was in the car?" Mr. Stott asked, his voice remote as he concentrated on the image in the teleidoscope.

"No, it was dark and I was scared of getting my head blown off. I just ran, well, glided, to your house."

"Probably wise. Some rival of Belinda's must have been keeping an eye on the shop, awaiting an opportunity. I wonder who else is in town."

Nate leaned back on the bed, which made him realize how tired he was. "She has this other guy, a big fat dude, who was barfing orange goop at us. It was so disgusting."

"Here we go," Mr. Stott said. "Have a peek."

Nate sat up and slid off the bed. This was the faintest image yet, convoluted letters formed by glittering silver particles:

MAP

IN

SHIP

"Map in ship," Nate read. "How did he set up all these messages?"

"A remarkable feat," Mr. Stott acknowledged. "Even if, as I suspect, he was something of a magician himself. I have never come across a mirror system quite like the one in this teleidoscope, with some deliberate imperfections built into it. I honestly can't guess how he pulled it off, especially with such subtlety."

"What does the clue mean?"

Mr. Stott put his eye to the teleidoscope again, coaxing the wheel forward little by little. "Locating a map would be a serious coup," Mr. Stott said. "The first half of the battle is learning where the treasure is hidden. After that, we can try to figure out how to acquire it."

Nate yawned. He knew it was important, but standing around and staring into a teleidoscope was not exactly keeping his adrenalin pumping.

"Success!" Mr. Stott finally reported. "Have a look."

The next words were formed by black specks against a psychedelic backdrop:

USS
STAR
GAZER

"The map is aboard the USS *Stargazer?*" Nate postulated.

"A reasonable guess," Mr. Stott said. "Let me keep looking."

Nate sat on the floor while Mr. Stott continued to nudge the wheel, scrutinizing each new kaleidoscopic vista. Nate leaned back. The floor felt comfortable. He thought about climbing onto the bed.

The next thing he knew, Mr. Stott was gently shaking his shoulder. Nate blinked blearily. "Find something?" Nate asked, trying to sound awake.

"Nothing new," Mr. Stott said. "I cycled back through all the four messages twice, using different lighting schemes. I think we've found all we're going to get, but I'll check again in the morning with fresh eyes."

"I guess I should get going," Nate said.

"Let me give you a lift in the truck," Mr. Stott offered. "You've had a traumatic night."

Mr. Stott led him out of a door in the kitchen and down three concrete steps to the driveway. He manually raised the garage door and went to the driver's seat of his truck. Nate climbed in the passenger door. "I suppose we can dispense with the music tonight," Mr. Stott said. "Four A.M. is a trifle early for ice cream sandwiches."

Nate snapped on his seatbelt. Mr. Stott pulled out of his driveway. "Tell me where you live, Nate."

"On Monroe in the Presidential Estates."

"Near Trevor and Pigeon," Mr. Stott said, nodding. "How about we avoid Greenway and go up the back way, on Mayflower? My guess is you've seen enough of the Sweet Tooth Ice Cream and Candy Shoppe for one night."

"Yes, please," Nate agreed.

"Now that you made your move, I'll have to remove my bathroom mirror," Mr. Stott said. "Can't give Belinda a chance to retaliate that way."

"Good idea," Nate replied.

They drove in silence for a moment. Nate felt unsettled. He kept expecting a car to close in behind them. They rounded a corner onto Mayflower.

"Don't worry about Trevor," Mr. Stott said. "That teleidoscope was the real deal. I'll start working on those clues, and we'll figure out a way to get him back."

"How?"

"The way I see it, we don't want to give away the clues until we follow up on them, find the map and the key. Then we can exchange the teleidoscope and the base for Trevor without handing Belinda the treasure. For all of our sakes, we must prevent her from gaining the power she seeks. That woman has a long memory."

"Think she might come after me?" Nate said.

"Belinda is not rash," Mr. Stott said, turning into the Presidential Estates from Mayflower. "More likely she'll spy on you, try to confirm the location of the teleidoscope before making a move. Since you no longer have the teleidoscope, that should work to our advantage. Try to relax. I'll get in touch when I know more. I expect I'll have a mission or two for you and your friends to perform before this is over."

"Do you have magic candy too?" Nate asked.

Mr. Stott winked. "I may not hand out power as readily as some, but I've been crafting enchantments for at least as long as Belinda. I've got a trick or two up my sleeve, never you fear. For now, hang on to this cell phone. I programmed in my number. I'll be in touch soon."

Nate accepted the phone. "What's your address?" Mr. Stott asked.

"3473," Nate said. "Up here on the left."

The ice cream truck pulled to a stop, brakes squeaking. "Get some sleep," Mr. Stott said.

"Thanks for the ride," Nate replied, hopping out of the truck and shutting the door.

Mr. Stott pulled away, and Nate went into his house. He had left the front door unlocked. He walked up the stairs to the bathroom, closed the door, sat on the edge of the bathtub, and cried. Once he got going, he found himself overwhelmed by violent sobs. It had all been so terrible, abandoning his friend to an unknown fate, almost getting captured himself. He wished he had never heard of Mrs. White or her magic candy.

He pulled himself together and used some toilet paper to blow his nose. This was far from over—he needed to keep his head. He used the toilet, and then washed his hands. After turning off the faucet, while shaking droplets from his fingers, he saw a face in the mirror.

A face besides his own.

The surprise made him gasp and jump back.

It was Trevor.

Nate spun, checking the room. Trevor was not in the bathroom with him. But he was in the mirror.

Nate turned to the mirror and waved. Trevor waved back, smiling wanly. He looked just as real as Nate's reflection. Who knew how he had escaped? All that mattered was that he had! Nate motioned for Trevor to come through the mirror.

Trevor shook his head, holding up empty hands.

Nate frowned. He dug the two remaining Mirror Mints out of his pocket and pointed at one.

Trevor shook his head.

"No mint?" Nate whispered.

"No mint," Trevor mouthed. If he had spoken the words out loud, Nate could not hear him.

Nate held up a finger and ran to his room. He opened his backpack and removed a notebook and a pen. Returning to the bathroom, he wrote:

She stranded you in there without a mint?

Trevor nodded.

I only have two. One gets me in, and the other only gets one of us out.

Trevor nodded, apparently having already worked that out.

You came straight to my bathroom once Mrs. White trapped you?

Trevor pointed to himself, then steepled his fingers to form a roof.

You went to your house first?

Trevor nodded, pumping his arms to convey that he had run there.

Did she hurt you?

He scrunched his face and turned one hand from side to side, indicating that she had hurt him somewhat.

Nate wrote quickly, his handwriting even less legible than usual.

The scope worked. We have clues. We're going to bargain to get you out of there.

Trevor held up both hands, fingers crossed.

Are you okay?

Trevor shrugged and gave a slight nod.

Do these letters look backwards?

Trevor shook his head.

Nate had to think about that one. The reflected words looked backwards to him. But Trevor was not looking at a reflection, he was looking at the actual paper, as if through a window. That made sense.

I'm sorry I left you. I panicked. I thought I'd get captured too.

Trevor stuck his thumbs up. Then he pantomimed as if he were looking through a telescope and gave a thumbs-up again.

We'll get you out. I promise.

Trevor nodded and winked. They stood there staring at each other awkwardly for a moment. How could Trevor be so close and so far away? Trevor leaned his head sideways, closed his eyes, and rested his hands against his cheek.

Sleepy?

He shook his head, pointed at Nate, and pantomimed like he was sleeping again.

Yeah, I'm tired. But I don't want to leave you.

Trevor shook his head and gestured again for Nate to sleep. Then he mouthed something that Nate didn't catch. Trevor pointed up at the light, and Nate understood.

I'll leave the light on.

Trevor smiled.

CHAPTER THIRTEEN

CHASING A SHIP

The cell phone did not ring until late Tuesday morning during class, beeping the melody of "Somewhere over the Rainbow." Nate hastily pressed the green answer button. "Hi."

"Can you talk?" asked Mr. Stott.

"I'm in class," Nate said softly. "But my teacher is on the fudge."

"Good. Still no definite leads on the Haags. At least twenty members of the family currently live in Colson. I've found names and addresses for most of them. Narrowing down the list of candidates might take some time. I do, however, have solid info on the ship."

"Where is it?"

"Among his many hobbies, Hanaver liked to construct model vessels. His masterpiece was an elaborate clipper housed inside a bottle. Guess what the name was."

"I don't want to say it out loud," Nate said.

"Right. The USS *Stargazer*. Not based on any actual ship I could find, although I came across a *Star Trek* vessel with that name. The model is currently owned by Victoria Colson, daughter of Ebner Mills, a grandson of Hanaver. Victoria is the wife of our current mayor, Todd Colson."

"What do we do?"

"I'll drive my route after school," Mr. Stott said. "Meet me with Pigeon and Summer at the bottom of Monroe Circle at about three-thirty."

"You got it."

"See you then." The line went dead.

Nate put away the phone. Both Pigeon and Summer were staring at him from across the room. He had called them on Saturday and explained what had happened to Trevor. Nate nodded to confirm that it was the call they had been expecting.

Nate had mostly laid low over the weekend, and had instructed Summer and Pigeon to do the same. If Mrs. White was watching, he did not want to be out in the open unnecessarily. His one exception had been the visit to Trevor's house on Sunday afternoon.

His stomach had been in knots when he knocked on the door, but he had known it was unfair to let Trevor's parents think their son might be dead. He could barely look Trevor's mom in the eye when she answered the door.

"Hi, Nate, are you here for Trevor?" To his astonishment, she had not sounded distressed.

"You could say that," Nate had replied.

She had placed her hands on her hips and sighed. "You know, I'm having the hardest time keeping track of that boy! He's always off on one errand or another. Seems like he's hardly ever home lately!"

Feeling a new level of respect for the white fudge, Nate had decided not to meddle any further, hoping that somehow they would rescue Trevor before his parents ever knew he had been in danger. Part of him doubted whether it would have been possible to convince them their son was missing, no matter how much evidence he presented.

Other than visiting Trevor's parents, updating Summer and Pigeon, and waiting in vain for Mr. Stott to call, Nate had spent the weekend attending to Trevor. He wrote him notes, showed him the Sunday funnies, and even put on a slapstick puppet show.

Trevor had pantomimed that he could not sleep inside the mirror realm. He spent many of the daylight hours exploring the void where he was trapped. Using Nate's bathroom mirror as his home base, he had visited his own house, Pigeon's, and had even gone across the creek to Summer's. He had vowed not to spy on Cheryl when she used the bathroom.

Nate had written to Trevor about how his parents seemed oblivious to his disappearance, and had detailed the clues the teleidoscope had revealed, along with the plans he and Mr. Stott were hatching. Trevor often seemed bored, but his spirits remained fairly buoyant, considering the circumstances. Nate made sure the bathroom light stayed on all night.

Snapping the cell phone closed, Nate pocketed it. The lunch bell was about to ring. Miss Doulin sat at her desk, watching the clock as eagerly as her students, the thin red second hand ticking up toward twelve. Nate wondered how many pieces of fudge she would be eating. If she was anything like his parents and sister, it would be a lot.

The second hand went vertical and the bell rang.

* * * * *

Summer sat down across from Pigeon and opened her lunch sack. She glanced at Nate, sitting alone at the far side of the lunch area, pulling a pear from his lunch bag. He still wanted to sit apart, in hopes that Mrs. White would hold him and Trevor solely responsible for stealing the teleidoscope. It was a nice thought, but Summer doubted whether they were fooling anyone.

She was still struggling to absorb what had happened to Trevor. It was nightmarish to think of him roaming from mirror to mirror, unable to sleep, no heartbeat, surrounded by darkness and silent windows to the world he had left behind. Summer had worried that Mrs. White might be dangerous, but Trevor's fate surpassed her worst expectations. What if they never got him out?

Summer unwrapped her turkey sandwich and took a bite. It tasted dry. Not enough meat, not enough mayo, the bread getting stale. Her dad used to make such good sandwiches! The white fudge was even ruining her lunchtime!

On her second bite, she paused mid-chew, watching Denny, Kyle, and Eric saunter over to stand behind Pigeon. Denny slapped a hand on his shoulder.

"Hey, Pigeon, what's for lunch?"

Pigeon looked at Summer, eyes wide. These were the first words Denny had spoken to him since the incident with the trick candy.

"You better take off," Summer said.

"You've got us all wrong," Denny said, acting wounded. "We're here to give Pigeon a treat. Sort of a payback for everything he's done for us."

Kyle set a waxy pink cube in front of Pigeon. "Yeah, Pigeon, this one is on us."

"Eat up," Eric said.

Summer slid a hand into her pocket.

"What is it?" Pigeon asked. "Laxatives?"

"Pigeon!" Denny said. "We're not going to poison you. We got this at the best candy store in town, the Sweet Tooth Ice Cream and Candy Shoppe. You really should have a taste."

"Why don't you guys take a hike?" Nate said, stalking toward them, hands clenched into fists.

"Dirt Face!" Denny said, spreading his arms. "I was wondering when you'd turn up. We have a present for you as well."

"Leave my friend alone," Nate said.

"We brought treats for all you guys," Denny said, grinning like a shark. "Where's Trevor?"

Nate lowered his shoulder and charged Denny. Eric reached out a hand, grazing Nate's shoulder, and a flash of electricity sent Nate twirling through the air. He landed on top of a lunch table a few yards away, his foot thumping the head of a Latino girl. Eric looked surprised at how effective the jolt had been.

"Whoa, Dirt Face!" Denny laughed. "Those were some smooth moves!"

Summer slapped her hand to her mouth, jumped over the lunch table, and swatted Denny on the back of his neck as he was still laughing. A sizzling flash sent him soaring forward in a flying somersault. He landed on his back on the concrete.

Pigeon also had Shock Bits in his hand now, Summer was reaching for another handful, and Kyle was digging in his pocket as well. Eric rushed over and crouched beside Denny. A short, pudgy yard duty, Ms. Figgoria, hustled over to them.

"Absolutely no fireworks at school!" the furious woman huffed. "Who set those off! I want names!"

Nate rolled off the table. He had warm lasagna mashed against his shirt and jeans from the pair of trays he had landed on. The girl he had accidentally kicked glared at him. Eric helped Denny to his feet.

"We don't have fireworks," Kyle said. "Ask my mom!"

"I saw a bright flash," Ms. Figgoria said. "Empty your pockets!"

Kyle, Summer, and Pigeon showed the yard duty their candy. She checked Eric and Denny as well. Apparently she had missed Nate's flight, because she paid him no heed. She studied the ground, hunting for remnants of fireworks. Ms. Figgoria got huffier as it became clear that there was no evidence of wrongdoing.

"You haven't tried the white fudge from Sweet Tooth, have you?" Kyle asked.

"I don't eat sugar," Ms. Figgoria replied. "And I don't tolerate nonsense. You kids better get your acts together."

"Later," Denny promised, patting Pigeon on the shoulder before strolling off with Eric and Kyle to eat lunch.

"Are you okay?" Summer asked Nate.

"I've been zapped by those Shock Bits more times than I'd like," Nate grumbled. "It's like getting kicked from every direction all at once."

"Summer shocked Denny back," Pigeon said.

"I sort of saw," Nate said. "What are they doing with Shock Bits?"

"Looks like they picked up our old after-school job," Summer said.

"As if things weren't bad enough," Nate moaned. "You guys have many Shock Bits left?"

"A decent amount," Pigeon said.

"I need to go to the rest room and wash up," Nate said. "Can I borrow a dose for safety?"

"Of course," Pigeon said. "How about two mouthfuls?"

"While you're handing out candy, do you have an extra Sweet Tooth I could borrow?" Summer asked.

"Sure," Pigeon said. "I've only used one so far."

"Let's hope they don't know about these yet," Summer said, placing the candy on her tongue.

She walked over to the table where Denny, Eric, and Kyle were sitting. Eric nudged Denny, who turned to confront Summer. "Touch me again and you'll regret it," he threatened.

"Don't mess with my friends. I just came over to warn you guys about Mrs. White. She's dangerous. Did you hear what she did to Trevor?"

"She told us how you guys betrayed her," Eric said. "Man, you morons spoiled a good thing."

"Our gain," Kyle said.

"She trapped Trevor as a reflection in a mirror," Summer said. "Maybe forever. Worse will happen to you guys. Count on it. You should quit taking candy from her."

They were all listening attentively. Eric even nodded. Denny suddenly shook his head. "She warned us about the Sweet Tooth junk, if that's what you're trying." The other two boys snapped out of the trance. "You almost had me going for a second."

"I'm just giving you fair warning," Summer said. "You're walking into a very messy situation."

"Only because you losers made the mess," Denny said. "Stop trying to warn us. Stop trying to talk to us. I understand you're jealous that we're getting all your candy. Tough luck. Stay out of our way, or you really will get hurt."

"I can't believe how much Mandy Meyers keeps staring at you," Summer said, changing the subject abruptly and making her tone much more conversational.

"Yeah?" Denny said, checking over his shoulder. Mandy Meyers was the sixth-grade girl who enjoyed the celebrity status of most desirable female at Mt. Diablo Elementary. Mandy was seated one table over. Summer had noticed that she was sort of facing Denny.

"That kind of window of opportunity closes fast," Summer said. "If you like Mandy, you should make a move." Summer deliberately said Mandy's name loudly, earning a glance from her, which Denny noticed.

"You think?" he asked, sitting up a little straighter.

"Girls like Mandy want a guy who knows how to take control of a situation. She doesn't want to play games. She wants a guy bold enough to fearlessly share his feelings."

"Lame as you are, you may be right," Denny said.

"Go for it," Kyle encouraged.

"You're the man," Eric said.

Denny got up and started walking around the lunch table. Summer could not believe he was falling for it. What a difference between proposing something he wanted to hear versus suggesting an idea he didn't want to believe! She would have to keep that in mind. She moved close enough to eavesdrop.

"I noticed you looking at me," Denny said to Mandy.

She stared up at him uncertainly. "Excuse me?"

"Don't be shy. I think you're a hottie too. Want to go out with me?"

Mandy looked befuddled. "No, I don't even know you."

"That's the idea, we'll get to know each other," Denny said, throwing in a wink.

"I think you need mental help," Mandy said, turning her back on him. Her friends snickered.

Denny retreated, face reddening. He glared at Summer, awareness registering in his eyes.

"You don't believe me when I tell the truth," Summer said. "But you totally gobble up the lie!"

"Don't worry," Denny replied. "You'll get yours."

* * * * *

The faded blue ice cream truck rolled forward, leaving behind a pair of young teenagers holding chocolate-dipped ice cream bars. Electronic music chimed, sounding like an amplified demo song from a cheap keyboard. Nate, Summer, and Pigeon did their best to look casual as the truck squeaked to a stop in front of them.

"Here are some familiar faces," Mr. Stott blustered. "How about some candy on the house?"

"Sure," Nate said.

"All of this candy is extremely difficult to make. Feel free to use it, but please do not waste it. Pigeon, this sack is full of Brain Feed. You will not eat this yourself. Brain Feed grants animals temporary human intelligence and communication skills. Most birds, mammals, and reptiles find it delicious. The effect should last about ten minutes. Brain Feed does not guarantee friendship, but you'll find that many animals will be cooperative. A big helping lasts no longer than a small one, so portion it sparingly. Pretend to give me money for it."

Pigeon acted like he was handing Mr. Stott money and accepted the bag.

"Summer, I call this gum Peak Performance. You get six sticks in a pack. While chewing it, you'll find yourself performing at the absolute limits of your physical capacity for as long as the flavor lasts. Not only will you sprint faster than you ever have, you will be able to continue at top speed without tiring. You'll find yourself almost perfect at dodging, aiming, balancing, and a wide array of acrobatic feats. A serious athlete would trade anything for a substance like this."

Summer pretended to pay and accepted the package of gum.

"Nate, these jawbreakers are Ironhides. Four in a bag. While they last, your body will have a durability that surpasses tempered steel. You'll be no heavier or faster or stronger, but you'll be very difficult to hurt. As with all enchanted consumables, don't mix any of these treats with other magical edibles. Use one type at a time."

"What are we supposed to do?" Nate asked, pretending to pay and accepting the four jawbreakers bundled in yellow plastic netting.

"Ever since William P. Colson founded this town, the Colson family has maintained a weighty presence here. They have amassed a fortune through mining and real estate. Their donations keep the town museum afloat and account for our fine public library. The Colson clan has provided the town with five mayors, including Todd Colson, who currently holds the office. His wife, Victoria, inherited a model clipper ship in a bottle called the USS *Stargazer*. We need that ship. Hanaver Mills hid the map to the treasure inside."

"Where do they keep the boat?" Summer asked.

"I don't know," Mr. Stott said. "Two of Hanaver's model ships are on display in the town museum, but neither one is the *Stargazer*. Todd and Victoria Colson live in the North Ridge area on 14 Sunset Lane.

Handsome house, big gate out front. Their two children are grown, so they live alone, along with whatever staff they retain. Victoria holds no day job; you should be able to find her at home."

"Do you think it's in their house?" Pigeon asked.

Mr. Stott's eyebrows jumped. "Very likely. Of all his models, Hanaver was fondest of the *Stargazer*. The ship probably resides in a place of honor."

"Should we break in?" Nate asked.

"You should perform reconnaissance first," Mr. Stott said. "But be quick about it."

"North Ridge is far," Pigeon said.

"You'll figure something out," Mr. Stott said. "Did Belinda give you a Sweet Tooth or two? Might be an opportune time to use one. We've already been talking too long. Bring the ship to me once you have it. I'll keep investigating the Haags. Call if you need me."

The Candy Wagon pulled away, music bleeping.

Nate looked at Pigeon. "This sounds like a job for Sweet Teeth and Brain Feed."

Pigeon folded his arms and shuffled his feet. "Both of my candies are good for reconnaissance."

"Think you could pose as an overeager student?" Nate asked. "Go bug the mayor?"

"Nobody would buy Pigeon as an eager student!" Summer joked.

"I don't know," Pigeon said. "Sounds risky."

"Or you can give me some of your candy and I'll do it," Nate said. "I think I could act studious in an emergency."

Pigeon pressed his lips together. "No, it's my candy, I should do it. If I act like it's for a school report, nobody can get angry. I can call my cousin. He'll give me a ride on his motorcycle."

"You sure?" Summer said.

Pigeon nodded. "I can't let Trevor down. If things go well, maybe I'll come back with the *Stargazer*. Worst case, I'll at least learn where it is."

"Okay," Nate said. "Call when you know something, or when you need us. You can do this, Pidge. It's right up your alley."

"Hey, if you're going to be on a motorcycle, you can finally get some use out of that jacket," Summer said.

"No way," Pigeon said. "Today, I need to look as nerdy as possible. I know just the sweater."

* * * * *

Nate leaned against his bathroom counter, scrawling in a notebook. He held up the page to show Trevor.

The Stargazer *is a ship in a bottle owned by the mayor of Colson. Pigeon is going to try to find out where he keeps it.*

Trevor pointed at himself and shaped his hands into binoculars.

The mayor lives in North Ridge. Pigeon acted like it was far.

Trevor frowned and nodded.

Guess what? Denny, Eric, and Kyle are now working for Mrs. White. Might not hurt to spy on them if you get the chance.

Trevor looked astounded by the news, then connected his thumb and forefinger to make an okay sign.

They used Shock Bits on me today at school. Summer shocked Denny, and used a Sweet Tooth to get him to ask out Mandy Meyers. Mandy totally denied him!

Nate could not hear the sound, but Trevor laughed hard.

"Somewhere over the Rainbow" started playing. Nate answered the cell phone. "Hello?"

"Glad I reached you, Nate," Mr. Stott said. "I need you to come to my house right away. There is someone I want you to meet, and something I want to give you."

"I'll be there in a few minutes."

"See you soon."

" 'Bye."

Trevor stared at Nate curiously.

I have to visit Mr. Stott. I guess he forgot to give me something. I'll be back in a while.

Trevor pointed at himself, made a walking motion with two fingers, and raised his hands to his eyes like binoculars.

Yes, go and spy. Later.

Trevor saluted and jogged out of view.

* * * * *

Pigeon held onto Nile, trying not to cling like he was scared as they leaned around a corner onto Sunset Place. Pigeon loved the exhilaration of riding a motorcycle, but cornering made him feel off-balance. Nile accelerated down the road, the sudden increase in speed making Pigeon's insides lurch.

All of the houses in the North Ridge community were remarkable structures with professionally landscaped yards, but number 14 at the end of the cul-de-sac was the most impressive of them all. A brick driveway flanked by white planters led from the black iron gates to a wide mansion made splendid by numerous turrets, chimneys, and balconies.

Nile came to a stop at the gate, dropping his feet to steady the motorcycle. "You want me to go up with you?" he asked.

"For this to work, I need to seem nerdy and pathetic," Pigeon explained. "You're too cool."

"All right," Nile said. "I'll keep an eye out until you get inside, then I'll check back every ten minutes or so. If I loiter too long in a neighborhood like this, somebody might call the cops."

Pigeon hopped down off the bike and removed his helmet. He wore a sky-blue button-down sweater and khakis. "Do I look pathetic?" he asked.

"No comment," Nile said.

Pigeon had told Nile that he was working on a report for school, and that he hoped the mayor might let him take some old Colson artifacts into his class. When Nile had come to pick him up, he had spotted a box of white fudge on the table and snuck a piece, confiding that he had become mildly addicted.

Running to the gate, Pigeon put a Sweet Tooth into his mouth and pressed the button on the intercom. He glanced up and noticed a security camera aimed at him.

"Colson residence," said a male voice. "May I ask your name?"

"I'm Paul Bowen. I'm hoping to talk to Mrs. Colson. I go to Mt. Diablo, and I'm working on a report about Hanaver Mills."

"Do you have an appointment?" the voice asked.

Pigeon hoped the Sweet Tooth would work through an intercom. "I'm only ten. I wasn't sure how I would make an appointment. I thought maybe I'd just drop by. Can't you let me see her? It will only take a couple of minutes."

"One moment."

Pigeon waited. He slid the Sweet Tooth around his mouth with his tongue.

The gates started opening on their own. Pigeon heard Nile riding away. "Come on in," the voice invited.

Pigeon followed the driveway to the elegant front door. A middle-aged man in a shirt and tie opened the door and admitted him. Pigeon stared up at a magnificent chandelier suspended above a grand staircase. A fat Persian cat, its long hair a tawny brown, relaxed on the stairs, licking a black paw. The man escorted Pigeon across the marble entryway and indicated a room off to one side. "You're welcome to wait in the parlor," the man said in a friendly, unpretentious manner. "Mrs. Colson is on a call, and may be a few minutes."

"Okay, thanks," Pigeon said, looking around the well-appointed sitting room.

"Be brief and polite," the man added in a confidential tone. He winked and exited, closing the door.

Pigeon hesitantly sat down on an ornate pink and black chair. The furniture looked almost too nice to touch. There were several paintings on the walls, mostly pastoral scenes.

After waiting for a minute or so, Pigeon rose and leaned an ear against the door. From his pocket he removed a plastic sandwich bag full of reddish-brown kibbles. The sack the Brain Feed had come in was too large for pockets, so Pigeon had downsized the bag.

Pigeon inched the door open and peeked out. The Persian cat was walking away down a hall, but paused when Pigeon hissed at it softly and shook some Brain Feed into his palm. Pigeon set a few bits of food on the floor near the door and backed away. The cat came forward, sniffed the food, ate it, then entered the room.

"That was quite good, have you any more?" the cat asked in an articulate female voice.

He did not know what he had expected, but hearing the cat suddenly speaking in perfect English left Pigeon momentarily speechless. "Sure, if you help me out," he finally managed.

"Do I strike you as an errand girl?" the cat sniffed, raising her head imperiously.

"I meant a favor," Pigeon said.

"I seldom grant favors, and certainly not in exchange for bribes." The cat slunk to the center of the room, furry tail swishing lazily behind her.

Pigeon remembered that he still had the Sweet Tooth in his mouth, and resolved to be more direct. "You must know this house very well," he said.

"None know it better," the cat declared.

"Have you seen a model ship inside a bottle?"

"Here in the house? Certainly not." The cat stretched.

"A really nice model, built by Hanaver Mills," he specified.

"By Hanaver? You might try the Colson Museum."

"This model isn't in the museum," Pigeon said, realizing that this line of questioning was getting him nowhere. "Is Mrs. Colson nice?"

"Nice? That depends. She can be affectionate and generous. She can be cold and ruthless. I quite like her."

"How about I give you some more of this food just to be kind," Pigeon said.

"How magnanimous of you," the cat said sarcastically.

Pigeon set a few more kibbles on the floor, and the cat ate them. "I must say, as sorry as it looks, this stuff has a most agreeable after-taste. Where did you get it?"

"Hard to explain," Pigeon said. "Look, I—"

At that moment Mrs. Colson came through the door, a slender woman in a smart gray suit, her hair short and stylish. Pigeon jumped up and tried not to look like he had been having a conversation with a cat. Mrs. Colson strode forward, extending a hand toward Pigeon with the breezy camaraderie of a practiced politician. "Victoria Colson, so nice to meet you, Paul."

"Thank you for letting me visit," Pigeon said, meeting her assertive grip limply.

Mrs. Colson bent down and picked up the cat. "How did you get in here, Jasmine?"

"My fault," Pigeon apologized. "I noticed her in the hall and opened the door. I like cats."

"More like you lured me in here with salty snacks," Jasmine purred.

"A fellow feline enthusiast," Mrs. Colson said with an automatic smile. She did not appear to have heard the cat speak. "Please, Paul, have a seat." He sat back down on the pink and black chair. Mrs. Colson alighted on the sofa, stroking Jasmine. "How may I help you?"

"I'm working on a project for school about the models Hanaver Mills built. He's your ancestor, right?"

"My great-great-grandfather, yes."

"I've seen the boats in the town museum, but I read that he had a favorite, a ship called the *Stargazer* housed inside a bottle. I'd love to have a look and maybe take a picture if you know where I can find it."

Mrs. Colson placed a manicured finger beside her lips. "I donated the *Stargazer* to the library as a display piece several years ago," she said thoughtfully. "I'm in there almost every week, but I can't say I've seen it. The model must have ended up in storage. You know who could help you is Leslie Wagner, the head librarian. I'll give you a note. Bravo for going the extra mile on your research! Wait here one moment."

"You got on her good side," Jasmine remarked as Mrs. Colson exited the room. "Victoria has always been a pushover for kids and animals. Funny all the interest in Hanaver lately."

"All the interest?" Pigeon asked.

"Some of his belongings were recently stolen from the Colson Museum," Jasmine said. "And of course Belinda White keeps asking Victoria about Hanaver Mills memorabilia."

"Belinda White?"

"She telephones on occasion," Jasmine said. "Belinda runs the new candy shop on Main. She sends us the most delicious complimentary treats: peanut brittle, chocolate macadamias, truffles, fudge . . . I would love to meet her face-to-face."

Mrs. Colson returned, heels clicking across the marble entryway. She stopped in the doorway, a piece of stationery in hand, and glanced at her delicate wristwatch. "If you get down to the library before six, you might catch Mrs. Wagner before she heads home."

Pigeon crossed to the doorway and accepted the pink slip of paper. "Thanks a lot, Mrs. Colson," he said.

"My pleasure," she replied, guiding him to the door.

"Come again, Paul," Jasmine called.

Pigeon turned and waved. Mrs. Colson closed the door. That had gone smoothly! He wondered if the Sweet Tooth had made Mrs. Colson so obliging, or if perhaps he would not have needed the candy in the first place. He hurried down the driveway as the gates swung open. With Nile nowhere in sight, he set off along Sunset Place.

Sliding a hand into his pocket, Pigeon fingered the Brain Feed. What a remarkable creation! Without the kibble, Jasmine could not possibly comprehend English, which meant that the Brain Feed not only granted her the ability of speech, it also allowed her to instantly and effortlessly make sense of previous human interactions she had witnessed. Plus, the magical kibble functioned so naturally that the cat had not seemed a bit amazed to be conversing with a person. Pigeon determined that after visiting the library he would have to spend some time getting to know his dog.

CHAPTER FOURTEEN
THE LIBRARY

Nate rapped on the door and Mr. Stott answered. "Come in, my boy," he said.

"What's going on?" Nate asked, stepping inside.

"I want to introduce you to a colleague of mine." Mr. Stott closed the door. He led Nate down the hall and paused outside a door across from his bedroom. "We magicians sometimes employ engineered apprentices. Assistants whom we imbue with power to make them more useful."

"Like the fat guy full of orange goop who works for Mrs. White," Nate said.

"Precisely. I don't as a rule tamper with my assistants, but many years ago, a loyal man who served me contracted a terminal illness. As the end neared, he urged me to preserve his life. The only hope within the parameters of my abilities was to drastically alter his physiology. I explained the hazards, and still he beseeched me to make an attempt.

"In many respects, the procedure went wrong. Although I

succeeded in sparing his life, it came at the price of his humanity. Physically he was ruined, and mentally he had changed as well, grown simpler. I can still communicate with him, which is why you are here. He renamed himself the Flatman. I tell you about him in advance because his appearance is unsettling. Upon seeing him for the first time, two people, to my recollection, have passed out, and others have become nauseated."

Mr. Stott opened the door. Nate walked into a dim room. Heavy drapes obscured the windows. A solid table stood in the middle of the room beside a wicker rocking chair. On the table sat a shallow aquarium filled halfway with fluid that reeked of formaldehyde. The Flatman floated on the surface of the fluid.

Half curious, half disgusted, Nate drew closer. The creature looked like a cross between a human being and a fried egg. About the size of a Frisbee, the Flatman was sheathed in pale human skin, complete with pores and faint wrinkles. He had one large eye, one small eye, and three misshapen slits—presumably two nostrils and a mouth. Four translucent fins flapped languidly, their form eerily reminiscent of hands and feet. The larger eye had a fleshy lid that opened and closed, while the smaller one perpetually stared. Nate could appreciate why people might pass out upon meeting the Flatman.

"Can he hear me?" Nate asked.

"Most assuredly," Mr. Stott said.

"Can he talk?"

"Not as you or I speak. After completing the botched transformation, I assumed my assistant would not want to continue in this state. But his will to live was extraordinary—to this day he claims he is glad to be alive. Along with all he lost, he did acquire some new abilities. One side effect of the changes I wrought is that his consciousness drifts across time, allowing him to glimpse the past and the future."

"Can he see outside this room?"

"He can see only places where he was or will be, and he has no conscious control over the ability. At times he becomes confused. The past is constant, but the future is always in motion. Some of the futures he glimpses never come to pass. Lately he has been observing a future without me in it to feed and take care of him. He has seen himself anonymously starving, unable to seek help. And then this afternoon he adamantly insisted I needed to give you the most powerful confection in my possession."

"Give it to me?" Nate asked. "Does he know me?"

"Perhaps he overheard your name during a prior visit. More likely, he has observed you in the future. He stubbornly maintains that giving you the Grains of Time will be my only hope for surviving the looming hostilities. When he acts this resolute, I have come to rely on his predictions." Mr. Stott held up a small hourglass on a silver chain. Ornately decorated, the hourglass contained blue sand in one chamber, red sand in the other, with a tiny yellow pellet plugging the gap between the two.

"What does it do?"

"I created the Grains of Time with the help of my master, who has since passed away. I do not believe I could devise another like it. Back then we took more pride in packaging our formulations, before the world fell in love with all things plastic and disposable. To function correctly, the grains must be consumed in the proper order—first blue, then red, then yellow. The blue will take you into the past, the red into the future, and the yellow will give you temporary dominion over the present. The three types of sand must be consumed in rapid succession or the spell will fail. Use the contents of this hourglass only in the moment of your most dire need. You will get only one chance."

Mr. Stott handed Nate the hourglass.

"Do I wear it around my neck?"

"That would seem sensible," Mr. Stott said.

"Are you sure you want to give this to me?"

"Sure enough. Tell me, has Pigeon had any luck locating the *Stargazer?*"

"I haven't heard back yet," Nate said. "Don't worry, we'll find it."

Mr. Stott scratched his beard and shifted his feet awkwardly. He cleared his throat, coughing lightly into his fist. "Nate, if something should happen to me in the coming days, I'm wondering if you might keep an eye on the Flatman for me. He eats fish flakes and canned cat food. The mixture he floats in is three parts water, one part formaldehyde. He can help you learn the details. If other forms of communication fail, one blink means yes, two means no. Could you do that for me?"

Nate looked over at the Flatman. A fleshy pancake with a disfigured face was about the last pet he would ever choose, but he supposed he could get used to it. "Okay. But let's try to avoid the need. You take care."

"Count on it," Mr. Stott said. "I simply prefer to cover my bases. If ever you require access to the house when I am not around, there is a way to bypass the defensive spells. Swear to me you will keep it private."

"I promise," Nate said.

"Ring the doorbell twice. Say, 'Archmus, I am a friend indeed.' Then ring the doorbell again. You should hear the locks in the door unfasten themselves. At that point, the house is yours. Got it?"

"Yes."

"Do it only if your need is dire and I am not answering the door."

"Okay," Nate said.

"You had better run along. If you can get the ship tonight, do it. The sooner we find the map, the sooner we can free Trevor. I'll continue narrowing down Haag family candidates."

"All right. See you later, Mr. Stott. See you, Flatman."

One of the fragile fins seemed to wave good-bye.

* * * * *

Summer counted her Flame Outs, ending up with a pile of fourteen. She knew how many she had, but wanted to conduct a careful inventory in preparation for breaking into the mayor's house. Summer, Pigeon, Nate, and Trevor each maintained a personal stash of candy. In addition to her Flame Outs, Summer had three doses of Shock Bits, eight Moon Rocks, six sticks of Peak Performance gum, and the extra Sun Stone.

Since she had so many, she frequently considered sharing her Flame Outs with the others, but worried that Mrs. White may have been right not to trust the boys with such potentially destructive candy. She could envision Nate and Pigeon burning down the entire town.

The telephone rang, and Summer picked it up. Her dad was not home yet, so she reached for a pen to take a message. "Atler residence."

"Summer, it's Pigeon."

"Wow, you're already done! Any luck?"

"I just got back from the town library."

"The library?" She started doodling a sailboat on the notepad by the phone.

"Mrs. Colson donated the ship to the library. And she wrote me a recommendation asking the head librarian to help me find it. I caught the librarian as she was leaving. She was really nice, maybe because the Sweet Tooth was helping, and we spent almost half an hour searching through three storage rooms. In the end, we found the *Stargazer*."

"Yes! Great job. Do you have it?"

"I tried to talk her into letting me take it home for the night, but she resisted the idea. I used a few different approaches, but quit when she started getting angry. In the end, she said I could come take videos or pictures of it whenever I want. It's pretty big, more like a ship in a jug than in a bottle. But I know right where it is. The only problem is, I'm going to look pretty guilty after we steal it tonight."

"Have you talked to Nate?" Summer asked.

"Not yet. I just got home. I'll call him. Let's meet on the path at one. Bring your bike."

"Okay. If I don't hear back, I'll assume that's the plan."

"Right. Oh, and Summer, the Brain Feed is amazing. I had this really coherent conversation with a cat. You won't believe it."

"That's cool."

"See you tonight."

" 'Bye."

* * * * *

Nate sat on the edge of his bed winding a yo-yo. He was trying to get the yo-yo to sleep, but it refused to hang and spin at the bottom of the string, and kept getting tangled instead. He tried again, throwing the yo-yo down, popping his wrist just before it finished unwinding. He timed it wrong. Not only did the yo-yo fail to sleep, it wound back up only halfway.

The failure was not too upsetting. Larger issues loomed in his mind. He and his friends were about to undertake another mission. This time they were invading a library. Each new mission felt more dangerous. Once Trevor had gotten trapped in the mirror, any semblance of fun had vanished. Magic candy was now only a tool to hopefully help undo the trouble they were in.

On prior occasions when Nate had felt overwhelmed by anxiety, he had always eventually ended up talking it over with his parents. They tended to be understanding and helpful. Sometimes they could make major worries fade away with simple reassurances or advice.

But he couldn't get help from his parents on this one. He had tried to broach the subject of Trevor in the mirror with his mom twice already, but she became instantly distracted. The white fudge created a daunting communication barrier.

Nate wondered what would happen if he pressed as hard as he could, doggedly compelling his parents to recognize what was happening. In a way, he was afraid to try. He did not want to learn that no matter how blunt he was or how hard he pushed, he was cut off from parental support when he needed it most. At the same time, if there was a chance of getting any help from them, the hour had arrived. He had never yearned more for his parents to intervene and bail him out of a predicament.

Setting the yo-yo down, Nate walked resolutely out of his room and down the stairs. He entered the family room, where his dad sat watching sports news.

"Dad, can we talk?"

Nate's dad snapped out of his television trance. "Sure, son, what's on your mind?"

"I've gotten involved in something really dangerous," Nate said. "I'm in way over my head. I need your help."

"Tell me about it," his dad said, eyes wandering toward the television screen.

"It has to do with the Sweet Tooth Ice Cream and Candy Shoppe," Nate said.

"Love that fudge."

"Dad, the white fudge is addictive. Not just because it tastes good. The fudge makes the people who eat it lose their focus and blinds them to what is going on around them."

"I gave some to my boss," his dad said. "He wants me to pick him up ten boxes of the stuff."

"Which you shouldn't do," Nate urged. "The lady who runs the candy shop, Mrs. White, is some kind of magician. The white fudge is unsafe. Dad, I think she might try to hurt me."

"Nothing wrong with eating fudge," his dad said. "Just don't go overboard. A little goes a long way."

Nate frowned. His dad had switched his attention to the baseball scores flickering across the screen. "Dad, Mrs. White is trying to kill me. I'm not talking about eating too many sweets and having a heart attack. I'm talking about murder."

His dad shifted in his seat and rubbed the side of his face. "Nate, I've had a long day, I don't have time for your stories."

"It isn't a story," Nate said, putting a Moon Rock in his mouth. He hopped into the air, twisting so that his body pressed flat against the ceiling before drifting down to the carpet. "Did you see that?"

"I told you, Nate," his dad huffed, "I've had a long day."

Nate leaped toward a wall, kicked off, and glided across the room. "Can you explain how I'm doing this?" Nate asked.

"Is there a show on you want to watch?" his dad asked impatiently. "Am I in your way? If you want the TV, you can ask me directly. I'm not a tyrant."

Nate spat out the Moon Rock. He stood watching his dad. Through word or action, there appeared to be no way to pierce the fudge-induced fog. "Never mind, it's no big deal."

"Okay, don't forget your homework," his dad advised.

"My teacher forgot to give us homework," Nate mumbled, walking from the room.

It was official. He was on his own.

* * * * *

The cool night air ruffled Nate's hair as he coasted down Monroe Circle. He saw Pigeon waiting on the path astride his bike. As Nate hopped the curb and skidded to a stop, he saw Summer pedaling down the path.

"Nice work finding the ship," Nate said to Pigeon.

"Thanks," Pigeon said. "The only hard part is, the library has an alarm system. But I can guide us straight to the *Stargazer.* I saw the key Mrs. Wagner used to open the supply room, and I saw the drawer in her desk where she keeps her key ring. Her office has a window on the ground floor, so if we break in through the window and snag her keys, we can be in and out in a couple of minutes."

Summer pulled up beside them. "You guys ready?"

"The library has an alarm," Nate told her. "Did you try to get the alarm code?" he asked Pigeon.

"When I tried to get Mrs. Wagner to let me take the boat home, she started acting suspicious of me," Pigeon said. "After she had started resisting the Sweet Tooth, I got nervous and couldn't think of even a vaguely plausible explanation for why she should give me the alarm code."

"So what do we do?" Summer asked.

"We try to get out before anybody responds to the alarm," Nate said. "Let's go."

They rode their bikes down the path and then turned onto Mayflower, which they followed until reaching a tree-lined street called Goodman Road. Not far down the road they came into view of the Nelson J. Colson Memorial Library, a sprawling, modern structure with lots of huge windows. The unusual slopes and angles of the contemporary library contrasted sharply with the neighboring old barn and fenced pastures. The decrepit barn stood near a paved road that branched out from the library parking lot and passed beneath an arched sign for Goodman Farm.

"What's with the farm?" Nate asked.

"It's cool," Summer said. "That's the original barn. It's mainly for show. The rest of the farm is more current. They have real animals, but they run it like a park so people can see how a farm works. You can milk cows, feed pigs, pet sheep, take a hayride, that sort of thing."

"My family likes to go there," Pigeon said.

"I've been there on field trips," Summer said.

"Gotcha," Nate said. "Where are we headed, Pigeon?"

"This way," he said, riding his bike onto the lush lawn encompassing the library. The grass was thick and ready to be mowed, making pedaling hard work. Pigeon gave up grinding forward and walked his bike over to the side of the library, leaning it against the wall behind a bush. Nate and Summer did likewise.

Pigeon led them along the side of the building, trudging through wood chips, weaving around shrubs and young trees. He peeked through a window. "Anybody bring a flashlight?" he asked.

"I forgot," Nate said.

"I have one," Summer said, removing a small black flashlight from her pocket.

Pigeon pressed the flashlight to the glass and clicked it on. "Not this one," he reported. "I pretended to be admiring Mrs. Wagner's view and unlocked her window. If she didn't notice, it'll make life easier."

After peering into the next window, Pigeon gave them a thumbs-up. Pressing his palms against the glass, he slid the window sideways. "Phew," he said. "If we'd had to break the glass, I would have looked ten times more guilty. If we're careful, they may not ever realize anything was taken, and I'll be off the hook."

The windowsill was about the height of their necks. Nate boosted Pigeon and Summer through, then grasped the windowsill, kicked off the wall, and pulled himself up. By the time he was standing in the office, Pigeon had the keys in hand. A steady beep filled the air.

Clutching the flashlight, Pigeon led them out of the office and down a hall. The beeping continued, warning them to punch in the code to disarm the alarm. They reached a staircase that went down to a basement and curved up to a second story. Pigeon led them up. Near the top of the staircase, the beeping stopped and an obnoxious alarm started blaring. Emergency lights flashed.

They ran along a hall at the top of the stairs. One side of the hall had several doors and a couple of drinking fountains. The other side overlooked orderly ranks of bookshelves on the first floor. The hall let them out near a reference desk in an airy room divided by row after row of shelves.

Pigeon raced back into the book stacks, fumbling with the keys. At the end of the shelves they reached a wall with a gray door. Pigeon jabbed a key into the doorknob and opened it. The windowless room beyond was cluttered with books, cardboard boxes, stacked chairs and desks, framed pictures, wheeled carts, a pair of overhead projectors, a film projector, a phony-looking suit of armor, and metal shelves stocked with fake flowers and other diverse knickknacks.

The alarm blaring incessantly, Pigeon directed them to a shelf in an obscure corner of the room where the USS *Stargazer* sailed inside a clear bottle beside a marble bust of Mark Twain.

"It's huge!" Nate shouted over the alarm. "That looks like a refill bottle for a water cooler!"

"I told you it was big," Pigeon said.

The bottle rested on curved wooden mountings to prevent it from rolling. Nate scooped his arms under the bottle and lifted it off the shelf. It was almost too heavy for him to carry. Not only was the bottle big, but the glass seemed thick. "Lend me a hand, Pidge," Nate grunted.

With Pigeon holding one end of the bottle, carrying the *Stargazer* was no problem. When they exited the storeroom, Pigeon kicked the door shut and made sure it was locked. They hurried between the bookshelves and hustled across an area full of tables and chairs near the resource desk.

Upon reaching the hall that led to the stairs, Nate and Pigeon stopped, the bottle cradled between them. Three figures waited in the hall, blocking their exit, lights pulsing around them. Denny, Eric, and Kyle.

"A boat, huh?" Denny called, striding forward. "Hand it over."

"What are you guys doing here?" Nate asked.

Denny rolled his eyes. "What do you think, Dirt Face? We got a call from Mrs. White and followed you. Give me the boat."

Summer took a baggie of Shock Bits out of her pocket and dumped some into her hand.

"Don't make this hard!" Denny yelled, pointing at her. "Trust me, we have candy you guys haven't seen."

"Jump through a window," Summer advised Nate, walking past him and putting the Shock Bits into her mouth.

Holding his end of the bottle with one hand, Nate snagged an Ironhide from his pocket. Like most jawbreakers, it felt smooth and hard against his tongue, and tasted sugary.

Denny shoved a small cookie past his lips. Eric and Kyle also each ate something. Kyle's fingers began sparking.

Denny began to swell. In seconds his oversized T-shirt looked small on him. His shoulders widened, his limbs grew longer and thicker, his belly expanded. Warts erupted on his face, and his nose plumped up like a potato. A sloping brow jutted over sunken eyes. He sprouted up to well over six feet tall, his frame filling out into the powerfully bloated physique of a professional lineman. Opening his inhumanly large mouth, he roared, drowning out the alarm and displaying dull yellow fangs.

"Run!" Summer shouted.

"Can you hold it?" Pigeon asked.

Nate hoisted the cumbersome bottle onto his shoulder and fled into the room with the bookshelves. Several large windows at the far side of the room offered a view of the old barn, dimly visible by the lights of the parking lot. As he studied the far wall, a particular window caught Nate's attention. It had a table beside it, which would provide the height he would need to leap through the glass.

As he ran, Nate questioned whether he really wanted to jump through a second-story window. He had the Ironhide in his mouth, but his skin did not feel any different. Then again, the bottle was heavy enough that it should be hurting his shoulder, but although he felt the pressure of the weight, there was no discomfort.

He heard another roar from Denny, alarmingly near. Even with his adrenalin pumping, the bottle was so heavy that he could barely manage, let alone run fast. Reaching the end of the room, Nate used a chair to step up onto the table near the tall window—a single pane of glass about four feet wide and eight feet tall. Trusting the jaw-breaker, knowing that if it was a dud he was about to die, Nate charged across the table and lunged at the window with all his strength, aiming beyond the glass.

Head, arms, bottle, and torso punched through, and for a terrible moment, he lost momentum and hung draped over a jagged sheet of glass, feeling the pressure against his waist, but no pain. Then the glass buckled beneath him and he tipped forward, plunging headfirst toward the patio below along with a swarm of transparent knives. Disoriented as he was, Nate tried to twist his body to cushion the ship, but he felt the bottle rupture in his embrace as he struck the concrete.

Without the Ironhide he would have impaled himself and broken his neck. With the Ironhide, he experienced the wild rush of the fall, and a tactile sensation of striking the patio, but no pain. Glass had shredded his shirt, and shards glittered on the concrete all around him, but he did not have a scratch or a bruise on his body.

Two of the *Stargazer's* masts had snapped, and a long crack traversed the bow, but otherwise the ship seemed mostly intact. Nate got up and ran away from the library, uncertain of where to go. He saw headlights, and recognized a police car coming down Goodman Road toward the library parking lot.

The nearest cover was the barn, so Nate ran toward the dilapidated structure. Without the heavy bottle, carrying the ship was no problem. Coming around to the side of the rundown building, he found a modern door. It was locked, but had window panes. He searched around for something to smash the glass, finally remembering that his hand would do just fine. He bashed his fist through a pane, receiving no scratch and feeling no pain, reached down, and unlocked the door.

Pushing the door open, he hurried inside and shoved it closed. Enough light filtered in from the parking lot through several high windows that he could faintly distinguish the strange forms of antiquated farming equipment on display around the room. Seeking a hiding place, Nate wove between obsolete plows and combines until he reached a rickety ladder that led up to a high loft. The rotten rungs creaked in protest as he ascended, cradling the *Stargazer* in one arm while climbing with the other.

When he reached the loft, Nate did not like the warped contours of the floor or the way the wood groaned beneath his weight. He reminded himself that if he fell, he just had to protect the ship, because his body would not suffer any injury. Emboldened by the thought, he proceeded to a hatch in the roof and started stacking old crates in order to reach it.

Summer gaped at the monstrous new version of Denny, knowing that Nate would never escape with the ship if she failed to slow him. She held up her hands menacingly, hoping he might find the prospect of a shock discouraging. He leered and strode forward. Glancing back, Summer saw Nate dashing away with the *Stargazer* braced on his shoulder. Pigeon was swallowing some Shock Bits of his own.

Denny tried to brush Summer aside, but when his hand met hers, electricity sizzled. He lurched backwards several paces and dropped to one knee. Rising, he let out a barbaric cry of resentment.

Kyle and Eric rushed at Summer. Electricity crackled between Kyle's fingers, and Eric no longer looked like himself. Though he was still roughly the same size, his skin had coarsened into green scales, his eyes were yellow and reptilian, his nose and mouth had merged into a snout, and sharp claws tipped his fingers.

Summer started chewing her first stick of Peak Performance gum as she backed away from her attackers. Kyle lunged at her, but she spun nimbly away from his grasp. Eric sprang forward, swinging a clawed hand. Summer ducked the swipe and grabbed his scaly upper arm in one hand, his forearm in the other. Heaving and pivoting, she swung him into Kyle, releasing his arm just before a blaze of electricity launched Eric into a bookshelf.

While Summer was occupied with Kyle and Eric, Denny had raced around the altercation in pursuit of Nate. Pigeon charged forward, fingers sparking, and tried to touch Denny, but the overgrown bully dodged around him and continued after Nate, roaring savagely. Pigeon swapped targets, tagging Kyle on the elbow and sending him flying.

Summer saw Nate crash through the window, hang suspended for an instant, and then topple out of view. Denny froze, stunned by the sight, probably not understanding that Nate was uninjured. Without knowing about the Ironhide, anyone would have expected to find Nate bloodied and dying on the ground below.

Kyle, Eric, Summer, and Pigeon all watched Denny edge forward and hesitantly peer through the empty window. "He's fine!" Denny growled. "He's up and running! Get the ship!"

Denny sprinted away from the window, back toward Summer and the others. Eric raced for the stairs, moving with remarkable speed. Pigeon ate another handful of Shock Bits and moved to block Denny. Kyle put his hand to his mouth and sprang at Pigeon. When they touched, lightning stabbed from the floor to the ceiling, blasting Pigeon and Kyle away from each other with much greater force than any Shock Bits jolt Summer had witnessed. With them having shocked each other, the effect had evidently been multiplied.

Without breaking stride, Denny picked up a table and hurled it at Summer. She rolled out of the way and ended up back on her feet, but Denny was already past her. Her reactions felt razor sharp. She had been diving out of the way before the table had left Denny's hands.

Pigeon sat up shakily, looking shell-shocked. "I'm going to help Nate," Summer yelled at him, already running after Denny. He was big, but swift. Even though she was running faster than she had ever sprinted, by the time she was in the hall, he was already down the stairs.

Summer noticed a bookshelf near the top of the stairs. Without pausing to worry, she vaulted over the railing, landed gracefully on top of the bookshelf, crouched, dangled from the edge, and dropped to the floor. The actions felt as simple as skipping down a sidewalk.

Dashing after Denny, not too far behind him, Summer heard glass shatter. Ahead of both of them, Eric had taken an emergency fire extinguisher from its case and hurled it through a sizable window. Eric sprang through the window, followed by Denny. Summer stopped to study the situation.

A police car idled in the parking lot. The officer was on the radio, but was ignoring the lizardlike boy and the hulking figure beside him. Denny gestured for Eric to check around the other side of the library and then ran toward the barn. Realizing that the officer was probably blinded by white fudge, Summer climbed through the window and chased after Denny.

"He's in here!" Denny bellowed upon reaching the door with the broken pane. He threw the door open and stormed inside.

Summer followed Denny into the dim barn, hearing him noisily blunder into old-fashioned farm machinery. Denny roared, and she heard metal squealing. Rushing around the edge of the room, Summer found the ladder and suspected that Nate might have headed that way. As she rapidly climbed, she heard Denny start scaling the ladder behind her. She hoped the unstable ladder might collapse under his weight, and took a Moon Rock from her pocket just in case.

When she reached the loft, Summer saw a suspicious pile of crates below a hatch in the ceiling and knew Nate had gone that way. She raced over to the crates and clambered up through the hatch. Nate stood across the roof, near the brink. "Nate!" she called in an urgent whisper.

"Summer? Where are they?"

"Right behind me," she said, dashing over to him.

"If I spit out the Ironhide and jump with a Moon Rock, do you think the boat will drag me down too fast?"

"Don't chance it," she said.

"The ship is already in bad shape," Nate said. "I don't want to demolish it."

"Aha!" boomed Denny from the hatch, boosting his bulky body through. "This is what they call a dead end."

Summer pulled something from her pocket.

"No more tricks," Denny warned. "Give me the boat."

Summer charged him, shouting as loud as she could.

Denny smirked and let out a tremendous bellow, a mighty cry that mingled the roar of a lion with the shriek of an eagle. As Denny roared, Summer winged the Sun Stone at him sidearm, a perfect throw into the center of his gaping mouth.

The roar abruptly ceased. Denny's hands went to his throat, and his knees began to wobble beneath the increased pull of gravity. His body snapped forward, slamming through the roof of the barn and then through the loft below, finally smashing the barn floor with a tremendous crunch.

"You threw a Sun Stone in his mouth?" Nate marveled.

"The gum really works," Summer said. "It felt like I couldn't miss. Let's hope he broke some bones."

"I hope you didn't kill him," Nate said.

The thought made Summer worried. That had not been her intent. Denny had seemed so big that nothing could hurt him, but she supposed a three-story fall propelled by increased gravity could potentially kill just about anything. "Mrs. White said the Sun Stones reinforce people so the extra gravity doesn't harm them. I bet that will protect him."

"Oh, no," Nate said.

Scaly Eric scrambled through the hatch, along with a taller, thinner version of Kyle. The new Kyle had spindly arms and legs, a long, narrow nose, and bluish skin. He had to be almost seven feet tall. "Careful," Eric hissed to Kyle. "The roof didn't hold Denny."

"What happened to you guys?" Nate asked.

"Creature Crackers," Kyle bragged, his voice raspier. "You guys don't stand a chance."

Summer spat out her gum and stuck a Flame Out in her mouth, planning to intimidate them with a warning shot. Heat radiated through her mouth—not the spiciness of hot candy but real heat, as if her tongue were a fiery coal. The temperature rapidly increased until it felt like her mouth was about to combust.

Tilting her head back, Summer expelled the candy up into the air. It emerged as a raging ball of fire, illuminating the night, growing larger as it soared higher. "Back off!" Summer yelled, staring down Eric and Kyle while readying another Flame Out.

"Summer!" Nate cried.

A quick glance skyward revealed that the fireball was falling back toward the roof of the barn. She had inadvertently shot it almost straight up. Eric and Kyle dove through the hatch. Summer raced toward the edge of the roof, a Moon Rock in her hand. She slapped the candy into her mouth as she jumped. Out of the corner of her eye she saw Nate fling himself off the roof and plummet to the ground below.

Behind her, the fireball landed, spreading across half the roof, the dry shingles welcoming the searing flames. A scorching wave of heat washed over Summer as she glided away from the burning barn. By the time she reached the parking lot, Summer landed hard enough that she dropped to her knees, banging them against the asphalt. Rising, she leapt over to where Nate stood holding the *Stargazer*, which now had deep splits running through the gashed hull.

"I landed on my back," he said. "It still got smashed up."

Summer could see an imprint in the ground where he had landed. "At least it's basically in one piece. Take the gum." She handed him a stick. "Run to Mr. Stott's. I'll find Pigeon."

"You think Denny will be all right?" Nate asked.

Summer gazed up at the barn. "Only the roof is burning so far. Eric and Kyle aren't chasing us yet. I'm sure they're helping him."

Nate spat out the jawbreaker and put the gum in his mouth. "Get away as fast as you can," he warned. "This is out of control."

Overhead, snapping and popping, the flames leapt higher, reflecting hellishly off the billowing smoke.

CHAPTER FIFTEEN
A SHORT-LIVED VICTORY

D izzy, dazed, ears ringing, Pigeon vaguely heard Summer shout
something about Nate, and saw her running after Denny. Across
the room, Kyle was sitting up, hands clamped to the sides of his
face. The redhead tried to stand but sank back to his knees.

Pigeon knew exactly how he felt.

Closing his eyes, he seemed to feel the room slowly rotate. The
blaring of the alarm competed with the internal ringing for the dis-
tinction of most annoying noise in the universe. As he bowed his head
and focused on his breathing, the rotating slowed and the ringing
diminished.

Pigeon opened his eyes in time to see Kyle leap from the window.
By the drifting quality of the jump, he could tell Kyle must have eaten
a Moon Rock. Pigeon took out a Moon Rock of his own and staggered to the window.

On the patio below, Kyle spat out the Moon Rock and stuck a

small cookie in his mouth. He started shooting upward, growing taller and thinner, limbs stretching, nose elongating.

"He's in here!" Denny cried from over beside the barn.

Pigeon saw Summer dashing into the barn after Denny. The new, taller, uglier Kyle ran over to the barn, where he was joined by the reptilian Eric.

Slipping his own Moon Rock into his mouth, Pigeon leapt from the window, soaring out over the patio and landing on the grass near the parking lot. The night air helped clear his head. Some distance away, a pair of horses watched the commotion from the pasture adjoining the barn. Pigeon started jumping in their direction, gliding across the field in long, gentle parabolas. One of the horses shied away at his approach; the other tossed its head and stamped a hoof.

Pigeon spat out the Moon Rock and dug some Brain Feed out of his pocket. The dappled gray horse was much bigger than it had appeared from a distance—Pigeon was nowhere near as tall as its back. He eased nearer to the horse, hand held out flat. The horse stepped toward him, lowering its head. The wet mouth brushed his palm as the horse ate the fragrant kibbles.

"You really aren't supposed to come into the pasture," the horse said in a friendly, masculine voice.

"It's an emergency," Pigeon said. "I need your help."

"With what?"

"I was wondering if I could ride you to go help my friends."

The horse chuckled. "Right. I get it. I'm a Percheron. Sure, they say we were bred to carry knights into battle, the tourists eat that up, but in real life, I pull the hay wagon, I make nice with the kids, I . . . whoa, check that out."

Pigeon turned around and saw a blazing ball of fire rising up from the top of the barn, expanding as it ascended. The ball slowed, hung in the air, and then fell, holding its shape until unfurling wildly across the roof, setting the shingles ablaze.

"What kind of trouble did you say?" the horse said soberly.

"We're trying to save the town from bad guys," Pigeon said.

"Hop on."

Pigeon stuck a Moon Rock into his mouth and lightly jumped up onto the broad back of the horse.

"You're light!" the horse exclaimed. "No wonder you can bounce around like a grasshopper. You'll want to grip with your knees. Go ahead and hang on to my mane."

The horse started cantering across the pasture. "How do we get out?" Pigeon asked.

"I've noticed a flimsy spot over here," the horse said, loping toward the library, then slowing at the fence. "Never thought I'd take advantage of it." A front hoof lashed out, and Pigeon heard a fencepost splitting. The hoof shot out a few more times, and the fence clattered down. The horse walked over the fallen wood. "Where are we going?"

"To that girl," Pigeon said, pointing at Summer. She was running toward him along the edge of the library parking lot. The horse trotted toward her.

"Pigeon!" Summer cried. "You're okay!"

"I was coming to get you," he said. "Need a lift?" He patted the horse's neck. "Can you handle her?"

"Easy as pie," the horse said.

"Use a Moon Rock," Pigeon suggested.

Summer put the candy in her mouth and floated up to sit behind Pigeon. "Let's get out of here," she said.

"Where's Nate?"

"Running the ship to Mr. Stott's house. I gave him some gum."

"What about our bikes?"

"Leave them," Summer said. "Denny, Eric, and Kyle have all changed into monsters."

"I saw," Pigeon said.

"I need a destination," the horse interrupted.

"Away from the library along that road," Pigeon said. "Speed is important."

"Off we go," the horse said, breaking into a fast canter. "What's the plan?"

"I'm hoping you can take us home," Pigeon called, wind in his face. They passed a police officer standing outside his car, gazing up at the burning barn. It was the same officer who had spoken to Pigeon at the cemetery. He paid them no heed.

"You got it," the horse said. "I've always wanted to see more of the town. I get to walk in the Fourth of July parade, but otherwise I never leave the farm."

"We really appreciate this," Summer said.

"Don't mention it," the horse laughed. "You're as light as the other one. I can hardly feel either of you. What a night! This is great, like a jailbreak. Hear the sirens?"

"Turn right up here," Pigeon instructed as they approached Mayflower, the whine of multiple sirens growing louder.

"Hang on," the horse said, increasing his gait to a full gallop.

* * * * *

Racing down a sidewalk on the far side of Mayflower, Nate could not believe how easy it was to maintain a full sprint. All his past experience combined to insist that his lungs should be burning, his legs should be aching, his side should be sore. Instead, he felt no more winded than he would on a leisurely stroll, leaving him free to enjoy the exhilaration of the night air in his face as he rushed along a side street in a dark neighborhood.

Before long the night came alive with the cry of sirens, but he doubted whether any of the emergency vehicles would travel the minor residential streets separating him from Mr. Stott's house. Holding the ship in both hands, he tried to run smoothly enough to avoid making the splits in the hull any worse. The once-handsome ship had sustained some serious damage. Nate just hoped they had not messed up whatever map it contained. He worried about how Mr. Stott might react to the broken masts, tattered sails, crushed hull, and whatever little pieces had fallen off.

Nate turned down Clover Lane, crossed a few empty streets, and soon found himself on Limerick Court, still running at top speed. It was amazing how much ground you could cover with a tireless sprint!

The sirens were behind him now, their cries waning as they arrived at their destination. Ahead the street was still and dark, no lights in the windows, no cars on the road. Then a light came on as the door of a parked sedan opened down the street, not far from Mr. Stott's house. Nate abandoned the sidewalk and spied on the car from behind a bush.

To his dismay, the big round guy from the candy shop got out. He appeared to converse with somebody before he ducked out of sight. Nate covered his mouth. They were planning to ambush him when he brought the map to Mr. Stott. He had almost sprinted into a trap.

Taking out his cell phone, Nate dialed Mr. Stott. The old magician picked up after a few rings. "Hello?"

"Mr. Stott?" Nate whispered. "Can you hear me?"

"Sure. What is it?"

"Mrs. White has her goons guarding your house. I think they're trying to ambush me."

"Are you in immediate danger?"

"No."

"You have the map?" Mr. Stott asked.

"It was rough, but yes, I think so. I have the *Stargazer*."

"Excellent! Nate, just go home. You can bring me the ship in the morning."

"Okay. Talk to you tomorrow."

Nate hung up. Staying low, running across front yards instead of on the sidewalk, he hurried away from Mr. Stott's. It made Nate glad to think of the big round guy waiting disappointedly for him to show up.

Nate sprinted along side streets until he reached Main. After waiting for a car to pass, he dashed across and cut through Summer's neighborhood. He ran up to Mayflower to avoid the creek, and then rushed along the jogging path toward Monroe Circle, senses alert.

When he reached the bottom of Monroe, Nate saw a gray horse walking down the middle of the street. The sight was so unusual that he retreated into the undergrowth by the creek and fell flat. He watched the horse wander onto the jogging path and clomp away toward Mayflower.

Once the horse was out of sight, Nate raced up the street to his house, flung open the door, and locked it behind him. He rushed around the ground floor, making sure all the windows and doors were locked, then did the same upstairs. He went to his bathroom, where the light remained on, but Trevor was not in the mirror. He flashed the light on and off and waited a moment, but his friend did not appear.

Nate went to his room and set the mangled ship in his closet. The *Stargazer* was a mess, but it was mostly in one piece. Even the broken masts were held to the boat by tangles of netting and string.

Nate took out his cell phone and called Summer. She answered on the second ring. "I'm glad you called," she said. "Did you deliver it?"

"No, the big guy from the candy shop was waiting to ambush me. It seemed like he had others with him. So I came home. I figured my mom could swing me by there on the way to school. Are you and Pidge okay?"

"We rode home on a talking horse," Summer said.

"I think I saw it!" Nate said. "Was it gray?"

"That's the one," Summer said. "He was really friendly."

"Nice use of the Brain Feed."

"We left our bikes behind, which might come back to bite us, but honestly, I'm just relieved we made it. That was scary."

"I know, what was with the monster candy? It was like Melting Pot Mixers on steroids!"

"It was freaky," Summer said. "Are you going to school tomorrow?"

"For sure," Nate said. "With all the people around, school is probably the safest place for us right now."

"I don't want to see Denny there," Summer said.

"Neither do I," Nate agreed. "You think he's okay?"

"I'm sure. Eric and Kyle would have been after us faster if they hadn't been helping him get unstuck."

"Maybe we can hide out during lunch," Nate said.

"Bring your candy just in case."

"Always. Hey, Summer, you were amazing tonight. You saved the day with that Sun Stone."

"What are friends for?" She sounded very pleased. "See you tomorrow."

"Yep."

He hung up.

His digital clock said it was not quite two-thirty. The whole escapade had taken place in less than ninety minutes. Nate spat his gum into the wastebasket by his bookcase and turned off the lights. He leaned back on his bed, told himself he would undress after he rested his eyes for a moment, and faded off to sleep.

* * * * *

Nate snapped awake, certain he had heard glass breaking. His room was dark; the clock read 3:46 A.M. He lay still, straining his ears, hearing only silence. Had it been a dream? He had smashed through a lot of glass earlier in the night—maybe his subconscious had been reliving the adventure.

He could not shake the conviction that the sound had been real, and decided he had better check it out. He reached over, clicked on his reading light, and saw a bubble floating over his bed. Chills raced down his back. It was the size of a baseball, like the bubble they had seen in the alley by the museum, like the bubble Pigeon had described hovering near the Nest.

Transfixed, he stared at the little sphere, uncertain exactly what it meant, knowing it was a bad sign. The floor in the hallway creaked. Terrified, Nate forced himself to move, plunging a hand into his pocket. The bubble streaked out the door. Nate got up, putting an Ironhide in his mouth, watching the doorway, wondering if he should call his parents.

The wrinkled wooden Indian from the candy shop walked into his room, clutching a tomahawk.

Nate screamed as he had never screamed before, an involuntary, desperate wail. The Indian reacted by running at him and hurling him onto his bed. The Indian sprang to the closet, tore open the door, crouched, and seized the *Stargazer*.

"No!" Nate yelled, diving off his bed, wrapping his arms around the painted buckskin jacket. The Indian fell against the wall, a couple of headdress feathers snapping off. Nate reached for the ship, and the Indian elbowed him in the face. The blow knocked him back, but it didn't hurt, so he hugged the Indian's legs as the chief tried to rise, and wrenched him to the ground.

The fallen Indian kicked Nate viciously, shoving him backwards, and scrambled across the floor toward the door. Unafraid to use his indestructible body as a projectile, Nate sprang onto his bed and leapt off, hitting the Indian with a flying tackle as he was rising.

The Indian released the *Stargazer*, picked up Nate, and rammed him into the bookcase, upsetting shelves and sending books and trophies cascading to the floor. Again Nate felt no pain and kept struggling, so the Indian clamped him in a headlock. The chokehold had no effect, and Nate managed to pick up the heavy Indian and thrust his head through the bedroom window. The Indian grabbed the windowsill and pushed off, falling to the floor beside Nate.

"Everything okay, champ?" Nate's dad asked, standing in the doorway in his undershirt and boxers.

"A wooden Indian is trying to kill me!" Nate hollered.

"It's just a dream, try to get some shut-eye."

No longer holding back, the Indian punched Nate in the face. The blow did not hurt, but it had enough force behind it to send him reeling. Nate landed on his hands and knees.

The Indian ran toward the door, grabbed the ship, and knocked over Nate's dad on the way out. Refusing to admit defeat, Nate gave chase.

"You guys need to settle down," his dad said as Nate ran by. "Your mom and I are trying to sleep."

The Indian was quick, but Nate had his chance on the stairs, diving from the top step and colliding with the wooden chief halfway down. They tumbled together, the *Stargazer* crunching beneath them, and landed in a tangle at the end of the staircase.

The Indian again abandoned the *Stargazer* to concentrate on Nate. The chief picked him up, carried him across the room, and flung him through the sliding glass door into the backyard. Nate got up and rushed back inside, chasing the Indian to the front door. When the Indian reached the door, the ship under one arm, Nate lunged, but the Indian turned and chopped him in the side of the head with the tomahawk.

As always, Nate felt no pain, but the fierce impact flung him brutally onto the living room carpeting. The Indian raced out the door. Nate got up and pursued him out onto the street, but soon found that in the open, the Indian ran considerably faster than he did. He gave up and watched the Indian dash to the bottom of the street and turn down the jogging path toward the candy shop.

Nate stared impotently at the empty street. He tried to devise a plan to fix things, but there was nothing he could do. The ship was gone.

He trudged back into his house, closing the front door. Cool air wafted in through the glassless sliding door. He pulled the curtain shut in front of it. A window in the family room was broken as well, presumably where the Indian had entered.

Nate climbed the stairs. He peeked into his parents' room.

"No more friends over on school nights," his dad stated in a harsh whisper.

"Okay," Nate said.

He returned to his room. Nate wanted to cry, but no tears would come. He had no idea what he would tell Summer and Pigeon, what he would tell Mr. Stott, what he would tell Trevor. He had failed everyone. Now Mrs. White had the advantage. If she found the treasure first, they were all doomed.

Nate plopped down on his bed, taking in the disaster his room had become. He spat out the Ironhide.

The *Stargazer* was gone.

CHAPTER SIXTEEN
THE SUBSTITUTE

The train of cars rolled forward a little at a time. Nate clutched the cell phone Mr. Stott had given him. The power was off in order to avoid receiving a call. His mom pulled forward, finally getting her turn alongside the curb at the front of Mt. Diablo Elementary.

"Here we are," she said. "Remember, come straight home after school."

"I will," Nate said.

He opened the door and got out, shouldering his backpack. His parents had concluded that the house was trashed because Nate had had friends over late. They had grounded him for a week. No television, no friends. In a way, he was glad they had at least noticed something, even if they had it all wrong.

Caught up in the flow of kids flooding into the school, Nate debated skipping his class. He wanted to hitchhike to San Francisco and stow away on a cargo ship bound for the Southern Hemisphere. Or maybe hop a train to a distant city and check himself into an orphanage. Or even just roam off into the wilderness, build a shack, and start a new life as a mysterious hermit. Anything to avoid admitting that the *Stargazer* had been stolen by Mrs. White.

In rebellion against his grandiose schemes, Nate's treacherous feet carried him toward his classroom. He looked at the cell phone. Should he call Mr. Stott? The sooner he confessed, the sooner they could formulate new plans. He put the phone away. He would tell Summer and Pigeon first; then they could all go tell Mr. Stott in person after school.

Nate entered Miss Doulin's classroom. He slouched into his seat, wondering how he was supposed to sit through another unprepared lesson, considering all the stress he was under. Only then did he notice that Miss Doulin was not sitting at the desk at the front of the class.

In her place sat a broad-shouldered man in an overcoat wearing a brown fedora with a black band. He had a strong jaw and heavy eyebrows. Nate instantly recognized him as the man who had chased him on the night they had stolen the pocket watch from the museum. Fear flooded through him. Somehow the man had tracked them down! Nate glanced over at Summer and Pigeon, already in their seats and looking as uncomfortable as he felt.

The bell rang.

Using a cane, the man stood up and limped to the chalkboard. Taking a piece of chalk from the tray, he wrote MR. DART in large capital letters before turning to regard the class.

"I'm Mr. Dart," he said in a confident voice. "Today I'll be standing in for Miss Doulin, who I am told was not feeling well. As long as you keep it to a low roar, I'll basically leave you alone to read or study or do whatever floats your boat. But first I want to share a few thoughts on an important subject."

He turned back to the chalkboard, erased his name, and wrote in imposing letters: DON'T TAKE CANDY FROM STRANGERS!

Nate squirmed.

"Now, that may not seem like news to anyone," Mr. Dart said. "This message, in various forms, has been drilled into children across many cultures for centuries. Why do you suppose this message gets repeated?"

April Flynn raised her hand. Mr. Dart nodded at her.

"Because strangers might lure you into their car to kidnap you," April said.

"A common response, and a real threat," Mr. Dart said. "Or maybe the stranger tampered with the candy and made it unsafe. I want to propose a lesser known reason. There are magicians in the world who are capable of creating powerful spells that work only on children. They blend these enchantments with candy to entice young-sters. These magicians consider children a disposable resource. They put kids in danger, get what they can from them, and then cast them aside when their usefulness has passed. None of these magicians can be trusted. They are not a new phenomenon. Some of the oldest chil-dren's tales contain warnings about them. Who knows the story of Hansel and Gretel?"

Several hands went up.

John Dart continued as if he had not asked the question. "Two children get lost in the woods and stumble upon a delicious house made of candy. Attracted by the sweets, the kids are captured by a witch, who continues feeding them treats. Why? The witch is fatten-ing them up so she can eat them."

Mr. Dart paused, staring at Nate, who dropped his gaze to his hands.

"Moral of the story? Don't take candy from strangers. You can find similar warnings in other tales. My message today is: Do not trust magicians who exploit children for gain."

Walt Gunther timidly raised his hand. Mr. Dart nodded at him.

"Are you sort of making up a fairy tale?" he asked, sounding concerned that Mr. Dart might be insane.

Mr. Dart smiled. "Something like that. I'm trying to prove a point to anyone who might be feeling confused about the issue. If any of you want to talk with me more on the subject, I'll be at my desk. Otherwise, find a task to perform quietly."

Mr. Dart returned to the desk and sat down. He took out a pen and began writing in a notebook.

Nate tapped his desk nervously with his pen. Whatever Mr. Dart was doing here, it was clear that he knew about the magicians and the candy. There was no point in trying to act naive. The man was on to them. It would be better to confront him directly. Mustering his courage, Nate got up and walked to the front of the room.

Mr. Dart looked up from his notebook. "Pull up a chair."

Nate grabbed a chair, glancing over at Summer and Pigeon. Summer pointed at herself and then at Mr. Dart. Nate shook his head. He did not want Summer or Pigeon to reveal themselves until he learned more about the unexpected substitute.

Nate sat down by Mr. Dart. "Do you know me?" Nate asked quietly.

"I do," Mr. Dart said in a deep, hard voice. "I don't know all the details, but I know you're in way over your head. If you'll fill me in, I can help."

"How do I know you're different from any of the other magicians?"

Mr. Dart almost smiled. "First of all, I'm no magician. Second, I'm not after what they're after. I'm only here to stop them. Third, unlike them, I'll tell you everything I know once I'm convinced you're on my side."

Nate rubbed his knees. "If that's all true, I may talk to you. But first you need to prove yourself."

Mr. Dart leaned back in his chair, thick fingers brushing the brim of his hat. "Look, I wouldn't be here if I didn't have a hunch you were basically a good kid. Belinda can be sly. She could cajole an honest kid into serving her. It seems clear you caught on to what she really is and that you were trying to fight back. Without help, it's a fight you'll lose. My guess is you're involved with Sebastian as well."

"He seems like a pretty good guy," Nate said.

Mr. Dart exhaled sharply, not quite a chuckle. "Compared to Belinda, yes, he is the lesser of two evils. But I expect he is keeping secrets, just as she did. Has he even told you what he is after?"

"An ancient treasure," Nate said.

"What ancient treasure?"

Nate shrugged.

"Do you understand that most of the treats these magicians prepare for you would not work on themselves? They're too old. It's the catch-22 of magic."

"Mr. Stott explained that."

"Do you understand that the unattainable miracle all magicians pursue is the ability to reduce their age? They can prolong their years, but they can't make themselves a second younger. If these wise old magicians could only turn back the clock, their power would increase exponentially."

"I sort of knew that, I guess."

Mr. Dart leaned closer and lowered his voice a little more. "Then it might interest you to know that the prize Belinda White and Sebastian Stott are seeking is a draught from the Fountain of Youth. Funny how neither of them mentioned it. Chew on that for a minute, and see if Sebastian still strikes you as such a nice guy."

Nate nodded thoughtfully. "Why do you care?"

By the look on his face, Nate sensed that Mr. Dart approved of the question. "I'm no magician, but magicians know me. I help keep them in line. I've fulfilled some important assignments, but nothing tops this. If either Belinda or Sebastian drinks that water and reverts to a younger state, it will be a really big problem. I'm not just talking about a problem for magicians, I'm talking about a problem for all humankind."

"How do I know this isn't a setup? You could be working for Mrs. White."

"Before we were formally introduced, I broke my leg helping you escape Mrs. White. I shot the dwarf."

"That was you in the car!"

"The dwarf was an Energizer. A Kinetic. He can store and release mechanical energy inside his body—jump with the force of fifty jumps, that sort of thing. He was storing up to follow you onto the roof of that antique store, so I simultaneously shot him with a rubber bullet and a crossbow. The quarrel from the crossbow struck him in the leg." Mr. Dart smiled. "Sort of knocked him off-kilter, and he leapt into the wall. Little guy busted himself up pretty good."

"How'd you break your leg?"

Mr. Dart studied him. He reached into a pocket of his coat and put a toothpick in his mouth. "I've been around long enough, my weakness is no big secret, although I'm never anxious to draw attention to it. I receive any injury that I directly inflict upon another. I punch you in the face, my nose bleeds. I break your leg, mine breaks too. I kill you . . . I die."

"Whoa," Nate said. "So you broke the dwarf's leg with the crossbow, and your leg broke! What about when the dwarf jumped into the wall?"

"That didn't count. He stored up and released the energy himself."

"Were you born like that?"

"I used to be an enforcer for the mob," Mr. Dart said. "We're talking back in the twenties. One time, we leaned on a guy who happened to be a magician. Not just any magician—pretty much the cream of the crop. We had no idea. He got the upper hand and killed the two guys I was working with. I was next. But he held off. He looks at me strangely and says, 'You've never killed a man.' I say, 'That's right.' He says, 'You've been using your gifts for unworthy purposes.' I say, 'Maybe.' He says, 'I killed the killers, but I'll offer you a way out. Not an easy way out, but a chance to live, a new life.' I ended up agreeing to his terms."

"What were they?" Nate asked, fascinated.

"He cursed me so that I would suffer whatever physical harm I inflicted on others. The curse slowed down my aging process—I age more gradually than most magicians, even. And the curse sped up how fast my body heals. This leg will be perfectly mended in a couple of days, even though the dwarf will be lame for months. After placing the curse, the spell caster introduced me to a person in charge of policing magicians, and I have done this job ever since."

"You went from criminal to policeman," Nate said.

"Something like that. I'm not proud of my unlawful background.

True, I never killed a man, but certain memories make me cringe. I may have been raised wrong, but I should have known better. The curse was just. I try to make up for my past errors by doing this job right."

"Why did you chase us the night we broke into the museum?" Nate asked.

"As far as I knew, you were in league with Belinda. I was just trying to gather information. You'll notice, I didn't hurt any of you. I could have."

Nate stared at him. "I'll admit, you're starting to convince me."

"I'm telling the truth," Mr. Dart said. "I can tell you more, but you need to meet me halfway. I need to know we're on the same side. I can't have the info I share with you leaking back to my enemies."

"Okay, we're getting close to the treasure," Nate said. "A guy named Hanaver Mills left clues."

"Hanaver is how my organization knows about the treasure," Mr. Dart said. "We believe he found it, but chose to help keep it hidden. He did not share exactly where it was located, although he told us what it was. Since my organization is run by magicians, we left the treasure alone. To claim it, even to hide it, would have been a conflict of interest. But somehow word finally leaked out. Now I have to plug the leak."

"You better hurry," Nate said. "Mrs. White stole the map to the treasure from me last night."

"You had a map!" Mr. Dart said, losing his composure for the first time. "Do you know the location of the treasure room?"

"The map was supposedly hidden inside a model ship built by Hanaver," Nate explained. "We stole the ship from the town library, but before we could investigate it, Mrs. White used a wooden Indian to steal the ship from my house."

Mr. Dart scrawled something in his notebook. "She may already know the position of the treasure. Are other kids still working for her?"

"The four of us who you chased that night at the museum quit working for her and started helping Mr. Stott," Nate said. "But she recruited three bullies from our school who are now helping her."

"Who are they?" Mr. Dart asked.

"Denny Clegg, Eric Andrews, and Kyle Knowles."

"Could you point them out to me?"

"Sure."

"What about the others working for Stott? How loyal are they?"

Nate glanced over at Summer. "We should bring them in on this. One is trapped as a reflection. The others are in this room, and, like me, they just want all of this to be over. If we help you, we need you to help us get our friend out of the mirror realm."

"I'll try my best," Mr. Dart said. "I had no idea anybody still knew how to access the space where reflections dwell."

"I've been there," Nate said.

"Well, yes, I'll do everything in my power to rescue your friend, and I'll not be claiming the water from the Fountain of Youth, or any of the other treasure. You would be welcome to destroy it. If there is gold, you would be welcome to keep it. I'm just here to stop the magicians from acquiring it."

"Hold on a second," Nate said.

He walked to Summer's desk and waved Pigeon over. "What's his story?" Summer asked.

Nate took a deep breath. "First off, I have something to confess. I lost the *Stargazer*. The wooden Indian from the candy shop broke into my house and stole it. I tried to stop him, but he was too strong."

"Then Mrs. White has the map," Pigeon said.

"I'm sorry," Nate said.

"That must have been scary," Summer said.

"It was the worst," Nate said. "My dad was watching and didn't even get what was happening. He thought I was roughhousing with friends. He just wanted me to quiet down."

"I'm sure you tried your best," Pigeon said. "I'm just glad the Indian wasn't in my house."

"I think this guy is for real," Nate said, tilting his head toward Mr. Dart. He recapped all the information John Dart had told him. "I know it's hard, but I don't see that we have any options except to trust him."

"Wow," Summer said. "I'd say we're lucky he found us. He may be our only hope."

"That's what I think," Nate said. "If it's a trick, it's the best one yet. He might actually be able to get us out of this."

"You really think Mr. Stott is a bad guy?" Pigeon asked.

"Mr. Dart said that Mr. Stott isn't bad like Mrs. White, but that he could become dangerous if he drinks from the Fountain of Youth. Considering that Mr. Stott didn't tell us what the treasure was, my guess is he plans to drink it. I think Mr. Dart is our safest bet."

"I'm in," Pigeon said. "Let's talk to him."

"Is that Denny?" Summer said, staring at a window near the door.

Nate turned and made brief eye contact with the bully. Nate, Summer, and Pigeon hurried to the window in time to see Denny running off. They shared a worried look.

"What was he up to?" Pigeon asked.

"I don't know," Nate muttered.

The three kids approached John Dart's desk.

"What was that about?" Mr. Dart asked.

"One of the bullies working for Mrs. White was peeking in the window," Nate reported. "Denny. Do you think he could have heard us?"

"No," Mr. Dart said. "But it would make sense for Belinda to spy on you. I doubt he could have recognized me, but we'll have to be careful."

"This is Summer and Pigeon," Nate said.

"The Japanese girl and the black kid," Mr. Dart said. "I'm John Dart. Call me John if you like. What other leads do we have?"

"The other big one is a clue left by Hanaver Mills," Nate said. "The House of Haag holds the key."

"That is a big lead," John said. "What do we know about the Haag family in Colson?"

"Mr. Stott said there are at least twenty Haags in town," Nate said. "He's been working on narrowing down the list."

"Does Belinda know about the Haags?" John asked.

"No," Pigeon said.

"So Sebastian knows about the Haags but lacks the map, while Belinda has the map but knows nothing about the Haag family," John summarized.

"Right," Nate said.

"What about henchmen?" John asked. "Who's working for Sebastian?"

"All I know about is a weird mutant called the Flatman," Nate said. "Mr. Stott called him an engineered apprentice."

"I've heard of the Flatman," John said. "Sebastian never worked with many associates. What about Belinda?"

"Obviously the dwarf," Nate said. "She also has a fat guy who can spit orange jelly. And maybe a guy with a huge birthmark."

"Engineered apprentices," John said. "We call the fat guy a Gusher, or a Slopgut. He has a symbiotic relationship with the gel inside of him. He can expel it in order to entrap or smother victims. The man with the birthmark is a Fuse. Every Fuse has different magical specialties. Each time he calls on his power, the birthmark spreads. When the mark covers his entire body, he dies. Hence the name. I actually captured the Fuse a few days ago. He won't talk, but at least he's out of play. What else can you tell me?"

Summer, Nate, and Pigeon exchanged glances. "That's about it," Pigeon said.

"We still have some candy from both of them," Nate said. "You might find us more useful than normal kids. We'll do whatever it takes to get Trevor back."

"I'll be honest, I'm not much of a babysitter," John said. "I've always liked the idea of children a lot more than the reality. But you three seem okay. I can definitely use your help to gather information. I'll try my best to keep you out of harm's way. Our first step will be to nab one of your bully friends and find out what he knows. I'll need you to point them out to me at the first opportunity. For now, go back to your desks. I look forward to working with you."

Nate returned to his seat.

Heather Nielson leaned over and whispered, "Is he as weird as he seems?"

"You can't imagine."

Fourth, fifth, and sixth grade kids flocked to the lunch tables. Seagulls wheeled and plunged overhead. One of the few clouds in the sky moved in front of the hot sun, providing temporary shade.

Nate, Summer, and Pigeon waited at one side of the lunch area. Beside them John Dart took a long drink from a bottle of Dr. Pepper. They had failed to spot Denny, Eric, or Kyle during first recess, and had begun to worry the boys might have ditched school. Just because they had seen Denny earlier did not guarantee that he had stuck around.

"It's convenient that you're a substitute teacher," Nate said, making conversation.

"I'm not," John said.

"How'd you get in here?" Pigeon asked.

"This morning at around five I went to Miss Doulin's house, tied her up, and shut her in a closet. She'll be fine. I grabbed her keys, skipped talking to anybody in the office, and took over her class. Helps that most of the faculty and office staff are on white fudge."

"There they are," Pigeon said, pointing out Denny and Eric. They had hot-lunch trays, and settled down together at a table full of sixth graders.

"No sign of the third one?" John asked.

They waited a few minutes, but Kyle did not join the others.

"Which of those two has the weaker will?" John asked.

"Eric," Summer said. "The kid sitting on the left. The other one, Denny, is pretty tough."

"You three go have lunch in the classroom. Here's the key."

"What are you going to do?" Nate asked.

"You'll see," John said.

Nate, Summer, and Pigeon returned to the classroom. They pushed three desks together and ate their lunches.

"I'm grounded," Nate said.

"Why?" Pigeon asked.

"In my fight with the Indian I trashed the house. Smashed my bookcase, shattered the window in my room, pulverized the sliding glass door. Fortunately I was sucking on an Ironhide. My parents somehow decided I'd had friends over and we had vandalized everything. I'm supposed to go directly home after school."

"You got busted even with them on the fudge?" Pigeon asked, sounding a little nervous.

"Yeah, but they had it all wrong," Nate said. "It took me wrestling a wooden Indian in front of my dad and doing severe damage to the house to even get noticed."

John entered the room. "You kids want to leave school early?" He walked to the front of the room, leaning on his cane. He erased DON'T TAKE CANDY FROM STRANGERS! and replaced it with STUDY QUIETLY UNTIL I RETURN.

"You're not returning," Pigeon guessed.

"Not very likely," John admitted. "Hurry up, I have Eric in the trunk."

"You're kidnapping him?" Summer asked.

"Don't worry, I took away all of his candy," John said. "Trust me, we're doing the weasel a favor. We'll take him home safe and sound when this is over."

Nate, Summer, and Pigeon collected their backpacks and followed John to the front of the school. He was driving an old Buick. The exterior was clean although the paint was chipped and scratched.

"Shotgun," Nate said, climbing into the front seat and sitting on the dry, cracked upholstery.

"Nine-millimeter handgun, actually, modified to shoot darts," John said, sliding in and starting the car. "Buckle up."

"Mine doesn't work," Pigeon said.

"Sit in the middle," John said.

Pigeon scooted over and buckled the lap belt.

"Where are we going?" Nate asked.

"The Paradise Inn," John said.

"Isn't that kind of a dump?" Pigeon asked.

"My third dive since hitting town," John said, turning onto Oak Grove Avenue. "We may have to make an extra stop before then. You kids have a traveling eye monitoring you."

"Traveling eye?" Pigeon asked.

"Some magicians can send a traveling eye to help them spy on distant events. This one looks like a bubble."

"I've seen it before!" Pigeon said.

"It showed up in my room before the Indian took the *Stargazer*," Nate said.

"Then the eye belongs to Belinda," John said. "Reach under your seat."

Nate reached under his seat and pulled out a crossbow. Instead of an arrow, the string held a small cup covered by a leather cap. It looked ready to fire.

"The weapon shoots forty silver pellets," John said. "I typically use it for other purposes, but it should get this job done. Have any of you kids ever fired a crossbow?"

The kids were silent.

"How about a rifle?"

Nate and Pigeon shook their heads.

"I have," Summer said. "My grandpa took me."

"I can't afford to shoot the eye myself," John said. He pulled into a large parking lot adjacent to a supermarket and several smaller stores, including a tanning salon, a Chinese buffet, and a copy shop. He parked in a vacant area near the back of the lot. "Nate, give Summer the crossbow. Summer, the eye is above and behind us to the right. It may be hard to identify against the blue sky. Aim by putting the bead at the front of the crossbow into the notch at the rear and lining it up with the target. You'll get only one shot."

"Then I'd better use some of this," Summer said, inserting a stick of Peak Performance gum into her mouth.

John reached back and released a mechanism on the crossbow. "The safety is off," he said. "Ready? On three. One . . . two . . . three!"

Summer pushed open her door, stepped out, and aimed the heavy crossbow. The baseball-sized bubble hovered right where John had described, about thirty feet off the ground, barely visible. Holding her breath, she pulled the trigger. The cup lurched forward, the leather cap slid off, and a cloud of pellets were catapulted into the air.

The bubble burst, and a red smear appeared on the parking lot beneath it. John got out and took a look at the smear. "Great job," he said, patting Summer on the back. "You shot her eye out. She'll think twice before sending the other one after us."

"You mean she actually lost an eye?" Summer asked.

"That's the risk she took," John said, taking the crossbow from her. "Hurry, hop in the car." He climbed behind the wheel and passed the unusual crossbow to Nate, who stowed it under the seat.

John revved the engine. Peeling out, they swerved back onto the street and drove away at well beyond the speed limit.

CHAPTER SEVENTEEN
HOUSE OF HAAG

The Paradise Inn consisted of a two-story horseshoe of rooms wrapped around a weedy parking lot. Opposite the office was a small gated swimming pool, deserted except for a few dirty deck chairs. A sun-bleached *Temporarily Out of Service* sign hung on the battered ice machine. The marquee bragged about the swimming pool and the cable TV.

John pulled the Buick into a spot and killed the engine. There were only three other cars in the lot. He got out, looked around, opened the trunk, and hauled Eric over to room 6. Stabbing a key into the lock, John thrust the door open.

The air-conditioning unit below the window was working hard to keep the room cool. John sat Eric on the edge of the bed. Eric looked sweaty and scared.

"I'm going to make this simple, Eric," John said. "You've become involved with a wanted criminal. If you don't tell me all you can about everything she is doing, you will never see anyone you love again."

"Who are you?" Eric asked, not very defiantly.

"You don't want to know," John said.

John stalked over to the closet and opened it. The man with the lurid birthmark sat inside wearing a straitjacket, duct tape over his mouth. John pulled a straitjacket off of a shelf and closed the door. Eric watched gravely.

"Ever try one of these on?" John asked, unfolding the straitjacket. Eric shook his head.

"Funny thing," John said. "Take a sane person, put on a strait-jacket, and it isn't long before he starts acting absolutely nuts. Let's see how it fits."

"I'll tell you stuff," Eric said.

"Start with the map," John recommended.

"I haven't seen it," Eric said. "She told us about it this morning. She said it was written on a piece of vellum she found in the ship's cabin."

"Vellum?" Pigeon asked.

Eric shrugged.

"Specially treated calfskin," John clarified. "Lasts for centuries. Go on."

"Mrs. White said she had to read it under a microscope. She said the treasure is somewhere beneath the school."

"Your school?" John asked. "Mt. Diablo?"

Eric nodded. "She wanted us to start checking out the school for underground tunnels. We haven't found anything yet. That's all I know."

"Why wasn't your friend Kyle at school?" John asked.

"I don't know," Eric said. "Maybe he was tired. He wasn't with us this morning."

"You guys got out of the barn okay?" Summer asked.

"No thanks to you losers," Eric said. "Denny almost bought it. He couldn't move, and we couldn't budge him. The roof was starting to come down when the candy finally wore off."

"What else can you tell me?" John probed. "Think hard. You're not just helping yourself, you're helping Denny and Kyle. You boys don't want to be mixed up with Belinda White, especially if she gains the power this treasure would grant her."

"That's all I know," Eric said.

"I hope so." John shook the straitjacket. "We can do this either of two ways: You can cooperate, or I can force you. The jacket really isn't as bad as I was saying. I don't plan to keep you here long."

"I'll cooperate."

John helped Eric into the straitjacket and duct-taped his mouth. "Have a seat in the bathroom for now," John said. "Unless you want to have a staring contest with the Fuse."

Eric went compliantly into the bathroom.

John, Nate, Summer, and Pigeon huddled together. "Are there any Haags affiliated with your school?" John asked.

"Gary Haag is the custodian," Pigeon said. "And there's a third-grade teacher named Mr. Haag."

"Are they related?" John asked.

"I don't think so," Pigeon said. "At least not closely."

"Do either of them have older relatives who once worked at the school?"

None of the kids had an answer. John started thumbing through a worn phone book.

"Nate, lend me your cell phone," John said. Nate handed over the phone, and John punched in a number. "Hi, yes, my son is in Mr.

Haag's third-grade class. I have an emergency situation on my hands. Is there any way I could speak with Mr. Haag? He isn't? No, that's all right. Remind me, what is Mr. Haag's first name? That's right. Thanks a lot." John returned the phone to Nate. "Mr. Haag is out today. Considering all that has been happening, his absence could mean a lot. Summer, call the school from the motel phone. Ask if Mr. Haag the custodian is in. You're his niece."

Summer crossed to the phone and picked it up. John told her the number and she dialed it. "Yes, is Mr. Haag the custodian there today? This is his niece. You did? No, no message, thanks." Summer hung up. "She saw him there like half an hour ago."

John started flipping through the phone book again. Finding the desired page, he ran a finger down a column of names. "Lester Haag," he said, tapping the entry. "Gotcha. Any of you three familiar with the custodian?"

"I know him pretty well," Pigeon said. "He's a nice guy. He was extra friendly back when nobody talked to me."

"We'll drop you at the school, Pigeon," John said. "Find out if the custodian had ancestors working there before him. If the moment feels right, ask about the key. If all else fails, find out if he is aware of any old passageways under the schools. The rest of us will pay Lester Haag a visit. My gut tells me Lester is our man."

"How'd you catch the Fuse?" Nate asked.

"Snuck up behind him when he was out alone one night," John said. "Not very gentlemanly, but so it goes. He can't access his power if I keep him gagged."

"What should we do about Eric?" Summer asked, inclining her head toward the bathroom.

"Give me one minute to make him more secure," John said. He

opened the closet, removed a length of rope, and disappeared into the bathroom. When John returned he reached under the mattress and pulled out a dart gun. He took a large crossbow from under the bed and a pair of throwing stars from a drawer. Grabbing the phone book, he strode swiftly to the door. "Away we go."

Nate, Summer, and Pigeon collected their backpacks and followed him out. John locked the door.

"Where'd you get all the weapons?" Nate asked.

"I know a guy," John said.

"If you can't kill people, why the huge arsenal?" Nate pursued.

"Weapons are what I know. Apart from my curse, there's nothing magical about me. I can use them for intimidation. I can use them to wound an enemy. I use tranquilizer darts and non-lethal bullets. My curse only applies to humans. If a magician conjures up creatures, or has familiar animals, I'm free to dispatch them. And, if the situation warrants, I can slay a single enemy. The price is just really steep."

They drove in silence and soon reached the school. Class would not let out for another hour.

"Pigeon," John said, "you know how to call Nate's cell phone?"

"Yeah."

"Here's some change." John opened an ashtray and handed Pigeon several quarters. "Call when you know something, or if you need anything."

"You got it," Pigeon said. "Good luck with Lester."

The Buick drove away.

Pigeon walked hesitantly into the school. He had never roamed Mt. Diablo Elementary during school hours without a hall pass. He hurried along the covered walkways, keeping an eye out for a custodial cart outside the rest rooms.

Aware that the custodian's office was by the cafeteria, Pigeon headed that way first. He entered the empty cafeteria and saw that the door to the custodian's office was closed. He ran over and gave a quick knock.

"Come in," said a voice.

Placing a Sweet Tooth in his mouth, Pigeon opened the door and stepped inside. Gary Haag sat with his feet on his desk, balancing a clipboard on his lap.

"Hey, Gary," Pigeon said.

"Pigeon, how are you?" He dropped his feet and stood up. "Can I help you with something?"

"I have kind of a weird question," Pigeon said.

"Shoot," Gary said.

"Do you have any relatives who worked here before you?"

"Yeah, my uncle used to be the custodian. He scored me my first job here. Why?"

"Just curious. Did he have any family who worked here before him?"

Gary gave Pigeon an unusual stare. Almost always a laid-back guy, he suddenly seemed suspicious. "He did. Why are you curious about that, Pigeon?"

"Do you know anything about a key?"

Gary got up, went to the door, peered out, and then shut it. "I have lots of keys. Why are you asking about a key, Pigeon?"

"A special key. A key your family protects."

Gary paled. His lips twitched. "You shouldn't talk about keys."

"I know about the treasure under the school," Pigeon said.

Gary closed his eyes and rubbed them. He leaned against the

door. "I know what you're talking about, Pigeon, but I'm not sure you do."

"I do," Pigeon said. "A lot of people here in town are after that key. You wouldn't believe what kind of people. I'm not one of the bad guys, I'm here to help."

Gary sighed. "Pigeon, when my great-uncle gave me the key, he warned me that one day somebody might come asking about it. He told me I had to kill that person."

It took Pigeon a moment to muster a response. "Gary, no, I'm not trying to steal the treasure."

"I hear you, Pigeon, but this is serious business. I may not come across as the sharpest knife in the drawer, but when it comes to the key, I don't mess around. The lives of my whole family are tied to that key."

"What do you mean?"

"You'd never believe me."

"I've seen some crazy stuff lately," Pigeon insisted. "Real magicians, candy that gives you powers, talking animals. I'll believe you."

Gary crossed his arms. "My family has protected the key for well over a hundred years. My great-great-great-grandfather Ebner Haag originally took on the responsibility. All of his direct descendents are held accountable. Only a few of us know about it. My great-uncle guarded the key for about forty years, then passed it to me. Pigeon, if you put the key in an oven, my family gets feverish. If you put the key in the cold, we start freezing. If you put the key under water, nobody in my family can breathe. I've seen it or I wouldn't believe it. My uncle tossed the key in a sink, and I started drowning. If the key fell into the wrong hands, somebody could kill us all, or at least blackmail us. Pigeon, unless I protect the key, we'll all suffer. And if anyone in my family uses the key to unlock the door . . . we all die."

"Be glad I found you first," Pigeon said. "There are powerful magicians who have almost figured out you have the key. I'm working with a guy named John Dart to keep them from stealing the treasure."

Gary rubbed a finger back and forth against his nostrils. Tears glistened in his eyes. "I can't do what my uncle said. I don't want to kill anybody, Pigeon. I really don't."

"Then don't," Pigeon said. "You can trust this John Dart guy. He won't let anybody harm your family."

"No, Pigeon, I can't trust anybody with this," Gary said. "I have to leave town. Look, I believe that you stumbled into this unluckily. I don't know what to do. I can't let you share what you know."

"Gary, lots of people know I'm here! They know all about you! You lose nothing by letting me go."

"I could lose time," Gary murmured. "Look, I won't hurt you, I believe you mean no harm, but I need to tie you up while I get away. Go sit in that chair."

Pigeon obeyed. "You should consider letting John Dart help you. I don't think you can hide from these magicians."

"I have a place in mind, and people who can help me," Gary said. He started using an extension cord to bind Pigeon to the chair.

"Please don't make it too tight," Pigeon said. "I have sensitive skin."

"Somebody will find you," Gary said, winding the cord snugly around Pigeon's chest and arms. "If you know what's best, you'll keep your mouth shut. If others are looking for me, let them do it on their own. If they hear about me from you, I promise, I'll make you pay."

He snagged another extension cord and started working on Pigeon's legs. Pigeon begged, "Gary, don't leave me here like this."

"Be glad you're alive," Gary said. "Don't try to get out. Let somebody find you."

Gary finished binding his legs and used a rag to gag him. "Sit tight, Pigeon. I'm sorry about this." He hurried out of the room, shutting the door.

As soon as the door closed, Pigeon started struggling. It soon became apparent that squirming free was going to take a lot of work. Despite his plea, the cords were quite tight. The gag trapped the Sweet Tooth in his mouth, and Pigeon began to feel like he was going to choke, so he chewed it as best he could and swallowed. The action seemed to cause no harm.

Jerking with his whole body, Pigeon began hopping the chair closer to the desk. The telephone was not far from the front edge. The chair was low enough, and he was short enough, that his head was not much higher than the phone. The cords were not wound high enough to prevent Pigeon from craning his neck.

By doggedly inching forward, he managed to position the chair close to the desk at an angle that allowed him to touch the phone with his face by tilting his head forward and sideways. He nudged the handset off the cradle, then began pecking numbers with his nose, proud that he remembered to dial 9 first for an outside line.

After pecking the final number, Pigeon leaned his ear as close to the handset as he could. He heard it ringing.

"Hello?" Nate answered.

"Ate!" Pigeon grunted, trying his best to enunciate in spite of the gag.

"Pigeon?"

"Ary as a ee!"

"What?"

"Ary as a ee!"

"Gary has the key?"

"Uh-huh."

"Where are you? Why do you sound like that?"

"Urry oo is ouse," Pigeon grunted.

"Hurry to his house?"

"Uh-huh."

"Where are—"

The line went dead. Had the cell phone dropped the call? Straining forward, Pigeon pressed his nose to the cradle and hung up the phone. There was no dial tone. He pecked 9. Still no dial tone.

He caught a flicker of motion on the floor. Turning his head, he saw the little plastic surgeon doll running toward the door. Pigeon yelled at it, his cry muffled by the gag.

The doll paused near the door and faced him. Pigeon struggled against the extension cords to no avail. The doll pointed at Pigeon's backpack, saluted, fell flat, and wormed under the door.

Pigeon lurched wildly against the extension cords. He had to get free! They had been spying on him! They knew everything he knew! The chair tipped over sideways. The painful shock of the fall left him momentarily dazed. The extension cords remained snug. From his uncomfortable position, Pigeon stared at the unplugged phone cord.

* * * * *

"Pigeon? You there? Pigeon? I lost him!" Nate hung up the phone and thumbed over to the received calls menu.

"Gary has the key?" Summer asked.

"That's what he told me," Nate said, calling Pigeon back. There was no answer. "He could hardly speak."

"Is he in trouble?"

"Sounded like it."

Nate and Summer were seated in the Buick a block away from Lester Haag's house. John had gone ahead alone to scout it out. Nate tried calling Pigeon again.

"We better get John," Summer said.

"Pigeon said we should hurry to Gary's house," Nate said. He put away the cell phone. "Whatever line he called on is suddenly out of commission."

"I'll grab John," Summer said.

"I'm coming," Nate said.

They got out of the Buick and hurried along Ingrim Place until they reached 2225, a modest home with a basketball hoop out front.

"Think he's inside?" Summer asked.

"John?" Nate called in a loud whisper. "John?" There was no answer. "Let's try the door."

They ran up to the porch, knocked, and waited. Nate was reaching for the doorbell when the door whipped open. John was down on one knee, crossbow ready. "I said to stay in the car," John said, lowering the weapon.

"We got a call from Pigeon," Nate said. "He could hardly talk, like his mouth was taped shut. He said Gary has the key. He said we should hurry to his house."

"Did he give an address?" John said, rushing from the house, running awkwardly, stabbing the ground with his cane to help support his left leg.

"No," Nate said, chasing John down the street.

"You'd think after eighty years on the job I'd have better instincts," John grumbled. "Looked like the Lester Haag family was on vacation."

When they arrived at the car, John tore open the phone book. He leafed through several pages, eyes intense. His finger traced down a column of names. "Gary," John said. "You two ever hear of Rosario Court?" Nate and Summer shook their heads. John yanked a map from the glove compartment and unfolded it. "Help me look."

The three of them huddled over the map of Colson, scanning street names. "Here," Summer said, poking the map.

"Good eyes," John said, tossing the map into the back and diving into the car. He started the engine before he was situated, grabbing for his seatbelt as they accelerated down the road. He ran a stop sign. Swerving onto a bigger road, he cut off a minivan, earning a prolonged honk. After getting pinned at a red light, he raced around an empty school bus, took a left onto a smaller street, and zoomed through a neighborhood at an irresponsible speed. A few more turns, tires whining, and they found themselves on Rosario Court, a short street bordered by twelve good-sized, two-story houses.

John pulled into a sloped driveway. "That could have been worse," he said. "Sit tight." Leaving the keys in the ignition, he got out and dashed toward the front door, using his cane to pole-vault onto the porch. Nate and Summer watched from the car.

Holding his crossbow behind his back, John pounded the door. A skinny woman with short graying hair answered. John spoke. The woman laughed and touched his arm, using her hands expressively as she replied. John said something else, and she said something back.

He said a few more words and limped away from the door, keeping the crossbow hidden.

John slid into the driver's seat. "This is the home of Gary senior," he said, backing out of the driveway. "His son Gary the custodian is unlisted. He lives at 3488 Winding Way."

"Near our school," Summer said.

"My fault," John growled. "Sloppy . . . slow."

The engine revved as they ignored another stop sign.

* * * * *

Methodically, persistently, trapped awkwardly on his side, Pigeon tried to wriggle free of the extension cords that trussed him to the chair. He squirmed, bucked, wrenched, and flexed. He was making progress—the cords felt looser than when he had started, but they had not yet relaxed enough for him to free either of his arms.

Pigeon heard conversing women approach the office. He screamed as best he could around the gag.

"Did you hear that?" one of the women said.

Encouraged, he screamed louder.

"Hello?" the voice called.

Pigeon grunted and shouted. "Elm! Elm ee, elm ee!"

The doorknob shook but did not open. It was locked.

"Are you all right?" the woman asked.

"Uh-uh, urry, elm ee!"

"Just a minute, we'll find somebody, hold on!"

Pigeon relaxed. There was no way he could squirm free of the cords before they found somebody to open the door. After a longer wait than he expected, a key rattled in the doorknob, and Ms. Jesky, the vice-principal, entered, followed by a pair of lunch ladies.

"Oh my goodness!" Ms. Jesky gasped, kneeling by Pigeon and tugging at the cords. When his arms were free, Pigeon yanked the gag from his mouth.

"I have to make an emergency call!" Pigeon insisted.

Ms. Jesky was still picking at the cords around his legs as he crawled forward to plug in the telephone.

*   *   *   *   *

The Buick screeched to a stop in front of 3488 Winding Way, an attractive, split-level home with a white porch swing out front. There was no vehicle in the driveway.

"Stay put," John said, exiting the car with the crossbow hidden behind his back. He limped briskly up the walkway to the front door and rapped on it with his cane.

Nate's cell phone rang. "Pigeon?"

"Nate, they know about Gary!"

The door to the house swung inward. A column of orange jelly filled the doorway. John launched a pair of quarrels from his crossbow as the gelatinous pillar sloshed forward, heaving him onto his back. His fedora fell off, and his cane clattered down the porch steps. John fought to his knees, wearing orange ooze from the neck down. Swinging his arms jerkily, he shook off globs of jelly and staggered to his feet. Blood fumed up from his shoulder within the translucent gelatin.

"Too late," Nate yelled, hanging up the phone. "We need Shock Bits!"

Summer was already shaking some into her palm. "I'm almost out."

As they dashed from the car, Nate put half of the Shock Bits Pigeon had given him into his mouth. Across the yard, the gelatin slurped upwards, engulfing John's head. Still flailing, he tumbled down the porch steps. The impact splashed apart some of the jelly, but the majority remained fastened to him. The blobs that had been jostled loose flowed across the ground to rejoin the squirmy central mass.

A tall, hideously deflated man stepped through the doorway, hand pressed to his bleeding shoulder. His lips parted as he launched a small jellyball at Summer, which liquefied when it shorted out her charge with a flash. A second jellyball missed Nate, but the third tagged him with a hiss and a crackle.

From inside the pulsing mass of gelatin, John aimed his dart gun at the man in the door, but it did not fire. John exhaled, stationary bubbles clustering in front of his face.

A baritone voice commenced chanting musically. The Fuse, his radiant birthmark slowly spreading, approached from down the street, arms spread wide, fingers splayed. The front lawn of 3488 Winding Way began to flutter and grow. Blades of grass enlarged into ropy green tentacles, snaking around Nate's legs, pinioning Summer's arms to her sides, plunging into the gelatin to entangle John.

Nate thrust an Ironhide into his mouth as the grass writhed higher, twisting and constricting. Saggy skin swaying, the tall man shuffled down the porch steps, crouched, and parted his thick lips. The orange gel abandoned John, leaving him wheezing in the winding grasp of the vines, and flowed toward the tall man.

The Fuse quit chanting and his birthmark stopped glowing,

having spread to vividly tattoo more of his face. Grassy vines wound tightly around Nate, Summer, and John from shoulders to ankles. With the Ironhide in his mouth, Nate felt no pain from the squeeze, but he was immobilized. He couldn't even wiggle his fingers.

The tall man swelled as his gaping mouth vacuumed up the orange gel, limp flaps of skin inflating until he was once again big and round. Behind him, Denny and Eric emerged from the house. "That was just sad," Denny laughed.

"Denny, don't do this, help us!" Summer cried.

Denny smirked. "Not my fault I'm playing for the winning team."

"Where's Gary?" John growled.

"Not here," Eric said. "But we know where he's going."

"He has family on the edge of town," Denny said. "Burt and Starla Haag—we'll have him soon."

"Can it," the Fuse spat. "Go fetch the straitjackets."

Denny and Eric ran off obediently, heading down the street.

"Well done, Mauricio," the Fuse said.

The big round man nodded, lips glossy with jelly residue.

"How'd you get out?" John asked.

The Fuse arched an eyebrow. "None of your business."

"I don't get it," John complained. "Your powers are null without your voice."

"Shut up," the Fuse said. "Maybe I pulled a Houdini, what do you care? You should have stuck to the shadows, John. Limping around in broad daylight doesn't suit you. Although, to your credit, you caught up to us much quicker than we expected."

Denny and Eric came running back up the street, each holding a stack of folded straitjackets. The Fuse investigated the jackets, selecting a large one and unfolding it. "John, I expect you'll make this easy. I can crush your little sidekicks with a word."

The Fuse mumbled, birthmark shimmering faintly, and the vines around John's upper body slackened and fell away. The Fuse patted John and discovered a tranquilizer gun tucked away inside of his overcoat, along with a few throwing stars. He passed the weapons to Mauricio. John submissively slipped his arms into the straitjacket, which the Fuse tightened.

"How does your own medicine taste?" Eric taunted.

"No gloating," the Fuse snapped. He mumbled again and the monstrous grass around John's legs came free from the ground. "Mauricio, bring the car."

The big round man strode away. The Fuse walked over to the Buick, opened the door, ducked inside, and came out holding the keys and the crossbow that hurled pellets. "Summer, you put on the next jacket," the Fuse said. "Again, be nice, or your friends will pay."

The Fuse chose a jacket, released the grass around Summer's upper body, and secured her in the white coat. As he had done with John, the Fuse uprooted the grass around her legs, leaving them snugly bound.

Mauricio pulled a black Hummer into the driveway. He got out and lumbered over to the Fuse. "Load John and the girl into the Buick," the Fuse said. "Then take Eric and Denny back to the shop."

"What about the boy?" Mauricio asked, jerking a thumb at Nate.

"John Dart has considerable value as a hostage," the Fuse said. "And keeping one of the brats could prove useful. We don't need two."

Mauricio heaved John Dart over one shoulder, dumped him into the Buick, fastened his seatbelt, and then lugged Summer over to the vehicle. Afterwards, the big man plodded over to the Hummer and drove away with Denny and Eric.

The Fuse waved a hand, and the vines binding Nate squeezed tighter and pulled him to the ground. He realized that the Fuse was trying to squeeze the breath out of him, so he pretended to go unconscious. Once he did so, the vines relaxed their grip. The Fuse entered the Buick and started the engine. When the car was out of earshot, Nate started squirming, and the grass binding him began to loosen. Grimly, Nate realized that he represented their last chance. The thought was overwhelming. Part of him wanted to just stay tied up there in the grass. How could he possibly succeed where people as experienced as John Dart had failed?

One hand came free and Nate started tearing at his grass bindings. The odds were against him, but at least he might have the element of surprise on his side.

* * * * *

Sniffling in the backseat of the Buick, Summer squirmed inside of her confining coat. Her nose was running but she could not wipe it. She tried her best to rub her nostrils against her shoulder. John sat stoically beside her, eyes straight ahead, a red stain slowly spreading on the shoulder of his straitjacket.

"Your shoulder," Summer said.

"Not much of a wound," John said. "I only grazed him. It was a tough shot."

Feeling frustrated, Summer twisted and wriggled.

"I'd hold still, Summer," the Fuse said. "I can still use your bindings to crush either of you at will. Behave, and you might get out of this alive."

"Every time you use your magic you get closer to dying," Summer said.

"Making the grass grow big and tie you up took some real power," the Fuse admitted. "Couldn't be helped. But manipulating the grass requires almost none."

"Why'd you have to leave Nate?" Summer said softly.

"Ahhh, missing your boyfriend already?" the Fuse snickered. "Want to know a secret? We already grabbed Gary Haag and his precious key! He was packing up when we arrived. He's in the Hummer. We told Nate what we needed him to hear. He thinks I tried to crush him, but it was obvious that his body was magically reinforced. I loosened his bindings as we were leaving. Setting him free with that misinformation will get Sebastian Stott out of the way. We can't have the old man meddling, not today. So sit back, relax. This will all be over soon."

CHAPTER EIGHTEEN

BLUE

Jogging along Winding Way, Nate went over his plan in his mind. It had not taken him long to determine that soliciting help from Mr. Stott was his best option. Nate had betrayed the old magician by turning to John Dart, but Mr. Stott still didn't want Mrs. White to get the treasure, and he had a vehicle. So, hopefully, after Nate brought him up to speed, all would be forgiven and they could chase down Gary Haag together. Even if it meant Mr. Stott ended up drinking water from the Fountain of Youth, that would be preferable to empowering Mrs. White. Unfortunately, Nate had left the cell phone in the Buick, or he could simply have telephoned.

Nate had considered using a Moon Rock to reach Mr. Stott's house faster, but in broad daylight he felt he would be too conspicuous. Not everyone in town was consuming white fudge. Besides, leaping with a Moon Rock wasn't that much faster than running. Thankfully, most of the way to Mr. Stott's place was downhill.

Sucking on the Ironhide, trotting under the hot sun, Nate was bulletproof, but he was sweaty. He panted and rubbed the stitch in his side, wishing for a stick of Summer's gum.

Eventually Nate diverged from Winding Way into Mr. Stott's neighborhood. He noticed some kids around his age walking home from school, and felt a little jealous. He longed to be equally oblivious to magic candy and magicians and engineered apprentices. Of course, all he had to do was go home and devour a box of white fudge!

Which was not an option. He had to save Trevor. He had to save Summer and John. At least he had to try. Before long somebody would probably have to save him. He wondered if Pigeon needed to be saved.

Nate slowed to a walk for a block, then picked up the pace again. He turned onto Limerick Court, sprinting past the last few houses. His chest was heaving when he reached Mr. Stott's house.

Mr. Stott opened the door before he knocked. "Come in," he said.

"I'm glad you're home," Nate panted, entering. "I was worried you might be off driving your route."

"I stuck around, hoping to hear from you," Mr. Stott said, fingering one of the black stripes in his beard. "I tried to contact you this morning, but the phone was off."

"I lost the phone," Nate said. "I lost a lot of things. We had the *Stargazer,* but Mrs. White recruited bullies from our school who tailed us to the library. We got the ship past them, and I was running it here using Peak Performance gum, but as you know, I saw the fat guy full of jelly waiting near your house in ambush. His name is Mauricio. So I took the ship home, planning to bring it here in the morning, but the wooden Indian from the candy shop came and stole it."

"I'm sorry to hear that," Mr. Stott said, his gaze steady.

"It gets worse. This guy named John Dart was my substitute teacher today."

The name *John Dart* gave Mr. Stott a start. "John Dart? Here in town?"

"He told us you guys are after a drink from the Fountain of Youth and that he had to stop you. He seemed honest, and filled in a lot of blanks, so we decided to help him. He kidnapped Eric, one of the bullies, and found out that the treasure room is under Mt. Diablo Elementary."

"Under the school?" Mr. Stott said. "Two Haags work at your school! One of them, Gary, is from the line that has been here in town since the old days. He was on my short list of suspects."

"Gary was the guy," Nate confirmed. "Summer and I went to his house with John to pick him up, but Mauricio and the dude with the birthmark beat us there. I barely got away, and they captured John and Summer. They missed nabbing Gary, but they know where he was going. Have you heard of Haags named Burt and Starla?"

Mr. Stott nodded. "They live a ways outside of town. We better get going. Run and say hello to the Flatman, and I'll meet you in the garage." He shook his keys and walked toward the door in his kitchen.

Nate hurried down the hall and peeked into the Flatman's room, feeling unsure what to say to the odd creature. "Hi, Flatman. Mr. Stott is taking me in his truck to chase some guy. I'll see you soon."

The Flatman's fins fluttered.

Nate ran to the garage, joining Mr. Stott in the truck. Mr. Stott hit the gas, leaving the garage door open as they rumbled onto Limerick Court.

"The Flatman told me you were coming and that you would need a ride," Mr. Stott said. "That's why I was ready and waiting."

"I just told him you were taking me in your truck," Nate said. "Which is probably what he saw."

"The birthmark guy is powerful," Nate warned. "John called him a Fuse. He made the grass turn huge and tangle us up."

"Nobody wants to contend with a Fuse," Mr. Stott said. "But Belinda has the map and knows where to find the key. This could be our last opportunity to derail her."

"I'm with you," Nate said. "This might be my only chance to save my friends."

"Burt and Starla live off the beaten path," Mr. Stott said. "Do you have much candy left?"

"A little," Nate said. "My second-to-last Ironhide faded to nothing while we were talking in your house. I have one left. They've been lifesavers."

"I wish I had more candy to offer you," Mr. Stott said. "Our best chance will be to beat Mrs. White's thugs to Burt and Starla's."

"We might make it," Nate said. "I came straight to you. It seemed like the others were taking John and Summer back to the candy shop."

"Let's hope you're right."

They drove out of town on Main Street, and then turned on Gold Coast Drive. The road wove among golden-brown hills and oak-filled valleys. Sprigs of wildflowers blossomed among the brush. Nate was impressed that on some stretches, Mr. Stott got the old truck up to over sixty miles per hour.

About ten minutes into the drive, a dirt road marked Orchard Lane branched off from Gold Coast Drive. "This is our last turn," Mr. Stott said. At first, the dirt road was flat and drivable, but the further they meandered into the hills, the more rutted the road became, and soon they were jouncing along at fifteen miles per hour.

"We getting close?" Nate asked.

Mr. Stott glanced at his odometer. "A few more miles," he said.

Nate repeatedly checked the big side mirrors, watching the empty road behind them, worried that their enemies could overtake them at any moment. The ice cream truck often slowed to less than ten miles per hour.

They were traversing a field where an old wooden bridge spanned a dry creekbed. Tall golden brush thrived everywhere, along with old oaks and a few huge bushes.

Off to one side of the road, a black Hummer pulled out of hiding from behind a screen of shrubs.

"Oh, no," Mr. Stott said.

The Hummer raced toward them, gaining speed as it bounced through the brush. Mr. Stott tried to accelerate, but the road was particularly rutted, and he almost overturned the top-heavy truck. Rocks scraped against the undercarriage. "What do we do?" Nate asked.

"Ironhide," Mr. Stott said.

Nate fished out his last Ironhide and put it in his mouth. It became evident that the Hummer meant to broadside them. Mr. Stott swerved off the road and accelerated, trying to avoid the collision, but the Hummer rammed into the side of the Candy Wagon near the rear. The truck spun and flipped upside down. Dreamlike and slow after the initial jolt, the inverted ice cream truck rocked and slammed down on its side.

Nate felt the sensation of rolling and whipping around violently, but his seatbelt held him in place and he experienced no pain. Mr. Stott also had his seatbelt on, but blood trickled down his forehead from where he had bashed the side window. The old magician looked dazed.

The Hummer raced off, spewing up dust on the dirt road. The impact had to have damaged it, but Nate could see only the back of the vehicle as he stared at it sideways through the starred glass of the front windshield. The passenger window was facing the sky. Mr. Stott's side of the truck was against the ground.

"Drove into a trap," Mr. Stott mumbled. He closed his eyes and pressed his fingers together, grunting. "There. Changed the gasoline . . . into water. So we won't explode."

"Are you okay?" Nate asked.

"Could have used an Ironhide," he smiled. "Not that it would have reinforced these old bones. I'm unwell."

"Can I do something?" Nate said.

"If I leave the vehicle, I'll die," Mr. Stott said. "My age will catch up with me. Let's see." He closed his eyes and pressed his fingers together again. Blood drizzled down into his beard. He bared his teeth, groaning, and suddenly changed into a coyote, a transition that occurred in a blink.

"Mr. Stott?" Nate asked.

"That's a bit more comfortable," the coyote said in Mr. Stott's voice. "I may be able to travel temporarily like this if it becomes life or death. But I can't change myself back. I'll require assistance. If I leave the truck in this state, in time my awareness will depart and I'll grow feral."

"What do I do?" Nate asked.

"I'd say this qualifies as a dire situation," the coyote said.

"The Grains of Time?"

"Might as well give it a shot. Now or never."

"You said blue first, then red, then yellow?"

"In rapid succession," the coyote said. "Past, future, and present."

"How long will I have?" Nate asked. "It won't do much good to go back in time if I'm stuck in a field in the middle of nowhere!"

"You'll go back a week or two for about an hour, forward a day or two for about an hour, and then you'll have about an hour with an advantage in the present," Mr. Stott said. "Your body won't travel through time. Nobody knows how to send matter across that gulf. But we can send a mind. You will find yourself occupying a vacant mind in the past, and a vacant mind in the future. The minds you occupy will have no idea you were there, no memory of what you did."

"Will it be somebody nearby?" Nate asked.

"The nearest ideal candidate," Mr. Stott said. "Colson remains the closest town. You'll probably end up there. Use your minutes wisely."

"What should I do?" Nate asked.

"All you can. You'll find you can't change the past—at least, I've never heard of anyone succeeding. Everything you do ends up being something that already happened. You'll see."

"So I can't do anything?"

"You can do a lot. Just because it already happened doesn't mean what you accomplished didn't matter. I'll confuse you more if I keep talking. Go back and do all you can in the time you have."

"What about the future?" Nate asked.

"You can change the future, but not while you're there. None of it has happened yet, you'll be visiting a possibility. Scour the future for information. The future you will experience is the future without you in it. You see, your mind travels into the future, leaving your body vacant, meaning you weren't a participant in how things turned out. Once you return to the present, you can try to make things work out differently. Never an easy task."

"What advantage will I have in the present?" Nate asked.

"Three selves," the Stott coyote said. "You'll return to this location, and for an hour or so, you will manifest as three people. All of them will be equally you. Everything will be copied, even your clothes and the items you carry. When time runs out, however far apart your three selves have traveled, you'll be drawn back together at a central point. You won't materialize in solid rock or anything, or up in the air, but the spell will reunite you as close as possible to the midpoint of the space separating the three selves."

"You're frying my brain," Nate said. "When time runs out, all my selves will teleport back to a central spot and I'll be one person again?"

"Yes, but you can't take anything with you that you didn't have when you split into three," Mr. Stott said. "I'll explain more when the time comes. For now, you better get going."

"Okay," Nate said, unscrewing the top of the hourglass.

"You'll want to spit out your Ironhide," the coyote cautioned. "Never a good idea to mix candy. Sometimes it's harmless, but it can be lethal."

Nate removed the Ironhide from his mouth. "I can't save it? It's my last one."

"Doesn't work that way. Taking it out undoes the spell. Make this count."

Nate tossed aside the Ironhide and raised the hourglass. "Down the hatch." He dumped the blue sand into his mouth. Instantly he felt like the truck was spinning, and he swooned. He experienced a brief sensation of floating, and then soared.

The next thing Nate knew, he was lying in an alley, opening his eyes. It was daytime. He sat up. His clothes were dirty and stank. He had a foul taste in his mouth. Rubbing his jaw, he found it stubbly, a sensation he had never experienced. He was a grown man!

Nate stood up, much taller than he had ever been. He felt unsteady, as if the wooziness from the blue sand were persisting. His head throbbed.

Stumbling out of the alley, Nate found himself next to the bar and grill on Main Street. The sun seemed brighter than usual. He stepped into the eatery.

"What time is it?" Nate called. He sounded like a grown-up!

"Almost three," a voice called back.

"What day?"

The voice chuckled. "Thursday."

"I mean what date?"

"September thirteenth."

Nate stepped out of the bar. Almost three on a school day. He should be walking home down Greenway! That wasn't far!

Nate rushed along Main, his head hurting, his equilibrium off. He pushed onward, determined to overcome the uncomfortable aftereffects of time travel. He cut down a side street. Looking up ahead, he saw several kids walking along Greenway, including a familiar foursome.

"Summer, Trevor, Pidge, Nate! Hold up! You have to listen to me."

His friends and his past self looked startled, and started murmuring to each other. Nate continued toward them, trying to ignore the pounding in his head.

"Stay away from Sweet Tooth," Nate warned, stumbling slightly. "You can't trust Mrs. White. She's dangerous. You can't trust anyone!"

"That's close enough," his past self demanded.

Nate halted. Although the scene was becoming eerily familiar, he persisted. "You have to let me explain. Nate, it's me. I'm you! I'm from the future!"

"Right," his past self said. "You don't look anything like me. How do you know my name?"

Mr. Stott had warned him that he would not be able to change the past. He had explained that everything he did would be something that had already happened. Which meant that trying to convince his friends he was a time traveler would be a dead end. He had already failed! With less than an hour to burn, he had to make the most of his time.

"I have no time," Nate said, plunging his hands into his wild hair. He looked at his past self. "What was I thinking? I forgot that you weren't going to believe me. I guess you guys don't want to come with me so I can fill you in on some things?"

"Sorry, we're not going anywhere with you," Summer said. It felt strange having her look at him coldly, like a dangerous stranger. It felt strange being so much taller than his friends. It felt strange looking down on himself from the perspective of another person.

"This guy harassing you?" the crossing guard called, approaching from down the street.

"I think he's drunk," Pigeon said.

Nate had a clear memory of this moment, thinking what a psycho the stranger must be, thinking how there was no way he would ever look like that slovenly bum. He remembered that the crossing guard had considered calling the police.

Nate threw up his hands, backing away. "No problem here, sorry to bother you kids." The stranger had predicted something that would happen. What had he said? Oh, yeah. "Keep in mind, robbing graves isn't right. I have things to do."

Nate dashed away down Greenway, in the same direction the homeless stranger had run. What had been the man's destination? How could he best use his time in the past? He could confront Mrs. White, but her henchmen were there and could certainly handle him, especially if he were alone, unarmed, and without candy. Besides, if he had succeeded doing something to Mrs. White, it would have already happened, right?

He considered his needs in the present. He was stranded in a field miles from town, with no houses around. If he was going to make a difference in the present, he needed a way back into town.

And suddenly it was clear what he needed to do. Of course! It was something he had already done. He just hoped it was something he had succeeded in doing. He would have to hurry.

Nate ran down a side street. He needed to double back, cross Main, and get into his neighborhood. But he couldn't use Greenway or he would spook the crossing guard and his past self.

He dashed along the nearest street that paralleled Greenway, raced across Main, and entered Summer's neighborhood. Racing through the middle-class development, he reached the creek. The rainstorm had not happened yet, so it was pretty low. He crossed the stream at a narrow point, managing to hop on rocks and avoid dousing his shoes.

Panting, Nate charged up the slope to the jogging path and trotted to Monroe Circle. He was getting so sweaty and nauseated that he walked up Monroe to his house. Pausing on the sidewalk, he stared at the front door. He knew just where his mom kept the keys, on the hook in the entry hall.

Still he hesitated. He remembered how this had traumatized his mom, and hated the thought of frightening her, but this was an emergency, and he knew the Explorer could handle the terrain where the ice cream truck was stranded. The SUV was an automatic, his dad had let him drive it short distances a couple of times, and he knew he could successfully steal it on short notice. He needed to do it! In fact, he felt certain that, in a sense, he already had.

Nate walked up to his front door and found it unlocked. Easing the door open, he heard his mom in the kitchen using the sink. He quietly closed the door and took the Explorer keys from the hook. He slunk over to the door to the garage and passed through it silently.

Sliding into the driver's seat, Nate rubbed his eyes. They felt itchy and sore back behind the eyeballs. In the rearview mirror he saw that they were bloodshot. He found it very unsettling to look in a mirror and see somebody else staring back.

He started the engine and clicked the garage-door opener at the same time. He gently pressed on the accelerator as the door went up. The engine revved but the Explorer did not move. He was still in park. He tried to shift to reverse, but the gear stick would not move. He pressed down the brake, and that did the trick. Shifting into reverse, he backed out of the garage, clicking the button to close the door behind him.

Switching into drive, Nate accelerated up Monroe and turned toward Mayflower. It was nice that he could comfortably reach the pedals. In fact, the seat was a little too close to the steering wheel, so he backed it up a few inches.

Now that he was under way, driving felt easier, although he didn't brake soon enough at Mayflower and ended up screeching several yards past the stop sign. He tried to use the turn signal and instead switched on the windshield wipers.

The stop sign at Main was approaching. He considered running it as John Dart had, but chickened out. It proved to be fortunate that he had hesitated, since he would have plowed into the side of a school bus. After a car honked to inform him it was his turn, Nate pulled out onto Main.

Cruising down the street, Nate found it troublesome to maintain a constant speed—he pushed the accelerator either too hard or too softly. Through experimentation he got better. By the time he turned onto Gold Coast Drive, he was feeling confident. He even used his blinker correctly!

The hills looked browner and drier than when he had driven this way with Mr. Stott. He saw no wildflowers. That rain had really freshened up the fields. The speed limit was 55, and he tried not to go over. At this point, getting pulled over for speeding would prove disastrous.

He watched for Orchard Lane, remembering that the road had been small and the sign not particularly obvious. He still felt a little unstable, and his head ached, but he managed to keep the wheel steady. He saw Orchard coming, put on his blinker, and turned.

The dirt road seemed to be in better repair than when he had traveled it with Mr. Stott. It was hard to be sure whether that was truly the case, or if the Explorer just handled the ruts a lot easier than the Candy Wagon had. He had lost all track of time, and began to worry he might skip back to the present at any moment.

Finally he reached the area where the ice cream truck had been ambushed. He saw the oak trees, the bushes, the dry creek with the little bridge. He drove through the dry brush on the opposite side of the road from where the Hummer had been hiding, heading for some voluminous bushes behind a bent oak tree.

Coming around to the back of the bushes, he found he could pull the Explorer into them some distance, screening the vehicle from view on three sides. He got out and locked the doors. The ground was firm and on a slight slope, so he hoped it would be a good place for the deserted Explorer to weather the rains.

Nate stuffed the keys a short ways into the tailpipe and ran off. With his remaining time, he wanted to put some distance between himself and the Explorer, so the man he was inhabiting would not discover the SUV when he regained his senses.

Feeling rested after the drive, he started out at an ambitious sprint, feeling the texture of the dirt road through the thin soles of his shoes. Soon Nate flagged to a brisk walk, throbbing pain hammering inside his forehead. He continued forward in spite of his weariness and discomfort.

Nate was well out of sight of where he had hidden the SUV when the fringes of his vision began to darken. He became so dizzy that he had to sit down. The darkness encroached from all sides until it seemed like he was peering at the world through a narrow tube.

The world spun and he swooned, soaring up into nothingness.

CHAPTER NINETEEN

RED

Nate came to himself seated in the overturned ice cream truck. "I'm back," he said to the coyote. "The headache is gone—what a relief!"

"To me it seemed you never left," the coyote said. "It happened in a twinkling. Hurry, use the red sand."

Nate unscrewed the other end of the hourglass. "I stashed a car nearby," Nate reported.

"Good thinking."

"Hope it's still there. Off I go!" He poured the sand into his mouth, swooned, and soared.

* * * * *

Nate opened his eyes. He was lying on a couch in front of a television, head cushioned on a decorative pillow. On the TV a judge was dispensing advice to a woman with poofy red hair, who was nodding reluctantly.

Nate sat up. His arms were pudgy and he had long nails. He could feel rolls of fat on his waist and chest. He was a woman!

Hustling to the kitchen, he found a clock. Instead of numbers, it had the hours represented by different species of bird. According to the clock, it was about blue jay past goldfinch. Which meant 3:25. Daylight flooded in through the open blinds, throwing shadow stripes on the kitchen floor, so he knew it was afternoon.

Nate noticed a set of keys on the counter. He grabbed them and headed for the door, pausing to take a look at himself in the bathroom mirror. His brown hair was tied up in a scarf. The face was chubby and friendly, a woman in her forties wearing too much makeup.

One of the keys was electronic. Scuttling out the door, Nate tapped the unlock button twice. He heard the locks click inside the silver Sentra parked in the driveway. Turning in a circle, Nate recognized the neighborhood—he wasn't far from the cemetery.

Nate tugged open the door of the car and got behind the wheel. Relieved that the car was an automatic, he started it up and backed out of the driveway. Mr. Stott had said the red sand would take him one or two days into the future. Whichever it was, at this time of day, his best bet would be Pigeon's house. Judging from the phone call before the ambush at Gary Haag's, Pigeon was his one friend who had not yet been captured. Hopefully that was still true.

Driving cautiously, Nate found the streets abnormally empty. He wound his way down to Mayflower and followed it to the Presidential Estates. Turning down Monroe, he parked alongside the curb where Pigeon lived.

He got out of the car and walked up to the door, fascinated by the feel of his softer, flabbier body. Nate rang the doorbell, waited, and rang it again. An old man opened the door who looked so much like Pigeon that Nate almost laughed. It had to be his grandfather, or maybe even great-grandfather.

"Can I help you?" the old man asked in a frail voice.

"I'm looking for Pigeon?" Nate said. His own voice surprised him. It was so feminine! He would have to get sprayed for cooties when he got back to normal.

The old man looked him up and down. "Do you know him?"

"Yes, this is really important."

The old man stared at Nate suspiciously. "How do you know him?"

"He's a really good friend of my son," Nate tried.

"What friend?"

"Nate Sutter."

The old man shook his head. "You're not Nate's mom. What is this? Who are you really?"

"Who are *you?*" Nate countered. "Pigeon never mentioned he had a grandpa living with him. How do you even know what Nate's mom looks like?"

"Okay. Try this on for size. I'm Pigeon, and I've never met you."

"Pigeon?" Nate said. "How far into the future did I go?"

"What are you talking about?"

"Pigeon, it's me, Nate Sutter. Mr. Stott helped me travel into the future and I ended up in this body."

Pigeon grinned. "No way. Prove it. What's the name of our club?"

"The Blue Falcons."

"What does Denny call you?"

"Dirt Face."

The grin broadened. "Wow, Nate, good to see you."

"What year is it?" Nate asked, wondering why none of the cars or houses looked futuristic.

"I saw you yesterday," Pigeon said. "I was aged by magic. Come in."

Nate entered Pigeon's house and found a seat on a sofa. Pigeon sat down carefully in an armchair. "What happened with Mrs. White?" Nate asked.

"She did it," Pigeon said. "She drank from the Fountain of Youth. I tried to stop her but I blew it."

"Pidge, you have to tell me everything you know. I'm only here for a little while, then I'll go back to yesterday. We might still be able to stop her."

"That would be great," Pigeon said. "Nate, it's terrible. She's turned into a little tyrant. Everyone who has been eating the white fudge is under her spell. Like the Sweet Teeth, but worse—they do whatever she says. My parents are actually at a special meeting down at the candy shop right now. She took over the town."

"How old did she end up?" Nate asked.

"She looks about our age. The age we were, I mean. Ten or eleven."

"How'd she do it?" Nate asked.

Pigeon settled back into the chair. "Where should I start? Kyle wasn't at school with Denny and Eric yesterday because he was inside the surgeon doll, the same one you used at the museum. I learned the whole story from him after I was caught. He snuck into our classroom and crawled into your backpack while you were speaking with Mr. Dart. That was why we saw Denny outside the window. Then at the Paradise Inn, Kyle heard we were looking for Haags, so he wanted to get back to Mrs. White with that info. When he heard John was going to drop me at the school, he managed to sneak from your backpack into mine. His goal was to bail out and find Denny, but before he could, I brought him with me into Gary Haag's office.

"When I talked to Gary, it became clear he was the guy with the key. Gary almost killed me for finding out his secret, but instead tied me up in his office. Kyle was still in my backpack, so he heard everything. Once Gary left, Kyle came out of the backpack and unplugged the phone. That was how I lost you when we were speaking. Then Kyle wriggled under the door and ran off.

"Turns out Kyle went straight to Denny, who called Mrs. White, who blew into Kyle's eye to break the connection with the doll. Kyle was actually at the candy shop, under her supervision. When he arose from his trance, Kyle told Mrs. White what he had heard, including who Gary was and where Eric and Wyatt were being held."

"Is Wyatt the Fuse?" Nate asked.

"Right," Pigeon said. "And the jelly man is named Mauricio. Mrs. White telephoned Mauricio, who rescued Eric and Wyatt, then picked up Denny. Miss Perlman, Denny's teacher, used to date Gary, so Denny got his address from her. They had just barely captured Gary and prepared their trap when you guys arrived."

"So they totally set me up," Nate groaned. "They knew they didn't knock me out. They let me get away! They said Gary had escaped to his relatives who lived outside of town. They knew I'd drag Mr. Stott out to the middle of nowhere. The perfect place for an ambush."

"Pretty much," Pigeon agreed.

"Then what?" Nate asked.

"Some lunch ladies found me. I plugged in the phone and called as quickly as I could, but I was too late. I knew that the treasure was at the school, and that Mrs. White probably had the key, so I went home for reinforcements. I gave my dog, Diego, some Brain Feed. We'd been having some really good talks, so I knew I could count on him. We returned to Mt. Diablo and spied.

"Mauricio arrived just after I got there. He had Denny, Eric, and Kyle with him. I found out later that they had used the key to blackmail Gary into telling them where the treasure room was hidden. See, the fate of the key is connected to everybody in Gary's family. For example, if they held the key underwater long enough, everyone in his family would drown, which Mrs. White knew, because Kyle overheard Gary telling me about it. Gary wasn't sure what would happen if somebody outside his family opened the door. He ended up spilling his guts, since it was his only hope to maybe save his family.

"Mauricio went straight to the cafeteria. Under some filing cabinets in Gary's office was a hatch that led down to a secret basement. After waiting for a while, I tried to follow them, but Wyatt, the Fuse, captured me and Diego with a couple of giant black widow spiders. Not long after, one of the spiders bit Diego and killed him." Here Pigeon had to pause, lower lip quivering.

"I'm sorry, Pigeon. I'll try to save Diego, too."

Pigeon nodded. He gave a small grin. Nate could tell that the grin was the best response he could muster without crying. He waited for Pigeon to compose himself, and then asked, "Where exactly did you get caught?"

Pigeon drew a shaky breath. "The Fuse was hiding in the cafeteria, back where they prepare the food."

"How did Wyatt get there?"

"I'm not sure," Pigeon said. "I didn't see him arrive with the others. He probably came separately. Might have been before, might have been after."

"Okay, I'll do all I can to prevent it from happening."

Pigeon nodded. "Anyway, Wyatt marched me down the hatch after them. He had used his powers earlier to knock down a wall. Beyond the wall was a tunnel that led to a door. Kyle had unlocked the door. Turning the key had transformed him into an old man. Through the door was a room. The water from the Fountain of Youth was inside a jeweled goblet resting on a pedestal. Mauricio entered the room to retrieve it and dropped dead. He changed into an old skeleton. They had suspected that a curse would fall on whoever turned the key, but had no idea that an aging curse transformed anyone who entered the room. Denny convinced Eric to go in, but he became an old man who couldn't walk, and collapsed on the floor.

"That was when I showed up with Wyatt. They made me go in after the goblet. That's how I got so old. I aged as soon as I entered the room, but at least I could still walk. When they sent me into the room, Diego went berserk. His Brain Feed had run out, but he was still trying to protect me. That was when one of the giant spiders bit him." Pigeon paused, took a shuddering breath, and wiped his nose with his sleeve.

"I'm so sorry," Nate said. "Remember, we'll try to prevent any of this from happening."

Pigeon nodded. "Wyatt worked his magic on the stem of a rose and it coiled around my neck. I could feel the thorns pricking me. He told me that if I tried to drink the water he would kill me instantly. I knew he could keep his word before I drank it, so I just dumped it out. The problem was, every time you dumped it out, the goblet was full again. The only way to drain it was to drink it. Afterwards it made sense—I mean, if there wasn't some sort of magic to prevent the water from spilling or evaporating, it would have been gone a long time ago."

"So they ended up with the water," Nate said.

"Yep," Pigeon said. "And I almost got strangled for dumping out the goblet, until they saw that it was spill-proof. I helped Eric out of the room, and Wyatt carried him to the car. We all drove back to the candy shop, where they were holding John, Summer, and Gary. We all got to watch Mrs. White turn into a ten-year-old. She was actually pretty cute."

"Then what?" Nate asked.

"Mrs. White asked John to swear loyalty to her and eat the fudge," Pigeon said. "He wouldn't, so she had Wyatt kill him. I didn't watch. Then she gave Summer the same offer. Summer accepted. I don't blame her. It was unbelievably scary. After eating the fudge, Summer was like a robot. She did whatever Mrs. White told her."

"And Gary?"

"Opening the door apparently broke the curse on his family," Pigeon said. "He was a free man for about twenty minutes, until he ate the fudge."

"What about you?" Nate asked.

"Mrs. White thanked me for the water and said that I had done enough. She didn't make me eat the fudge. She didn't seem to think I could cause any trouble, since I was so old. And she would have been right, except that you came forward in time and found me. She has become so powerful, I doubt anybody could stop her at this point. I don't think she considered that somebody might be able to go back and stop her before she was invulnerable. But here you are. And here I am."

"Anything else?" Nate asked.

Pigeon shrugged. "I talked to Kyle afterwards. He was old too, and Mrs. White didn't make him young, she just dismissed us. Denny was mad she didn't heal Eric and Kyle, so she made him eat white fudge. Like with me, she didn't make Kyle eat the fudge. She just sent him away. Kyle was bitter, and we ended up having our first good talk, a couple of eighty-year-old kids. He filled me in on how everything had happened from his point of view, and I explained some of the details he had missed."

"What about Trevor?" Nate asked.

"Still in the mirrors," Pigeon said. "He has come to my mirror a few times. I told him the gist of what happened. He keeps hoping you'll show up back at your place."

"Is there anything else I should know?" Nate asked. "Anything else that might be useful? We get a second shot at this. If it goes right, we can make it all end differently."

"Would that mean I'd cease to exist?" Pigeon asked pensively. "This me, I mean?"

"Sort of. Not really. Just this last day will cease to exist. Hopefully we can fix it so you'll never end up old."

"Then what happens to this me?"

"This you will never happen," Nate said. "This you isn't real yet. This you is just a possibility. This is the you without my help."

"I hope you can do it," Pigeon said. "I'd love to erase this past day. Do you have any Ironhides left?"

"No, and just one dose of Shock Bits."

"We'll think of something," Pigeon said. "Try to watch out for Diego."

"I'll do my best," Nate said.

"Is it weird being a girl?"

"Not as weird as I would have imagined," Nate said. "I almost forget if I'm not talking. Is it weird being old?"

"Not too bad," Pigeon said. "You have to move around more carefully."

"What time is it?" Nate asked.

Pigeon got up and looked at a clock in the other room. "Just after four."

"I still may be able to find out more," Nate said. "Thanks. You can't think of anything else?"

"You know all I know."

"See you yesterday."

"I hope so."

Nate rushed to the door and got back into the Sentra. Where to next? His mind was whirling with the information Pigeon had shared. John was dead! Summer was a mindless fudge zombie! Mrs. White had become as powerful as everyone had feared. Now that Nate knew how it had happened, he wished he could think of an obvious way to prevent it.

Driving out of the Presidential Estates, he was struck with a thought. Since he now realized how crucial it was, maybe he should visit the Flatman and plant the idea of giving the Grains of Time to his past self. The thought sparked an internal debate. On one hand, he already had the Grains of Time, so what could it matter to plant the idea? On the other hand, here he was with an opportunity to suggest the idea—shouldn't he do it just to be safe?

Without another more urgent destination in mind, Nate drove to Limerick Court. He got out of his car, rang the doorbell twice, said,

"Archmus, I am a friend indeed," then rang the doorbell again. He heard the locks inside the door clicking.

Pushing open the front door, Nate entered the quiet house. He passed down the hall to the room where the Flatman lived, opened the door, and approached the basin where the fleshy pancake floated, fins curling languidly.

"Hi, Flatman," Nate said. "You may not recognize me, but I'm Nate. I've been missing ever since Mr. Stott took me to find Gary yesterday. I take it Mr. Stott hasn't been back."

The larger eye blinked. One of the slits puckered.

"I'll take that as a yes," Nate said. He glanced around, saw a small can of fish flakes, and shook several into the bowl as he talked. "Look, if you want to save Mr. Stott, and all of us, you have to tell him to give Nate the Grains of Time. Nate. I'm actually a fifth grader. And a boy. Anyhow, the Grains of Time are how I'm here now. Things are a mess. We were ambushed. If Mr. Stott hadn't given me the sand, we'd already be sunk. I had the Grains of Time because you told him. So be sure to tell him. In the past. Got it?"

The eye blinked.

"Great. In this future, Mrs. White ended up drinking from the Fountain of Youth. Do you have any advice on how to stop her?"

The eye blinked twice.

"Thought I'd ask," Nate said. "I'd better be going. I'll be traveling back to the present to fix things soon. You sit tight."

On his way out, Nate saw that it was 4:15. He trotted out to the Sentra. With only a few minutes left, he decided to check out the candy shop, see if that meeting was still in progress.

He drove down Greenway, but had to pull over and park before he reached Main. The intersection was thronged with fudge fanatics. Male and female, black and white, young, old, and middle-aged.

Nate got out of the car and joined the crowd. They were all pressing toward the Sweet Tooth Ice Cream and Candy Shoppe, trying to get nearer. Messages came percolating through the multitude, repeated from person to person.

"Linda said Tammy Speckler will be in charge of everyone who lives in Redwood Homes."

"Linda said the next wave of fudge will be parceled out on Saturday!"

"Linda said if we work together we can accomplish anything."

After hanging around at the edge of the mob for a few minutes, Nate gathered that they were gearing up to widen the distribution of white fudge to neighboring communities, with team leaders and awards for those who dispensed the most. The crowd seemed zealous to hear and obey Linda's commands.

"I have an important message for Linda!" Nate cried in a strident voice.

His words flowed forward through the crowd. People craned to get a look at him as his words were repeated all the way to the front. The crowd parted around him, allowing him to walk into the store. He started to feel a little woozy, the same sensation that had preceded his departure from the past.

A young girl stood on the counter wearing a red dress and a ruffled white apron. A pink satin patch covered one eye. She wore white ribbons in her auburn hair, and had a light spray of freckles across her nose and cheeks. Pigeon was right—even with the patch, she was pretty cute.

"I hear you bring a message," she said imperiously as Nate walked down the impromptu aisle.

Nate felt dizzy. He wanted to sit down. Instead, he glared at the little girl standing on the counter. "Belinda, enjoy this now, because none of it is ever going to happen."

The girl frowned. "I'm Linda," she said. "Who are you?"

"Somebody willing to do anything to prevent all of this." Nate blinked several times. Blackness was creeping in from all directions.

"Too late," the girl said, smirking. "Care for some fudge?"

"See you yesterday," Nate said, looking at her through a tunnel.

The little girl's eyes narrowed, and then widened. "You!" he heard her say as he fell backwards into darkness. He began to soar, and then slowed, feeling compressed, like he was folding in on himself. He had not experienced this uncomfortable sensation previously. Without form, Nate struggled. With a final burst of exertion that he could not explain, he was soaring again, leaving everything behind, dwindling into nothing.

CHAPTER TWENTY

YELLOW

"I should have warned you," said the coyote embodiment of Mr. Stott. "You went to see Belinda, didn't you?"

Nate nodded, back in the Candy Wagon, feeling unexpectedly weary. He wiped drool from his lips. "She won," he mumbled. "She was young. She had control over everybody who had eaten the fudge."

"You almost didn't make it back," the coyote said. "Belinda must not have realized who you were until the last moment; otherwise you wouldn't be here. Having regained her youth, she had become the most powerful magician in history. Puissant enough to override any enchantment of mine. I should have forewarned you to avoid her. I did what I could to pull from this end. You were thrashing around and foaming at the mouth."

"Can she still get to us?" Nate asked.

"You were visiting a possibility," the coyote said. "Now that you're back, the possibility does not yet exist. You should be safe for the moment. Just make sure you stop her."

"Now I have to eat the yellow," Nate said.

"Right. Did you learn what you needed?"

"I don't know. I hope so. I know how Mrs. White succeeded. I'm still working out the details of how to prevent everything from happening the same. I'm not sure if this is something I can do, Mr. Stott."

"You have to try," the coyote said. "You've come this far, Nate. At least you have a chance of stopping her. You've already done better than most people would have. Try to stay calm. During the drive back into town you'll have to try to piece everything together and come up with a plan."

"We'll see," Nate said, shaking his head. "The magic guarding the water from the Fountain of Youth makes people age. Pigeon looked like he was in his eighties. If that happens again, could he be cured?"

"Aging due to a spell is different from natural aging," the coyote said. "It would be beyond my capabilities, but I know that some types of aging magic can be reversed."

"I'll try to keep it from happening in the first place," Nate said.

"You need to eat the yellow sand promptly, but let me explain a thing or two first," the coyote said. "This magic does not produce clones. It will divide you into three linked manifestations of the same individual. If one gets hurt, they all suffer the same injury, because they are the same person. If one uses magic candy, they will all exhibit the effects. If one self uses a certain candy while another self ingests a different treat, you risk the side effects of mixing magic."

"Will my candy be linked also?" Nate asked.

"Yes, the same way you are," the coyote said. "Everything the yellow sand splits into three is connected. You will not triple your candy supply. If one of your selves eats a particular candy, the corresponding candy will vanish from the other two selves as it is chewed and digested. If you use up the magic of a candy and spit it out, the other two corresponding candies will become useless."

"And you said before that I can't keep anything I find, because only linked items will teleport with me when my selves reunite," Nate said.

"I think you've got the idea," the coyote said. "Hurry and finish the sand. You may want to go outside—it will get cramped in here with two more of you."

Nate held up the hourglass, examining the sphere of yellow sand trapped in the central chamber. "Do I break the glass to get it out?"

"We merged the yellow sand into a solid lump to keep the rest of the sand separate. You'll find that the glass is edible—just chew it all up and swallow. Nate, this is a tough assignment. Good luck."

"Thanks," Nate said. "I'll do my best."

With the Candy Wagon on its side, the passenger door was facing the sky. Hanging the hourglass chain back around his neck, Nate unclipped his seatbelt, stood on the side of his seat, and pushed the door open. He boosted himself up onto the side of the truck, surprised by how far away the brushy ground looked.

Nate crouched and dropped into the brush, rolling when he struck the dirt to help break the fall. The glass portion of the hourglass did not feel edible, but, trusting Mr. Stott, Nate put it in his mouth and chewed it up. The glass was sugary, like fragile rock candy. The sourness of the yellow sand made his mouth pucker.

As Nate swallowed, he realized that he was staring at two other exact replicas of himself who were also swallowing. In unison, the three Nates raised a hand, waved, and said, "Hi."

They laughed at the simultaneous action, and then all together said, "It's going to be fun working with such studly guys."

Again the three Nates laughed. "Seriously," they said. "We better get going."

The three Nates all ran toward the bushes where they had hidden the Explorer. "I hope it's still there," they all said.

"We need to stop speaking all at once," they complained, chuckling at how they couldn't get out of sync. "Great minds think alike," they muttered.

Racing around to the back of the bushes, they found the Explorer parked where they had left it. The tires had sunk into the ground a little, but otherwise the vehicle looked fine. They crouched together. The nearest Nate poked a finger into the tailpipe and retrieved the keys.

"We need to figure out a way to tell ourselves apart," they all said. "How about the Nate holding the keys is number one? Okay, sounds good."

"You'll be Two," One said, pointing. "And you'll be Three. Remember, we're all the same guy. We need to trust that about each other as we split up." Nate thumbed the unlock button twice. "I'll drive."

"Shotgun," the other two Nates called simultaneously.

"Two, you take shotgun," One said.

They loaded into the SUV, and One started the engine. "The pedals are a lot harder to reach," One said, adjusting the seat as much as possible.

"Need me to work the pedals?" Two asked.

"I think I can manage," One said, backing out from the bushes, stretching to both reach the pedals and see over the steering wheel. "We're not tall, but we're not tiny."

"Do we all have the same plan in mind?" Three asked.

"What are you thinking?" One and Two inquired.

"We'll probably want to split up to make the most of our advantage," Three said. "One of us should go to the school to meet up with Pigeon and try to make that turn out better, hopefully ending up with the goblet." One and Two nodded.

"Another of us should go to the candy shop," Three continued. "We know that Mauricio and Wyatt will both be gone, along with Denny, Eric, and Kyle. While they're away, we might have a chance to free Summer and John, which could create a second chance to intercept the goblet if the Nate at the school fails."

"Still with you," the other Nates said.

"And, as I know we've been thinking, the last of us should go home and use a Mirror Mint to try to save Trevor."

"It'll be risky," One said, guiding the SUV along the dirt road. The road was significantly more rutted than when he had driven the Explorer along it earlier. The rains must have caused the erosion.

"We have two mints," Two said. "We use one to get into the mirror, and give Trevor the other to get out."

"And we hope that by having two of us outside the mirror, the one inside will teleport out when we reunite at a central point," Three concluded.

"We have to try," they all said.

"Who goes where?" Three asked.

"Let's go by number, in the order you laid out the plan," One said. "I'll go to the school, Two will lurk around the Candy Shoppe, and Three will go into the mirror."

"Not that the mirror is the riskiest part," Three grumbled.

"They're all risky," Two said. "If any of us get hurt, we all get hurt."

"What if being in the mirror keeps me from getting drawn back to you guys when we're supposed to reunite?" Three said. "I could exist as a Nate duplicate trapped in the mirror forever. I'm just as much Nate as you guys!"

"I bet we'll either all get sucked into the mirror, or you'll get sucked out," One speculated.

"Easy to say when you're not the guy in the mirror," Three muttered. "One of us has to take the risk—I'll do it. But if I end up stuck in there, you guys better never rest until you get me out."

"We won't," One and Two promised.

"I know you won't," Three sighed. "I wouldn't."

"We should drop off One first," Two said. "He most needs to be early. Then drop me off near the store, then Three can take the car home."

"Sounds like a plan," One said. "I'll drive to the back of the school. I don't want to risk being spotted by entering from the front."

"Let's spend some time thinking separately about our own missions," Two said.

"Good idea," One and Three agreed.

The truck bounced along the rutted road for a while in silence.

"Are we getting close to the paved road?" Three asked.

"Not far," One said.

They continued for some time without speaking.

"I thought up a joke," Three announced. "Want to hear it?"

"You're supposed to be planning for your mission," Two said.

"My mission is easy," Three said. "Go into the mirror, give Trevor the candy, and wait."

"There's Gold Coast Drive," One said as the street came into view.

"What has three heads, six arms, and half a brain?" Three asked. One and Two answered in unison. "Nate Sutter."

* * * * *

"I've never actually bitten anyone," Diego said. "I mean, I've fantasized about it, but now that I might have to actually do it, the thought makes me a little squeamish."

"You'll do great," Pigeon said, patting his Labrador reassuringly as they hurried up the ramp at the rear of Mt. Diablo Elementary.

"Most of my food isn't much more than meaty porridge," the dog said. "I'm not complaining, it tastes good, but it doesn't really test my teeth. Do you think I could break skin?"

"For sure," Pigeon said. "You just need more confidence. Don't you think I'm worried too? How am I supposed to succeed where everybody else failed? But we have to give it a shot. The bad guys will probably show up here soon to claim their treasure. We have the element of surprise on our side. If we're stealthy, we might find a way to stop them."

"I can do stealthy," Diego assured him. "You wouldn't believe how many birds I've almost caught."

Pigeon knelt just before they reached the top of the ramp. He held out some Brain Feed in his palm. "You better have a little more," Pigeon said. "I don't want you to relapse."

Diego ate the kibbles. "You say I get all slobbery and stop responding to your commands?"

"Pretty much," Pigeon said. "Without the Brain Feed, your only tricks are *sit* and *shake*. And I have to help you shake by grabbing your paw."

"Funny, I can't picture that. If you say so."

"Don't let me forget to give you more in a few minutes," Pigeon said.

They arrived at the top of the ramp to find Nate racing toward them. Nate stopped running and waved his arms.

Pigeon rushed over to greet Nate. "Am I glad to see you!" Pigeon gushed.

"Me too," Nate said. "I was starting to worry I'd missed you. I've been searching all over."

"Where are Summer and John?" Pigeon asked.

"They were captured," Nate said. "Only I got away. I have a lot to explain. Where were you going to wait for the bad guys?"

"We were planning to set up a stakeout over by the Dumpster," Diego said, making Nate jump.

"Forgot about the talking dog," Nate said. "Okay, you two didn't get caught there last time, so that sounds good." They started walking across a playing field toward the front of the school.

"Last time?" Pigeon asked.

"I used the Grains of Time that Mr. Stott gave me," Nate explained. "I've been to the past and the future. Remember that bum who bugged us when we were walking home that time? It really was me. My mind traveled back into his body."

"No way," Pigeon said.

"What bum?" Diego asked.

"Long story," Nate said. "I also went to the future where Belinda had succeeded in drinking from the Fountain of Youth. Pigeon, in that future, you and Diego tried to stop her unaided. Diego got killed, and you were changed into an old man."

"You weren't here?" Pigeon said.

"The future I saw was the future without me in it. But I'm here this time, and I know what went wrong. Hopefully we can do things differently and make everything turn out better."

"How'd I get killed?" Diego asked.

"Mauricio showed up with Denny, Eric, and Kyle. They went to the janitor's office and used a hidden entrance to get into a secret basement. When you guys tried to follow, Wyatt ambushed you with giant black widow spiders. He captured Pigeon and later killed you, Diego."

"Wyatt?" Pigeon asked.

"Wyatt is the Fuse, Mauricio is the jelly guy," Nate said.

"What should we do differently?" Pigeon asked.

"First let's run to the Dumpster," Nate said, picking up the pace.

Pigeon ran along behind, slowly falling back. As they raced through the school, he noticed that there were still teachers in some of the classrooms. It was strange to think that for most people, this was just another ordinary day. When they reached the parking lot, several cars remained. Nate, Diego, and Pigeon all ducked into the chain-link cage that surrounded the Dumpster.

"Does this feel good?" Nate asked. "Is this where you would have stayed to spy on their arrival?"

"I think so," Pigeon said.

"Once they arrive, we partly just need to lay low longer," Nate said. "Instead of following them, we should set up an ambush. Turning the key to open the treasure room door will age Kyle. Entering the room will kill Mauricio. Then Eric will enter the room and end up an invalid. That was when they sent you, Pigeon, into the room to retrieve the goblet with the water from the Fountain of

Youth. That was how you turned old. If we stay out of the way, Denny will have to retrieve it, and he'll end up old also."

"Then what?" Pigeon asked.

"If Denny fails, we'll be ahead of the game. The others are too old to retrieve the goblet; entering the room would kill them like it killed Mauricio. If Denny succeeds, we'll have to jump him and Wyatt and take back the goblet. Denny will be old and frail. We'll have to shock Wyatt or something. Do you have any Shock Bits left?"

"One dose," Pigeon said. "Do you have any?"

"I have one also. Remember, with Wyatt, we have to zap him quickly, or he'll use his magic on us. Once we have the goblet, we can't just pour out the water. A protective spell keeps the goblet full until somebody actually drinks it. I was hoping Diego might volunteer to down the water. Wouldn't you like to be a puppy again?"

"I'm only what, six years old?" Diego said. "What if I get so young I cease to exist?"

"That could happen if any of us drink it," Nate said. "But in dog years you're like forty-two, making you the oldest by far."

"What if the water doesn't take dog years into account?" Diego asked. "Then I'd be the youngest."

"We have to get rid of this water," Nate said. "After Mrs. White turns young, everyone who has tasted the white fudge will fall under her control. And she'll start preparing to distribute white fudge to the world."

"How come the dog is more disposable than the human?" Diego complained.

"There has to be another way," Pigeon said.

They stood in awkward silence for a moment.

"I'm kidding, Pidge," Diego said reluctantly. "I know how much this matters to you. I'd do anything you asked of me, you know that. You want me to lap up the water?"

Pigeon dug more Brain Feed out of his pocket and fed it to Diego. He stroked the dog's black fur. "Yeah, we need you to do this. Hopefully it will work out for the best."

"Right," Diego said, trying to sound brave. "It'll be fun to be a puppy again."

A black Hummer with one side of the front bashed in came zooming along Oak Grove Avenue and squealed into the parking lot. Nate crouched out of sight behind the Dumpster as Pigeon peeked out through the fence.

"It's them," Pigeon whispered. "Mauricio, Denny, Eric, and Kyle. Where's the Fuse?"

"He didn't arrive with them," Nate replied quietly.

"They're heading into the school," Pigeon reported. "Going toward the cafeteria, just like you said."

"We need to be patient," Nate said. "They have to get into the janitor's office, move some filing cabinets to find the hatch, climb down, get to the door, open it, and have a few of them get old."

"Where do you want to ambush them?" Pigeon asked after a minute.

"Are they out of sight yet?" Nate asked.

"Yes."

Nate came out from behind the Dumpster and surveyed the area. "We should hide behind the Hummer. That way Wyatt will come close enough for us to shock him. We'll have to strike quickly."

"I wish you had another Ironhide," Pigeon said.

"Sorry," Nate said.

"I can hide under the Hummer," Diego offered. "I'll rush out and distract him, go for his legs, then you guys can move in and deliver the shock."

"Sounds good," Nate said.

"What's the difference between waiting over here and waiting behind the Hummer?" Pigeon asked.

"Nothing, I guess," Nate said. "Except if we hide at the Hummer, we'll already be in position, just in case."

"That's what I was thinking," Pigeon agreed.

Staying low, they dashed across the parking lot and squatted behind the Hummer. Diego crawled underneath and then crawled back out. "I'll go back under when the time comes," Diego said.

Pigeon gave Diego a few more kibbles of Brain Food.

"There are two other versions of me running around town," Nate said.

"What?" Pigeon asked.

"The yellow sand of the Grains of Time split me into three," Nate explained. "The other two dropped me off at the back of the school a few minutes before I found you. One of me is staking out the candy shop to help Summer and John, and the other is going to try to help Trevor. In a little while we'll all get drawn back together at a central location."

"Are you the real Nate?" Pigeon asked.

"We're all the real Nate," Nate said. "It's complicated."

They waited in silence. After some time, Pigeon gave Diego more Brain Feed.

"How's life as a dog?" Nate asked.

"No complaints," Diego said. "Nice home, good family, plenty to eat, attention when I want it, time to myself when I want it. I've always wondered though, Pigeon, why'd you give me a Spanish name?"

"Dad got you in San Diego," Pigeon said.

"Ah," Diego said. "I missed that somehow. Makes sense."

Chanting commenced behind them. They turned in time to see the Fuse approaching, arms spread wide, birthmark blazing. In front of him on the asphalt, three black widow spiders expanded to horrific proportions, each reaching the size of a small car, most of the mass residing in their bulbous abdomens.

While Nate tucked his candy into his pants, and Pigeon fumbled for his Shock Bits, the glossy spiders pounced, adroitly binding them in sticky threads. Diego barked. Once the kids were bound, the gargantuan spiders backed off.

"On your feet," Wyatt said. "I have total control of these adult female black widow spiders. At this size, I don't think I need to explain what their venom would do to you."

Nate and Pigeon shared a terrified glance. This was not supposed to happen.

* * * * *

Nate number three entered his bathroom and found Trevor waiting in the mirror. Trevor looked relieved to see him and waved. Nate waved back and popped in a Mirror Mint.

Nate had considered bringing a pile of comic books into the mirror with him, in case he ended up stranded. Then he had remembered that he would not be able to see anything in the darkness. If he was going to read anything, somebody would have to hold it up to the mirror from the outside.

Climbing onto the counter, Nate tested the mirror. It felt pliable, flexing inward as he pressed his hand against it. Biting down hard on the mint, Nate crossed through into the cold darkness.

"What are you doing?" Trevor asked excitedly. "Did you find extra mints?"

"I still only had two," Nate said. "I want you to use the last one."

"But then you'll be trapped!"

Nate explained about being split into three selves, and his theory that when the selves reunited, he would be pulled out of the mirror realm.

"Sounds risky," Trevor said.

"At least it gives both of us a chance," Nate said. "Otherwise you'd be hopeless."

"What should I do when I get out?" Trevor asked.

"Do you have any candy left?" Nate asked.

"They took it all," Trevor said.

"Maybe you can go give me a hand at the school or the candy shop." Nate hastily outlined what had happened to the others and what was going on.

"Sounds like you might need more help at the school," Trevor said.

"You better hurry," Nate encouraged, finding Trevor's hand in the darkness and giving him the mint.

"If you end up trapped, I'll get you out," Trevor promised.

"Okay," Nate said. "I'll be waiting here."

Trevor bit down on the final Mirror Mint and crawled through the mirror onto Nate's bathroom counter. Dropping to the floor, he clutched his side. Wincing into the mirror at Nate, he waved and exited the bathroom.

Pigeon glanced over his shoulder at the eight eyes of the massive spider following him, his view of the black widow blurred by tears. The sleek, silent arachnid followed him dispassionately, legs working in creepy coordination. Webbing bound his arms to his sides.

Pigeon hung his head. Not much had changed from the way Nate had described things going the first time. The only difference was that instead of just Pigeon and Diego getting captured, now there were three prisoners.

Diego padded along beside him. Was his dog going to die again? Pigeon wished he had never given the Labrador Brain Feed. He wished he had not come to know his dog on such a personal level. He wished Diego was still slobbering out in the backyard.

"How did you find us?" Nate asked as Wyatt marched them into the custodial office.

"What's it to you?" Wyatt asked.

"Weren't you in the cafeteria?" Nate asked.

The Fuse huffed. "Part of the time. A good sentry stays in motion. I spotted you running over to the Hummer, and moved into position while you were jabbering."

Two of the three spiders descended through the dark square on the floor of the custodial office, lowering themselves with silky strands of webbing, one of them carrying Diego. Wyatt uttered a few musical words, and the webs binding Nate and Pigeon fell away. The boys descended a rope ladder through the opening. The ladder was longer than Pigeon expected, and it twisted as he climbed down. Wyatt clicked on a large flashlight. Pigeon reached the dirt floor and moved out of Nate's way. Powdery dust plumed up with each step, making the flashlight beam look almost tangible. The two enormous black widows waited silently as the third lowered herself into the darkness.

Wyatt descended last, the flashlight hanging from a belt loop. When he landed on the ground, he summoned two of the spiders with a gesture. Their spinnerets quivered, and soon Pigeon and Nate had their arms bound to their sides again by sticky webs. The Fuse jerked a thumb to indicate which way they should proceed.

The ancient walls of the basement were fashioned out of stone. On the far side of the room, part of the wall had collapsed to reveal a tunnel sloping away into darkness. Pigeon led the way with Diego, followed by Nate, followed by the spiders, followed by the Fuse. The air smelled so richly of dirt and stone that Pigeon could almost taste it.

"No heroics, Diego," Nate murmured. "We know how it ends if you try anything."

"I hear you," Diego said.

"Stop gabbing," Wyatt demanded from behind them.

The air grew more chilly the deeper they descended. Denny called from up ahead, "Who is that?"

"Wyatt," the Fuse responded. "I caught Nate and Pigeon."

"We can see the magic water," Denny said. "Mauricio died when he entered the room. He turned into a pile of bones. Eric went in and became an old man. He can't walk. Kyle's already old from opening the door—I think the room would age him into bones like Mauricio. Mrs. White warned that strange things might happen to us, but promised she could fix whatever happened once she had the magic water. That's the truth, right?"

"Right," Wyatt said.

Pigeon rounded a bend in the tunnel and Denny came into view, holding a small flashlight. An elderly version of Eric lay beyond a stone doorway beside a rotted pile of human bones. Kyle leaned against the wall, breathing erratically. He looked too old to be standing.

"We'll send in one of these two next," Wyatt said. "You've done well so far, Denny."

"I'll go," Nate said.

Pigeon wanted to make a similar offer, but the words were stuck in his mouth. He wrung his hands. "I can do it," he managed in a small voice.

Nate shot Pigeon an insistent look. The look conveyed a desperate need to be the one who went into the room, something more than heroism. Pigeon realized Nate might have a plan. "I'm more responsible for starting this whole mess," Nate said. "I want to finish it, not Pigeon. Besides, the dog might not react well if Pigeon goes in there."

"If you're volunteering, you're more than welcome," Wyatt said. "Just don't try to get smart." The Fuse held a rose up to Nate's neck and mumbled a chant. His birthmark brightened and spread more, covering almost all of his face. The stem of the rose elongated and snaked around Nate's neck, sharp thorns needling his skin. "If you attempt to drink the water, I'll finish you before it touches your lips." The Fuse intoned more soft words, and the webbing binding Nate's arms to his torso dissolved. "Do this right, and maybe Mrs. White will show mercy after she regains her youth."

"I won't be holding my breath," Nate said.

Pigeon peered through the doorway. The room was bare save for a black stone pedestal on the far side. Atop the pedestal rested an ornate golden goblet set with glittering gemstones. There was nowhere to hide. Pigeon could not foresee what Nate might have in mind.

"See you, Pidge," Nate said, giving his friend's shoulder a squeeze.

Nate kicked off his shoes. Scowling, Nate rubbed his eyebrows. Pigeon thought they suddenly looked singed. Nate touched his elbow, getting blood on his fingertips.

"Get a move on," Wyatt demanded.

Nate paused a moment longer, as if bracing himself, then strode forward. The instant Nate stepped into the room, he started growing taller and withering. Loose clothes became much too tight, the sleeves and pant legs much too short. Liver spots appeared on his wrinkled hands. His hair thinned and became a silvery white. He hunched forward, walking with a stoop. At least he could still walk.

Nate looked back, the thorny collar snug around his wrinkled neck. Pigeon could hardly recognize his friend. His face was longer, his nose bigger and droopier, his eyebrows bushier. Limp folds dangled below his chin, and deep creases marred his face. But the eyes were Nate's, and the smile.

"I always hoped to grow old gracefully," Nate chuckled, his voice deeper and more fragile.

"Get the water," Wyatt demanded.

Diego whined. Pigeon crouched beside the dog.

Nate shuffled toward the pedestal, taking small, cautious steps. Upon arriving at the pedestal, he hovered over the goblet for a moment, as if staring into it.

"Hurry up," Wyatt ordered.

Nate picked up the goblet and turned around, shuffling back over to them. Pigeon kept waiting for the trick. As he neared the doorway, Nate put a hand to his head and swayed. Steadying himself, he stepped through the doorway and handed the goblet to Denny.

"Well done, let's get out of here," Wyatt said.

Pigeon stared at Nate, watching for a sign, straining to guess what Nate expected from him.

"I'm not feeling so well," Nate said, massaging his temples.

"Pull Eric out here," Wyatt commanded.

Nodding, Nate crouched, grabbed Eric's shriveled legs, and dragged him out of the treasure room. Then Nate sat down and buried his face in his hands.

"Get up!" Wyatt barked.

Nate turned translucent, became blurry, and vanished. The thorny stem fell to the ground. Diego barked.

"What happened?" Denny asked.

"Must have been a curse," Pigeon said.

Denny looked uncertainly at the jeweled goblet.

"Doesn't matter," Wyatt said, crouching to pick up Eric. "We need to get back."

Pigeon glanced at the goblet. It was so close! Nate had warned that spilling it would do no good. Maybe Nate had thought of a trick to pull now that his selves had reunited. Or maybe he had no plan, and was simply being heroic.

The Fuse raised his hands palms outward and chanted briefly. The three black widows shrank down to their original tiny statures. Wyatt stomped on them.

"Don't get any ideas, Pigeon boy," Wyatt said. "This is over. Don't make me do unnecessary violence to you or your mutt. Come on."

Pigeon followed him away from the treasure room.

* * * * *

Nate number two stood at a window inside the antique store across from the Sweet Tooth Ice Cream and Candy Shoppe. He kept waiting to see Mauricio or Wyatt leave along with Denny, Eric, and Kyle, but a lot of time had passed, and he began to fret that he had missed their departure.

A *Closed* sign hung in the candy shop window. Nate had watched a steady stream of people approach the shop, jiggle the door, peer through the glass, and turn away in disappointment.

Before taking up his position inside the antique store, Nate had confirmed that the back door of the antique store was locked. He had circled the candy shop, furtively searching for an unlocked window and finding none. He knew that spells protected the candy shop from unauthorized intruders, so he had saved a direct assault as a last resort.

A husky bald man with a goatee shook the candy shop door. The man checked his watch and banged on the glass. Shaking his head disgustedly, the man stalked away.

Nate had been spying on the candy shop for almost thirty minutes. His hour had to be waning. If he was going to risk a direct assault on the shop, he knew it was now or never.

Since he had no money on him, Nate picked up a heavy bronze candlestick without paying and walked out. He jaywalked across Main and flung the candlestick through one of the large plate-glass windows. Huge sheets of glass fell, dissolving into shards and splinters as they hit the ground.

An enormous sound followed, like the blast of a ship's horn, accompanied by a searing flash of light and heat. Nate fell over backwards, landing in the street and scraping his right elbow. Picking himself up, he approached the window. He used the sole of his shoe to try to push away some of the remaining glass. When his foot touched the glass, a tremendous shock sent him spinning to the ground. Nate lay on the sidewalk in a stupor, fingers twitching. He had underestimated the defenses of the shop.

After a few deep breaths, Nate sat up. Despite the violent jolt, no lasting harm appeared to have occurred. As he began to rise, Nate started to grow and age. His shoes squeezed his feet, and Nate tore them off with liver-spotted hands. Rising painfully, he hobbled away from the broken window.

Why was he old? This was not part of the plan! Had everything fallen apart?

He leaned against a light pole to catch his breath. Cars roared by on Main, indifferent to his internal anguish. Time was running out, and he could think of nothing useful to do.

* * * * *

Out of breath and sweaty, his ribs screaming in pain, Trevor found the door to the school cafeteria unlocked. It was almost strange to feel his heart beating again. In the mirror realm, he had been able to run all he wanted without getting tired. In all his time there, Trevor had not felt his heart beat once, even when he had jogged a long distance with his fingers pressed to his neck as an experiment.

He dashed inside the cafeteria to the custodial office and found that door unlocked as well. Inside he discovered a square hole in the floor and a rope ladder. Hurriedly Trevor pulled up the rope ladder and tipped over a filing cabinet to cover the hole.

Trevor exited the cafeteria and checked the parking lot. He arrived just in time to witness the black Hummer driving away.

He slumped down and a black Labrador approached him, nudging him with a wet, black nose.

"Diego?" Trevor asked, recognizing the purple collar. "What are you doing here?"

The dog had no response.

CHAPTER TWENTY-ONE
THE GOBLET

Nate materialized on a side street not far from Main. Fortunately there were no cars speeding down the road the moment he appeared. His shoes sat nearby. Groaning, Nate picked up his shoes and shuffled over to the edge of the street.

He had three sets of memories colliding in his mind. Memories of giant black widow spiders spinning webs around him and of aging as he entered the treasure room. Memories of breaking one of the candy shop windows. Memories of waiting behind the mirror, staring out at his empty bathroom, hoping he would not be trapped in the frigid blackness forever.

It took a few moments to reconcile the different recollections. The incident with the candlestick and the candy store window explained how his eyebrows had gotten singed and where the scrape on his elbow had come from. Two of his selves had not felt the shock when he had kicked the glass—apparently only the actual changes to his body were universally experienced, not sensations. He remembered his panic in the mirror realm as his body began to age.

After sorting through the various memories, Nate began to feel whole again. He still had some candy, though he doubted it would work now that he was old. He tried to get a Moon Rock out of his pocket to experiment, but his pants were so tight, and his fingers so arthritic, that he failed.

All Nate knew was that he wanted to get to the candy shop to see how everything ended. He shambled along the side street until he reached Main, then turned in the direction of the candy shop. He waited at a crosswalk until the traffic ebbed. Many cars lined up waiting as he slowly traversed the intersection. He was hurrying as best he could, but his old legs grew tired so quickly!

After having paused several times to rest on a bench or squat on some stairs, Nate arrived at the candy shop. The window remained broken. The closed sign was still on display.

Through the broken window Nate could hear voices in the back. "Hey!" Nate called. "Hey! It's Nate! Let me in!"

A moment later Mrs. White pushed through the batwing doors, wearing a black eye patch. "Nate, how good of you to join us!" she said. She unlocked the front doors and opened them, admitting him. "I didn't expect to see you again. You arrived just in time for the grand finale! I understand I have you to thank for claiming my prize."

"You could say that," Nate agreed in a meek voice.

Mrs. White closed the door, locked it, and offered Nate her arm. He let her escort him into the back. Summer, John, and Gary were tied up sitting on the floor. Pigeon was there too, webs still binding his arms to his sides. They gazed at Nate in despair. Old Kyle was seated on a chair beside Denny. Wyatt stood beside a worktable where the ornate goblet rested, clipping his fingernails.

"Look who came for a visit," Mrs. White said elatedly. "Our *old* friend Nate! I've always been taught to show respect for my elders, so Denny, please pull him up a chair front and center."

Denny retrieved a chair and Nate sat down directly in front of the goblet.

"Friends," Mrs. White said. "In this humble room, in this obscure town, you are about to witness the dawn of a new era. All of you will be invited to serve me. Those who refuse will face nightmarish consequences. The rest of us are about to embark on a journey that surpasses anything you could possibly imagine. Decades of hiding and studying and preparing have finally reached their culmination!"

Mrs. White seized the goblet and raised it high. "To a new beginning," she cried exultantly, and began gulping down the water. She continued drinking until she held out an empty goblet for all to see.

The change began almost immediately. Her stature diminished. Wrinkles smoothed away. Faint freckles came into being. Her clothes hung baggy on her smaller frame. Within a moment, Mrs. White looked ten years old.

Nate leaned forward, eyes narrowed, hands clenched into fists. Denny coughed, muffling the sound as best he could. Everyone in the room watched the young girl in expectant silence.

Her jubilant expression faded. The eye patch fell down around her neck, revealing a vacant socket. The young girl looked around at everyone, no recognition in her eye. She seemed flustered and disoriented. "Who are you?" she finally asked in a small, hesitant voice. "Where am I?"

Using the worktable for leverage, Nate stood up. "You are a lucky little girl," he said, his age adding a certain dignity to his voice. "Not everyone gets an opportunity to start over with a Clean Slate!"

There was a moment of utter silence. Then John Dart threw his head back and laughed.

Wyatt approached the young girl. "Belinda?"

"Is that my name?" the girl asked. She reached up a hand, touched her vacant eye socket, and jerked it away. "What happened to me? Who are you people?"

Wyatt glared fiercely at Nate. "You put a Clean Slate into the goblet?"

"I still had the one Mrs. White intended for us to use on Mr. Stott," Nate said. "Before the spider wrapped me up, I tucked it into the waistband of my underpants. It was my last resort. You didn't even search me for candy."

Wyatt shook his head. He rubbed a hand against the worktable. A rueful grin crept onto his face. "This probably ranks as the best sucker punch I've ever seen," he murmured to himself.

Wyatt cracked his knuckles. He fixed Nate with a steady gaze. "I'm not glad you did it," he growled. "But it's done. There's no going back. I've seen the Clean Slate in action before. This is over. Her mind is irretrievable."

"What are you talking about?" the little girl asked.

Wyatt crouched. "You lost your memory," he explained. "You have no family. Maybe some of these people can help you find a foster home."

John Dart stood up, hands bound behind his back. He walked toward the Fuse. "What's your move, Wyatt?"

"Not a step closer, John," the Fuse said. "Far as I'm concerned, this whole endeavor is a bust. If I didn't think you'd hunt me down, I might take my leave quietly."

"From the look of things, you're running out of unmarked skin," John said. "My guess is Belinda promised to restore you with her augmented powers."

"I've got enough juice left to take all of you with me," Wyatt spat.

"Maybe," John said. "But why perish? Let me take you in."

"Not a chance," Wyatt said, backing away. "Never underestimate a Fuse. You'd do well to give me your word you won't pursue me, and let me depart in peace."

John looked around the room, making eye contact with Nate and the kids. "You realize I can't speak for my employers," John said.

"I'm more worried about you than them," the Fuse said. "I've made it personal with you. I'm going to trust that your employers have bigger fish to fry than a Fuse who bet on the wrong horse and has almost burned out."

John looked wretched. "All right, for the sake of the kids, I pledge I won't chase you if you leave immediately."

The Fuse smirked, dipping his head. "That's all I needed to hear. Look after little Linda, would you?"

Wyatt ambled out the back door. Nate heard him thumping up the stairs.

John turned to face Nate, a warm smile spreading across his lips. "Nate, I can't believe it, you're one in a million."

Nate grinned as Pigeon, Summer, and Gary shouted words of approval. It was sort of pathetic to watch people tied up on the floor trying to cheer. But he appreciated the sentiment.

"What about me?" Kyle said, standing feebly. "What about Eric?"

"She wasn't going to change you back," Nate said. "I used magic to visit the future. She was going to enslave all of us, including you, Denny. Where is Eric, anyway?"

"Upstairs with the dwarf," Denny said. "They're both in bed. They're too injured to be on their feet."

"We'll have to go pick up Mr. Stott," Nate said. "He's stranded as a coyote in his ice cream truck. Without his help, we wouldn't have stopped her."

"What about Trevor?" Summer asked.

"I got him out of the mirror," Nate said. "I'll tell you all about it later. Right now I feel really tired."

Denny pounded a fist into his palm. "Dirt Face, I've got to say, I didn't know you had it in you."

"Nate," John said, "I've never been so thoroughly defeated. We were all helpless. I have to agree with Denny, I didn't see a way out of this. You have my eternal respect and admiration."

"Thanks," Nate said, sitting down. "I'd do it all again if I had to, but ideally, I'd rather not spend the rest of my life as an old man."

"Don't worry," John said with a wink. "I know a guy."

NEW JOBS FOR JOHN

You guys need any more bean dip?" the coyote inquired.

"I'm stuffed," Trevor said, rubbing the side of the brace encasing his ribs.

"You sure?" the coyote version of Mr. Stott persisted. "I have several more cans in the pantry." They were all seated in Mr. Stott's living room. Half-empty bags of chips littered the coffee table, along with a platter of bagels, several tubs of cream cheese, a bowl with remnants of onion dip, an empty bean-dip container, and a dozen paper cups.

"How about you, Gramps?" Summer asked Nate. "Still hungry?"

Leaning forward on the couch, Nate poked Summer in the thigh with his cane. "I warned you," he growled. "If you get to call me Gramps, I get to jab you." Elderly Kyle, sitting beside him, chuckled and coughed.

"We won't get to call you Gramps much longer," Pigeon said. "What time is John getting here, anyhow?"

Kyle checked his watch. "Any minute."

"How about Old Timer?" Trevor tried.

Nate tried to prod him, but Trevor was out of reach.

"Or Old Man Sutter," Summer said, moving away from Nate. "Or Geezer. Or Fossil. Or Dinosaur."

"Nathanosaurus," Pigeon proposed.

"Laugh it up," Nate grumbled.

"Up until a few days ago, I would have been hesitant to let John Dart set a foot in this house," the coyote interjected. "He has a sinister reputation in our circles. But if he hadn't arranged to have my truck towed here, I'd probably be roaming the hills chasing rabbits by now. He seems to be genuinely trying to set everything right."

"Is John bringing Linda?" Pigeon asked.

"I believe so," the coyote said.

"You wouldn't want her to leave without saying good-bye," Nate teased.

Pigeon blushed and looked away.

"Pigeon, don't you think having a thing for her is a little twisted?" Trevor said. "After all, she tried to kill us."

"Not kill us," Pigeon corrected. "She was mainly just trying to turn us into mindless slaves. And it wasn't her, not really. Belinda is gone. Linda is a new person."

"I think he's into the eye patch," Summer said.

"It matches his leather jacket," Nate observed.

"The patch is sort of cute," Pigeon mumbled.

"I want to be best man at the wedding," Trevor joked.

"You'll have to ask John's permission," Summer said. "He already treats her like a daughter."

There came a heavy knock at the door.

"Speak of the devil and he appears," the coyote exclaimed.

Pigeon crossed the room to answer the door, but it opened before he arrived. Linda entered, wearing a black eye patch, followed by John, who held a plate stacked with miniature quiches.

"Hey, guys," Linda said with a small wave. They had all hung out a few times since she had lost her memory. Sweet, friendly, and a little shy, Linda had offered no hint of recalling her former identity.

"Hi, Linda," Pigeon stammered.

She beamed at him.

"No dip left?" John complained.

"I have some in the cupboard," the coyote said.

"I'll help you grab it," Trevor offered, walking out of the room.

"I brought little quiches," John said, setting the plate on the coffee table.

"What are quiches?" Nate asked.

"You'll like them," Summer said. "They're soft. You can gum them."

She was out of reach, so Nate stood up and shuffled toward her, brandishing his cane. Laughing, she ran away from him. "Come back here, you whippersnapper!" Nate called in his most cantankerous voice.

Summer cowered behind John. "Can't you shoot him or something?"

"You're on your own," John said, raising both hands and backing away. Summer shrieked as Nate swatted her leg with his cane.

Trevor and the coyote returned with a can of bean dip. "What happened this time?" Trevor asked, popping the tab on the bean dip and tearing off the lid.

"She said I have to gum my food," Nate huffed, panting.

"Don't worry, Nate," John said. "I'll have you chewing like a pro again before you know it."

"Did you bring him?" Kyle asked.

John reached into a bag and pulled out some tortilla chips. He scooped up some of the pasty brown bean dip and put the chips in his mouth. "I just got off the phone with him," John said around the crunchy mouthful. "He'll be here any minute. Nate is a lucky boy. Mozag does not normally make house calls. He was impressed by my report, and wanted to see personally to Nate's well-being. No offense, Kyle, but he's not here for you. You and Eric will have to journey with me to the lair where the Council meets."

"Why not fix me while he's here?"

"The Council wants you and Eric to account for your actions before offering any assistance," John explained. "They'll make Sebastian explain his role in all of this as well. I'm confident they'll restore all of you in the end, though I imagine they'll have a punishment in mind for you and Eric."

"Punishment?" Kyle blurted.

John shrugged. "Nothing compared to losing the best years of your life, I assure you."

"Where does the Council meet?" Kyle asked.

"Ohio."

"You prepared the vehicle so I can ride in it?" the coyote asked.

"It will serve as a temporary lair," John said, snatching more chips. "Should be quite a road trip. Two eighty-year-old kids, a little girl with amnesia, and a talking coyote."

"I want to come," Pigeon said.

"Who would you sit by?" Trevor asked innocently.

Pigeon blushed vividly.

"After this, I'll be able to add some new items to my resume," John mused. "Geriatric nurse, baby-sitter, and zookeeper. Oh, and antiques dealer—I think I found a buyer for the goblet."

"I actually wouldn't mind coming with you also," Trevor said. "My folks have been in a nasty mood all week, arguing and shouting. Mom sent me to bed without dinner for flipping through the channels too quickly. Dad grounded me from riding my bike for sprinkling too much food in the fish tank!"

"My dad sleeps all the time," Summer said. "He quit shaving and showering. He's called into work twice already so he can mope around the house in his pajamas. He's never acted so depressed."

"My mom has been eating nonstop," Pigeon said. "Lately she's been downing brownie batter and milkshakes. And she's more over-protective than ever. Technically I'm never supposed to see you guys again. Right now she thinks I'm studying at the library."

"Everybody deals with white fudge withdrawal differently," the coyote said. "It will pass in another week or so."

"See, Nate," John said. "At least you haven't had cranky parents to contend with."

"They think I'm missing," Nate said.

"They contacted the police last week, once the fudge started wearing off," John acknowledged. "But you can hardly visit them in your current state. We'll have you back to normal shortly, and then you can enjoy a happy reunion."

There came a knock at the door. John bounded over and pulled it open. A short old man with bushy white sideburns and a stained Chicago Cubs cap entered holding a platter of sardines. "Sorry I'm late, I'm no good with directions."

"We're honored by your presence, Mozag," John said solemnly.

Mozag waved him away. "Where's our young hero?"

John gestured at Nate.

"Not so young anymore," Nate said.

Mozag squinted at him, deep crow's-feet spreading from the corners of his eyes. "You aren't nearly as old as you appear. The application of the artificial years was even sloppier than I expected. This treatment will do wonders."

Nate gave him an incredulous look. "Sardines?"

"Excuse me?" Mozag asked. Then he glanced down at the platter in his hands. "Oh, no, these are for the others. And you as well. And me. Hard to call it a party without sardines."

"If you say so," Nate said.

Mozag handed the platter to John and removed a fortune cookie from his pocket. He handed the cookie to Nate. "Don't crack it open," Mozag instructed. "Eat it in a single bite. Chew it well."

"Is there a fortune inside?" Trevor asked.

Mozag studied Trevor, eyeing him up and down. "Nate will get about seventy years back by consuming it, so yes, I would say that the contents of that cookie are definitely worth a fortune."

"Just eat it?" Nate asked. "Right now?"

"No time like the present," Mozag said.

"I don't have any teeth," Nate said.

Mozag smiled. "Let it soak in your mouth for a moment."

Nate put the cookie in his mouth, and waited while his saliva gradually softened it. The cookie tasted slightly sugary as he waited. Finally, when the cookie began to feel mushy, Nate started chewing. The inside of the cookie was pasty and salty, not hollow like he had expected. It tasted like there was sausage in the cookie, and corn, and raisins. Finally he swallowed it. "All done," he announced.

Mozag squinted at him. "Feel any different?"

"My stomach feels a little sore," Nate said. Suddenly he began to tingle. The sensation intensified until it burned through all the tissue of his body. His stature diminished. Wrinkles smoothed away and age spots faded. His features became less droopy. His clothes and shoes became loose. Nate stared at his young hands in giddy disbelief.

"It worked!" Pigeon cried triumphantly.

"Almost perfect," Mozag said, looking at Nate closely. "You're about seven hours older than you would have been otherwise. Close as I could manage."

"He looks a little green," Summer pointed out.

"You're right!" Trevor echoed. "In his cheeks and around his eyes."

"Green is good," Mozag said. "A necessary side effect. The coloring will fade away soon."

"How long will it take?" Nate wondered.

"Three to five days," Mozag said.

"Five days!" Nate exclaimed.

"Breaking a curse is no small matter," Mozag said. "Five days with greenish skin is a small price to pay. While you're waiting, help yourself to the sardines."

Mozag grabbed a sardine off the platter and dropped the entire fish into his mouth. He turned and walked toward the door.

"Thank you," Nate called.

"Don't mention it," Mozag replied. "You bailed us out of a tough spot. It's the least I can do. Don't forget the temporary preview of your winter years. What a rare opportunity. It will take quite a while to earn your way back. John, a pleasure, as always. The Council will tie up your other loose ends."

"Thank you," John said, bowing slightly.

Mozag waved a dismissive hand and walked out the door.

"You sure Nate isn't stuck with a green complexion?" Kyle asked after the door closed.

John nodded. "You were just in the presence of arguably the most powerful magician in the world. The spell will hold. And the Council knows its business as well. We'll get Sebastian back on two feet, find a home for Linda, and restore you and Eric to your proper ages."

"How did Mozag get here?" Pigeon questioned. "I thought magicians needed to remain in their lairs."

"You don't miss much," John said. "He came in a portable lair. And, of course, this is a lair. Plus, that Cubs hat he was wearing is almost as good as a lair. It grants him abnormal mobility for a magician."

"It looked old," Trevor said.

"He's caught eleven foul balls in that hat, all at Wrigley," John said.

"Let's get going," Kyle said. "I'm antsy."

"Relax," John assured him. "The hard part is over. This trip will be a piece of cake."

"Can I use the rest room before we get started?" Linda asked.

"Of course," the coyote said. "Down the hall on the left. There's no mirror. It's a long story."

Linda walked off down the hall.

"What about you, Sebastian?" John asked. "Want me to let you out back before we get rolling?"

"Actually, sure, if you don't mind."

John and the coyote went into the kitchen.

"Well, guys," Nate said, tossing his cane aside, "I guess we did it."

They huddled together in a group hug.

"Thanks for saving us, Nate," Pigeon said seriously.

"You can stop saying that," Nate said. "A million times is enough."

"I'm not sure we'll ever stop saying it," Summer said.

"We all owe you big," Trevor added.

"Including Diego," Pigeon said.

"I'm just happy to put all of this behind me," Nate said.

"All of it except the jeweled goblet," Summer reminded him.

"John thinks he might be able to get a lot of cash for it," Pigeon said.

Nate shrugged. "He said any gold we found was ours to keep. We'll see."

"Think he'll really split the money between us?" Trevor asked quietly.

"I think he keeps his promises," Nate said.

Linda returned from the bathroom, and John entered alongside the coyote. "Should we get rolling?" John inquired.

"Yes," Kyle replied. "Before I die of old age!"

ACKNOWLEDGMENTS

Perhaps more than any other book of mine so far, *The Candy Shop War* has benefited from feedback gathered from readers and editors. Entire sections of the book were completely transformed multiple times. The reactions I received reshaped the story in ways that helped it become clearer, more inventive, and more appropriate for use in schools.

Key people who provided feedback include Chris Schoebinger, Lisa Mangum, Emily Watts, Caleb Freeman, Josh Freeman, Chandler Labrum, Mary, Pam, Liz, Cherie, and Summer.

In fifth grade I lived in a Northern California town, having moved there the year before. This story owes a lot to that town. Although all of the characters are fictitious, the memories of the adventures I tried to find there with my own club of underage thrill seekers helped spawn this book.

It is tough to name everybody who deserves to be mentioned in a section like this. I need to place some emphasis on the publicity and marketing team at Shadow Mountain and the great work they have been doing. Gail Halladay, Angie Godfrey, Liz Carlston, MaryAnn Jones, Tiffany Williams, and Roberta Ceccherini-Nelli have been making great things happen with getting the word out for this book as well as my Fablehaven series. I owe a special thanks to my sister Summer, who has been working for my publisher booking my tour and traveling with me. Her help has been invaluable to the success my books have been enjoying.

Thanks also need to go out to others at Shadow Mountain. Chris Schoebinger—the guy can manage a project. I appreciate the skills of Emily Watts, editor; Brandon Dorman, illustrator; Richard Erickson and Sheryl Dickert, designers; and Laurie Cook, typographer.

I have to give a special nod to my Uncle Tuck, who loaned me the Flatman from a strange nightmare he had years ago. That guy has some weird things in his head. I hope he'll lend me other odd ideas in the future.

I've been taking some heat for naming certain family members and not others. Since I owe a lot to all of my family, here I go. Parents: Pam and Gary. Siblings: Summer, Bryson, Tiffany, and Ty. Grandparents: Cy, Marge, John, and Gladys. Uncles: Tuck, Danny, Chuck, Dave, and Bob. Aunts: Kim, Trudy, Jody, and Pam. Cousins: Travis, Jason, Mike, Matt, Ashley, Stephanie, Lindsay, Curt, Jason, Dave, Sheena, Nicole, Marisha, and Tanu. I love and appreciate all of you!

Of course my wife and kids need a special acknowledgment. Mary, Sadie, and Chase put up with Daddy traveling a lot to do assemblies at schools, to speak at libraries, and to sign books. I dread when my work takes me away from them, and I love them deeply.

As always, thank you for picking up this book. Without readers, I'd be a crazy guy typing alone in a room. Some of you have expressed concern that this book is releasing before the Fablehaven series is even halfway done. Don't worry, I'm working hard! My goal is to release books 3, 4, and 5 in consecutive years. Keep on reading and I'll keep on writing!

READING GUIDE

1. Losing the ability to get help from their families limited the options for Nate, Summer, Trevor, and Pigeon. How does your family support you during hard times? Who would you turn to if your family was unable to help?

2. In what ways did Nate, Summer, Trevor, and Pigeon watch out for one another? What have you done recently to show loyalty to a friend?

3. Between Nate, Summer, Trevor, and Pigeon, who would you most want as a friend? Why?

4. Trust was a big issue in this story. Why did the kids trust Mrs. White? How did she lose that trust? Why did they trust Sebastian? Why did they trust John? Who did you trust most as a reader? Why?

5. The kids in the story had to deal with bullies. Summer, Trevor, and Pigeon used a passive approach, giving in to their demands. Nate stood up to them—and sometimes suffered unhappy

consequences. What do you think is the best approach for handling bullies?

6. Which of the magic candies in the book would you want most? Which would you want least? Why?

7. If you could invent a type of magic candy, what magical ability or power would it have? What would you call it?

8. What do you imagine the pets you know would say if given Brain Feed?

9. If you had an endless supply of Ironhide jawbreakers, what profession would you choose? Why?

10. If you had a bag of magical candy corn that had the power of suggestion, who would you talk to? What would you say?

11. Sweet Tooth's white fudge was extremely addictive, thus compelling customers to want more. What treat or food do you find addictive? How many days could you go without eating it?

12. Do your parents pay enough attention to you, or does it seem like they're eating too much white fudge? Explain. If you could spend the whole day with your mom or dad, what would you do?

13. If you knew you were going to be trapped inside the mirror world for an indefinite period of time and could bring only what you could fit inside your school backpack, what would you bring?

14. If you could go back to any time in your life for an hour, what time would you visit? What would you change or do?

15. Do you think it would be ethical to give Clean Slates to people convicted of certain crimes? Why or why not?

ABOUT THE AUTHOR

Brandon Mull, *New York Times* bestselling author of *Fablehaven*, travels the country visiting schools, promoting literacy, and sharing his message that "Imagination Can Take You Places." In his youth, Brandon won a gold medal at a pudding-eating contest in the park behind his grandma's house. His long-standing love affair with sweets continues to this day.